THE MISSING
AMERICAN

By Kwei Quartey

The Missing American

THE MISSING AMERICAN

KWEI QUARTEY

Allison & Busby Limited
11 Wardour Mews
London W1F 8AN
allisonandbusby.com

First published in Great Britain by Allison & Busby in 2020.
This paperback edition published by Allison & Busby in 2020.

Published by arrangement with Soho Press, New York,
with the assistance of Rights People, London

Copyright © 2020 by Kwei Quartey

A CIP catalogue record for this book is available from
the British Library.

10 9 8 7 6 5 4 3 2 1

ISBN 978-0-7490-2573-1

Typeset in 11/16 pt Sabon LT Pro by
Allison & Busby Ltd.

The paper used for this Allison & Busby publication
has been produced from trees that have been legally sourced
from well-managed and credibly certified forests.

Printed and bound by
CPI Group (UK) Ltd, Croydon, CR0 4YY

To Ahmed Hussein-Suale,
a Ghanaian journalist martyred on
Wednesday 16th January, 2019

PART ONE

PART ONE

CHAPTER ONE

4th January, Sekondi-Takoradi, Ghana

Lying flat with the stock of the long-range rifle pressed firmly against his shoulder, the assassin positioned himself on the gable roof of the UT Bank building off Shippers Council Road. His legs were stretched straight out in a V on either side of the roof's ridge. He would have preferred a flat surface, but the advantages of this location easily outweighed any drawbacks. From this angle, he had an unobstructed view of the road through the Zeiss scope.

He waited. When the moment arrived, he would place the pad of his right index finger on the trigger rather than the crease between the first and second joints. That could result in a sideways torque on squeezing the trigger. So too could wrapping the thumb around the buttstock. Leave the thumb on the stock pointing forward towards the end of the barrel – that was what he had learnt in his first days as an officer in the Ghana Police Service's SWAT Panther Unit. Now, two years later, he was one of the best marksmen among his peers. Unfortunately, GPS talk was cheap, and they never put their money where their mouth was. Only the sniper's freelance work, like this assignment, bought him the good life – a nice car, good clothes, new furniture. And women, of course.

Political rallies in Ghana are a serious business. There's blaring music, dancing troupes, and handkerchief-waving groups of women in matching outfits. Gangs of ferocious biker youths careen erratically through the streets, sometimes colliding with cars and each other, but these excitable young men, their bodies soused with adrenaline, leap right back up and keep riding.

So it was for Bernard Evans-Aidoo campaigning in the city of Sekondi-Takoradi against incumbent President Bannerman. Big, charismatic, and dressed flamboyantly in his signature red, black, white, and green – the colours of the National Democratic Congress party, the NDC. Evans-Aidoo stood out of the sunroof of his black Benz and waved to the thrilled crowds lining Shippers Council Road. A full brass band, rocking and high-stepping in rhythmic unison, preceded the slow-moving vehicle, and behind the car was a bunch of random kids and teenagers whirling and jumping up and down with unspecified exuberance. Every so often, the Benz paused and Evans-Aidoo got out with surprising agility to press palms with his fans. He saw the worshipping, idolising expression in their eyes as they stretched out their hands to be blessed by his touch.

It was the candidate's third stop for the day: Axim, Tarkwa, and now Sekondi-Takoradi. There had been the inevitable delays at the two prior rallies and Evans-Aidoo and the entourage were late. Even though they had started the parade before dusk, darkness had descended quickly around 6 p.m., as it always does at the equator. But that was no impediment. The campaign had a vehicle with a generator and bright lights that travelled at the head of the procession, sharply spotlighting the popular man who had set the youth on fire with his promises. He had pledged first, to sack every single corrupt official in the Bannerman government; second, to shunt away some of Ghana's petroleum and natural gas revenue into programmes that would benefit ordinary men and women, particularly the largely unemployed youth. It was a classic taking from the rich to give to the poor. These young people, so hungry for a livelihood, truly loved Evans-Aidoo, and they had waited for him for hours in the ferocious sun. Now he was here, and he didn't disappoint as he put on this dazzling show. He was larger than life, physically and symbolically.

The cacophony from the cheering crowds, the band, and the noisy mobile generator prevented anyone from hearing a distinct gunshot. Evans-Aidoo's body dropped so suddenly from view that few people grasped that anything was wrong.

But inside the Benz, terror unfolded. Evans-Aidoo had collapsed like a sack of yams into the lap of his campaign manager, who let out a high-pitched scream as the minister's blood sprayed her and the tan leather seats. The bodyguard in the front scrambled into the back seat to shield his boss. The chauffeur craned to look behind. 'What happened? What happened?'

'*Drive forward!*' the bodyguard shouted. '*Drive!*'

The Benz shot forward and crossed the street's centre line. Tyres squealing, it skirted the generator vehicle and kept going. People at the roadside were screaming, but it was not jubilation any more. It was panic. Something bad had happened, but no one knew exactly what.

The manager in the Benz was shrieking, her head turned away from the sight of Evans-Aidoo limp and half wedged behind the passenger seat. The bodyguard tried to lift his boss's head, but it was slick with blood and brain matter and it slipped from his hands.

Hyperventilating and gripping the steering wheel like death itself, the chauffeur said, 'Where? Where?'

'Takoradi Hospital,' the bodyguard stammered. He was close to weeping. '*Hurry!*'

ONE DAY EARLIER

CHAPTER TWO

3rd January, Accra, Ghana

With darkened windows, sirens going, and small flags of Ghana flapping on their hoods, three shiny black SUVs raced along Independence Avenue. Ordinary mortals on the street knew the drill and pulled their vehicles to the side to give the VIP free passage.

In this case, the dignitary taking precedence over the plebes of Accra was the Inspector General of Police, James Akrofi, who was in the back seat of the middle vehicle. He didn't look up from his work as he made last-minute changes to the draft of his Ghana Police Service Report to the Blue-Ribbon Commission on the Eradication of Corruption in Ghana. It was a mouthful, but before President J. K. Bannerman had been elected to power almost four years ago by an overwhelming majority of Ghanaian voters, he had campaigned consistently on that one bedevilling issue: corruption. Tapping into a lurking sense among Ghana's citizens that the nation was slipping backward like a truck mired in muck, Bannerman had persuaded Ghanaians that corruption was standing in the way of every individual's development and prosperity. 'Ghana fails when corruption prevails', his albeit clumsy slogan, had caught on. Bannerman had promised the nation a new era of The Clean and Enlightened Society. The people reached out to him with the fervour of a parched man in the Sahara yearning for an oasis.

To be honest, like the engine of an antique car, the anti-corruption machine had been slow to start. Now, as Bannerman's first term was ending and the political parties were revving up for the upcoming presidential and parliamentary elections at the end of the year, the president's track record had been spotty – some even said too little, too late. There was some truth to the characterisation that implementation was not Bannerman's strong suit and that he was more of an idealist than a pragmatist. Privately, Akrofi thought the truth was somewhere in the middle. The bottom line was that Bannerman was now vulnerable to one man: Bernard Evans-Aidoo.

The SUV convoy swept through the gates of Jubilee House and sped across the vast square towards the presidential palace, which was built in the shape of the golden stool of the *Asantehene*. The Office of the President was expecting Akrofi, so from the palace entrance to the final security door of President Bannerman's inner sanctum, passage was quick and all the checkpoints along the way essentially a formality. Everyone knew who the Inspector General of

Police was: one of Bannerman's closest friends and advisors.

Mr President, sixty-three, had a stern but avuncular demeanour, his charcoal-ash hair suggesting wisdom. He strode forward, hand outstretched. 'James! *Ete sen?*'

'*Nyame adom*, J. K.,' Akrofi said, grasping the hand with a firm, enthusiastic grip. Their eyes met and held, a testament to the strong bond between them.

'Good to see you, good to see you,' Bannerman said. 'Come, let's sit down.'

Akrofi followed the president several metres across the crimson carpet with Ghana's coat of arms in the centre. They had a 360-degree view of Accra through the tinted, floor-to-ceiling bulletproof glass, the cost of which had no doubt contributed to the bloated $50 million cost of the palace. But Akrofi didn't find that necessarily bad. In what country was it not fashionable to complain about the extravagant residences of the ruling class?

Out of respect, Akrofi waited for the leader of the nation to sit down before he did. 'How are dear Josephine and the children?' Bannerman asked, turning his body halfway towards his friend.

'Everybody is doing well, by His Grace, thank you,' Akrofi said. 'Josephine is in DC at the moment winning friends and influencing people, so to speak, and then she will be in England to see Kwame.'

Bannerman's expression softened. 'How is he doing these days?'

Akrofi lowered his gaze with a touch of sadness. 'You know. He has his good and bad days.'

'Yes, of course. I have faith that one day he will be well by God's grace.'

'Thank you, J. K. I appreciate your good wishes.'

'You are always welcome,' Bannerman said. 'So, let's see what you have for me.' Akrofi handed him the folder with the report and the president read it through once.

'Outstanding,' he said at length. 'This is simply first class and I like your four-part plan to eliminate corruption at the top. I think you've done a lot to change the culture of middle management and the junior officers, but now it's time to target the upper echelons.'

'You have my sincere word I will endeavour to do so,' Akrofi said. 'I admire what you are trying to do for the country.'

He and Bannerman had been in law school together, and high school and college before that. Akrofi had heavily supported his friend's presidential campaign and Bannerman had promised him the IGP post in return. One didn't rise to that position. It was a civilian appointment made entirely at the president's wishes.

Bannerman rose to place the documents on his rosewood desk imported from Italy, and then turned to the view from the south-west window. Accra's afternoon traffic was as clogged as bad plumbing. From here, one could just see the roof of the Ghana Police Service headquarters. On the other side of the double-lane Ring Road East, several embassies nestled among the trees.

Akrofi came to stand beside the president.

'You and I are cut from the same cloth,' Bannerman

said quietly. 'So, you understand how much I want this. Obviously, I can't abolish corruption completely, but I want Ghanaians to come to regard it in a different way – as a kind of cancer that has metastasised to all parts of society. Now it must be surgically removed everywhere it is found. Then things will begin to change.'

Akrofi nodded. 'I do understand.'

'We will drum anti-corruption into the Ghanaian psyche,' Bannerman said. 'Billboards, radio, TV, social media. I'll have rappers and football players endorse the plan. With their help, I'll create a new consciousness.' He looked at Akrofi. 'We are warriors against a worthy foe, but together, we can vanquish.'

'By "worthy foe" you mean corruption? Or Evans-Aidoo?'

'Corruption. Evans-Aidoo can't sustain his position in the polls. This business about him redistributing oil wealth to the citizens is nonsense. We are not Norway.'

'No country is – except Norway,' Akrofi said with a wry smile. 'I'm a little concerned about him though, because his followers believe him and there are more and more of them every day. It's all false hope, for sure, but the nature of people is that they cling to that.'

Akrofi waited for his friend to respond. Instead, Bannerman turned away with his head down and hands thrust deeply in his pockets. Akrofi had an awful foreboding that if Bernard Evans-Aidoo wasn't stopped, Bannerman's presidency would be over.

19

CHAPTER THREE

Nii Kwei was a '*sakawa* boy', meaning he made his money through Internet swindles. '*Saka*' was the Hausa word for 'to put in', referring to adding items to the virtual shopping cart. Nii was well-educated, having completed his BA in political science at the University of Ghana, but that field didn't exactly invite a tsunami of job offers. Nii Kwei's options were limited to being either unemployed or underemployed, and he alternated between those two glum circumstances for about a year after graduation.

Whenever Nii looked back on his past, he remembered clear as crystal the day his fortunes changed. Coming out of a Max Mart, he bumped into an old secondary schoolmate called Isaac and was stunned to see that Isaac owned a late model Lexus SUV – a bright red one at that. Isaac had been a loser jock prankster at school with no academic prospects. In fact, he barely scraped through senior high with grades that would never have got him into college or a trade school. How in the world was he driving his own

Lexus? Nii Kwei drove an old, dent-rich Toyota Corolla – when his brother could lend it to him, that is.

'So where do you work now?' Nii Kwei asked Isaac, his conversational tone belying his curiosity.

'Internet stuff, you know,' Isaac said.

'No, I don't know. What kind of Internet stuff?'

'Like overseas business.'

The glint of the giant gold chain on Isaac's wrist caught Nii Kwei's eye and held it for a moment. 'Come on, Isaac,' he said in Ga. Switching to the vernacular always helped. 'We were mates, so be straight with me. What are you doing?'

Isaac glanced around as if someone might be watching them, or maybe it was just a dramatic flourish. 'OK, let's sit inside my car and talk.'

My God, Nii thought as he got in. He ran his fingers over the precisely stitched tan leather seats and stared at the Lexus's high-tech dashboard, which looked like an airplane cockpit and came with a navigation system. *Why can't I have this luxury too?*

In the bliss of the Lexus's air conditioning, Isaac told Nii about the world of *sakawa* – Internet fraud with the backing of magical powers that could make you enormously successful at making money through several scams. You accessed magical powers through an intermediary like a traditional priest, aka fetish priest. It used to be people went to a man of God – either a Christian pastor or a *mallam* – to request those powers, but either the MOG or God Himself was slow because the magic took too long to materialise. Fetish priests were fast. They jumped on the project immediately, and before you knew it, the *sakawa* boy was up and away like a racehorse.

But the price the fetish exacted from his supplicant was high. Sacrificing a couple of chickens to the gods was standard, but that was the easy part. The difficulty came with the more exotic rituals the fetish might demand of the *sakawa* boy. Certain items were highly treasured by the gods, and if a *sakawa* boy truly desired any modicum of success, he needed to bring those to the priest. The most prized offerings included the hair of either an *oburoni* or an albino, the thighbone of a child, a person's lips, and male or female genitalia. The best way to procure these body parts was to have an arrangement with someone at the mortuary in a large hospital.

Isaac detailed how one of his fetish priests asked him to have sex with three different women every day for a week and provide video evidence. Failure to obey the fetish could result in an instant loss of income, sickness, death, or all the above.

'But how do you actually make money?' Nii asked Isaac. 'Is it like the 419?'

In the infamous '419' scams, a made-up Nigerian oil tycoon emails you and promises you a percentage of millions of dollars if you send him a mere $5,000.

'That's the one everyone knows,' Isaac said with a smile. 'Nigerians invented it and it still works, but Ghanaians have taken it to a new, higher level and we're now better at it than they are. We have several techniques now.'

Isaac told Nii Kwei about the Iraq war vet scam: an American marine is stranded in Turkey/Jordan/Qatar en route back home to the US from his rotation. The authorities have seized the vet's passport and the only way he can get out is to pay $3,000, but he has no way of getting his hands on that kind of money. Can you, the recipient of this desperate email, help? His life could be in danger if he doesn't pay up within the next seventy-two hours. He will reimburse you as soon as he returns stateside.

There were others: romance cons, lottery scams, identity theft, credit card fraud, inheritance scams, business venture scams, Yahoo and Facebook scams – take your pick. The only thing more amazing than the amount of money one could rake in through these illegal channels was just how gullible these white people could be – especially Americans. Some of them had read and *knew* about these Internet cons, and yet still they allowed themselves to be duped. Amazing.

But the gold scam was the king. This brought in thousands and thousands of dollars. Arab people fall for this one a lot because they love gold. The Chinese? Forget it. They're so good, they can scam the scammers.

The gold scam begins with the search for a suitable overseas scam target, known as the *mugu*, which literally means 'fool'. Let's call him 'Joe'. Perhaps Joe is a gold investor or otherwise interested in gold. It's a good idea to give Joe's name and his picture to a fetish priest to check (by spiritual means) if Joe is a good target. The *sakawa* boy entices Joe to Ghana with the promise of a sale of twenty-four carat gold from the country's rich reserves of the magical, glittering metal. The goal is to get Joe to Ghana to make a purchase of twenty to forty kilos of gold ore. Joe's independent testing shows the ore contains gold, but somewhere in the process, a member of the 'scam team' switches the container, and what Joe pays for is, in fact, dirt with copper shavings that give the 'ore' a sufficiently golden appearance. When he returns to the States, he finds he has paid upwards of $200,000 for worthless material.

Isaac had participated in more than one gold scam. In fact, in one of them, it was his job to make the notorious 'switch' at a moment the *mugu* was distracted by someone else in the room.

'You don't feel bad about taking people's money like that?' Nii Kwei asked.

Isaac looked at him with a mixture of charity and pity. 'You studied political science at the university, right?'

'Yes.'

'Didn't they teach you about the exploitation of Ghana and Africa by white people?'

'Of course,' Nii Kwei said. 'Everyone knows about that, but most of these people you take money from didn't directly exploit us—'

'What?' Isaac interrupted. 'But they are the direct beneficiaries of exploitation through the ages, so they are just as guilty. They owe us the money, all those white people. They have stolen our gold, diamonds, timber, oil – and of course, our people. They took us away as slaves, and do you know they are still taking our nurses and doctors—'

'Nurses and doctors run away from Ghana of their own free will,' Nii pointed out. 'They want a better life, so why not? Me too, if I can go to *aburokyire*, I'll go. And so will you!'

Isaac sucked on his teeth and shook his head. 'So, they can use me like a slave? I don't think so.'

'But there are good people there too,' Nii Kwei argued. 'Who knows, maybe you are robbing some poor old white lady who contributes to aid organisations working in Africa.'

'You say what? Poor old white lady.' Isaac doubled over with mirth. 'You're funny, Nii. An American poor person is rich compared to us. It doesn't cost them anything. They don't even feel it.'

Nii Kwei suspired and looked out his window for a moment. This wasn't an argument he could win, and besides, Isaac was not wildly off the mark regarding foreign exploitation. Still, for Nii, the leap to duping individuals of their money was a problem. And yet, despite Nii's reservations, he felt himself being sucked in. Just look at this Lexus, he kept thinking. My God.

'Do you think I can do it?' he asked Isaac. 'The *sakawa*, I mean. I'm not saying I want to – just wondering.'

'But of course!' Isaac exclaimed. 'Nii, you are smart. You're wasting your life right now. Look, just try it for some few months and then you can decide whether you want to continue or not.'

Notwithstanding guidance from Isaac, those first few months of becoming a *sakawa* boy were not easy for Nii Kwei. Isaac

25

showed Nii Kwei the ropes and introduced him to someone called Kweku Ponsu. He was the traditional priest who was to become Nii Kwei's default spiritualist. Ponsu put Nii Kwei through initiation rites that were a trial by fire. More than once, Nii was on the verge of quitting, but he endured.

Now, three years on, Isaac (ironically) had found his way to Germany and Nii had his own shiny black Range Rover and was training his own mentee, Bruno. He was rough and unpolished, like a piece of wood gouged off a baobab tree. Nii had to get Bruno to understand the mentality of white people. Nii had learnt all about that at the University of Ghana, where he had hung out with a fair number of white students and had had an affair with an American professor, Susan Hadley. At the time, Hadley was visiting on a guest professorship from Boston. Nii Kwei often went to see her at her campus bungalow several times a week to fuck until they both collapsed. Now that Susan had returned to the States, Nii often missed her.

CHAPTER FOUR

4th January, Atimpoku, Ghana

Bobbing his head to the rhythm of *hiplife* blasting from the Rover's eight-speaker music system, Nii drove north to Atimpoku. He arrived at the frenetic *tro-tro* junction just past two in the afternoon and stopped to buy *abolo*, crisp *one-man-thousand*, and fiery *shito*. While he ate, he watched the noisy chaos – travellers coming and going, *tro-tros* pulling out in a cloud of dust and smoke, and traders swarming the incoming ones in the hope of selling something. The irony was they were all selling the same items.

Chasing his meal with Alvaro pineapple soda, Nii came away from the junction and drove farther on to find a parking space next to the Adome Hotel. After alighting, he followed the would-be pavement bordering the southward road for about four hundred metres, then turned right up a steep hill through a space between two houses. Most of the flatlands east of the road near the Volta Lake were already built up, so everyone was constructing on the hill now. People at the top had the most money, of course, including Kweku Ponsu. Three separate, low-slung buildings with long verandas, one of them still in construction, comprised the sprawling property. Parked in front were six of Ponsu's vehicles, a mix of SUVs and sedans. In addition to this Atimpoku location, Ponsu had a practice in Accra. Unlike the frenetic Atimpoku junction, it was quiet here with the only sounds being those of goats and sheep bleating, chickens clucking, and kids playing.

Two women were doing laundry on the veranda of the centre building, one bucket for the wash, one for the rinse. They looked up as Nii appeared.

'Good afternoon,' he said in bad Twi. As a Ga, he spoke Twi with an awful accent. 'Nii Kwei,' said the older one with a smile, 'how are you?'

'I'm fine, and you? Please, is Mr Ponsu in?'

She got up, wiping her hands in the fold of the cloth around her waist. 'I'm coming, eh?' She went briefly inside the house, re-emerging to beckon to Nii. 'Mr Ponsu says you can come.' It took Nii's eyes a few seconds to adjust to the room's dimness. Ponsu, swaddled in yards of resplendent *kente* cloth, sat in the corner on a traditional wooden stool as he texted on his smartphone. A violent gas lamp explosion when he was a child had scarred his face and chest for life, but he had undergone restorative plastic surgery in the United States recently, and his blotchy, tight skin had improved considerably.

Ponsu eschewed the term, 'fetish priest'. It was the white man's language and had always had a derogatory connotation. He preferred 'traditional priest', a fitting name considering Ponsu repeatedly rattled Ghana's conservative clergy and the Pentecostal ministers by accusing them of fraud and false prophecy. People either hated Ponsu's guts or believed in him with all their heart. To Nii Kwei, Ponsu was like a father who commanded fear, respect, and sometimes even love.

'Good afternoon, Papa boss,' Nii said, touching his forehead in salute.

'How are you?' Ponsu's tone was nasal, as though his vocal cords were placed in the back of his nose.

'I'm good, please.'

'Sit,' Ponsu said, indicating a stool opposite him. 'How are you faring?'

Nii cleared his throat. 'Not so bad.'

'What have you brought me?'

Nii took out a bulging, folded envelope from his pocket, stood up, and gave it to Ponsu, who took out the *cedi* bills and counted them. He looked up for an explanation. 'This is all?' he asked, his tenor flat and disapproving.

Nii was squirming inside. 'Papa, I will get more. The money hasn't been coming as fast as I want. I don't know what's wrong.'

'You are having difficulties because the gods are not so pleased with you,' Ponsu declared.

That pronouncement engendered dread in Nii. He flicked his tongue across his lips. 'Yes please, Papa.'

'In next two weeks, bring two chickens as an offering.'

Nii nodded.

'And,' Ponsu continued, 'hair from a white woman.'

Nii started. 'Please, Papa – you say?'

'Hair from a white woman.'

'What about albino?' Nii suggested. He could buy that in town. It was expensive but available.

'*No!*' Ponsu shook his head. 'Are you deaf? I say a white woman and you are trying to tell me "albino". Foolish. You will sleep with a white woman and get the hair. And her underwear too with her fluids. Then the gods will know you are serious. If you don't bring it, you know what can happen.'

Yes, Nii was aware. Loss of livelihood, riches, prestige – and, sometimes, of life. 'I will bring it, Papa.'

'And your boy, is he learning?' Ponsu asked.

'Please, you mean Bruno? He is learning fast.'

'If he is ready, then you bring him to me next time. He should bring two chickens for the sacrifice.'

'Yes please.'

'You can go now.'

Nii left, shaken. He needed to ask God – the head of all gods – for help. He had to find a white woman.

CHAPTER FIVE

5th January, Accra, Ghana

That night, Nii went to The Republic off Oxford Street. It was a loud bar and club with a DJ who spun *hiplife* and hip hop. When the place was packed, which was always, patrons spilt out onto the street. The waiters sped about between tables serving up mixed drinks and yam fries. The crowd was a mix of Ghanaians and people from all over the world. White American girls loved coming here to get some black-man penis. The Americans always acted all cool but if you watched them carefully you could see their eyes eating up tall, young Ghanaian guys like vultures devouring carrion.

Nii spotted three white women sharing space with a few other people at a table next to the small dance area. One woman was on the chunky side, and the second was thin with almost no breasts. But it was the third woman who held Nii's attention. She was pretty, on the dark side of blonde with hair cascading to her shoulders. A lot of hair.

Nii approached them, switching on his charm and Americanising his accent and pronunciation. Reese was the pretty one, and Nii concentrated his attention on her. He used some of the American expressions and idioms he'd learnt from Susan Hadley.

Reese seemed to be responding to his flirtations, but after a while, Nii noticed the other two were being obstructive, especially the chunky one, Sheila, who kept sending him disparaging looks. She seemed to be trying to 'protect' Reese, or else she was just plain jealous. He couldn't even get Reese's number because of that fucking Sheila. All the same, he did give Reese the number to his two mobiles.

Abruptly, Sheila signalled to the others it was time to go, and Nii had a bad feeling she wanted to get the other two away from him. *Why?* He put it down to prejudice. When they left him with an empty 'Nice meeting you', he felt rejected and then angry. Reese gave him a glance back as they left, and he prayed she would text him when she had a moment alone.

He got home relatively early – just after midnight – and went to bed feeling annoyed and anxious. What was the next step to getting to sleep with a white girl and getting a snippet of her hair? To no avail, he checked his phone again for a text from Reese.

He slept until past ten in the morning, waking up to a phone alert. His heart leapt at the thought it might be Reese, but it wasn't. Even better, it was Susan Hadley who was in town at the Golden Tulip Hotel and wanted to see him.

CHAPTER SIX

When Susan Hadley, PhD, had first visited Ghana, she had been a tenured physicist at Boston University. At the time, she was fifty-two, recently divorced, and disillusioned. The divorce had been brutal.

Susan needed a change of pace and environment – a radical one. So, she signed up for a two-year visiting professorship at the University of Ghana. She'd never stepped foot on the continent of Africa, so it was a culture shock – the kind of jolt she needed. Something as dissimilar to Boston as possible. She wanted to do a 'mind cleanse', the mental equivalent of juicing.

Among the things she learnt to get used to in Ghana was being called 'Mama' – even in public – by young Ghanaians she didn't even know. It wasn't an insult. It was a term of deference and often affection. True, it reminded her she wasn't a spring chicken any more, but she learnt to roll with it. For one thing, her age commanded a lot more respect than it ever had at home, where 'Ma'am' was sometimes used as a slight.

Susan was ready and willing for new experiences. The heat and humidity and all that black skin around her woke up something inside and the number of men she slept with surprised even her. But Nii Kwei was her prince. They met at one of those staff-student mixes. He was in his last year of political science and he was bright, eloquent, and funny. Sarcasm is not used as much in Ghanaian humour as it is in American, but Nii Kwei knew how to do it.

Susan was decades past romantic cat-and-mouse games and playing hard to get. The very night of the mixer, she cut to the chase and invited Nii Kwei to her on-campus bungalow where they had sex half the night. My God, he was good. Her multiple climaxes with him left her as limp as a dishrag. Her lectures the following day were a little uneven, but someone commented on how well she looked.

At first, she wasn't wildly excited about Nii calling her 'Mummy'. She felt weird about it and rolled her eyes. But for all his quirks, Nii was loyal and affectionate. He didn't have much money, but he always brought her little gifts from the market or the mall. It was his smell that got her – earthy, yet fresh and essential.

When her two years were up, Nii was morose about losing Susan. She was more sanguine, however, and promised to come back to Ghana as soon as she could.

'Promise and swear to call me when you return,' Nii demanded.

'I promise and swear,' she said.

* * *

And now, she was back – older and not in quite the same frame of mind as before. Nii would be around twenty-six now, and when Susan opened her hotel room door to him, she saw that some of his boyishness had gone. He had a neatly trimmed beard now, and his body seemed more solid – more like a man's than a boy's. They embraced each other for a while.

'I've missed you so much,' he told her. 'Come, let's talk.'

They sat together on the sofa. Nii explained that he hadn't done anything with his BA in political science. In fact, it had been worthless to him, and he had been through a rough patch of unemployment before getting into 'information technology', as he put it.

'Oh, that's great!' she exclaimed. 'And you look like you're doing very well. Those clothes you're wearing are an upgrade! Oh, my God, you're even handsomer than before.'

He laughed. 'Thanks, my love. And what about you? How is work?'

Susan was still teaching at BU. Her oldest daughter had had a baby.

'You look so good,' he said softly. 'Can I kiss you?'

They kissed for a long time, and then Nii told Susan to hang on tight while he lifted her and carried her to the bed.

Nii Kwei seemed to Susan to have more finesse than she remembered – at least at the start. But after several minutes, some of the old roughness returned with something new besides. He talked dirty, which she had never heard from

35

him before, and he mixed English with Ga, producing a steamy, heady mix of brutally erotic language. She was transported to an intense high, only hazily aware that she was shrieking and crying and begging him to do it harder and faster, which he did until they had migrated across the bed to the edge of the other side. He pulled them both back from the brink before they fell off.

When both were spent, Nii went to sleep for a while. She watched him and relished the glossy blackness of his skin, which both absorbed and reflected light. He stirred and pulled her close, so he was behind her and she fitted into the concavity of his body.

'Your hair is lighter these days,' he said.

She chuckled. 'You mean greyer?'

'No, I didn't mean that.' He kissed her. 'I like it. Can I have some?'

She lifted her head to look at him. 'Really?'

'Yes, yes. That's what I want. I know someone who can make a bracelet from it. I will wear it and you'll be with me all the time.'

'How weird and sweet,' she said. 'OK, but just a little bit. I'm not exactly blessed with flowing tresses.'

She got up and dug around in her things, finding a small pair of scissors in her first aid kit.

He snipped a little from the back, where the hair was longer. 'Thank you, my love.'

36

CHAPTER SEVEN

6th January, Accra, Ghana

Emma Djan was no good at sleeping. She lifted her head in the darkness and looked at her phone: 2.54 a.m., the worst possible time to be awake. She made the best of it, rising to make some milky tea with a chunk of sweet bread to go with it.

At five, she took a shower to refresh herself and reverse the oppressing warmth of the night. The rainy season, which brought cooler weather, would not be for several months. Until then, Emma would need these bracing morning showers, pathetic as they were because of insufficient water pressure. The Ghana Water Company gave preference to the foreign embassies, upscale hotels, and posh areas of the city like Airport Residential and Trasacco Valley. Emma's part of town, Madina, didn't make the list.

Apart from the slow-running water, the bathroom was adequate at best but frequently less than. Overall, her lodgings were scanty, with the kitchen and sitting room practically one space and the bedroom not much more than a cubbyhole. And yet the rent took easily three-quarters of Emma's salary, first because housing in Accra, Ghana's capital, was exorbitant at any level, rich or poor, and second because as a constable in the Ghana Police Service, or GPS, Emma didn't earn much.

The measly compensation from the GPS would always be the way it was. You had to accept it and live. That Ghanaian police officers were constantly looking for a handout from the citizenry wasn't even a secret any more. Cops' paltry salary was both a reason and excuse for greed, need, and corruption. Everyone, from the lowly constable to the exalted police commissioner, was guilty, and they knew the public knew.

Emma checked her reflection in the mirror, making sure her conservative grey skirt and cream blouse were spotless and impeccably pressed. She felt she was too skinny. Her problem, as friends and family pointed out without relent, was that she 'never ate anything'. Not quite true, but she did often skip meals without noticing.

She left the house, walking quickly along the unpaved and uneven pavement. This time of the morning, already warm and humid, the streets were full of children in their uniforms hurrying to school and workers rushing to get to work on time. Accra's traffic could foil them yet.

At the Kaneshie lorry park, *tro-tro* drivers and their assistants, called 'mates', competed ferociously for passengers. Hustling potential riders, they yelled out their final destinations in an iconic singsong voice. Emma found her *tro-tro* and squeezed past other passengers to a tattered seat with ratty foam and exposed springs. When the mate had packed the vehicle as full as physically possible, he signalled the driver with a bang on the roof and the journey started. The minivan, like almost all other *tro-tros*, was in an advanced state of disrepair – no maintenance whatsoever, Emma imagined. Essentially, she and the eighteen-or-so other riders had just agreed to a high risk of death or mutilation going from point A to B.

The Criminal Investigation Department, CID, building had a new coat of sun-yellow paint, but it could not conceal its age. Seven stories high, it had monotonous rows of old style, dusty louvre windows with occasional modernised plate glass sliders.

A sentry box and armed guard stood to the left of the front security gate and everyone including senior officers underwent an immediate pat down on entry to the premises. From there, it was on to the lobby of the building accommodating an assortment of people on all kinds of business.

Headed to the second floor, Emma went up the steps, which were so worn they slanted downward. Emma was a true novice with the Ghana Police Service in general and the CID in particular. Twenty-six, she had graduated from the police academy only four months before. She had always dreamt of being a homicide detective. That was what her late father had been. The atmosphere in Daddy's office milling with detectives, the stacks of folders piled high on desks, the capture of suspects and the questioning of witnesses, a glimpse into this case or that – as a girl, Emma had taken it all in by some unconscious process of osmosis infused with fascination.

'Daddy, how did you catch the bad man?' she would ask him, sitting on his knee.

He had never waved her away with that well-known adult dismissiveness towards a child: 'You wouldn't understand. I'll tell you when you grow up.' He would explain it all to her in a way that made sense. And when she nodded with understanding and satisfaction, he smiled and gave her a kiss on her forehead. She would laugh and run off to play.

Daddy had been her hero – he still was. His sudden death at the age of only fifty-five had left the two women in his life – Emma and her mother – bereft. He had never taken his hypertension seriously enough. One morning at work, he collapsed – dead almost instantly from an engulfing haemorrhage of the brain.

On graduation, Constable Emma Djan quickly discovered she would be assigned a department at the discretion of the GPS alone. New recruits didn't get to indicate their preferences, if they had any. Emma's fervent hope she would join Homicide didn't materialise: her station was to be the Commercial Crimes Unit (CCU). She and fourteen other officers investigated the acquisition of land or homes through fraudulent transactions, trespass, document forgery, and so on. Land grabs and property theft were rampant in Ghana. Getting to the bottom of it was tedious, mind-numbing work. Most of the cases remained open for months to years.

Emma's heart was not in it. She wasn't under any illusion that murder investigations didn't involve monotonous paperwork, but the motives behind commercial crimes didn't grab her the way murder did.

She pushed the CCU door open and went in with a flat, unenthusiastic feeling that meant she would rather be somewhere else. She was more than on time. Only two other workers were already there. The rest would straggle in over the next hour or two. Stolen property wasn't going anywhere. There was no pressure to get to a crime scene before evidence was destroyed.

'Morning, morning,' Emma said brightly to her co-workers. She tried to put the best face on it.

They replied without much enthusiasm as Emma took a seat at the table she shared with several colleagues. The whole unit was depressed and depressing. She tackled the folder at the top of her file – dreary records about this complainant and that defendant. She wished she was Homicide *Detective* Constable Djan. 'DC Djan' had a nice ring.

When she had first joined CID as a recruit in the CCU, she had begun working with her officemates with reasonable keenness. They showed her the ropes, but with scant hand-holding. 'This is like this, and that is like that; now get to work.' In only her third week in the unit, it hit Emma right between the eyes that she couldn't possibly continue this. She was dying a slow death in boredom purgatory. Several days followed during which she drummed up the courage to approach her superior officer, Inspector Kuma, in his office, which wasn't much more than a small space in the corner of the unit.

'Yes?' he had asked irritably as she knocked on his open door. He was youthful in the face and rotund in the body. Too much *banku*.

Emma came forward to a respectable distance from Kuma's desk, deferentially keeping her hands behind her back. 'Please, sir,' she whispered, 'I want to know if I can also train in the Homicide Division.' She didn't dare say 'transfer to Homicide', because it would sound like she didn't like Inspector Kuma or his department – which was true but not a good thought to express out loud.

'What?' he snapped. 'Train in Homicide? What is wrong with you? You think you can just go wherever you like? Why do you want to do that?'

'Please, I like it,' Emma said.

'How do you know? Have you been a homicide detective before?'

'No please, but my father was one.'

'So, because he was in Homicide, you think you know you will like it?' Kuma laughed. 'It's in the blood, is that what you are trying to say?'

'Yes please.'

'Who is your father?'

'Chief Superintendent Emmanuel Djan. He passed away six years ago.'

'Oh, sorry,' Kuma said, with a surprising amount of sympathy in his tone. 'Where was he stationed?'

'At Kumasi – Manhyia District Headquarters.'

'Did he know our director?'

By that, Kuma meant Commissioner Alex Andoh, the director-general of CID. Next to the inspector general of police, he was one of the most powerful and influential men in the police hierarchy. 'Director-General' was his position, while 'Commissioner' was his police rank and the titles were used interchangeably.

'Please, I'm not sure,' Emma said, her fingers twisting around each other behind her. 'I don't think so.'

'Look, Constable Djan,' Kuma said, 'you can't just change your department like that, eh? Maybe one of your father's associates can talk to DCOP Laryea in charge of recruit assignments, but as for me, I can't help you. Sorry.'

'OK, sir. Thank you, sir.'

Kuma dismissed Emma and she went away surprisingly uplifted because there might have been something to Kuma's idea. She was lost in thought as she sat down, her work temporarily forgotten. Commander Seidu, the head of the Kumasi Regional Headquarters, had always liked and respected Daddy and had been deeply affected by his death. Emma made the decision to call Seidu.

But in the months that followed, nothing seemed to result from contacting Commander Seidu. He had said he would see what he could do for her and Emma knew him well enough to know he had meant it, but in retrospect she realised she had set her hopes too high. Slowly, she was becoming accustomed to the grind and tedium of the CCU, and her desire to become a detective constable in Homicide, albeit still there, began to wane. The reality that it wasn't going to happen sank in. The question she had begun to pose to herself now was whether she wanted to remain with the Ghana Police Service at all.

Near closing time, Kuma called Emma to his office. 'Report to DCOP Laryea's office,' he said curtly.

'Please, now?'

'No, next week. Of course now!' he thundered. 'What's wrong with you?'

'Yes please. Sorry, sir.'

Emma nearly tripped over her own feet as she made haste out of the unit.

CHAPTER EIGHT

Deputy Commissioner of Police (DCOP) is among the top ranks in the GPS, and so for Emma it was nerve-wracking to face Cleophus Laryea in his expansive, fifth-floor office, chilled by an efficient air conditioner high up on the wall. Receding, patchy hair and a face lined with creases confirmed his seniority. A pair of spectacles perched halfway down his broad nose, and when he looked up over them, his eyes were intense and piercing.

'Be seated, Constable Djan,' he said quietly, pointing at one of a pair of chairs in front of his desk. She sat down without a word and waited, her heart in her stomach. She suspected this was about her request to move to Homicide, but was it going to be good news or bad?

'I have heard from Commander Seidu in Kumasi on two occasions now,' Laryea began, his voice as deep as a village borehole. 'He informed me of your interest in working in the Homicide Division.' He looked over his spectacles. 'Is that still the case?'

'Yes please, sir,' Emma said.

'He spoke very highly of your father.'

'Thank you, sir.'

'Why do you want to work in Homicide?'

'Please, as I followed my father's work until the day he died, I came to learn the ways of working as a detective, and I liked it very much. I have wanted to do it for a long time. I feel the connection with people is stronger and more important than . . .'

Laryea removed his glasses. 'Than what?'

Emma squirmed. 'Than what I'm doing now,' she said in barely a whisper.

His eyes sliced through her. 'Are you having any kind of conflicts or difficulties in the CCU you wish to tell me about?'

'No please,' Emma said hurriedly. 'Everything is fine.'

Laryea nodded. 'I asked Inspector Kuma about you and he said you are a diligent worker.'

Emma's heart fluttered. Maybe Kuma wasn't so bad after all. 'Thank you, sir.'

'I will approve your transfer to Homicide,' Laryea said. 'As a matter of fact, they do need some female presence, and so that will be good.'

'Thank you, sir,' Emma said, hardly able to believe what she was hearing. Was there a *but* coming?

'But,' Laryea said, 'the final decision lies with Commissioner Andoh.'

'Yes please,' Emma said, her elation beginning to dissipate.

'I've discussed it with him already.' Laryea looked at his watch. 'It may be too late, but let me see if he's in the office and if he can see you now.'

Emma's disquiet spiralled into outright terror. She was to *meet* Commissioner Andoh in person? For a junior officer like her, the director-general was God himself.

Laryea got on his mobile and after a few seconds said, 'Yes, sir. I have interviewed her. Yes, I believe she is, but of course, it is ultimately your decision. Yes, sir. Thank you, sir.' He put away his phone and looked back at Emma. 'He says you can go up now.' Laryea must have detected her anxiety. 'Don't be fearful, Djan. The director would never summon you if he wasn't open to your request. You should understand that.'

'Yes please,' she said, slightly reassured but no less nervous.

'Just be yourself, as you have been with me and you'll be OK.'

'Yes please. Thank you very much, sir.'

Like an anxious mountain climber, Emma went up two flights to the seventh floor, the summit of the CID building. Sergeant Thelma Bright, Commissioner Andoh's decades-long assistant, showed Emma into the room. It was, as she had expected, larger than any other she had seen at CID. The carpet was plush. Pictures of the commissioner – one a full portrait by himself, the others with various luminaries including Ghana's president – adorned the walls.

Andoh's desk was dark, polished, and massive. Half a dozen chairs were arranged in a line about three metres away from it. Part of the director-general's role was to give audience to select members of the public who had a particularly serious matter or grievance to bring to his attention.

In size, the commissioner matched his desk and the large leather executive chair that supported his heft. Resplendent in a dark-blue uniform with impressive insignia on his chest and epaulettes, he was writing something, and he didn't look up.

'Sit down there, please,' Bright said to Emma, indicating one of the chairs.

Emma didn't make a sound as she took a seat. She realised she was holding her breath. Bright remained standing with her hands respectfully behind her back.

After a short while, the commissioner glanced up at her, but not at Emma. 'You may go, Thelma. Thank you. Goodnight.'

'Goodnight, sir.'

Thelma left, closing the door quietly behind her. Andoh continued to write as if Emma were not there. Then he capped his pen, leant back, and looked her over. Like Laryea, he was greying, but his face was much pudgier, with heavy jowls. 'Yes, Constable Djan. How can I help you?'

Emma didn't know how to begin.

Andoh saved her the trouble. 'DCOP Laryea tells me you want to transfer to the Homicide Division. Do you know you can't do whatever you want here at CID?'

'Yes please,' she whispered.

'You think you're special just because your father was a homicide detective?' He sounded contemptuous, which made Emma want to shrink.

'No please.'

'Eh? Speak up.'

'No, sir.'

'How do you think you will personally benefit the Homicide Division?'

Emma was undecided on how to answer. Should she continue to cower or speak her mind? 'Please, I understand there aren't many women in that unit.'

He pressed his lips together. 'That's your reason?'

'Please, I believe it's my destiny.'

Andoh looked incredulous for a moment and then began to laugh. 'You are funny,' he said. 'Funny and naive. But one thing is that you are motivated, and that is good.'

Emma felt a small wave of relief.

'If you are to get this position,' Andoh said, 'then you must perform well and to my satisfaction. Do you understand?'

'Yes please. I will.'

He inclined his head. 'Are you sure you can look at dead bodies? You look too soft.'

'No please,' Emma said with a tinge of indignation. 'I'm not soft.'

'Come here and let me show you some photographs of murder crime scenes and we will see how you react,' the commissioner said. 'Bring the chair over with you.'

'Yes, sir.'

Emma sat to his left and he brought a laptop in front of them from the right side of the desk. After some clicks, he brought up several gruesome photographs – people butchered to death by blunt force or deep machete wounds; a woman with her throat cut almost clean through; a man hanging from a tree branch.

'These are all real cases the Homicide Division has seen,' Andoh said, looking at her. 'How do you find them?'

Emma was leaning forward with fascination. 'This one has a very personal signature,' she murmured, pointing at the woman with the severed neck. 'Maybe her husband or boyfriend, or a family member.'

'You know about signature,' Andoh said, clearly surprised. He nodded. 'Anyway, you are correct. In fact, it was the husband who murdered her. He thought she was committing adultery with the neighbour. Good job.'

'Thank you, sir,' Emma said. Her heart was racing with excitement. He seemed impressed. This was working out beyond her dreams.

'What about this one?' he asked, clicking to another image and at the same time resting his large hand on Emma's right thigh. She flinched, startled. The commissioner's attitude towards her had transformed. Now he was friendly, even intimate. Perhaps he was just being kind, but she felt uncomfortable.

'Constable Djan?' he pressed, and his hand shifted a little higher on her thigh. 'What do you think?'

'Well,' she said, flustered and distracted, 'from his injuries, it seems he was dragged to the location where he was found.'

Andoh was watching her closely. 'Something like that.' He stood up, towering over her. She found him intimidating. 'Come with me,' he said.

Uncertain, she rose to follow him to a door in the back of the room that she had not noticed till now. He unlocked it, opened it, and stepped inside. 'Come,' he said, as he saw her hesitation.

Emma went in cautiously and saw it was a small bathroom and changing area in the middle of which was a chair with a cushioned seat and cane back.

'This is my private chamber,' Andoh said. 'Sometimes I need to change into ceremonial clothes for visiting dignitaries.'

'Yes please,' Emma said. 'It's nice.'

'Please sit over there.' He pointed to the chair.

'Sir?'

'Sit down on the chair.'

Emma did so uneasily, not clear what was going on. Andoh approached her.

'You remember how I said you must perform well to my satisfaction?' he said, caressing her face.

Oh God, she thought. *Please, not this.*

He circled around to the back of the chair. 'Well, now is the time.'

She went rigid as his heavy hand slipped into her blouse, fondling one breast, and then the other. His finger wormed into her bra to stroke her nipple back and forth like a windshield wiper.

'Your skin is so soft and beautiful,' he said, breathing heavily. 'If all goes well, you can start in the Homicide Division tomorrow, OK? I'm sure you will work out there very well.'

Emma let out a whimper. 'Please sir.'

'What is it?'

'I beg you, sir.'

He chortled. 'Beg me for what? To make love to you?'

She began to cry.

'Why are you crying?' he demanded. 'What are the tears for? Are you a small girl?' He sounded annoyed. 'Stand up. Come on, stand up.'

Emma covered her face in shame, hyperventilating as Andoh unbuttoned her blouse. His jowls were in her face. He tried to kiss her, but she pulled her head back. He tugged his pants and shorts down to his thighs. She caught a glimpse of his erect penis and turned her head away quickly, utterly mortified and repulsed.

'Take off your dress,' he ordered.

She shook her head, pleading with him. 'No please. I beg you, sir.'

'Stop this,' he said, his tone becoming harsh. 'Do what I say.'

He pulled her forcefully to the ground with one hand and began working her dress up with the other. Emma resisted. He leant on her, his big body suppressing her struggles.

What was happening? *Why was this happening?*

Her panic rose to a crescendo and she screamed.

'No one can hear you,' Andoh muttered. 'If you try to tell anyone about this, they won't believe you and you will be disgraced.'

He was trying to tug her underwear down, but that didn't work, so he tore it instead. Emma looked away, weeping as he grunted and huffed, moving his big body into position. She remembered what Daddy had said. *Go for his eyes, his balls.*

'Let me take off my dress properly for you,' she said, her voice shaking. 'I can do it for you, sir.'

Andoh pulled back, appearing surprised at her apparent new willingness. He lifted his weight off her, freeing up her hands. Like a striking cobra, she jabbed her right index finger into his left eye socket hard and quick. He recoiled with a gasp of pain and fell back, his hand pressed over the left side of his face. Emma jumped up, nearly falling as she bolted for the door. The commissioner lay on the floor bellowing like a wounded cow. *Run*, she told herself. *Run*.

Without looking back or shutting the door behind her, Emma exited Andoh's office into the dim, deserted corridor, along which ran open louvre windows and mosquito netting. Outside, darkness had fallen.

She ran down the stairs. Almost everyone had gone home, but one or two people coming up in the opposite direction gave her a curious look. The women's bathroom on the second floor was open. She went into a stall, locked it, threw up in the bowl, and then leant weakly against one wall. She was bewildered. Was this real?

Her hands were shaking as she tried to button up her blouse. She broke down, taking deep, whooping breaths between each cycle of sobs.

'Hello?' a woman's voice said from the other side of the door.

Emma held her breath to stop crying, but small whimpers still escaped her throat. The woman knocked on the stall door gently. 'Are you OK?'

'I'm . . . I'm fine,' Emma stammered.

'What's wrong? Do you need to go to the hospital?'

Emma struggled to lighten her voice. 'No, madam, everything is fine. It's just . . . well, I've received some bad news. A relative has died.'

'Oh,' the woman said, sounding like she didn't believe it. 'Can I help you somehow? It seems like you're hurt.'

'No, no please, I'm all right.'

The woman was silent for a moment. 'All right,' she said finally. 'Take care, OK? And I'm sorry for what happened.'

'Thank you, madam.'

The woman left. As warm as it was in the uncooled bathroom – none had air conditioning – Emma began to shiver so violently it frightened her.

Now, she wanted to leave, but she was terrified she might bump into Andoh coming down the stairs. Briefly, she began to cry again, but then she pulled herself together. She had to get out of here. Tiptoeing to the bathroom door, she opened it slightly and listened for a long time. Nothing – no footsteps. The commissioner had likely departed.

Go now, she told herself.

She flew down the steps, almost tripping at one point. When she got to the ground floor, she half ran to the security gate, but slowed down as she got there in order to look somewhat normal.

'Goodnight,' she said to the sentry with forced cheerfulness.

He responded with a disinterested nod. The sentries were never particularly friendly.

Emma stood at the side of Ring Road East feeling paralysed and unreal. She was barely aware of the rush of evening traffic, the *tro-tro* mates yelling out, and the buzz of pedestrians making their way home.

Emma's ferocious shivering began again. She was in profound shock. Her vision darkened and she felt herself spinning. And then she collapsed.

CHAPTER NINE

At almost the same instant Emma hit the ground, she regained consciousness, but she was momentarily confused. What was going on? Why had everyone crowded around her?

'You fainted,' a woman said. 'Are you OK?'

Emma tried to scramble up, but the woman made her stay down. 'Relax, eh? Relax, please.'

'She should go to the hospital,' a man said.

'Can you take her?' the woman asked him.

'Yes,' he said. 'My car is just here. I can bring it.'

'No, no,' Emma protested. 'No, I'm fine. Please, I just want to go home. I'm fine.'

'You're not fine,' the woman insisted.

'It's, it's because I didn't eat the whole day,' Emma offered, grasping for any justification at all. This was embarrassing – all these people staring at her.

'She can drink this,' someone else said, producing a can of Milo chocolate milk. He popped the top and offered it to her.

Emma sat up now and took the can. She hated chocolate milk, but she drank it anyway.

'Better?' the woman asked.

Emma nodded. 'Please, I'd like to get up now.'

They helped her to her feet. For a moment she felt unsteady, but she recovered quickly. 'Where do you live?' the woman asked her.

'Madina. I'll take a cab there.'

'I will get one for you,' the Milo man said. 'Just wait, please.'

He flagged down a cab and opened the rear door. The woman helped Emma in. 'Thank you very much, madam,' Emma said. 'I appreciate it.'

'Be careful, eh?' the woman said. 'When you get home, eat plenty *banku*.' They both laughed.

At home, Emma showered, lathering up several times with her most fragrant soap until she was sure she couldn't detect the commissioner's odour on her. But she felt dirty sitting at the side of her bed, her short, nappy hair still wet. She shuddered. She had no desire to eat *banku*, as the kind woman had suggested, or anything else for that matter. She didn't want to eat, sleep, watch TV, or socialise on Instagram. Emma didn't want to do anything. She sat unmoving in the silent room like a block of wood – lifeless and empty. She was confused. She couldn't sort out what had occurred. It was as if she were looking at a pile of twisted, knotted ropes that she had no idea how to untangle.

She lay down, leaving the light on, but the incident began to replay in her head, so she sat up to shake it. After thirty minutes in a kind of suspended, undefined state, Emma tried to sleep again. A couple of hours later, she jerked awake, gasping and looking around for the rapist. She cried again, and then went to the kitchen to make some tea, dunking sweet bread in it. When she finished, she folded her arms on the table and rested her head. She woke again and took herself to bed.

Before five, the nightmare repeated and she rose, grateful the morning was finally here.

In the *tro-tro*, Emma felt detached and outside herself. Her hearing seemed muffled, as if her cranium was full of cotton balls – dull and muted. The passenger beside her had to nudge her to make her aware that the mate was holding out his hand for the fare. She alighted on Ring Road East and crossed to the CID building. She didn't want to look up at the seventh floor. As she went up the steps to the second, she was gripped with apprehension that Commissioner Andoh might be behind her or coming down in the opposite direction.

When Emma got to her unit, she avoided making eye contact with her co-workers, muttering good morning in a subdued tone quite unlike her. She could feel the curious glances, the double takes, and quite irrationally she felt as though her co-workers might be able to tell that she had been violated. Maybe somehow the whole of CID knew? Tears welled up and she felt humiliation engulf her. She wished she could stay in hiding at home but calling in sick wasn't an option at the GPS – unless you had an iron-clad doctor's note to back you up.

Inspector Kuma came in at 10.30 a.m. In her peripheral vision she watched to see if he was looking at her, but he didn't seem to be. At 10.45 a.m., when he called her into his office and told her to shut the door and take a seat, Emma knew something bad was about to take place. She kept her eyes down, but she stole a glance at Kuma to find him looking at her with distaste. *He knows*, she thought.

'I did everything I could to help you,' Kuma said, 'and then you turn around and speak badly of me and DCOP Laryea to Commissioner Andoh.'

Emma was bewildered. 'But please, I didn't say anything against you. Or the DCOP.'

'You are a liar,' Kuma said, curling his lip. 'I don't like liars. What a disgrace. We don't tolerate the likes of you in my department. The DCOP wants to see you in his office right now. He will speak to you, and then as of today, you will no longer be working at CID. Whatever personal belongings you have here, take them with you and get out.'

Emma left the inspector's office trying to hold back her tears, but everyone in the unit could tell she was crying. The room was quiet as a church and all eyes followed her first to her desk where she retrieved her backpack, and then to the door as she left with a crushing feeling of shame.

It seemed a long trek to DCOP Laryea's office. She knocked and entered at his command. When he saw her tearstained face and puffy eyes, he looked alarmed.

'Sit down, Djan,' he said, rising from his chair.

Emma did so and began immediately to weep, her face buried in her palms. Laryea pulled his chair around from behind the desk and sat down about a metre away from her, waiting quietly until she was able to rein in her emotions somewhat.

'I'm sorry, sir,' she whispered.

'It's OK.' Laryea leant forward, forearms on his thighs. 'But what is going on? The director called me this morning to say you cast aspersions upon me and Inspector Kuma, and that you were in general very disrespectful when you spoke to him yesterday evening. Why did you do that?'

'But I didn't, sir!' Emma said, outrage finding its way into her voice for the first time. 'Please, I never did.'

Anger was rising to replace anguish now because she was beginning to see clearly that Andoh was simply taking revenge against her. He had offered her a position in Homicide in return for sex, but she had not complied. In addition, she had injured his eye.

Laryea studied her. 'Then, what happened when you went to see Commissioner Andoh?' he asked quietly.

Emma hesitated. On no account would she *ever* reveal the truth, for who would believe her? Even to her, when the incident flashed through her mind, it seemed unreal or impossible. All this morning during eerie moments of self-doubt, she wondered if she was recalling the event accurately. Worst of all, people might say she was a temptress who had deliberately aroused the man. With heavy guilt, she thought about how closely she had sat next to the commissioner at his desk. She should not have done that.

'I was—' she began, and then rephrased. 'Maybe I didn't show Commissioner Andoh enough respect.'

Laryea frowned. 'How or why would that be the case? If anything, you are beyond respectful. How many "sirs" and "pleases" can you pack in one sentence?'

'Yes, sir,' she said, looking down at her hands as her fingers twisted around one another. Laryea watched her for a few moments. She did not meet his gaze.

'Something happened,' the DCOP said finally. 'I don't know exactly what and you don't have to tell me, but something did happen.' He took a breath and heaved a sigh. 'Nevertheless, I regret to say that on orders of the director, I have to relieve you of your duties. As of now, you are no longer an employee of the Ghana Police Service and you are disallowed from ever holding a position in the organisation. Is that clear?'

Emma's eyes were still downcast. 'Yes, sir.'

'You are dismissed.'

Emma rose slowly and walked to the door with her mind leaden, static, and without direction.

'Wait a minute,' Laryea said. She turned. The DCOP, his up-pointing right index finger suspended, was pondering.

'Yes, sir?'

'Something has just occurred to me.' Laryea stared at her intently. 'Would you be interested in becoming a private investigator?'

Emma was unclear. 'Please, I don't quite get you, sir. Private investigator?'

'I have a friend, Yemo Sowah, who owns a private detective agency in Accra,' Laryea said steadily. 'He might be able to employ you. I think you would be good at it.'

Emma felt a surge of interest – eagerness, even. 'Please, what do they do there?'

'Mostly missing persons, marital infidelity, theft, gathering evidence for lawyers, and so on. Not many murders, to be honest, but at least you can do detective work.'

'Yes please,' Emma said with a sudden, big smile.

'But I'm not guaranteeing you will get a job, Djan,' Laryea said hastily. 'I'm just saying *maybe*. I will call him first, and if he's interested, he'll get in touch with you.'

'Thank you very much, sir.' Emma's voice shook. 'You have really tried to help me. I really appreciate everything you've done for me. God bless you.'

Laryea brushed it aside. 'Not at all. Look, the best of luck to you, wherever your destiny might take you.'

CHAPTER TEN

9th January

Nii delivered Susan's underwear and a lock of her hair to Ponsu in a small, clear plastic bag. The priest nodded approval. The two chickens Nii had brought along were squawking from the inside of an old rice sack. Ponsu looked inside and grabbed one of the fowls – a dirty white hen that lost a few feathers as it struggled to get away. Pressing the hen down on a flat stone, Ponsu quickly cut its head off. The creature's legs and wings went through a series of violent spasms.

'Stand there,' he said to Nii, pointing at a spot in the courtyard, around which several dwellings were built. The occupants looked on with interest.

Holding the chicken's neck down, Ponsu made a circle of blood around Nii, finally laying the bird at Nii's feet.

The second chicken got different treatment. First, its beak was tied firmly shut with a length of twine. After its decapitation, Ponsu let it run around like a cavorting drunkard until it collapsed in the dirt. He looked at the severed head and then turned to Nii. 'Tonight, you come with me to the Awudome Cemetery.'

They arrived past one o'clock in the morning. The sound of traffic from nearby Ring Road West was soft compared to the daytime tumult. Nii didn't like cemeteries, and certainly not in the dead of night. He was shivering, not from cold but from fear. Ponsu, leading the way with the anaemic beam of a mobile phone, appeared unaffected. He had obviously been to Awudome Cemetery several times. It was a huge expanse of land, but the priest appeared to know where he was going. Nii followed him in lockstep to preclude even the slightest chance that he lose sight of the priest and find himself lost in the dark among the dead. The crosses and headstones were dark shadows and Nii could have sworn he saw some of them moving. Every so often, he stiffened and looked behind him as he thought he heard something or someone moving in the brush.

At last, Ponsu stopped at the corner of the cemetery closest to Awudome Road. 'Dig a hole here for the chicken head,' he instructed Nii, handing him a crudely fashioned wooden trowel.

Nii went to work. Ponsu's phone light was fading with its waning battery.

'It's OK,' Ponsu said, once Nii had dug deeply enough. 'Stand there.'

Nii went rigid as he saw where Ponsu was pointing. 'Please, you want me to stand on the grave?'

'Yes. The chicken's beak is tied so that your *sakawa* victims can never say no to you. They will try, but they won't be able to resist, no matter how much money you ask them for. So, you must stand on a grave and have no fear.'

Nii tried not to appear flustered, but his legs were shaking the entire time he stood on that gravestone, and it seemed an eternity before Ponsu allowed him to get down.

'Within two weeks,' the priest declared, 'you will see the money start to flow.'

CHAPTER ELEVEN

18th January, Washington, DC

Gordon Tilson was on Facebook Messenger with a man called Frank, who, like Gordon, was a widower. But unlike Gordon, Frank's loss was recent – only a month or so – whereas Gordon had lost his Regina to cancer thirteen years ago. The Facebook page, Widows & Widowers, was a forum and support group.

Gordon had never loved a woman more than Regina – except his mother, that is. He had met her while on Peace Corps duty in Ghana in the 1980s when he was twentyish and both black and white Americans were flocking to that West African country for entirely different reasons.

Gordon fell for Regina hook, line, and sinker. Her skin was a deep, resilient black while he, a redhead, invariably turned an uncomfortable pink in the pitiless equatorial heat and humidity. She wasn't that impressed with his overtures at first. Culturally they were miles apart, but his comical antics (he was quite the prankster) and his decent attempts at speaking Twi, Ghana's most commonly spoken indigenous language, amused and intrigued her. She enjoyed his deep interest in Ghanaian culture and his fervour to learn as much as possible about it. When Gordon's Peace Corps assignment was up, he told her he wouldn't leave without her. Besides, it turned out Regina was pregnant, and Gordon was certainly the father. Nine months later when the baby emerged crying at the top of his lungs, they christened him Derek with the Ghanaian middle name of Yaw, for Thursday. He was to be Gordon's first and only child.

Regina's slow, anguished death from ovarian cancer reached into Gordon's soul and ripped out his beating heart like a bloodthirsty warrior. He didn't think he could live without the woman he had called his Old Faithful. Now his Facebook friend was going through the same experience, and so Gordon was kind and supportive to Frank, who had just typed on Messenger: *I keep waking up at night and looking over at the empty space in the bed expecting to see her. But she's not there. It leaves me so desolate. Did that ever happen to you?*

All the time, Gordon wrote.

How did you deal with it?

I won't pretend it was easy.

A few moments passed before Frank said anything. Then, *Sometimes I don't want to get over it.*

Yes. Guilt over starting to feel OK. I had that too. But it does get better. In fact, it will pass.

Gordon's WhatsApp line on his phone rang and he felt a surge of eagerness as he saw who it was. *Helena.*

* * *

Among the features of a beautiful African woman, it was the space between the eyebrows and its transition to the nose that beguiled Gordon most. Its unromantic medical name is the *glabella*. In a white woman, the glabella is forced into the narrowness of the nose, but in an African, it remains open and subtle the way a smooth plain dips gently into a shallow valley. The eyes of an African woman appear uncluttered by the dictates of a high nose bridge.

Helena Barfour, the woman messaging Gordon now, was a picture-perfect example of that feature he loved so much. It was last year – he remembered exactly when: two days before Thanksgiving – that she had sent a friend request to him. His breath had caught at the sight of her image. He wanted to trace his fingers lightly over her glabella and soft eyebrows. Her colouring was on the dark side of medium, which Gordon also liked. He had little interest in light-skinned black women, or 'copper-coloured', as they say in Ghana, where fair skin is highly favoured.

On Messenger, Helena had related to Gordon that she was a widow, hence her joining the Facebook group. She was a new member at the time, but her husband had died four years before. It wasn't that she hadn't known about the Widow & Widowers page. Rather, it was that she had had little or no interest prior to now.

Why now, if I may ask? Gordon wrote.

I felt I will never find another David, my late husband, Helena replied, and Gordon recalled with nostalgia how Ghanaians use 'will' and 'would' interchangeably. It made him miss Regina, and indeed Ghana.

I isolated myself, she continued. *But then I realised that what my youngest sister had told me repeatedly was true. No, there will never be another David, but that doesn't mean there are no more worthy men in the world to meet. No one is talking about marriage. It's about companionship with someone you like and may grow to love.*

A very wise younger sister lol, Gordon responded.

Yes, she is – Stella, my favourite. She's very dear to me.

That's wonderful. How many siblings do you have?

Three sisters and two brothers.

Do they all live in Accra?

Except one brother in Takoradi. He works on an oil rig.

Ah, I see. May I say something, Helena?

Of course you may, Gordon.

You are breathtakingly beautiful.

Thank you so much, my dear.

You're very welcome.

And you too, she added, *your pic on Facebook is very handsome.*

You're kind, but I'm just a guy getting old. Gordon added a regret emoticon.

Don't say that. You're in your fifties, right? That's not old at all.

Fifties! Lol, I wish! I'm sixty-two.

Age is just a number. To me, you don't seem like sixty-two at all.

Thanks, Helena.

Do you know what I would love? she wrote. *It's just an idea – maybe you wouldn't like it.*

Tell me.

I was thinking if we can Skype one of these days. I will like to see you and we can chat.

But of course! I would love that too.

My laptop is not working so well, but my brother is fixing it so in a couple of days we can do it. I will let you know.

What about doing some video calls on WhatsApp?

Oh, sorry – my camera phone is very bad, so you won't see me well. I'm saving up for an iPhone, but for now I think Skype will be OK.

Sure, Gordon wrote. *I look forward to it.*

That was how Gordon remembered his last Thanksgiving as so special. It marked the beginning of his profound love affair with Helena. Since then, they had been in almost daily contact with each other through a combination of WhatsApp and Skype. The video connections were often unreliable, given Ghana's network challenges, and sometimes the audio and images were out of sync. Nevertheless, Helena enchanted Gordon and continued to do so. And now that she was calling, he needed to cut his Messenger chat.

Gordon picked up the line. 'Hi, Helena. Can you hold on one second? I'll be right with you.'

Can I catch up with you later? he typed to Frank.

Of course, buddy. Thanks for having my back.

Gordon went back to his phone. 'Sorry about that. How are you, love?'

'Something terrible has happened,' she said, her voice trembling. 'Stella has been in a bad accident.'

'Oh no.'

'Last night while coming home with some friends, a drunk man came driving on the street the wrong way and hit the car. One friend died on scene and the other one survived OK, but Stella is hurt very badly, in the ICU right now. The doctors have done one operation to stabilise her, but they say she has internal organ injury, so they need to go back for a second operation.'

'I'm so sorry,' Gordon said. 'How are you holding up?'

'I'm OK. But the problem is the doctors need to get paid first before they do the second operation.'

'What? How so? Isn't it an emergency?'

'You don't know how Ghana is now, my dear. You knew the old Ghana, now everything is money. These hospitals and doctors are not in the business of charity.'

Gordon was about to get on a moral high horse about the Hippocratic oath and all that but quickly checked himself. It was a separate discussion and unhelpful besides.

'So, are you going to be able to pay?' he asked. 'How much?'

'Five thousand *cedis* to start. My extended family are trying to scrape the money together.'

About a thousand dollars, Gordon thought. Not pocket change, but not that much by American standards either. 'Let me help, Helena.'

'No,' she said firmly. 'I don't want to use you that way. That's not fair.'

'How is it using me?' he said, but gently. 'It's not as if you're asking me to buy you jewellery. This is a matter of life and death. This is your beloved sister, worth every penny and much, much more.'

'God bless you, Gordon.' He could hear she was holding back tears.

'But of course, Helena. And I'll send you the full amount.'

Internet scams had made money transfer companies like Western Union suspicious of large sums wired to Ghana and Nigeria. They would likely decline Gordon's transfer, so an interbank transaction was the only way to do it. Helena texted him the details of her account in Accra and then he began getting dressed to go out to his bank. As he changed into his long johns, he heard the door of his townhouse opening downstairs. That would be Derek paying one of his semi-regular visits.

'Dad?'

'Up here.'

Derek walked in and they gave each other a manly bear hug. At forty-three, Derek was a younger version of his father although his skin tone was a golden brown (paler in the wintertime) against Gordon's white, and Derek's curly hair was an espresso colour where his dad's was ginger red. Most of the similarity was in the sharp jaw and their eyes, both possessing greenish irises and heavy lids people sometimes called bedroom eyes. They bore an implied suggestion of languid sex on a lazy Sunday morning. That was what initially got the attention of Claire, the woman Derek eventually married and later divorced.

'What's up?' Derek asked, plopping his long frame onto Gordon's recliner and pushing the seat back. 'Were you going out?'

'Just some errands,' Gordon said, sitting down to put on his socks. 'Nothing special.'

Derek scrutinised his father a moment. 'You OK? You seem a little preoccupied.'

Gordon shrugged and made a show of nonchalance. 'Not really. I'm OK.'

Derek nodded. 'What you been up to?'

'Nothing much. I was online with Frank a little while ago.'

'How's he doing?'

Gordon shook his head. 'Very rough for him right now.'

'How about you, Dad?' Derek said, his forehead creasing. 'All this helping people stress you out any? You know what they say – the caregiver needs care too.'

'True.' Gordon shoved his feet into his shoes. 'It's not too intense, though. I can always pull away from it if I need to. It's not as if Frank lives next door and comes running in every minute. He lives in California, for God's sake.'

'Yeah. Funny you've never even met him in person. The Facebook definition of "friend".'

They went on to talk about other matters. Claire, Derek's ex-wife, was being 'difficult', as he put it. But Simone, their daughter, was doing well in school. Derek wished she could be with him all the time, but he had to be content with the present arrangement and the uneasy truce with his ex-wife.

At length, Gordon looked at his watch. 'I'd better get moving. You wanna stay till I get back?'

'Nah,' Derek said. 'I need to get going myself.'

Gordon went to his bank and set up the wire transfer to go out that afternoon. On Massachusetts Avenue at Dupont Circle, he cast a look, with a touch of wistfulness, at the bookstore he used to own up until eight years ago, Tilson Books. Dupont Circle had always been expensive over the two decades that Gordon ran the store, but it got even more so as the coffee joints, Shake Shacks, and Krispy Kremes of the world moved in. The 2008 economic crash was a death knell and Gordon sold out for a respectable amount. His investments had been good, and he was comfortable – very. Now, under new management, Tilson Books included the obligatory cafe with high-priced, frou-frou drinks, something Gordon had eschewed. If he had acquiesced to that kind of stuff, who knows? He might still have the bookstore. But no regrets, no looking back.

Gordon had come to know a lot of influential people in the city. Before Amazon became the juggernaut bookseller, readers came in seeking books of all kinds – sometimes rare – and Gordon would either have the works in stock or could get a hold of them. That fostered friendships and great conversations. The most celebrated of writers had made appearances at Tilson's, including Toni Morrison, making the bookstore a very big deal. Now the place was perhaps less 'serious'. Some of the writers who came through would not have been Gordon's personal choice, but times had changed. A lot of heat and noise – like an ephemeral fireworks display.

CHAPTER TWELVE

19th January

Through his marriage to Regina, Gordon Tilson had come to know quite a few of the many Ghanaians living along the east coast, particularly in New Jersey, New York, and Washington, DC. Regina had kept company with a well-connected clique of them, like those in the diplomatic corps. It meant getting invited to embassy parties and somewhat more obscure bashes like the Ghana Physicians and Surgeons Foundation of North America inaugural dinner and dance. The events had been more important to Regina than to Gordon, but he had almost always tagged along and gone with the flow. If she was happy, Gordon was too.

Regina had been a terrific entertainer herself. In the good old days, she had orchestrated buffets and dinner parties at home, bringing together a good mix of her friends and Gordon's. After her death, he remained on many invite lists, and that's how, even without Regina, he continued to be a guest at many Ghanaian-flavoured events.

Saturday afternoon, Gordon went to one such party at the Ghana Embassy on International Drive, NW. Several other embassies sat along that opulent stretch of real estate. The Ghanaian Ambassador, Herbert Opare, was holding a cultural event, which, as far as Gordon could gather, aimed to attract more investment in Ghana.

The embassy's winter room was the venue – swank decor, irresistible finger food with an African touch, and well-dressed people. The crowd was mixed – American and Ghanaian, white and black. Gordon's gaze tended towards the Ghanaian women, who, hands down, wore the best outfits. Their artful headdresses fascinated him especially.

'Gordon!'

Like a speed bump, the voice jolted him out of his distracted state. Ambassador Opare was in front of him with an outstretched hand. He was tall with broad, flat facial features, gold-rimmed glasses, and a suave navy-blue suit.

'Good to see you again, Ambassador Herbert,' Gordon said. 'Thank you for having me.'

'You know it's my tremendous pleasure,' Opare said. 'A gathering here is nothing without you.'

'Thank you – nice of you to say,' Gordon said. 'How is Angelina?' Angelina was Opare's wife.

'She's very well, thank you for asking. She's somewhere around here – I'm sure you'll meet up with her shortly. Great to see you again. You're looking well.'

Opare moved on to other guests. About thirty minutes later, he made an introductory welcoming speech, and then a Ghanaian guest professor at Howard

University's Centre for African Studies gave a riveting demonstration of the fine art of Ghana's traditional talking drums. It reminded Gordon of festivals he had attended in small Ghanaian towns where the infectious singing and drumming had brought him to his feet, but he had never realised that in a pair of talking drums, the one with the higher octave was the 'female' and the other was the 'male'. A conversation, like in a marriage – a good one, at least.

The entertainment portion over, it was time for the feast. The guests attacked the buffet table with the ferocity of invading bees. A woman next to Gordon was helping herself to kebabs. He caught just a hint of perfume from her – something classic and understated. He took her in without staring. In iridescent blue and pink that only a Ghanaian woman would dare sport and make it work, she was almost as tall as he.

'Looks impossibly delicious,' he said to her, referring to the food and realising the double entendre too late.

She smiled at him. He thought she was in her late forties, although she could have been older. Her lipstick was ruby red. She had a small gap between her front teeth. He found her unconventional beauty wildly alluring.

'It certainly does,' she responded. He immediately recognised the class of Ghanaian accent well – educated and well-travelled.

'I'm Gordon, by the way,' he said.

'Hello, Gordon. I'm Josephine. It's a pleasure.'

'Likewise. Is there any *shito*?'

'Oh!' She looked both surprised and rather delighted. 'You know that word.'

'I spent years in Ghana in the Peace Corps,' he told her, 'and ended up marrying a Ghanaian woman, may she rest in peace.'

'Oh, my condolences,' she said, her expression taking on real sympathy.

'Thank you,' Gordon said. 'Anyway, all that said, I love hot pepper – especially *kpakpo shito*.'

'Wow,' she said. 'Hardcore.'

They laughed together as she found the *shito* and dabbed about half a teaspoon onto his plate. 'Is that enough?'

'A tiny bit more,' he said, inclining his head. 'Thank you.'

'You're welcome, and I'm impressed.'

'But I promise you, I *will* turn red as a tomato as I eat it.'

'I would like to see that,' she said, laughing. 'Would you join my friends and me at our table? Or are you committed elsewhere?'

'Not at all,' he said. 'Happy to.'

She was with two couples, one Ghanaian and the other black American. Gordon wondered where Josephine's husband was, safely presuming she had one. It was rare for a Ghanaian woman of her age to be unmarried. Gordon turned out to be right. In the following hour or so of conversation, he learnt Josephine was married to Ghana's Inspector General of Police, the highest law enforcement position there. No wonder she frequently went on trips to Europe, Canada, and the United States. Such perks came along with that kind of status in Ghana.

Gordon was surprised, if not disturbed, by the desire he was experiencing for Josephine. It was the kind of fanged lust that could eat a man alive. He wanted to invite her somewhere for coffee or a drink or dinner – anything – but his sensible side warned him not to begin what he could not finish. Josephine was a married woman, and in a few days, she would be returning to Ghana.

But she had a surprise for Gordon. As they were about to part ways, she offered to give him her contact information in Ghana. 'You must visit soon,' she said as he fumbled with his phone too eagerly. 'So much has changed since you were last there.'

He handed her his phone and she put in her digits. 'Actually,' she said, as if the idea had just occurred to her, 'I might as well give you my US number while I'm at it.'

Gordon felt a rush of heady excitement, like a teenager becoming smitten. 'Thank you,' he said. 'Don't be surprised if I call sooner than expected.' He tried to pull it off as a little joke, but it seemed to fall flat.

She humoured him, however. 'But I would *love* such a surprise. It would be wonderful.'

She was smiling and meeting his eyes. *There it is*, he thought.

She *is* flirting with me. His heart did a somersault.

CHAPTER THIRTEEN

20th January

In the evening, Gordon stopped by for a drink with Casper 'Cas' Guttenberg, his oldest and best friend from college. They sat and drank wine in Cas's luxurious flat at The Wharf with his old dog dozing at his feet. Cas, who had been a chain-smoker as long as Gordon could remember, was small, frail, and brittle, like a parched twig. His name befitted his completely white hair and ghostly pale skin. He and Gordon were close in age, but Cas was the older – and in Gordon's respectful opinion, the wiser – of the two. For decades up until retirement, he had been an investigative reporter of note for the *Washington Observer*. Now he did episodic freelance work for them at his leisure. Crippling arthritis of the hands made typing near impossible, so Cas used a voice recognition system to write his articles. Gordon would never forget that he owed a great deal of his success in DC to Cas's support and guidance.

The two men talked politics – both having the inside track of the Washington game – and then family. Gordon admired his friend for his breadth of knowledge, but the awkward truth that no one said out loud was that Casper hadn't produced a captivating newspaper piece – paper or online – in more than a year. Gordon, wanting to help his friend in some way without appearing patronising, was always on the lookout for some unique story that could potentially rocket Cas to prominence again, but beyond the usual insanity of politics inside the Beltway, there seemed to be nothing extraordinary. Gordon had the feeling that Casper, too, was waiting for something special to come along – but *what*, though?

'How are those fingers holding up these days?' Gordon asked.

Casper shrugged. 'Winter nights are the worst. I hate going anywhere in the evenings.'

Gordon nodded in sympathy. 'I hear ya.'

'And you?' Cas asked. 'Hey, how was the event at the Ghana Embassy yesterday?'

'Very nice,' Gordon said. 'Met a wonderful Ghanaian lady there.'

'Is that right?' Cas said, eyes dancing a bit. 'Name?'

'Josephine. She's in DC for a few more days. Married to the Inspector General of Police in Ghana.'

'So,' Cas said, 'romance in the air?'

'Did I mention she was married?' Gordon said dryly.

'What's your point?'

Gordon laughed.

'You going to see her before she leaves?' Cas asked.

'Thinking 'bout it. I guess I'd like to. Maybe take her

to dinner or something. No sex or anything like that.'

Cas seemed amused. 'Hey, I'm not the damn Pope. No moral judgements here.'

Gordon chuckled and took a healthy sip of wine. 'But speaking of marriage,' he went on, 'I wanted to share something with you – see what you think. I've been chatting online with a woman who really intrigues me.'

'Do tell.'

'She's Ghanaian, actually.'

Cas raised his eyebrows. 'Two Ghanaian women in a row. You're on a roll, pal.'

'Yeah, whatever. Her name is Helena – she lives in Ghana, not in the States. Back in November, just before Thanksgiving, she came to the Widows & Widowers Facebook page and requested to friend me, as they say. She lost her husband four years ago.'

'Oh. What's she like?'

'Well, gorgeous, to start. She's forty-nine, although her voice sounds younger on the phone. She manages a restaurant in Accra.'

Cas nodded. 'You must enjoy talking to her. Your face lit up just now.'

Gordon smiled. 'I do, I really do. But she's been struck by misfortune. About three weeks ago, her sister Stella was in a car crash with one fatality. Stella was in the ICU for ten days and then went to a step-down unit.'

'So, she survived,' Casper said. 'Thank God for that. More wine?'

'Just a little.'

Cas poured him some. 'What's the health care like over there?'

'It's good if you can afford a private hospital.'

'Helena have money?'

'Not that kind. I've had to help her out.'

'Well, that's good of you. What has it run you so far?'

'Going on three thousand dollars, but I'll need to send some more. It's not just the ICU costs, Helena has to buy a lot of the medicines in town and take them to the hospital herself. That includes IV meds.'

'Really?' Casper said, rubbing his chin. 'Imagine our having to do that in the States. Literally go shopping on behalf of the hospital and your loved one.'

'Yes.'

There was a brief silence between them. 'What's bugging you about the whole thing?' Cas asked. 'I'm reading something in your demeanour.'

'I don't know,' Gordon said, blowing air through his cheeks. 'I've been feeling like I should go to Ghana. To support Helena, and also because it will make things financially much easier if I take some dollars and open a bank account there that we can draw from as needed.'

'Well, why not?' Cas said with enthusiasm. 'I think that would be admirable of you – to render that kind of support to someone in need.'

'Really?'

'Absolutely! Why do you seem so surprised?'

'Not surprised as such. More like happy you feel that way.'

84

'Look, you've been to Ghana before. You're no stranger, and who knows?' Cas grinned. 'You might get lucky again and marry another Ghanaian woman.'

Gordon laughed, but the idea stirred him. Cas's support felt good, and Gordon was closer to making up his mind to make the trip to Ghana. The prospect of meeting Helena in person was heady.

Cas got up and put his winter coat on. 'Where you going?' Gordon asked.

'Balcony,' Cas said. 'Gotta have a smoke.'

CHAPTER FOURTEEN

21st January, Accra, Ghana

The *tro-tro*'s final stop was Tudu Station. As Emma and fifteen-or-so other passengers got off, she took a breath, relieved to have left the crammed minivan, only to cough from a lungful of *tro-tro* exhaust.

Tudu Road, part of old town Accra, was all industry and commerce: warehouses, loading docks, banks, electronics stores, and pavement stalls. Emma passed a man haggling with a merchant in front of a tower of cheap, China-made toys. Near Zenith Bank, she sidestepped a menacing motorcycle circumventing traffic by riding on the verge. Ghanaian pedestrians have eyes in the sides and the backs of their heads.

She turned west, walking into the mid-afternoon sun. At the double-laned Nkrumah Avenue, Emma waited for a break in the traffic to run across to the old Cocoa Marketing Board building people called Cocobod. It had been impressive in its day, but was no match now for the modern, glossy, glass high-rises dotting Accra's new and growing skyline: a showy kind of development while many old societal values remained the same as in the forgoing centuries.

Metres down from Cocobod, Emma entered the slum of the same name. You wouldn't want to be found dead there, but you could. It was its own small city with crime packed within its walls like a cancerous brain slowly swelling inside its skull – fights with broken-bottle shards, knifings, rapes, and sometimes murders. Most of these took place at night, so Emma was watchful but not afraid. For safety, though, she kept her folded jackknife in the right front pocket of her jeans, as she did whenever she went to a hazardous area of town, and there were quite a few of those. No man attempting to assault her would escape with anything less than a slashed face or a punctured throat. Her father had shown Emma how to fight off a man – just as he had done with Commissioner Andoh – and how to use a knife effectively for her protection.

Emma didn't like coming to this part of town, but to see her stepbrother Bruno, she had no choice. He had lived – thrived, really – in Cocobod for years. Each time she visited him, she hoped Bruno had decided to turn his life around. Even before he was a teenager, he had been prone to truancy and mischief. Daddy couldn't stand Bruno. He threw the boy out of the house and into the jaws of Accra's streets where Bruno learnt to steal, rob, swindle, fight, and use drugs. Now twenty-two, he had had more than his share of trouble with the law.

While Daddy regarded Bruno as a 'bad seed', Emma had never hated her stepbrother and he had always loved her as his sister. He was physically powerful and could even be dangerous, but towards her he was as sweet as honey straight from the hive.

Just like everyone else going to and fro, Emma negotiated the unpaved, meandering, narrow pathways between illegally and badly constructed wooden shacks. If a blaze broke out now and burnt most of the place down, it wouldn't be the first time. The stench of a choked sewage gutter blended with the delicious aroma of *tatale* being fried somewhere. Emma realised, again, that she had barely eaten the whole day.

She arrived at Bruno's shack. The door was padlocked, meaning he was out somewhere, which Emma had been afraid of. She had texted him earlier and he had told her he would be home, but Bruno was flaky much of the time. She looked around. A woman with a baby secured to her back was throwing dirty dishwater from a pan into the gutter. Emma approached her. 'Good afternoon, madam. Please, do you know Bruno?'

The woman had a dead, milky eye on the left and the pinched face of a grasscutter. 'Bruno?' she said. 'Yes, I know him.'

'Have you seen him today?'

'I saw him going that way,' she said, pointing vaguely. Emma followed the woman's direction more or less, wandering into a spot with a crumbling brick wall, from behind which wafted the sharp, unmistakable smell of *wee* – marijuana. *Perhaps Bruno is here*, she thought wryly, because Bruno and the drug were as inseparable as best friends. She circled the wall and found a grimy gap to squeeze through into the compound within. The marijuana in the air hit her airways and she coughed a few times.

About six guys sat around the perimeter of the compound, some sharing joints. Emma spotted Bruno reclining against the wall in a spot of shade next to a young man he appeared to know. Bruno sat up as he saw her and furtively pocketed his smoke after extinguishing it with his fingertips.

'*Ei*, sis!' he exclaimed, jumping up. 'What are you doing here?'

'Looking for you,' she said, dusting off her clothes.

He bent to embrace her with his six-foot frame of dense musculature. He had a diagonal scar across his forehead from a knife fight when he was sixteen or seventeen. He wasn't handsome until he smiled, and then he appeared a different man. 'Who told you I was here?' he asked.

'A woman back there,' she said. 'How are you, Bruno?'

'I'm good, sis,' he said, his voice softening. 'But I've missed you, *paa*.'

'Don't lie,' she teased him. 'You don't even think about me.'

'Ohh, sis!' he said, flashing that smile. 'How can you say that?' He followed her glance at the guy he had been sitting beside. 'That's my boy. Hey, Nii Kwei, moddafocka, make you stop smoking and greet my sister Emma.'

'Sorry, oo!' Nii Kwei got to his feet and approached. 'Good afternoon, Emma.'

Nii Kwei had coarse *Ga* features and was slight in physique – Bruno's exact opposite. Emma shook hands, saying little as she took him in quickly. He had a gold loop in his ear and two gold chains around his neck hanging low over his exposed chest. His black-and-red chequered shirt matched with tight black jeans, which stopped at his bare ankles above apparently brand-new red and white Nike trainers.

'Can I talk to you outside?' she said to Bruno.

He accompanied her out of the compound. 'So watup, sis?'

She caught an odd inflection and frowned. 'What is this American boy accent you're trying to do?'

He laughed with some embarrassment. 'Come on, sis.'

'What have you been up to?'

'Well, you know, I dey here, that's all.'

'Did you manage to get a job yet?'

Bruno crossed his big arms over his chest. 'I get construction job last month.'

'Congrats!' Emma said.

He shook his head. 'But they said they don't need me any more.'

'Oh,' she said with disappointment. 'So, what are you planning now? If anything?'

He hesitated. 'I want to go into Internet business with Nii Kwei.'

Alarms raised in Emma's head. 'What Internet business? Look, don't think I don't know what that Nii Kwei is all about. He's a *sakawa* boy, right?'

'No,' Bruno said, too indignantly.

'What no? Look at his clothes. What kind of car does he drive?' Bruno looked at the ground and muttered something.

'What?' Emma said. 'I didn't hear you.'

'Range Rover.'

'*Range Rover!*' Emma exclaimed. 'What did I tell you? How old is he? Twenty-seven?'

'Yeah,' Bruno said, squirming.

'And what normal guy his age can afford a Range Rover except a *sakawa* boy? Don't get involved with him, Bruno. Please, I beg you.'

'It's OK, Emma,' Bruno said, chewing on the inside of his cheek. 'Don't worry, OK? Nothing bad go happen.'

'Get a legitimate job, Bruno,' she pleaded, putting her hand on his forearm. 'Try to settle down into something honest for a change, eh?'

He flipped over his palm. 'Which job are you talking about? There are none in Ghana.' Bruno's statement wasn't far from the truth, but that wasn't the discussion.

'I just want you to turn your life around,' she said, staying on topic.

'I will, I will. It's just that . . .'

'That what?'

Bruno released a big breath. 'I don't know. Let's talk about you for a while. You're giving me too much tough time.'

She laughed.

'How is your work with the police?' he asked, determined to change the focus.

Emma turned the corners of her mouth down. 'They sacked me.'

Bruno's mouth dropped open. '*What?* When? Why?'

'Two weeks now. Long story.'

For a moment, Commissioner Andoh's assault played in her mind, but she forced it out. 'Oh, sorry, sis,' Bruno said with sympathy. He took her hand. 'Are you OK?'

Emma shrugged.

'I know what that means,' Bruno said. 'You're not really OK.'

'I will be,' Emma said with a sigh. 'Anyway, I've managed to get a part-time job at the Accra Mall in the Apple store. I start next week.'

'Ah, cool. At least you have that.'

Emma didn't mention that she had been hoping to hear from DCOP Laryea's friend, Yemo Sowah. She was beginning to lose hope. Wouldn't he have called by now?

'Come with me and let's chop *waakye*, your favourite,' Bruno said, brightening. 'I'm hungry.'

'Of course you are,' she said with a snort. 'It's all that *wee*.'

He giggled all the way to the *waakye* stand.

CHAPTER FIFTEEN

22nd January, Washington, DC

It was the night before Josephine was to leave. Gordon had begged her not to do so without his treating her to dinner, at least. 'Who knows?' he had told her on the phone. 'I may not see you again for a long time. Or ever, even.'

He knew she would accept. Her initial bashfulness was all a cute act. It made their interaction more interesting – exciting, even. They both enjoyed it.

At first, Gordon suggested going to one of the highly sought-after restaurants in Georgetown, but from his subconscious came another idea. 'Or you could try my *fufu* and groundnut stew,' he suggested.

'Are you serious?' Josephine said. 'You can make that?'

'I can. My late wife, Regina, taught me, so I learnt from the best.'

'How could I possibly resist?' Josephine said.

In truth, it had been a long time since Gordon had made groundnut stew and he had to look up some recipes on the

Internet to refresh his memory. The most important first step was to buy the least-processed peanut butter possible. The *fufu* wasn't an issue since one could easily buy the powdered, just-add-water version. Real *fufu* involved strenuous pounding with mortar and pestle. He ran over to Afrik International Food Market in Hyattsville, MD, for the plantain *fufu* flour. There was more traffic than Gordon had anticipated and when he returned to begin cooking in his recently renovated kitchen, he found himself short on time.

He was therefore quite nervous at first when Josephine arrived – not as ready as he had wanted to be. He was split between conversing with her and finishing up the meal.

'Can I help at all, Gordon?' she asked.

'Well, it's almost ready, actually.' He hesitated and then gave in. 'Would you mind checking the *fufu* though?'

She was happy to do so. 'A little more water and stirring,' she advised.

He thought how achingly lovely she was in a dark, formfitting outfit and heels. He had a thing for heels.

'This is a beautiful kitchen,' she remarked, as she shaped the *fufu* into a smooth, glutinous mass.

'Thank you,' he said.

They ate in the dining room. Gordon dimmed the lights and lit two candles. Josephine nodded in approval after trying her first mouthful. 'You have really tried,' she said, the Ghanaian way of saying *You've done a terrific job*.

'Thank you,' he said. His chest was swelling with

pride. He felt so good that she was here and that he had made this special meal for their mutual enjoyment.

'So, are you flying directly to Accra?' Gordon asked her as they tucked in. It really did taste good.

'No,' she replied, taking a dainty spoonful. 'I'll stop in the UK.'

'Ah. To see friends?'

'Yes,' she said. 'And to see our son, Kwame.'

'Is he in school there?'

She smiled a little. 'Actually, it's an institution called Warwickshire Home. Kwame is autistic. He's been there for many years.'

'Oh. How often do you get to see him?'

'Three or four times a year,' Josephine said. 'I still feel guilty that it couldn't be more often, but you see, in Ghana he wouldn't receive adequate care. James – my husband – and I made the decision long ago to move him to the UK.'

'I see,' Gordon said, studying her and trying to read her emotions. A lot was there, but he sensed she was keeping it shrouded. 'How is Kwame doing?'

'As well as can be expected,' she said, more happily. 'He talks somewhat now. For years, he could not.'

'That must have been a joyful achievement for him,' Gordon said, pausing from eating.

Josephine looked at him with appreciation. 'You're the first person who has ever said that – as if you know him. Because it *was* joyful. He had a big, big smile. Most people just say 'oh, great' or something inane like that.'

Gordon nodded. 'That's people for you.' He was feeling drawn to her like a powerful magnetic force. 'I would love to meet Kwame.'

'Really?' Josephine said. 'You would like each other. James doesn't ever talk about him.'

'Oh,' Gordon said.

She nodded. 'Yes. Once Kwame was out of his sight in England, he never wanted to see him again.'

'I'm sorry,' Gordon said. 'That must be hard on you.'

'James is a good man,' Josephine said, 'but I find his feelings about Kwame hurtful.'

'Yes,' Gordon said.

'It may be why I'm dedicated to supporting institutions in Ghana that cater to the mentally and physically disabled,' she said. 'I'm a patron of a centre for autistic children in Accra. I helped the owner set it up about four years ago. One of the reasons I've been here in DC is to lobby for funding.'

'I see.' He hesitated. 'Can I help out?'

'I would love that,' she said with fervour. 'Whatever is in your heart, Gordon. Any donation is welcome. I'll text you the information on the centre.'

'Please do. I'd love to participate.'

'Thank you.'

They both wanted to move on to more light-hearted conversation, and they did. Gordon regaled her with tales of his exploits and adventures with Regina when he was a young, carefree fool in Ghana. Josephine laughed long and hard all the way through the lemon chiffon dessert, which Gordon had *not* made. He offered Josephine more wine, but she had had enough.

Against his repeated objections, she insisted on clearing the table, loading the dishwasher, and generally cleaning up while he made coffee. 'It's the least I could do,' she said. By now she had kicked off her heels and was padding around in her stockinged feet.

He put a record – soft jazz – on a very expensive turntable.

'My goodness,' Josephine said, staring at it. 'A long time since I've seen one of those.'

'I'm a die-hard vinyl lover,' Gordon told her. 'Old-fashioned and proud of it.'

They sat together on the sofa, talking and sipping coffee.

'Thank you for coming,' he said to her, taking her hand. 'You've made me very happy.'

'It's been wonderful,' she said.

They kissed for a while. When he stood up with his hand outstretched, she took it and followed him to the bedroom. The jazz played as they undressed.

'Condom?' she murmured.

'Yes,' he said.

'Good boy,' she said, and they both giggled.

They caressed each other, and she was impressed by his size.

'Not bad for a white boy?' he asked.

'Not at all.'

He used his lips and tongue to pleasure her and she gasped and said she had never had that done before. He was happy to believe it, even if it wasn't true.

Wrapped around his back, her thighs were marvellously powerful, like Regina's. Gordon remembered now what it had been like in those days long ago. The glory and the ecstasy of being with an African woman. No comparison.

CHAPTER SIXTEEN

26th January, Heathrow, London

Duty free shops in US airports were OK, but Josephine preferred the magic of the European and UK versions. She picked up Belgian chocolates, German pastries, French perfumes, English treacle tarts, a couple of high-end handbags, and gifts her two girls had specifically requested.

Then she settled into the opulent British Airways business class lounge to wait for her flight, helping herself to breakfast, coffee, and sinful desserts.

Like other well-off people, Josephine was always aware of a level of comfort wrapping around her like a warm, waterproof coat impervious to the elements. Through James, the Akrofis were blessed with affluence. He provided for them with a resolute sense of duty. So, it wasn't without some guilt that Josephine thought about the extraordinary, lust-drenched time she had spent with Gordon four nights ago. But she rationalised it as a one-off in a foreign land, not at all germane to her 'real life' in Ghana. She wasn't having a true affair. Before Gordon, she hadn't had any good sex in several years. James wasn't exactly the poster boy for virility – not any more, at least, and he would *never* pleasure her orally the way Gordon had done. Ghanaian men had a generally lousy reputation when it came to foreplay, and as for postcoital cuddling, that would happen when snow fell at the equator. Regina had certainly known what she was doing when she married Gordon, Josephine reflected.

In addition, whereas Gordon had expressed a wish to meet Kwame, James had shunned the child, probably because of his ingrained traditional beliefs about children like Kwame – 'devil children' and the like. As Josephine had told Gordon, this was the most wounding aspect of her marriage to James.

Josephine had two life regrets, both related to childbirth. Kwame was the first. That was more of a misfortune than a mistake. In the first postpartum weeks and months, it wasn't clear anything was amiss, but by a year old, Kwame had missed several milestones. He didn't return anyone's gaze, and sometimes he had bizarre bouts of high-pitched, intense screaming.

Their paediatrician brought up the spectre of autism one day, from which James and Josephine recoiled with horror and outright dismissal. As many well-off Ghanaians do when faced with a dire medical question, James and Josephine took off with Kwame to the UK for an evaluation and second opinion on the child's conditions. After administering a battery of tests, the Harley Street consultant pronounced the verdict: 'I'm afraid I have rather bad news, Mr and Mrs Akrofi,' he told them with perfect, upper-class inflection. 'Your little boy is autistic.'

The kind of care Kwame would need – physical, psychological, emotional – for the best possible outcome for his life was barely available in Ghana. Accra had three autism centres at the most. So, the Akrofis never brought Kwame back with them to Ghana. Josephine's brother, who had lived in England for decades and was a UK citizen, agreed to become the boy's legal guardian. Even though it was for the best that Kwame stayed in England, the pain Josephine felt about not being able to take care of her own son never really left her.

The second lament was without question a life mistake. Josephine had been very young back then and she didn't realise – or was in denial over the possibility – that she was pregnant until the fifth month. She went on to have the baby boy, but it was really Josephine's sister who ended up rearing him. Josephine rarely saw him or his father. She had never revealed to James that she had had a child out of wedlock. She was ashamed of it. As far as Josephine was concerned, that would remain a secret for ever.

Her other two children with James were a success story, however. Two girls, utterly brilliant throughout their schooling, one finishing law and the other starting medical school. A doctor and a lawyer in the family. Nothing could be more perfect than that.

CHAPTER SEVENTEEN

26th January, Accra, Ghana

Apart from a minor disturbance back in economy, which Josephine barely heard as she slept in her business class flat bed, the flight into Accra was uneventful. Night had fallen but the new international Terminal 3 was lit up and glistening like a crystal palace. Josephine breezed through VIP customs. Her driver was waiting for her on the other side, using his special pass to enter a normally restricted area.

From the airport, Josephine's 4×4 vehicle with flashing lights got her back home more quickly than it would mere mortals and she pulled into the guarded compound of the Akrofi home within an hour of landing.

While the houseboy took the luggage in, James came out to meet her. 'How are you, love?' he said, hugging her and giving her a robust kiss on the cheek. 'I've missed you.'

'Me too, love,' she said.

'Tired after the long trip?'

'Just a little.'

They held hands as they went into the house. 'If you're hungry, Araba has made something,' James told her.

'Maybe in an hour or so,' Josephine said, slipping her heels off in the foyer. Her feet ached and it felt so good to walk in her stockings. With a sigh of relief, she flopped onto the sofa in the sitting room as Araba, the diminutive maid, appeared.

'Good evening, madam. You are welcome.'

'Thank you, Araba.'

'Please, will you take something to eat?'

'Just bring me some water with ice. Be sure it's Bel-Aqua. I can't drink that awful Voltic.' She looked pointedly at James, but he only laughed. They each swore by their favourite brands of bottled water and claimed they could taste the difference.

'Yes, madam.'

James didn't want anything, and Araba left.

'So great to see you, Josie,' he said, leaning over to kiss her again. 'Did you have a successful trip?'

'Yes, I think so,' she said, rubbing her feet.

'Here, let me do that,' he said, swinging her feet into his lap. 'You just relax.'

'Ah, thank you so much,' she said. James really did do a good massage. 'I got at least three people to pledge to the Autism Foundation and a couple more of them probably will once I get back to them tomorrow to remind them.'

'Excellent.'

'I met them at the party Herbert had at the embassy.'

'Party?'

'Yes, James. I texted you about it. Do you even read my messages?'

'But of course I do, my darling queen.'

She shot him a look askance, sitting up again as Araba brought her water with ice. 'What's new in your world?' she asked.

'Nothing, really. J. K. and I have been talking a lot. He's going full speed ahead with his anti-corruption scheme, and now that Evans-Aidoo is dead, J. K. probably has the election in the palm of his hand. Aidoo's running mate is very weak.'

'Yes, I understand.' Josephine hesitated. 'I think you mentioned once that J. K. is turning more of his attention to the higher echelons in the police?'

'Right,' he said, searching her face. 'You look worried.'

'No, not really,' she said, which wasn't true. 'Just wonder if it will affect what we do and how we do it.'

'I wouldn't worry about that. Things are pretty secure.'

'OK then.' Josephine was persuaded, at least for now. 'And the search for Aidoo's killer? How is that going?'

'Not very well,' James said. 'The police seem to have no leads at all.'

They were quiet for a moment. At length, Josephine spoke. 'Love? I was thinking. If I was to achieve my dream of the Autism Centre taking in a few boarders and coming up to world standard, would you consider having Kwame moved from England back here?'

He frowned. 'Why would you even consider that? How would we ever provide the same standard of care? And you know how much he depends on a set routine for peace of mind. Come on, Josie.' He moved closer and put his arms around her. 'We've done the best for him. He's safe and secure where he is. And that's what we should care about most.'

What James said made intellectual sense, but it failed to assuage the guilt eating at Josephine's soul.

CHAPTER EIGHTEEN

5th February, Washington, DC

Derek called out from the bottom of the stairs. 'Dad?'

No reply came. Derek went up to his father's room, but it was empty. He crossed to the window and saw his father dozing off in a deckchair in the solarium below. A weak winter sun had emerged. As Derek turned to leave the room, the open screen of Gordon's desktop caught his eye. It was Dad's Widows & Widowers Facebook page with a Messenger window open at the bottom right. Derek lingered, sneaking a look. He shouldn't be infringing on his father's privacy like this, and for an instant, Derek's curiosity clashed with guilt. Curiosity won. The last message in the window was from someone called Helena Barfour at 2.16 p.m., about forty minutes ago: *How are you today, my love?*

Gordon, presumably away from the computer at the time, hadn't yet responded. But what drew Derek's attention were the antecedent messages. Inexorably drawn in, he scrolled up farther, and farther still. 'What the fuck,' he muttered.

Pulling away as he caught the sound of his father's footsteps downstairs, Derek left the room to the balustrade in the hallway. 'Hey, Dad.'

Gordon emerged from the kitchen and looked up. 'Oh, hi, son. Didn't know you were here. I was out back.'

'Yeah, I saw you taking a nap.' Derek went downstairs and joined his father.

'Coffee?' Gordon offered.

'Sure. Thanks.'

They sat at the centre counter in the kitchen and talked about this and that, but Derek was preoccupied with what he had just seen. 'So, Dad,' he began when a pause in the conversation gave him the chance, 'when I came in, I went upstairs looking for you, and that Widowers Facebook page was open on your computer.'

'Oh, yeah,' Gordon said. 'Forgot to close it. What about it?'

'Look, what's on there is your business, and you know I don't make it a habit to pry.'

'But on this occasion, you did?'

'Yeah,' Derek admitted. 'On your Messenger – someone called Helena? Who's that?'

'Just a Facebook friend,' Gordon said.

'OK, but you're sending money to her?'

'So, what, you went through my entire conversation with her?' Gordon said tersely.

'Not that I feel good about it,' Derek said, 'but it's done now, and I can't put the toothpaste back in the tube. I mean, what's the story with this Helena? Where is she located?'

'In Ghana.'

'In Ghana!' Derek exclaimed.

'Yeah – Accra.'

'But the money, Dad? What's with that?'

'Listen, we've been talking for a couple months now, OK?' Gordon said, defensiveness creeping into his voice. 'She's a wonderful lady – understanding, gracious. I spend all my time helping people out on Facebook, but there's no one there who listens to *me* when I want to pour my heart out. No one.'

'Dad,' Derek said, with a slight quiver in his voice, 'you've got *me*. I don't count?'

'Of course you do,' Gordon said, his voice softening. 'I didn't mean it that way. I'm talking about the Facebook people and my role in the group. I'm like some big hero, but they gotta realise I'm made of flesh and blood too. So, sue me if there's someone like Helena who not only shares feelings with me but allows me to vent.'

'But I asked you before if you ever felt overwhelmed with this Facebook mentoring you do and you made it sound like you were doing just fine.'

'I did,' Gordon conceded. 'Bravado, I guess.'

'But back to the money,' Derek said. He'd allowed the discussion to veer off. 'You've sent this Helena or whoever something like, what, a couple thousand dollars by now?'

'Her sister was in a car crash – got banged up pretty bad,' Gordon explained. 'She can't get surgery unless they produce cash up front. You know how it is in Ghana. We've been there, right?'

'What, she doesn't have family? They can't put some money together? What does Helena do for a living?'

'Assistant manager at a restaurant,' Gordon said, taking a sip of coffee. 'I don't know about the rest of her family, but Helena's not earning the kind of money that she could access emergency funds. So, I offered to help. Look, it's really tough for people out there.'

Derek was filled with suspicion. 'Dad, this could be a scam.'

'Why do you say that?' Gordon said, frowning.

'It has scam written all over it. That's what all these Ghanaian and Nigerian guys are doing these days – you know that.'

Gordon winced. 'That was kind of a racist comment, don't you think? I wouldn't have expected that from you, especially since your late mother was Ghanaian. You're half Ghanaian, remember?'

'It's not racist,' Derek said, setting his jaw. 'It's the dirty truth. And please leave Mama out of this. It's got nothing to do with her. Fact is, these scams are at an all-time high and a big chunk of them are out of Ghana and Nigeria. There isn't a financial institution that doesn't shudder at anything to do with Ghana or Nigeria.'

'There's plenty of corruption right here in the United States,' Gordon said. 'We have our own con men.'

Derek flipped his palms up. 'Did I say we didn't? You're deflecting the issue, which is that you're sending money to someone you don't know. It's a *huge* no-no.'

Gordon flared. 'Two months, Derek. In fact, *more* than two months I've been talking to Helena. We've spoken on the phone, we've texted on WhatsApp, we've Skyped. I've *seen* her with my own eyes, live and talking to me. She didn't even ask me for any money. I was the one who offered.'

Derek was unmoved. 'You know what you should do? Ask this Helena or whatever her name is to take a selfie of herself and the so-called injured sister and see if she does.'

'Jesus Christ, Derek,' Gordon muttered.

'Dad, they've set you up. All that Skype stuff? They just use webcam software.'

'I know that,' Gordon said, annoyed. 'And sure, I'm no Internet wizard, but I'm not stupid either and I think I can pretty much tell when something's a hoax. Helena is not a hoax. I can guarantee you that.'

'When you Skyped with her,' Derek probed, 'you didn't have any strange pauses or inappropriate facial expressions or answers to your questions?'

Gordon shook his head. 'We've only Skyped a little. More contact on the phone.'

'And when you call, she immediately picks up?'

'Yes, of course.'

For a moment, Derek entertained the possibility that this could be real. Could it be? No, he was certain his dad was being duped.

'Is that all you've sent her?' Derek asked. 'The money, I mean. Is there more I don't know about?'

'That's all,' Gordon said sullenly. 'And stop treating me like a child. I don't like it.'

'I'm sorry, Dad,' Derek said. 'I didn't mean to. It's

just—' He finished with a sigh. 'But can you promise me you won't send any more money?'

'She told me her sister is doing better, so there's not going to be much need.'

'Until the next thing,' Derek countered. 'A funeral or some shit like that. You know them and their funerals.'

'I'm distressed by your tone,' Gordon said, shaking his head. 'So much contempt.'

'Just keeping it real.'

An unpleasant silence fell between them. Derek got up abruptly. 'Gotta go,' he muttered. 'No more money, OK? Her sister's accident, or whatever, isn't your problem.'

His jaw clamped, Gordon walked his son to the front door in silence. Physically they were in proximity, but emotionally they were miles apart. Once Derek had left, Gordon sat at the kitchen table to brood. Who was right here – Gordon or his son? Or maybe it wasn't an issue of right versus wrong but rather of perspective. Derek was suspicious, cynical, and sceptical. Gordon was accepting, open, and more benevolently inclined. Or was his heady liaison with Josephine colouring his judgement about Helena? Gordon rested his head on his hands and groaned. He was confused, and he knew it.

CHAPTER NINETEEN

14th February

Derek heard a notification from his phone and rolled over on the sofa with a grunt. He'd fallen asleep in front of the TV. He looked at the phone screen: 10.17 p.m. and a text from his father.

> *Derek, it's time to do what my soul tells me. Helena and I have talked it over carefully, and the decision is made. I'm texting you from Dulles, about to fly out to Accra, where I'll be finally meeting Helena tomorrow morning. I don't know what the future holds for us, but for now, this is our destiny. I am deeply, deeply in love with a very lovely lady. I'll be fine, son. Take care. Love you.*

'What the fuck.' Derek sat up and read the message again. 'Dad,' he said, as though Gordon was sitting next to him, 'don't do this.'

Derek tried calling his father and wasn't surprised that

he didn't pick up. *Dad*, he thought, *have you gone crazy?* But then maybe it was *Derek* being irrational. What if Helena *was* real? To be fair, besides what Derek had seen on Dad's Messenger, he hadn't been privy to their extensive and private conversations.

Perhaps Derek was the one making the mistake. *I hope so*, he thought. *I hope so*. But a moment later, he shook his head. This bullshit can't be real. It's a con. Derek's impulse was to shoot his father a what-the-hell-are-you-doing message, but he realised there was no point to that. Dad was gone and for the moment there was nothing Derek could do to get him back. Best to put a more affirmative spin on it.

He picked up his phone again and replied.

Hi, Dad – got your text. Thanks for letting me know. Not sure what phone you'll be using in Ghana, so I'm emailing. It's your absolute prerogative to do what you feel is right for you. I know we've argued over this, but I still wish you the best and I'm praying your instincts on this are right and mine wrong. Just want you to be careful out there. You, Mom, and I were in Ghana decades ago, but from what I read, a lot has changed in the country since then. Please, please let me know how you're doing or if you need anything. You know I'll do my best for you. Text me asap. Take care. Love ya.

What next? *Cas.*

Derek called Casper Guttenberg. 'Have you heard from my dad?'

'I was about to call you. I just read his email that he's headed to Ghana to meet this woman, Helena.'

'Did you know anything about it?' Derek asked.

'He mentioned the lady to me sometime last month, that he was thinking about meeting up with her in Ghana, but I didn't think he was seriously planning anything this soon. How about you? Did he talk to you?'

'Yes, but not voluntarily,' Derek said. 'I found out by accident and told him I thought it was a scam. I still do. What if someone's luring him out there to rob him or something?'

'Why jump to the worst scenario possible? Your dad's a savvy guy. Let's give him a few days to sort things out. Who knows, this might be a new and happy chapter in his life.'

Derek was not as sanguine as the old man, but for now he was willing to adopt the more positive outlook and pray it came true.

CHAPTER TWENTY

15th February, Accra, Ghana

When the Boeing 767 broke through the morning's light cloud cover over Accra, Gordon remembered how the savanna scrub dotted the laterite soils of the region, but he realised with surprise, almost shock, that the once uninhabited expanses of land that had surrounded the metropolitan area were now crowded with buildings, roads, and highways. He recognised the University of Ghana campus with its iconic tower on the hill, but not much else. What had happened to the boundary between city and suburb?

Eagerness to see this development from ground level and the anticipation of finally meeting his new woman in person set up a level of excitement Gordon had not even expected himself. Touchdown at 8.15 a.m. was a respectable ten minutes late. With its three terminals, Kotoka Airport was now several-fold larger than when Gordon had last seen it. Terminal 3, the international one, had a glittering glass facade and modern jetways. It used to be that deplaning was by staircase. Now, in this sealed environment, Gordon missed that first blast of hot, humid air one used to get on emerging from the aircraft – the announcement that yes, you really *are* in tropical Africa.

Immigration was uneventful, the officer warming to Gordon when he told her he had been in Ghana with the Peace Corps decades ago. As Gordon picked up his luggage, his eagerness grew as he pictured Helena waiting for him outside when he exited.

In the wide arrivals hall, family, friends, and chauffeurs waited behind the barrier. Gordon scanned the crowd, his heart beating hard as he searched for Helena's beautiful face. He knew she was quite tall, and he visualised her in a light, flowery blouse and a pair of slimly fitted slacks – or perhaps a knee-length skirt. He didn't spot her yet, but there was still quite a distance before he got to the back of the crowd several rows deep. Around him, people hugged and cried out with joy as they reunited with loved ones. Reaching the end of the phalanx, Gordon circled the periphery, checking to see if he and Helena might have missed each other somehow. He still couldn't find her.

He felt a burst of anxiety but told himself to calm down. Helena was probably close by or running a little late. He texted her on WhatsApp, and then tried calling to no avail. The number rang for a while, and then cut off sharply. He was wondering what to do next when someone tapped him on the shoulder. Gordon turned to find a smallish man with a luminous smile. 'Please, are you Mr Tilson?' he said.

'Yes, I am.'

'Welcome, welcome to Ghana. My name is Robert. I'm

here to take you to Kempinski Hotel. You walked past me up at the meeting point, but I saw you searching around and guessed it might be you.'

'Oh, yes,' Gordon said, blanking for a moment. He had forgotten he had given his flight information to the hotel. 'Thank you. Actually, I was expecting someone to pick me up.'

'Please, someone?'

'Well, she's a friend,' Gordon stammered, still looking around for Helena. He felt disoriented.

'Oh,' Robert said, thrown off course. 'Will you prefer to wait for her?'

Gordon reasoned he'd better take the shuttle. He could always reach Helena later. Anyway, *she* was late, not him. He realised he was irritated. 'No, it's fine,' he said. 'I'll come with you.'

'Good, sir. Let me take your bags,' Robert said, grabbing Gordon's luggage. 'This way, please.'

Leaving the arrivals hall to the car park nearby, Gordon walked alongside Robert, who made small conversation about the trip. The vehicle was a light blue van with the Kempinski logo on the side. Robert loaded the luggage into the boot. Gordon got into the van to join two passengers – both white – who were already there.

As they drove away from the airport with its brand-new road signs and branching exits, Gordon noted the cluster of high-rises changing the cityscape. Like ungainly giant birds, cranes dotted the horizon. Nothing in his recollection of Accra was here. Nothing appeared familiar. Nor did he recall the giant billboards at the sides of the road – ads for phones, luxury flats, fancy clothing. Billboard hell, Gordon thought.

They were in the heart of morning rush hour with traffic at a crawl, giving the itinerant vendors their chance to sell the day's newspapers, shoes, world maps, puppies, cold drinks, ice cream, home tools, and cheap Chinese trinkets. The traders moved easily within the dense lines of cars.

Thoughts of Helena shifted Gordon's focus away from the bustle around him. For the first time, an out-of-body *Why are you here?* sense filled him, and his mind cast back, annoyingly, to Derek's warnings. Once again, he texted Helena, but it was as if his message disappeared into a void.

Only these doubts prevented Gordon from wholeheartedly enjoying the magnificence of the Kempinski lobby, which had marble floors and a towering ceiling suspending a giant chandelier from its centre. After checking in, a bellboy took his luggage up.

His room was just as lovely – polished wood floors, cappuccino-coloured closets, and a capacious bathroom. He might even use the bidet, he thought absently and with some humour.

When he texted Helena again and received no reply, he tossed the phone onto the precisely made king-size bed and stood in the middle of the floor wondering if he was in a dream. A bad one.

CHAPTER TWENTY-ONE

17th February, Washington, DC

Three days after Gordon had left, Derek received an email from him.

> *Derek,*
> *No doubt you're worried sick about me. I wanted to let you know I'm doing OK – no, better than that because I met up with Helena and we're having a wonderful time getting to know each other. Don't have a picture yet, but I'll send one soon! Don't worry about anything. It's working out fine. I'm at the Kempinski Hotel in Accra, which is first class. I've put you on WhatsApp, which everyone uses here, so download it and then we can send each other messages.*
> *Dad*

Gordon had included his phone number in Ghana. Unconvinced by his father's anaemic reassurance, Derek read the message again. The email glossed over the details, like varnish over blemished wood. A wonderful time getting to know each other? He didn't have a picture 'yet'?

Derek tried the phone number. It rang several times and cut off with a prim, British-accented woman letting Derek know that the number he was trying to reach was not available and he should please try again later.

Next, Derek called Cas, who didn't answer but got back ten minutes later. 'What's going on?'

'Dad emailed me, said he was doing fine and had met the wonderful lady or whatever.'

'Oh, that's great!' Cas said.

'I don't believe it,' Derek said. 'The message sounds fishy, like he hasn't really met Helena and is either playing for time or too embarrassed to admit it.'

'Oh,' Cas said, with little inflection. 'Well, can you send his WhatsApp contact number to me? I'll try calling and texting him as well.'

'Thank you, Cas.'

Derek googled 'American in Ghana', and 'Gordon Tilson, Ghana', checking for a chance news item. Nothing came up, but by serendipity, Derek found himself reading descriptions of the different types of online scams. A common theme chilled him: the number of otherwise intelligent, rational Americans and Europeans who fell for them. A retiree from Maryland spent almost all her life savings on a supposedly stranded Iraq war vet. A guy in New York fell for a scheme to buy gold ingots in Ghana, only to find himself robbed of his money and no gold to show for it.

Derek discovered something else: a bizarre phenomenon called *sakawa* – the use of magical powers to achieve high success in the con business. *Sakawa* involved going through an intermediary like a traditional priest who might prescribe bizarre, even revolting, rituals to achieve the desired goal. Derek's lip curled as he read about the panoply of human and animal body parts used as sacrificial offerings to the gods, and in one case, a bloodstained rag from a traumatically penetrated virgin. Fucking crazy nonsense, Derek thought. At the same time, the claim that even normally smart, logical people could not resist the power of *sakawa* struck him. The irony was not lost because here was Gordon falling for something Derek would never have expected him to.

For five days, Derek heard nothing from his father. At night he slept fitfully, sometimes waking to turn on the light and sit wondering. On the sixth day, at around ten in the morning, Derek received the WhatsApp call he had been praying for.

'Hi, son,' Gordon said, his voice as taut as a stretched rubber band about to snap.

'Dad. Thank God. Are you OK? Where are you?'

'I'm fine. I'm still at the Kempinski Hotel in Accra. Nice place, five star – all the trimmings.'

'OK, that's cool,' Derek said impatiently, 'but what's going on?'

His father took such a long time to respond that Derek thought the line had cut. 'Hello?'

'I didn't really meet Helena,' Gordon said. 'I lied to you because I was so embarrassed. You were right, I was wrong. I called and texted her for days. The number's a dud. I've been had.'

'Shit,' Derek said. 'Jesus.'

'Right.'

'Dad, I'm sorry.' Gordon was silent, but Derek could sense the heaviness of his brooding. 'Fuck. Dad, I don't know what to say.'

'How about, "I told you so"?' Gordon said with resignation. 'You might as well, since that's what you're thinking.'

'Dad. Come on. I'm not the enemy here.'

'I know, I know. Sorry. Cheap shot.'

'Don't worry about it. So, what happened exactly when you arrived in Ghana?'

'Not a whole lot,' Gordon said with a bitter laugh. 'No Helena at the airport, no Helena reachable by phone, WhatsApp, email, you name it. I waited for that message or phone call to come, but it never did. I feel like such a goddamn *fool*. I've been scammed. I'm one of *those* idiots who's been duped by some fucking teenager sitting in front of a computer in some shitty Internet cafe. I don't think I'll ever live this down.'

'You can, and you will,' Derek said. 'I'm here for you.'

'Thank you. Feels good to hear that.'

'Of course.'

'It's weird. Every so often I feel this little glimmer of hope. That she'll call. My mind clinging by its fingernails to a futile hope.'

'I imagine that's a normal reaction,' Derek said. 'You're coming back home as soon as you can, right?'

'I'll need to go to the Delta office in town to find out the earliest flight I can get back. Today's Saturday and Monday is a national holiday here, so it'll have to be Tuesday.'

'OK,' Derek said. 'Meanwhile, just relax at the hotel, take it easy. And don't talk to anyone about this, either.'

Gordon grunted. 'As if I would even want to. Have you spoken to Cas?'

'Last night. Just wanted to know if he'd heard any news.'

'I'll call him. I know he's been trying to reach me.'

'Yeah,' Derek said. 'He's been worried. He cares about you.'

'I know. But me . . . well, I'm an asshole.'

'If you don't stop beating yourself up about this,' Derek said, 'Imma beat the crap out of you.'

To their mutual relief, that flash of humour worked, and they had a laugh. 'OK, son,' Gordon said. 'I guess I'll hang up now. I'll text you tomorrow.'

'Sure. Love you, Dad.'

CHAPTER TWENTY-TWO

After getting off the line with Derek, Gordon sat listless and depressed at the edge of the bed in his hotel room. He thought he might go downstairs to the bar for something to drink, and then eat dinner at the Papillon Restaurant, but he wasn't that hungry. Maybe later, after he got in touch with Cas. Gordon tried his number but got only voicemail. He got up and sat at the desk where his laptop was open. Rather than talk on the phone, Gordon would pour out his woes into an email to Cas. Sometimes writing was more therapeutic than talking.

> *Hey, Cas, how are you, buddy? I know you've been trying to get hold of me and I'm sorry I've been MIA. Spoke with Derek earlier on and told him what's happened here in Ghana. Bottom line is he was right. There's no Helena. Her number has dropped off the face of the earth. I've been duped big time. I fell for the kind of thing that in the past I would have*

said was an obvious ruse that only an uneducated dumbass would fall for. Funny when it happens to you. I believed what I wanted to believe, and so here I am. My feelings are all mixed up – anger, shame, embarrassment, depression, emptiness, the whole shebang. It's surreal, like I'm not in my body.

I'd set my trip for two months, but as I told Derek, I'll get the earliest possible flight back when the Delta office opens after the long weekend. It's a holiday here on Monday. Derek just wants me back asap. This is a classic case of 'I told you so', even though he didn't say that out loud, but he did warn me this might happen.

Hope you're well. Talk soon.

He went down to the Gallery Bar where a bunch of Brits and a couple of Ghanaians were drinking beer and watching a football match on the widescreen TV above the bar. Gordon had a scotch on the rocks and sat quietly in a booth by himself. After that he went to Cedar Garden and had kofta kebab. When he returned to his room, an email from Cas was waiting for him.

Gordon – listen, sorry to hear about this, but I have a different take on it than what Derek probably has. So, you got duped, so what? Big fucking deal. Look, shit happens, right? Chalk it up to one of those regrettable experiences that's not going to ruin your life and, in the end, won't make the slightest damn difference. In a few years it will all be a distant memory. Why hurry back? is my question. I know there's probably a lot that's changed in Ghana since you were last there, so cut your losses and just have a damn good vacation! Go sightseeing somewhere, look up some resorts or whatever. Don't they have some animal parks or something? What's happened isn't the worst thing that could happen to a guy! OK, so you're out a few thousand dollars, but you could lose that just as well in Vegas for God's sake. Hell, you could even embrace the whole experience and blog about it, I don't know. Call me if you like, and we'll talk, but I say sleep on it. In the morning things might seem quite different.

Gordon couldn't help smiling. That's Cas, all right. Always had a different and refreshing perspective, like seeing an object as a cube from one angle and realising it looked like a pyramid from another.

Before Gordon went to bed, he sent another email to Cas in reply.

Interesting perspective. Let me think about it.

In the morning, Gordon had a reply from Cas, who would be fast asleep by now, DC time.

I gotta proposal for you. Call me early afternoon Ghanian time.

Gordon noticed tangentially that Cas had left out the second of the three *a*'s in 'Ghanaian', a common mistake. But more to the point, what 'proposal' was Cas talking about? Gordon waited until around two that afternoon and then called.

'How you feeling today?' Cas asked.

'A little better, actually.'

'I'm glad to hear it,' Cas said. 'What's the temperature over there?'

'Must be in the nineties – it's the humidity that kills you. I saw on CNN we're having our first blizzard for the season in DC?'

'Pretty dramatic. I haven't been out in two days.'

'Well, stay safe. Don't want you slipping on an icy pavement.' Gordon cut to the chase. 'What's this "proposal" you referenced in your email?'

'So, it's going to sound pretty outlandish at the beginning, but hear me out.'

'OK.'

'At first my feeling was, fine, so you got duped, now let's move on. But I've been reading tons of articles online about these scam setups and thinking, well, let's hold our horses a second. Our impression of a bunch of teenagers and young men working out of shitty Internet cafes doesn't do justice to the whole picture. A few of these individuals do get picked up and thrown into jail, but the rule rather than the exception is that there are very few prosecutions, never mind convictions. And the reason why that's so is not because the scammers are so slick or that the authorities are powerless to stop them, it's that the police authorities are in on the game themselves.'

'I imagine that could be true,' Gordon agreed. 'Corrupt police isn't news, really.'

'Sure, but there's another, maybe even larger factor influencing why so few of these cases are prosecuted,' Cas went on. 'Something not immediately obvious is that Americans, Europeans, or whoever has been a victim of one of these scams, *rarely* turn up in Ghana to take action and try to prosecute. Why? Well, it's mostly fear of travelling to a country they know nothing about or of getting tangled up in a police system that's likely to be corrupt and possibly violent.'

'Yes, that makes sense,' Gordon agreed. 'I suppose I'd never thought of it that way.'

'Right, right,' Cas said, his crackly voice taking on some eagerness. 'So then, the police see nothing's going to happen and they reach some kind of agreement with the scammers to release them in return for some money. Even if the case goes to court, if the complainant repeatedly doesn't show up, the court eventually dismisses the case.'

'OK,' Gordon said, still waiting for the punchline, 'so . . . so what? You're saying that my case is different because I'm here in Ghana.'

'Bingo,' Cas said with satisfaction. 'This is one hell of a golden opportunity to nail this shit.'

'Hold on a second. Yesterday it was, "fuck it all, live and let live". Today I'm the new sheriff in town here to fix all the evils?'

'I'm saying you're in a unique position to make a difference, is all I'm saying,' Cas responded. 'You can alter the paradigm. It's like a big block of stone everyone's been walking past and ignoring for years until one day a sculptor comes along and shapes it into a statue.'

'Nice metaphor,' Gordon said, 'but what if one day the damn statue falls over and crushes the sculptor? In other words, what if I go after this thing and end up getting hurt?'

'I don't think it has to be that way,' Cas said. 'You won't be inventing the wheel. First, there's a guy called Sana Sana in Ghana—'

'Who?'

'Sana Sana. I know, weird name, but anyway he's a Ghanaian investigative reporter who does exposés on prominent people – mostly corrupt politicians. He's done some TED talks in the States and he's working on a documentary on these scams right now. He's got a bunch of resources at his command. If you could get a hold of him and work with him, he might even be able to track down the people who duped you. I'll text you the YouTube link.

'Second, for what it's worth, I think you should go to the police about this. Just making a report is an important first step because they're going to say, "OK, this guy is here right in front of us, and he's serious."

'Third, what about that woman you told me you met at the Ghanaian ambassador's? Didn't you say she's the wife of the attorney general or whatever?'

'Josephine. Wife of the Inspector General of Police.'

'Yes, that. Jesus, Gordon. You have a contact intimately connected with the top law enforcement guy there and you're not going to use that opportunity? How many people do you think have ever been in such a strategic position?'

Gordon chewed on the inside of his cheek. To be honest, he had ruled out meeting up with Josephine, not to mention her husband. He cleared his throat. 'I didn't tell you this, but I had sex with Josephine.' Silence from the other end. Gordon continued. 'So, I fucked her, and now I'm here in Ghana looking for *another* woman who, by the way, doesn't exist? How awkward are the optics on that?'

'OK, well,' Cas said, recovering, 'that's still no reason not to get in touch with her. You're both grown-ups. Whatever happened, happened. This is another matter altogether.'

Undecided and mixed up, Gordon heaved a sigh.

'The thing is, you're embarrassed about this,' Cas persevered, 'and I don't blame you. But this is what scammers rely on – your shame and embarrassment. They're master manipulators. You're *not* the culprit here, you're the victim. And it's time to turn it around and become a survivor, goddammit.'

Gordon was half persuaded.

'I don't think we can let this go,' Cas added. 'And whatever the outcome, when you get back to the States, we're going to document the whole thing.'

'That's what this is about, Cas? So you can get a piece in the *Post*?'

'The way I see it is a co-authorship. You've got the raw material and I'm going to shape it to produce a riveting piece. Preferably in two parts.'

'I'll give it some thought. Derek's going to have an issue with it, though. He's not going to see why I should turn into Kurt Wallander.'

'All you're going to tell him is that you've decided to make the best of it and take a vacation in Ghana. Nothing wrong with that. And *I'm* certainly not going to tell him about my idea. I'd like to stay on his good side.'

Gordon smiled. 'As you should.'

After they ended the conversation, Cas sent him the link he had mentioned. Gordon found one YouTube video after another featuring Sana Sana, whose exposés were sponsored by BBC News. From there, Gordon spent almost two hours reading horror stories from people all over the world who had been scammed of their money through various ruses out of Ghana. The more Gordon saw, the angrier he became. Like all those other chumps, he'd been well and truly hoodwinked. He sat back and thought about Cas's declaration that Gordon had 'one hell of a golden opportunity to nail this shit'. He was beginning to see Cas's point of view.

In the morning, Gordon realised he had slept peacefully through the night for the first time since arriving in Ghana. He knew why, too. Before going to bed, he had decided to go along with Cas's idea. Whereas before he had been demoralised, now he felt empowered, and that had put his mind unexpectedly at ease. Slipping into one of Kempinski's complimentary dressing gowns, Gordon sat at the desk and sent a short message to Cas: *OK, it's on. I'll take the 'vacation'*.

But to Derek, Gordon had to write something diplomatic and much more explanatory.

Hi, Derek – this will no doubt come as something of a surprise, but thinking over my situation, I've decided to make lemonade out of lemons, as it were. Yes, I was conned, but it's water under the bridge at this point. I'm here now, and there's no real reason why I shouldn't at least try to enjoy myself and stay out the rest of the time I'd previously scheduled. Especially since I'll likely forfeit the return portion on my ticket if I change the date – I'll basically be buying a new one-way ticket – and why should I have to do that? Of course I'm mad with whoever did this to me, but it doesn't mean I have to hate the whole country of Ghana and everyone in it. Hope you understand, son. Don't worry, I'll be fine.

Thanks.

PART TWO

PART TWO

CHAPTER TWENTY-THREE

3rd April, Atimpoku, Ghana

They had told Kafui it would be brutal. Mama, Auntie Mary, Cousin Gladys – all of them had warned Kafui the first three months would be hell with Yao, the new baby. 'He'll cry all night,' they said.

Trouble was, Yao had passed that time marker and still had not slept a single night straight through.

'Shh.' Kafui tried to soothe him, rocking the baby gently in the dark. 'What's wrong, Yao? Is it your stomach?'

Fiercely, he pushed away the breast Kafui offered. He wasn't hungry and seemed frustrated his mother couldn't figure out his problem.

Leonard, Kafui's husband, was trying to get some sleep on the floor in the opposite corner of the pocked floor of the hut. He lifted his head and looked at the silhouette of his wife cuddling their firstborn. '*Please*, Kafui. Take him outside, eh? Let me sleep!' He worked two jobs, so he was exasperated and tired. The heat of the night was insufferable and he would have to be up again in barely two hours.

Kafui, too, had work to do later – a cleaning job at one of the nice houses near the Volta River, where *oburonis* liked to stay. But Yao knew nothing about that, nor the detriment sleepless nights caused his parents. Kafui gathered him in her arms and went out to the compound, which was barely cooler than inside the house. Four other households shared the space for cooking and washing. Everyone was asleep except Kafui and her boy, whose all-out crying had quieted now to whimpering, as if he were gradually accepting the comfort of his mother.

She supported Yao in the crook of her right elbow, jiggling him in rhythm to her gait. She walked to the edge of the roundabout off which roads north, south, and east radiated like sunrays. The Adome Hotel stood strategically at the circle with its name scrawled in fading black paint on a background of splotchy green. Yellow streetlights cast a ghostly hue on the roads. Traffic was rare at this time of the night, but in a few hours the Atimpoku lorry park would spring to life as travellers stopped for refreshments and bus transfers.

'You need to sleep, boy,' Kafui said, rocking Yao like a slow pendulum. As of midnight, he was four months old to the day – born on 3rd December. She watched his eyes drift closed and his tiny, perfectly formed lashes come together like the leaves of a touch-me-not plant. At last, Kafui thought. But she would linger awhile to ensure Yao slept on. He had been known to wake up the moment he was laid down on his sleeping pad. She brushed his soft, silky forehead lightly with her fingertips and smiled down at him, her chest swelling with love. Before Yao, Kafui had miscarried, so she took him as a gift from God.

She looked up as a black SUV approached from a northerly direction and took a sharp left turn east towards the Adome Bridge spanning the width of the river. Upstream from Atimpoku and the bridge, the hydroelectric dam at Akosombo hummed with power as it held back the largest man-made lake in the world.

The bridge lamps, some of them extinguished and unreplaced, illuminated the SUV as it receded into the distance. Kafui saw the brake lights come on as the vehicle stopped. She could just make out two people alighting, one each from the driver's and passenger side. They went to the rear, opened the boot, and dragged out a long, heavy-looking sack of about two metres in length. One man at each end, they carried it to the side of the bridge and struggled to lift it up to the railing. Sagging in the middle, the sack seemed to move around somewhat and Kafui had an eerie notion that a human body was inside it. The men heaved the load over the railing and Kafui heard the faint splash seconds later. She shuddered, aware of the urban legends detailing human sacrifices to the river god.

Kafui turned away and hurried back home. Whatever had taken place on that bridge, she wanted nothing to do with it.

CHAPTER TWENTY-FOUR

6th April

Out of Africa
The lucrative African underworld of Internet scammers
that brings pain and ruin to well-meaning Westerners

By Casper Guttenberg

PART ONE
*Modern online romance scams are premeditated
crimes that steal millions – potentially billions –
of dollars from vulnerable people all over the US,
Canada, and Europe. Rarely caught or prosecuted,
the scammers sit safely at computers in countries
like Ghana and Nigeria while hunting for prey
on social networks. Their victims are often left
financially and psychologically damaged, and are
sometimes so embarrassed that they are disinclined
to come forward even when they realise they've
been duped.*

Contrary to a prevailing impression, people who fall prey to scams are not poor decision makers or even uneducated or stupid. They may have successful businesses or professional careers, but, as a University of Exeter study showed, they tend to be unduly open to persuasion by others, whether due to upbringing or life experiences.

GT, a long-time resident of Washington, DC (his name is withheld here for security reasons), built an online relationship with someone in Ghana who appeared on a Facebook page as a beautiful Ghanaian woman, 'Helena'. Later, 'she' would become his confidante and 'lover'. The emotional bond established, GT did not find requests for money from this person outlandish, suspicious, or unreasonable. Some six weeks ago, GT set off for Ghana to meet the new love of his life. When he arrived, he discovered the bitter, cruel truth: this Helena did/does not exist. At last count, he had sent 'her' around $4,000 to help her with what emerged to be concocted medical expenses. The elaborate story was that Helena's 'sister' had been involved in a catastrophic vehicle crash that had landed her in a steeply priced Intensive Care Unit. In a country where cash is still king, those costs must be borne fully by the patient and the family. That part was certainly true.

Unlike most scam victims whose connection to the scammer generally does not proceed beyond the online space, GT took the step to meet Helena in person. Of note, GT, a widower who lost his decades-long Ghanaian wife to ovarian cancer years ago, had been to Ghana before more than once, the first time being a Peace Corps mission in the 1980s.

GT therefore had a feel for Ghana that few Westerners do, and now that he was in the country, GT was afforded the rare, potential opportunity to confront those who had conned him. Not the kind of person to take abuse lying down, GT has remained in the country to investigate his own victimisation.

Derek's frown grew deeper as he read this online article, which included several stock photos of the 'poverty-stricken' Ghana in contrast to the 'wealthy less-than-one-per-cent'. He was baffled. From his perspective, the piece was out of left field. It was plainly the story of his father's experience, but who had made the decision to publish it in the *Washington Observer*, and why hadn't Derek known about it beforehand? Neither Gordon nor Cas had mentioned it before. Although initially opposed, Derek had come to accept his father's rationale for staying in Ghana. Through March, Gordon had sent emails and text messages to keep Derek informed: Dad had moved out of the Kempinski Hotel to a bed and breakfast, he'd rented a vehicle with a driver who was taking him around

Accra and the usual touristy places. All that was fine, but now, what in fuck's name did '*GT has remained in the country to investigate his own victimisation*' mean?

Derek called Cas, but it went to voicemail. Several hours passed before Cas returned the call.

'I saw your article called "Out of Africa",' Derek said. 'I mean, it *was* your article, right?'

'Yes, that's correct,' Cas said. 'What did you think?'

Derek was tempted to say 'not much' but he refrained. 'I'm confused,' he said instead. 'When did we discuss writing a piece about my father in Ghana? Had you planned this beforehand?'

'Your father and I talked about it and we decided to collaborate on a piece. My editor approved, so we went ahead with it.'

'When was this?'

'Last month sometime.'

Why was his tone so vague? 'Last month?' Derek said. 'And neither of you mentioned it to me?'

'I assumed Gordon had discussed it with you,' Cas said. 'He said he would. He might just have been too preoccupied.'

'When did he tell you he would talk to me about it?' Derek questioned, trying to nail this down.

'Look, I don't remember exactly, Derek,' Cas said with some impatience. 'Hey, I'm an old man. I can't keep all these dates in my head.'

He was trying to pass it off as a joke, but Derek was far from amused. 'Sorry, but something just doesn't add up. What's going on? Just level with me. Did the two of you plan this from the very beginning and decide to keep me out of it?'

'It's not like that at all,' Cas protested. 'Please don't think of it that way. We felt this would be an opportunity to explore the Internet scam phenomenon.'

'So, he's staying in Ghana to carry out some kind of investigation? This is ludicrous.'

'Look, Derek,' Cas said, his voice tightening, 'your father wants to get to the bottom of who did this to him, and I don't blame him. Why should he lie down and take it? Why should these conmen assholes get away with this kind of shit?'

Derek swore under his breath. He was angry and bewildered. Why hadn't his father shared this crazy plan to remain in Ghana to investigate who had defrauded him? Derek found himself grimly answering his own question: *Because it's crazy, that's why*. Crazy enough to make Derek smell a rat. And Cas was the rat.

Derek took in a good breath and let it out quickly in a mixture of weariness and frustration. And now something else was troubling him. 'Has Dad communicated with you in the past couple of days?' he asked Cas. 'He hasn't been answering any of my messages.'

'If I recall, he emailed me at the end of March sometime. I expect he'll drop you a line soon.'

Cas said he had to go and ended the call. Derek returned to the *Observer* article and stared at it until the text and images blurred and his mind was brimming with suspicion.

Had Cas manipulated Gordon into staying in Ghana in order to get a write-up in the *Observer* out of it? And an even starker, more cynical thought struck Derek and left him cold. Had Cas engineered this entire situation from the start?

CHAPTER TWENTY-FIVE

14th April, Accra, Ghana

Emma returned home after a day at the mall selling Apple devices. It was almost ten. She cooked dinner with the TV news on in the background.

Her phone rang, but she didn't recognise the number. 'Hello?'

'Emma Djan?'

'Who is speaking, please?'

'My name is Yemo Sowah.'

For a brief second, Emma forgot who that was, but then she remembered and her heart leapt. 'Oh, yes, sir. Good evening, sir.'

'Sorry to call so late, Miss Djan.' His voice was soft and a little husky, like wet leaves.

'It's no problem, please.' Emma sat down.

'DCOP Laryea called me about three months ago. He said you had left the police service but he recommended you highly.'

'Thank you, sir.'

'At the time, I had no vacancy, but I now have an open position. Are you still interested?'

Emma felt giddy. 'Yes, sir.' Her voice came out hoarse, so she cleared her throat and repeated herself.

'Good,' he said. 'I'd like to see you tomorrow morning, if possible.'

'Of course, sir.'

'Do you have a job elsewhere?' Sowah asked.

'No please,' she lied. She wasn't going to let anything jeopardise her shot at this.

'Excellent. Then I'll see you at eight sharp.'

At seven in the morning, Emma arrived at the Sowah Private Investigators Agency at 101 Limomo Walk in Asylum Down, a district named because it was a short distance downhill from the psychiatric hospital. She was so early it was no surprise the office wasn't open yet. The front door had a frosted glass pane emblazoned with the agency's name.

Idly scrolling through the news feed on her phone, Emma hung around. At about seven-thirty, a smartly dressed woman with flawless braids and impossibly high heels approached the door with keys in hand.

'Good morning,' she said, giving the visitor an enquiring look.

'Good morning, madam. My name is Emma Djan.'

'Oh, yes, I remember,' the woman said, unlocking the door. 'The boss said to expect you. I'm Beverly, his assistant. You can come in and wait for him.'

They entered a foyer and Beverly turned on the lights. 'Please have a seat,' she said to Emma, pointing to the seating area at one end.

A desk with a computer, printer, and filing cabinet in an alcove on the opposite side of the foyer turned out to be where Beverly did her work. It was comfortable but rather small.

Apart from offering Emma some water, Beverly said almost nothing as she set up for the day. But at precisely 8 a.m., she beckoned to Emma. 'Please follow me.'

Beverly unlocked a second door which opened into an open area with workstations and computers. The five desks were laden with large envelopes and dog-eared folders. Beverly's heels clicked precisely with her quick, efficient steps as she led Emma down a short corridor. At the end of that was an open door where Beverly put her head in and announced Emma's arrival.

'Very good. Please let her come in.' It was the live version of Sowah's phone voice.

Emma was nervous, and she didn't relax much when she saw Yemo Sowah. He reminded her of an uncle she had. Sowah was compact and dressed in a bright white shirt and dark tie. His crown was completely bald, leaving only trimmed, greying hair on each side of his head.

He got out of his chair. 'Good morning, Miss Djan,' he said. 'Sorry, is it "Miss"?'

'Yes please. Good morning, sir.'

They shook hands. His palm was small but rather rough. He gestured to a striking ruby-red sofa in the corner. 'Let's sit and talk, shall we?'

He took a seat opposite her in an office chair with a straight back. She noticed how impeccably polished his shoes were.

'Thank you for being on time, by the way,' he said with a smile. 'It's a good start.'

'Thank you, sir,' Emma said, her hands tightly folded in her lap.

Sowah read her body language. 'Relax, Miss Djan,' he said. 'It's not that bad.'

She laughed nervously.

'Where did you school?' he asked.

'Kumasi Wesley Girls High,' Emma replied.

'Oh, nice,' Sowah said. 'And your father was at Manhyia Headquarters in Kumasi, I understand. With the Homicide unit there.'

'Yes please.'

'When did you move to Accra?'

'After he died about six years ago, I moved here to find better work and support my mother. I stayed with one of my aunts for a while. My mother remained behind. I tried to persuade her to come with me to Accra, but she loves Kumasi too much.'

'Did you consider going to university?'

'Yes please. But money problems.' Emma made a face of regret.

'Understood,' Sowah said, nodding. 'At any rate, here you are, a relatively recent police academy graduate. Congrats.'

'Thank you, sir.'

'How did you like working at the Commercial Crimes Unit at CID?'

This was where it was going to become uncomfortable. 'The work was a little bit tedious,' Emma said, but hurried to add, 'the people were fine, just the work.'

'Sure,' he said.

She was dreading his next question. *He's going to ask me why I left.*

But Sowah didn't. 'I was with CID for about ten years,' he said. 'DCOP Laryea was my very good mate and we have kept in touch all these years. But I left CID because I wanted the freedom to work without bosses constantly looking over my shoulder and curtailing my every initiative. So, I founded this agency. It will be thirty years this year. Older than you.' He gave a one-sided smile.

'We do a lot of paperwork here,' Sowah continued, 'but the foundation of our activities continues to be contact with people. In missing persons cases, we sometimes must go as far as the Northern or Upper East Regions not only to find someone, but to locate another person who knew or knows the missing person. You know, here in Ghana we haven't quite reached the point where addresses are connected with driver's licences or voter IDs and so on – although we are headed in that direction. But we Ghanaians move all over the place and sometimes never inform anyone. When we do background checks for banks, we talk to people in person or on the phone. Sometimes you'll be calling them every single day and they won't even mind you.

You must go to find *them*. So, patience and curiosity are two qualities you need to work here.'

She nodded. 'Yes, sir.'

'As is punctuality and honesty,' he went on. 'We have five detectives – you make six – and they all know that second to lying, what I hate most is lateness. I know people always say GMT means "Ghana Mean Time" and you can therefore show up whenever you please, but we don't go by that system here. I hope that's clear. If you ever must be late due to unforeseen circumstances, you need to let me know as soon as you can.'

'Yes please.'

'Now, you will want to know about salary.' Sowah leant to the side and took a sheet of paper from his desk. 'Take a look at the breakdown.'

Emma studied the neat tables in the document. The remuneration was so much greater than what she had been getting at GPS – or working in an Apple store for that matter – she had to make sure she wasn't reading it incorrectly.

'Please,' she said haltingly, 'excuse me, this number here – is that per month?'

'No – every two weeks,' he said.

She tried not to let her jaw drop but he must have sensed what was going through her mind. 'Don't get a wrong picture,' he said. 'You are being paid for very hard work. Sometimes you may be here till nine or ten at night as well as the weekends.'

'Yes, sir. I understand.'

'Oh, I forgot something,' he said. 'In regard to what DCOP Laryea told me about you and your keen interest in murder, I must be honest with you, murder cases don't even remotely comprise the bulk of our work. Those tend to go over to CID. The world over, that is generally the case with private investigator agencies. That might be a disappointment for you, and I will understand if you would like to seek other opportunities.'

She shook her head. 'No please. I want to work here.'

'Good,' Sowah said, looking gratified. 'One of the reasons I want you to join us is that we have no female detectives, which is embarrassing in this day and age.'

Emma smiled with some pride. She was something of a pioneer, then.

'Now, do you have any questions for me?' he asked.

'Please, will I be with one of the other detectives to understand how everything works?'

'Good question. I will have you shadow all of them for a few weeks, but I will always be supervising and keeping a close watch. If you have any problems, come to me.'

'Yes please.'

'Last question. Can you start tomorrow?'

'Yes, sir.'

CHAPTER TWENTY-SIX

17th April

After church on Sunday, Nii joined a group of *sakawa* friends to hang out and work on their scams. They had a small place in the sprawling suburb of Dansoman. Except for an ancient, battered swivel chair with a wheel missing, and a desk with uneven legs, the room had no furniture, and the young men lay on the floor along with their phones, laptops, power banks, and a tangle of wires and connectors.

They chatted, joked around, and poked fun at each other even as they surfed and typed, trying to entrap potential victims. Bruno was here this time, staying close to Nii to learn *sakawa* fundamentals. One of Bruno's first lessons was mastering the art of creating a fake person with the combination of a sham Facebook profile, a designated WhatsApp phone, and judicious use of fake webcam software on Skype. The profile pictures on Facebook, WhatsApp, and Skype all had to match, of course. The skill was in getting the *mugu* to believe what he or she was hearing, even if suspicious at the beginning. Most important was to be armed with the spiritual power bestowed by the traditional priest, in this case Ponsu, so that even the smartest *oburoni* would never be able to resist sending more and more money. That's what started to happen with the white man, Mr Gordon, before he travelled to Ghana. He thought he was conversing with a beautiful Ghanaian woman. Nii Kwei, with the spiritual powers invested in him, made Gordon believe he was seeing and hearing what he really wasn't.

Nii instructed Bruno how to use Skype with ManyCam, which replaces a real webcam. ManyCam can use either an Internet image or a pre-recorded video. Nii recommended the latter. Easily available in Ghana, they save the scammer the time and trouble searching the Internet. Professionals make these short videos that appear to show someone on webcam talking to you.

'So,' Nii continued, 'I get plenty plenty videos I upload to ManyCam and I name the files so not to get confused.' He and his *sakawa* colleagues almost invariably used the accepted pidgin English of the streets when talking to each other. 'When I call the man on Skype, what he go see is some fine woman smiling at him. I tell him say my computer microphone no dey work well, so make we type instead. And I tell him say because of Ghana network the image make slow compared to the typing. So, for example, if the *mugu* say something serious but the woman on the Skype is smiling, he go ask why she make smile when he dey tell her something serious.'

'Oh, OK,' Bruno said, nodding.

'Make you no spend plenty time on Skype' – Nii warned – 'like maybe just some five minutes, then you cut the video and text the *mugu* tell him say the network is bad so you can't do Skype or WhatsApp video. But you can still send him some pictures. If he want naked pictures too, we have to send them. Also, we get women who can answer the phone for us, or if not, then we don't pick the call and later we text him to say the network is down.'

'But for that man Mr Gordon, why you no put white girl for profile instead of Ghanaian one?' Bruno asked.

Nii shook his head. 'Dat one be different kind target. This *mugu* no dey want white girl, you understand me? He like black woman, African woman. If you want to catch a dog, you bring meat, not grass. Wait, make I show you something.'

On his Samsung – the latest model – Nii pulled up a Facebook page called BWWM – Black Women, White Men. He scrolled. A white American man and his Ghanaian wife were decked out in *kente* outfits. All the couples were beautiful in some way, and their children even more so.

'This is how you can use Facebook,' Nii explained. 'Look at the likes for this pic. Click on the men who have liked the pic and see if you go get one who is single and looking for a woman. That's who you will try your hand, but first you go check his profile to see what kind of job he has. He should be someone who get plenty money. Then, you go message him – not as yourself, oo. I mean using the fake profile you made with the photo of a beautiful African woman. You take a screenshot of the same woman you use for the Skype. Then, you get to know him, and then after some small time pass, you start asking for money, and then more and more.'

'He won't suspect?' Bruno said.

'If you have the spiritual powers,' Nii said, 'he can never suspect. He will be somehow confused and just keep sending the cash.'

'So, like me, for example, can I get the powers?'

'Of course, but you have to work with Kweku Ponsu. To start, you will take two chickens to him—' Nii stopped talking and looked up as he heard male voices and the scuffle of boots. He put a finger to his lips to tell the others to shut up, ran low to the window, looked out, and then swung back. '*Police!*'

The boys scrambled to their feet, trying to put all their devices away. Too late.

The door exploded open and four police officers charged in yelling, their automatic weapons pointed. Thinking quickly and clearly, Nii dropped to the ground flat on his stomach, arms outstretched. A couple of his companions weren't so lucky. The officers clubbed them down into submission.

'Get them all!' a harsh female voice ordered, a sound resembling a piece of metal dragged over rutted asphalt. Nii didn't need to look up to see who she was. Detective Inspector Doris Damptey. She and Nii Kwei knew each other well. He relaxed, climbing down from his fight-or-flight state.

The officers cuffed the *sakawa* bunch and ordered them to sit up. The boys kept their gaze down – all except Nii Kwei.

'*Heh!*' Damptey yelled at them. 'Look up! Foolish *sakawa* boys. Do you think we don't know all about you people and your evil ways?'

Her legs were set far apart like pillars at the corners of her box frame. If a headmistress and Gaboon Viper got together, DI Doris Damptey would be the result: authoritarian, slow-moving, and venomous.

Nii smiled secretly. 'We beg you, oo, madam,' he said with exaggerated penitence.

She sucked her teeth in disdain. 'You say you beg me? Ah, stupid! We are going to take you to Dansoman station right now and then you will see how to really beg. *Kwasea!* This *sakawa* thing you are doing is *bad*.'

'We are sorry,' Nii said. 'We won't do it again.'

'Yes, because you will be in jail,' Damptey said, curling her lip.

'I beg you, madam.'

'Empty begging doesn't do anything while we are all hungry,' Damptey said. The officers, silent, folded their arms and leant against the wall.

Nii looked at his companions and back to Damptey. 'Maybe I can help you chop small.'

'Five hundred,' she said.

'I only have three,' Nii Kwei lied. Damptey wouldn't check.

'OK, OK,' Damptey said impatiently. She signalled her officers to uncuff Nii first and then his mates. Nii counted out bills from his wallet and gave them to Damptey, whose greedy eyes had lit up.

The officers marched all but Nii outside, where a handful of press photographers was idly waiting. Tomorrow morning, the boys would be in the papers, demonstrating what a great job the Ghana police were doing to stamp out this growing menace to society.

CHAPTER TWENTY-SEVEN

18th April

Emma had been apprehensive she might feel the sting of male supremacy from her five male co-workers, but Yemo Sowah set the tone in which gender didn't determine status: only experience, knowledge, and hard work. In any case, Sowah protected her from any bad treatment whatsoever. Nailed to the wall was a code of conduct that included respect, kindness, patience, honesty, willingness to be corrected, and taking responsibility for one's mistakes.

Barring emergencies, Sowah held a briefing every morning at 8 a.m. for updates on old cases and assignments of new. He started Emma off with a standard background check on a man a branch of Zenith Bank was interested in hiring.

The Sowah Agency had a Toyota sedan for office use, and if needed, Sowah's Kia SUV. This ratio of vehicles to investigators was a thousand times better than that of the Ghana Police Service. Sowah more or less promptly reimbursed his investigators' out-of-pocket travel expenses if they didn't have an official vehicle available.

Seven forty-five Monday morning, Emma got down from the *tro-tro* at her stop on Paradise Street two blocks from work. She stopped a paperboy and got the *Daily Graphic* and *The Ghanaian Chronicle*, the latter the more radical and outspoken of the two, the former still the best-selling paper in the country. She glanced at its front page as she walked the last few metres to work, looked again, and froze in place. The headline, WAR ON SAKAWA, accompanied a picture of a group of disgraced young men.

'Oh, no,' Emma whispered. 'Bruno.'

He was the second from the left, scowling at the camera in defiance.

Emma began to read the article through, but she didn't want to be a second late to work, so she hurried the last few steps to the staff room and sat down to read it there. The raid was part of President J. K. Bannerman's ambitious and sweeping initiative to cut out Ghana's cancer of fraud and corruption. Clearly, he was enlisting the help of the papers and other media to get the word out. This group of *sakawa* boys had been taken to Dansoman Police Station to be charged and jailed.

As Emma dived into the *Chronicle*'s piece, the other investigators straggled in. She smiled and greeted them cordially, but inside she was thinking about Bruno and was furious. This was exactly what she had been warning him about: *Stay out of trouble, get a legit job*.

Emma wasn't the only one who had seen the item on

the raid. Jojo, the youngest of the other investigators, was reading a copy of the *Ghanaian Times*, which had also front-paged the news. 'Catch five or six of these worthless guys and you say you're fighting the evil of *sakawa*,' he said in disdain.

It wasn't until six that evening that Emma was able to get to Dansoman Police Station. It was a two-storey building painted in the GPS's signature yellow and blue. A miscellaneous crowd hung around the front. Emma went to the small charge office, where the desk sergeant was a cordial but businesslike woman. 'Yes, we have Bruno Asare here,' she said, checking her logbook in response to Emma's enquiry. 'You want to see him?'

'Yes please, madam.'

'And who are you?'

'His sister.'

The sergeant shot her a doubtful look but didn't probe further. Instead, she turned and yelled back to the jail officer, who marched out a few minutes later with a sullen Bruno.

'You can talk to him over there,' the sergeant said to Emma, indicating the end of the counter.

'Sis, what are you doing here?' Bruno said in an undertone as she came up to him.

'That's not the right question,' Emma said angrily, trying to keep her voice down. 'The question should be what *you* are doing here?'

Bruno was deadpan. 'I haven't done anything.'

'Don't lie to me. It was all in the papers today – pictures of you and those *sakawa* boys. Didn't I tell you they would get you in trouble?'

Glumly, Bruno looked away.

'Were you with that Nii Kwei I met the other day?' Emma asked.

Bruno nodded.

'Is he also at this station?'

'No, I've not seen him,' Bruno said. 'Maybe they took him to somewhere else. I'm not sure. But the rest of us are here.'

It was possible that this station's jail was at capacity, Emma reasoned, although that normally never stopped anyone packing in a few more prisoners.

'Can you get me out?' Bruno asked her, making sad eyes at her.

Emma bristled. 'No! I will not. You got yourself into this trouble, and you'll have to get yourself out. Maybe you'll finally learn your lesson. It serves you right, Bruno.'

Emma noticed the desk sergeant staring at Bruno as she talked to someone on the phone. At intervals, she nodded and said, 'Yes, madam.' After ending the call, she beckoned to Bruno. 'Come.'

The sergeant opened a large ledger. 'Sign here,' she said, pressing her index finger to a space down the column.

Puzzled, Bruno signed.

'You may go,' the sergeant said, looking at him with both offhandedness and distaste.

'Please, you say?'

She raised her voice. 'You may go! Are you deaf?'

'Yes, madam. No, madam. Thank you.'

A corporal lifted the barrier at the counter and incredibly, Bruno walked out scot-free.

CHAPTER TWENTY-EIGHT

Sana Sana was a mysterious if not forbidding figure. He was Ghana's most famous journalist, yet very few people had ever seen the face hidden behind a curtain of thick wires or threaded beads hanging from the brim of a hat. On occasion, he had removed the mask in front of an eager TV audience only to reveal a prosthetic face underneath.

He kept his identity a firm secret because over the years he had broken dozens of stories of corruption and organised crime all over Ghana. He was the mastermind behind daring undercover operations that exposed not only the most influential personalities in the country, but murderous rituals practised in remote parts. Sana's most recent exposé had blown up the corrupt world of football game-fixing in Ghana. His motto was, 'name, shame, and jail'. His enemies were criminals in both high and low places, and as he once said at a TED talk in Europe, if he ever revealed himself to the crooks, he would be dead within days.

Even Sana's undercover agents and reporters never saw his face until he was sure they were trustworthy, but in the end, no one could be trusted a hundred per cent. Everyone was a potential Judas. Technically, so was Bruno, Sana's most recent employee, but that would be surprising. The story of Bruno, in brief, was that his ship was heading straight to the rocks and would have crashed into them had Sana not steered it back on course and into safe harbour. One of Sana's agents had discovered him while investigating a corruption scandal involving street beggars. He used Bruno to get more information. Now Sana employed Bruno often. Yes, he was still on the street, but his skills were redirected towards unearthing the evil that powerful men and women do.

Bruno's association with Sana Sana was best left as classified as possible, because almost everything Sana did was a secret.

The night Bruno got out of jail, he met up with the master journalist at a secret location. Sana listened to his account of the raid and the way Nii Kwei was taken aside and not jailed.

'He probably knows her and regularly dashes her chop money,' Sana said. 'And because he gave her and the officers the three hundred *cedis*, you were all released from jail later on.'

'Yes,' Bruno confirmed. 'Someone called the lady sergeant in the charge office and told her to release me.'

'It might have been DI Damptey or someone above her. That's what I'm especially interested in – the higher-up people. Her rank is inspector, which is nothing. I want to expose the people at the top, like the commissioners. That way we gradually work our way up to the guy they call the *Sakawa Godfather*.'

'The one we are dying to know who he is,' Bruno said.

'Yes,' Sana said with a nod that made his beads jingle. 'I want you to start asking Nii Kwei what he knows about the Godfather, but just be cool and casual.'

'Sure.'

'Tell me more about Emma, your stepsister. She came to see you at the Dansoman jail.'

'Yes please,' Bruno said. 'She's a good woman. She always tries to help me, and she wants me to do better for myself.'

'Have you told her about our project?'

'No please.'

'Good.' Sana nodded. 'You said Emma used to work at CID.'

'Yes please, but now she has taken a job as a private investigator.'

'Ah, I see. Interesting. Which agency?'

'Please, I've forgotten the name, but I know it's in Asylum Down.'

'Then that must be Yemo Sowah's agency,' Sana said. 'I know him.'

Bruno could feel Sana studying him from behind his veil.

'How are you?' Sana asked. 'Are you OK?'

'Yes please.'

'When do you plan to see Kweku Ponsu?' Sana asked.

'Please, I will go with Nii Kwei, so let me check with him and I will let you know.'

'Find out how much money he pays Ponsu.'

'Yes please.'

Sana fished for his wallet and counted out several ten-*cedi* bills, which he handed to Bruno. 'Here you are. Good work so far. Now on to the next level.'

Two days passed before Bruno and Nii could get together again to smoke. Hoping to loosen Nii's tongue, Bruno let him take most of the hits.

'The police people no beat you in the jail?' Nii asked him, his eyes narrowing against a plume of marijuana smoke.

Bruno shook his head. 'Not at all.'

'Good.'

'Why they no take you to jail?' Bruno asked. 'The lady policeman – Madam Damptey – do you know her?'

'Yah,' Nii said, as if in a pleasant dream. 'For long time.'

'Ah, OK,' Bruno said. 'Then that's why. Did you tell her about me?'

Nii took the dwindling stump of weed back and inhaled. 'Yes. That's why they released you first from jail.'

'*Ei!*' Bruno exclaimed, clapping his friend on the back. 'Then you have power, oo!'

Nii smiled, but only briefly. 'There are plenty people with more power than me. It's time for me to tell you everything about how it works, but don't talk to anybody about what I tell you. It's a secret you must keep if you want to be successful. You understand?'

'Yes, my brodda.'

'I've waited to see if I can trust you, and it seems I can.'

'Thank you.'

'OK,' Nii began, 'I pay Madam some money just like other *sakawa* boys pay her and other officers. If I get in trouble, whether *sakawa* or another thing, she protects me. That's why she told her officers not to arrest me.'

'Won't the officers suspect?'

Nii shrugged. 'And so what? They can't say or do anything. If she's in charge of a raid, she's highest in rank. Even, she might have dashed some of her officers something small so they don't say anything.'

'Ah, OK.'

'Even when she takes us to police station, they will release us maybe after one night or just a few hours because these raids are just for show. They take pictures of us for the papers and TV just so that the IGP and the president can say they are fighting against *sakawa*.'

'I see,' Bruno said. 'But what will happen if Madam's bosses find out she is doing this?'

Nii laughed. 'Oh, but some of them know already. Even, they are taking money too. Like her boss, Mr Quaino. Madam gives him something out of the money she gets from the *sakawa* boys. Quaino too, he has someone above him he also pays. And it goes on like that to the top.'

'Who is at the top?'

'They call him "Godfather", but not many people know who he is. It's better we don't know, because if Godfather falls, he will take everyone with him. The less you know, the more innocent you are.'

'Have you met him?'

'That one I can't tell you. If I've met him, it's a secret. If I haven't met him, it's also a secret.'

'So, Godfather and Kweku Ponsu, who is more powerful?'

'Godfather, of course,' Nii answered. 'And he's richer than anyone because he controls everything and gets money from police officers who support the *sakawa* boys all over Ghana.'

Bruno chewed the inside of his lip. 'I want to meet Godfather.'

'You have to be one of the best *sakawa* to do that. Only Kweku Ponsu can decide if you are good enough.'

'OK, then I will impress Ponsu.'

Nii smirked and said, 'It's just not that easy.'

CHAPTER TWENTY-NINE

20th April, Washington, DC

Ambassador Herbert Opare held a Meet the Press event at his residence, a chance for Ghanaian and American journalism students in both the US and Ghana to rub shoulders with the likes of writers and editors at the *Washington Observer* and the *Baltimore Sun* and perhaps look into career opportunities as well.

Herbert and Madam Ambassador Angelina Opare relished these intercultural exchanges and excelled at hosting them. Circulating waiters served hors d'oeuvres and wine to the mingling guests, a nicely balanced group of white and black, American and Ghanaian. Angelina, eloquent and elegant, floated from group to group chatting and engaging in deft repartee.

Herbert caught up with Marc Samuels, chief editor at the *Washington Observer*. He was sipping wine with Casper Guttenberg. This was convenient because the ambassador wanted to speak to them both.

'Would you join me for brandy later on in the Sun Room?' he invited them.

'We'd love to,' Marc said, looking pleasantly flushed already.

'Excellent,' Herbert said. 'I'll find you once most of the guests have departed.'

Once the room was buzzing with a comfortable rhythm, Herbert made his welcoming remarks: how Ghana was as committed to democracy and freedom of the press as the United States, and how political debate was alive and well in both countries. Yet both had their failings, and that was why it was vital that journalists from both sides meet to exchange ideas.

Then it was the turn of Marc and his counterpart at the *Baltimore Sun* to address guests briefly, after which a young American and Ghanaian journalist each spoke. By 8 p.m., the gathering was winding down and Herbert was saying goodbyes. He slipped away, allowing Angelina to close out the evening, and found Marc and Cas.

'How do you think it went?' Herbert said as he ushered them into the Sun Room, named for the skylight that conveyed an ice crystal illumination to the space during springtime. The rust-coloured carpet was plush, accenting the espresso of the wood floor and the pale olive upholstery of the armchairs.

'I thought it was excellent,' Marc said. 'These young men and women have fire in the belly. It's gratifying.'

'I agree,' Herbert said, gesturing his guests to sit. 'What can I offer you?'

Marc wasn't one to turn down some good brandy, and he'd shared several fine bottles with Herbert before. One might have guessed from Marc's corpulent frame that he liked good food and drink, and one would be correct. Casper, a smoker and coffee addict, was Marc's physical opposite. He was Marc's designated driver tonight, so there would be no brandy for him.

The three men settled in to talk, Herbert steering the conversation to the *Washington Observer*, where digital subscriptions were on the rise and had surpassed the one-million mark – still well behind the *New York Times*, though.

'I was interested by Cas's piece a couple of weeks ago about online scams,' Herbert said, pouring Marc a little more brandy.

'Oh yes?' Casper said. 'What did you think of it?'

'Top quality, of course,' Herbert said. 'Caused quite a stir on Ghanaweb.com, which posted excerpts of the piece and had a commentary.'

'What's Ghanaweb?' Cas asked.

'It's an all-media website,' Herbert explained. 'Radio, TV, videos, social networks, and so on. But what makes it stand out are the no-holds-barred comments underneath the features. The Ghanaweb audience is like a bunch of gunmen firing their weapons indiscriminately and not caring who gets hurt.'

'Oh, really?' Marc said, interested. 'What was the response to the *Observer* piece?'

'From what I could tell,' Herbert said, 'it broke down

into three categories. People who condemned these *sakawa* fraudsters, those who castigated and/or mocked the victims, and finally those who blame the scandal entirely on the present ruling party. Everything is politics in Ghana. I should let you know that President Bannerman has called me about the article.'

'The president himself?' Cas said. 'What did he say?'

'Well, he was concerned. You know, he has a comprehensive anti-corruption campaign in full swing. He asked if I had been aware this article was coming out in the paper. I told him, no. He went on further to say that, as an ambassador, I need to be reassuring potential American investors that the Ghanaian government is cracking down on corruption.'

'Corruption in Ghana has given the country a black eye internationally,' Marc said. 'Would you agree?'

'Yes, I would,' Herbert said. 'But back to the article – I'm curious why it's penned by Casper, who is not even in Ghana. Shouldn't it be someone who is actually there?'

Marc appeared uncomfortable. 'We do have someone there – an American who was a victim of one of these scams. He's agreed to carry out enquiries for us, and Cas is putting the two-part series together based on his experiences.'

'Who is this man?' Herbert asked.

'I can tell you once I have your assurance that you won't pass on the information,' Marc said.

'Of course.'

'His name is Gordon Tilson,' Casper said. 'He was fooled by a romance con out of Ghana and now he wants to tell his story in the *Washington Observer*. I'm writing it for him.'

'How long will Mr Tilson be there?'

Casper and Marc exchanged uneasy glances.

'What's going on?' Herbert asked, looking from one man to the other.

'Well,' Casper said, his craggy face creasing up, 'the problem is we haven't heard from Gordon in more than two weeks. We can't reach him. He's gone completely silent and we've no idea where he is.'

CHAPTER THIRTY

15th May, Accra, Ghana

Emma had successfully completed another background check. The client was going into business and wanted to be sure his intended partner was clean. He was. Her enquiries had taken her out of Accra to the Brong-Ahafo town of Sunyani.

She was happy in this job. She had a clearly defined role, encouraging colleagues, and a patient, supportive boss. She was free from long statement forms and reports in sextuplicate. With Sowah's computerised system for filing data and reports, the agency was able to cut tedious work to a minimum. Sowah had been there for Emma every step of the way. He was committed to giving her work that would challenge her sufficiently while not exposing her to anything dangerous.

Emma found comfort in the daily routine. The Thursday morning that brought a case to Emma that she could never have predicted, she was trying to eject the memory of her date the night before. It hadn't gone well.

At best, the man had bored her. At worst, he had appeared interested mostly in sleeping with her, which was out of the question. Emma was a virgin and intended to stay that way until after marriage – whenever that would be.

Her love life, if she could even call it that, was something of a muddle. Sometimes she fretted over it, but for the most part she shrugged. She had fulfilment elsewhere in her world, for example, her volunteer work with children at the Autism Centre in central Accra. Emma's Sunday afternoons were generally free, and after church, she hurried to the Autism Centre to help with the children. A dedicated, loving, and courageous woman with an autistic son of her own, who was about eight years old, ran the centre.

Emma was three hours into her work when she looked up to see a visitor who had just walked in and now stood at the doorframe. He was an *oburoni*, for sure. His greenish eyes got her attention. He was tall and very fair in colour, with curly hair receding from the forehead just a bit. He had a rugged beard with rare streaks of grey. His waistline had expanded a little beyond bounds, but it looked good on him.

'Good morning,' the man said, his gaze settling on Emma. Beverly was out for the morning.

'Good morning, sir.' She stood up. 'Can I help you?'

'I'm looking for' – he glanced at a scrap of paper in his hand – 'Yemo Sowah. Is he here?'

He sounded American to Emma. 'Yes please,' she said, approaching. 'But he's in a meeting at the moment. Is he expecting you?'

He smiled. 'I don't think so.'

The other investigators had looked up from their work with interest.

'Please have a seat.' Emma gestured at the chairs in the anteroom. 'I will let him know you are here. Please, your name?'

'Sorry – I should have said. I'm Derek Tilson.'

Emma knocked on Sowah's office door and opened it. He was meeting with a couple of clients. 'Please, sir, sorry to bother you. A man called Derek Tilson is here to see you.'

Sowah raised his eyebrows. 'Derek who?'

'Tilson. He doesn't have an appointment.'

'OK. I should be finished here in about twenty minutes.'

Emma went back to the anteroom, where the newcomer was glancing through the day's newspapers on the side table. 'Mr Sowah will be with you shortly.'

He smiled briefly and nodded. 'Thanks.'

'May I offer you some water?'

Derek declined.

From her desk, Emma stole a glance at Tilson as he waited. She wondered what the visit was about. Sowah came out with his two guests after about thirty minutes and escorted them out. Emma was waiting for him in the anteroom when he returned.

'Sir, this is Mr Derek Tilson.'

The two men shook hands. 'You can call me Derek.'

'It's a pleasure,' Sowah said. 'Please, come with me.'

He shepherded Tilson into his office and shut the door.

A few minutes later, Sowah stuck his head outside the door. 'Emma, please come. Bring your notepad.'

She hurried to join them, sitting in the second chair opposite Sowah and not knowing what to expect.

'Emma,' Sowah said, 'Mr Tilson is reporting his father missing. I want you to take notes.' He looked at Tilson. 'So far, my understanding is that your father arrived in Accra three months ago supposedly to meet a woman called Helena, who we don't know really exists or not, but strongly suspect she does not, correct?'

'Yes,' Tilson said. 'I was convinced that she was part of a scam and I told my dad that. We argued about it. He was convinced Helena was real and he was in love with her. He Skyped and called her over a period towards the end of November last year until February 14th – Valentine's Day, strangely appropriate – when he took off for Ghana without warning. After he got to Accra, he messaged me to say he had met Helena and was "having a good time", as he put it. But then a few days later he confessed there was no Helena at all. He was furious as well as despondent and embarrassed. I told him just get out and come on home. He seemed to agree at the time, but after he had thought about it for a couple of days, he changed his mind, decided to stay in Ghana and simply make it a vacation.'

'Did that surprise you?' Sowah said.

'Yes,' Derek said. 'It seemed like an about-face. After Dad realised he'd been a victim of a hoax, he seemed only to want to return to the States.'

'Yes, I see,' Sowah said. 'On the other hand, would it seem so out of character for him to decide to make the best of it and take a vacation? After all, he's paid for the whole thing – why not? And you mentioned he was in Ghana as a Peace Corps officer many years ago, so perhaps he wanted to experience the new Ghana?'

'That's exactly the reason he gave me, and although I wasn't in favour of his decision initially, I eventually made peace with it. Actually, for a moment I wondered if maybe my father had met yet *another* woman and didn't want to tell me about her.'

'Ah,' Sowah said, a smile creeping to his lips. Something was farcical about that idea and once Derek began to laugh, Sowah and Emma joined in.

'OK, maybe not,' Derek said, growing serious again. 'Getting back to the story, the month of March passed and it seemed like the situation was settling down. Then, in the first week of April, I read an article by a family friend in which he describes my father's experience with this scam and further reveals that my dad is staying in Ghana to *investigate* the crime against him.'

'Oh,' Sowah said. 'Was that true?'

'Exactly my question,' Derek said. 'So I called Mr Guttenberg – the author of the piece – about it and he told me he and my dad had decided that he might as well stay in Ghana to find out who had perpetrated the fraud on him.'

'This was obviously news to you,' Sowah said.

'Out of the blue,' Derek agreed. 'Casper Guttenberg

is an old friend of my dad's and for reasons beyond me, my father thinks the world of him. I firmly believe Mr Guttenberg wants to get a story out of my dad's ordeal and that he's the guy who encouraged my father to stay longer in Ghana. That would explain Dad's odd change of mind.'

'Very possibly,' Sowah said. 'When was the very last day you heard from your father?'

'April 2nd,' Derek answered. 'I should backtrack a bit to fill you in. When Dad first arrived in Ghana on February 15th, he checked in at the Kempinski Hotel and stayed for two weeks.

'Then, around March 1st, he decided to move to a bed and breakfast in Accra called Flamingo Lodge. He said he wanted something more like a home and less like a hotel. I was in touch with him every couple of days until March 27th, when he told me he was taking a trip to Akosombo for a week's stay at a place called Riverview Cottage on the Volta.

'He WhatsApped me on April 2nd to say he would be going back to Accra the following day. That was the last I heard from him, but I kept trying to reach him.' Derek shook his head. 'Nothing happened until April 10th, when the Flamingo owner called me to say Dad hadn't returned as expected and she wondered if I knew where he was. He had given her my phone number as his emergency contact.'

'Are you getting all these dates, Emma?' Sowah asked. 'Because I'm going to ask you to diagram the chronology.'

'Yes, sir,' she said nervously. Sowah was a stickler for dates and accuracy.

'What's the homeowner's name, please?' he asked Derek.

'Poem Van Landewyck. She's a Dutch woman who's lived in Ghana practically all her life.' Tilson pulled out his smartphone and scrolled. 'I've spoken to her, but I haven't met her in person yet. Here's her contact info.' He stood up and showed the screen to Emma to jot down the name and phone number. She caught a whisper of the light fragrance Derek was wearing.

'Thank you, sir,' she said.

'Going to Akosombo,' Sowah said to Derek, 'is that the sort of thing your father would do?'

Derek smiled. 'He loved it there for as long as I remember. When I was a kid and we visited Ghana from the States, Dad always took us up there for a few days. We'd go out on the lake, do some fishing, sometimes just anchor and relax on the water. So, yeah, it's something he might do.'

'I see,' Sowah said. 'So then, when he stopped responding to your texts and emails, you became concerned.'

Derek nodded, and Emma noticed how his curls caught and reflected the light from the window. 'I managed to get through to the American Embassy in Accra,' Derek continued, 'and believe me, it wasn't easy. Anyway, they said they'd do what they could, but this kind of thing falls under the jurisdiction of the local authorities and so their hands were tied somewhat. I felt I had no choice, then. I had to come look for Dad myself.'

'When did you arrive?'

'May 2nd,' Derek said. 'First, I went to the Kempinski Hotel and they confirmed Dad had checked out March 2nd, and they said they weren't aware of any issues during his stay. Then, I went up to the Riverview place in Akosombo to talk to the manager, who said Dad had notified him he would be checking out April 3rd. But he was nowhere to be found that morning when the driver came to pick him up, and his luggage was gone as well. That suggested to me a home invasion – a robbery or burglary. So at this point, I went to the local police station – they hadn't heard anything, so I gave them a statement, and then I went to CID Headquarters here in Accra and gave a statement to a Detective Inspector Doris something – I forgot the last name.'

'Damptey?' Sowah said.

'Yes, her.' Emma caught exasperation in his tone. 'She was less than responsive, to put it mildly. Maybe she doesn't consider it a priority to look for some American guy who's been duped by a scam.'

'When did you last speak to her?'

'Last week. She had nothing to tell me. Not even if she had started working on any leads. I felt like I was talking to a brick wall. I spoke to one of my Ghanaian cousins who told me if I had wanted anything done, I should have given Damptey some money at the start.'

Sowah grimaced. 'Unfortunately, that is how our country runs now. Money above honour, duty, or integrity.'

Derek nodded. 'And I noticed that exact motto up in your waiting room – honour, duty, and integrity.'

'It's our guiding principle,' Sowah said evenly. 'If you can't abide, you have to leave.'

'That's good to hear in this environment,' Derek said. 'When did Ghana get like this? Maybe I was too young to pay attention when I was here as a kid, but I don't remember the country or the people like this back then.'

'Well, it wasn't,' Sowah agreed. 'I've been around much longer than you have, and I can say with certainty that money is more of a motivator for Ghanaians than it ever was. Money runs everything. Honest or corrupt, it doesn't matter, and the police are possibly the worst offenders.'

Derek looked disheartened. 'That's discouraging.'

'Indeed,' Sowah said.

'What's causing it? All this corruption, I mean.'

Sowah deflected his gaze for a moment and then shook his head. 'Our society is ridden with this cancer.' He pulled in his breath and released it harshly. 'Anyway, even with money, Damptey might not have prioritised you, as you say. The police service is underfunded and choked with old cases. Not that I'm excusing them, but both Emma and I have worked in the Ghana Police Service, so we know what conditions are like.'

'Oh, really,' Derek said, looking at Emma with interest.

'Perhaps I should have asked you much earlier,' Sowah said to Derek, 'but how did you find us, sir?'

'Once I figured out I wasn't getting anything with DI Damptey,' Derek said, 'I searched online to see if there were any private detectives who could help and came across the International Association of Private

Investigators website. They listed you and your agency as one of only two in Accra that's fully licensed and vetted. That's how I found you.'

Sowah smiled. 'Thank you. Yes, the IAPI often sends us referrals. Derek, I would prefer to believe this conundrum will have a happy, reasonable conclusion, but we must be realistic and hope for the best while preparing for the worst.'

Derek nodded, his jaw hardening and his eyes downcast. For his sake, Emma sent up a silent prayer.

CHAPTER THIRTY-ONE

17th May

Sunday afternoon after church, Emma took a couple of *tro-tro*s to reach the Autism Centre at the junction of Barnes Road and William Tubman Avenue. She was in a huff because the driver's mate on the *tro-tro* had been slow – deliberately in Emma's mind – about rendering the correct change. But once she arrived at the Centre, she forgot the trivialities of Accra travel.

It was a modest place, but still far better off than the other autism institutions in the country. The rectangular brick building on the left was a small, converted home with a playroom, classroom, and an administrative office-cum-staff lounge/meeting room. The courtyard had a pair of swings, a slide, a climbing net, and two mini football goals on each side of the yard. The sky was darkening with rain clouds, so everyone was inside.

'Auntie' Rose Clarkson, the owner and director of the centre, was a hands-on woman who didn't mind working the weekends. She had only one staff member on with her on Sundays. Speech, art, and music therapy made up much of the activity during the week, but it was on the relatively unstructured Sunday when many of the permanent staff were off that Auntie Rose needed more volunteer help.

Rose's own eighteen-year-old son, Timothy, had autism. When he was born, Rose was living in Connecticut with her then husband, whom she later divorced. But at the time, Rose was thrown into the turbulence of learning how to manage an autistic child, and it wasn't easy. When Rose had to return to Ghana some ten years ago to care for her own mother, she faced the harsh reality that there wasn't a single institution that would care for Timothy at the level he had enjoyed in the US. On top of that, the stigma facing parents – especially a single mother like Rose – was severe. Rose knew she wasn't the only mother suffering. There were others like her. That's why she founded the Accra Autism Centre.

'Glad you're here,' Rose said as Emma came in. 'Kojo needs you.'

Emma had a rapport with thirteen-year-old Kojo, officially the Centre's first autistic child (after Timothy) to register. Kojo's mother, Abena, was Emma's best friend and the conduit through which Emma had been introduced to autism and the Centre. Thereafter, Emma became a regular volunteer. This afternoon, he was rocking, flapping his hands, wiggling his fingers, and grimacing, which meant he was in a moderately agitated state that might – or might not – deteriorate into a sensory meltdown.

Emma eased Kojo away to the adjoining office, shutting the door behind her with a foot and moving to a corner of the room. She sat on the floor and he followed. It was quieter and darker in here than outside and Emma hoped decreasing visual and auditory stimulation would help. After about five minutes, he was less active, rocking only slightly, but his eyes were still far away, lost in that world of his that no one else could enter.

'Better?' Emma said softly.

She didn't expect a verbal response because Kojo was nonverbal and had never uttered a sound beyond an indistinct moan. They sat quietly together awhile as Emma reflected that while Kojo and the other Autism Spectrum Disorder children at the centre were blessed to have this safe place, they were but a tiny proportion of ASD Ghanaians in need. And Rose operated on a shoestring budget, depending on donations and volunteers. She seemed to be constantly on the verge of having to close down, but something or someone always came along to rescue her at the last minute. One of those saviours was Josephine Akrofi, the IGP's wife. Mrs Akrofi was the Centre's strongest patron.

Kojo was much calmer now, so Emma took him back to the outer room.

Rose looked at her with a smile. 'I knew you could do it. He loves you, that boy.'

After Kojo was settled on the floor with a picture book, Emma sat beside Rose at the table in the centre of the room.

'I have some exciting news,' Rose said. 'I wanted to make sure it would happen first, and now it looks like it will.'

'Oh, really! I can't wait to hear.'

'As you probably know,' Rose began, 'there's research suggesting that some autistic kids do well interacting with screen images. The topic is a little controversial, but some nonverbal children are able indicate their needs using mobile apps – like on a tablet, for example. And the ability to express themselves relieves them of a lot of frustration.'

Emma nodded. 'Yes, I've read something about that.'

'So,' Rose said slowly, enjoying the suspense she was creating, 'I asked Madame Akrofi if she could help the Centre acquire a tablet we can try on some of our kids. Guess what? She did even better than that. She got us *four* tablets.'

'That's wonderful!' Emma exclaimed, clapping her hands together.

'Yes, it is,' Rose said, elated. 'So, what we plan is a ceremony later this week at which Mrs Akrofi will be presenting us with the gifts. She's arranging for some newspaper and TV press so that we can highlight the Centre and use the opportunity for not only publicity, but education of the public as well.'

'That will be great,' Emma said. 'I'm eager to see what Kojo does with the tablets.'

'Me too,' Rose said. Her demeanour changed to grave. 'This year, we have to be very aggressive about raising funds. The lease on the property is up in fourteen months, and if I don't pay the landlord, we're going to be out.'

For Emma and Rose, that would be an unthinkable catastrophe. What would Kojo and the other children do without Auntie Rose's Autism Centre?

CHAPTER THIRTY-TWO

18th May

Drumming his fingers on his desk, Sowah said, 'Our job is to find Gordon Tilson, so let's begin. First, Emma, we need to trace Gordon's path, starting with the Kempinski Hotel. That's where you'll go this morning. You'll speak to the manager and anyone else who saw or encountered Mr Tilson. You should check the restaurants there, the security guys, and so on. Call me to brief me and don't leave the hotel until we've discussed it.'

'Yes, sir.'

'Keep a record of your Uber charges so I can reimburse you.'

'Thank you, sir.'

Two security guards stood on duty at the gated entrance of the Kempinski Hotel, which looked like a fortress. Emma went in the pedestrian entrance and nodded at the guards, who responded with a look of only passing interest. She had no backpack or object of potential suspicion. On the inside of the gate, the wide driveway branched like a 'Y' to a large parking structure on the right and to the left around the decorative fountain in front of the hotel. Several black limousines stood in a neat line to one side of the entrance. Emma raised her eyebrows at the sight of several uniformed police officers clustered around two marked vans. Armoured vehicles belonging to the Panther Unit's SWAT team were stationed in a cul-de-sac off the driveway directly opposite the hotel. Emma noticed a sniper in black keeping a lookout from the roof.

Emma gave all this a wide berth as she approached the entrance, but she turned as someone called out her name. Standing beside one of the intimidating vehicles, a heavily armed SWAT guy was waving at her. 'Me?' she asked by gesture. He nodded. Emma wondered if she'd done something wrong, so it was with some tentativeness that she walked over where the man stood with two similarly black-clad colleagues. She didn't recognise any of them.

'Do you know me?' he asked.

She squinted at him. 'I don't think so.'

'We should change that, then,' he said. He was in his early thirties, and absurdly handsome, Emma thought. She tried not to melt somewhat under the deep gaze of his smoky, long-lashed eyes.

'Why, you know me?' she asked.

'I've seen you at CID before. I'm Dazz Nunoo. And you?'

'Emma Djan. But I'm not with CID any more.'

'Ah, OK. You left us?'

'Yes. Now I work for Sowah Private Investigators.'

He nodded. 'Nice. How is it over there?'

'I really like it.'

Dazz gestured at his companions. 'Meet my mates – Edwin and Courage.'

Edwin was tall, angular, and unsmiling. Courage was heavyset and more jovial in appearance. Must be Ewe, Emma thought. They loved names like Grace, Charity, Marvellous, Hope, Peace, and so on. She sized Courage up. Not bad looking, really. He wore his weight well.

'How long have you been with the SWAT?' Emma asked Dazz.

'Like three years.'

'What's going on today?' Emma asked, looking around. 'All these police guys and SWAT?'

'President of Gabon arriving for some kind of international conference,' Dazz explained. 'And what brings you here too?'

'We have a case – a missing American man.'

'Oh?' Dazz said with mild interest. 'Name?'

'Gordon Tilson. Ring any bells?'

Dazz turned the corners of his mouth down and shook his head. He looked at Courage and Edwin, who indicated the same.

'His son Derek has come down from the States looking for him,' Emma continued. 'On arrival in Ghana, Gordon first checked into Kempinski, so that's why I'm here.'

'I see,' Dazz said, nodding. 'If I hear anything, I'll text you.' He got his phone out. 'What's your number?'

He tapped it in with his thumbs as Emma recited it.

Courage got out his own phone and leant over to see the number on Dazz's, but Dazz moved it out of reach. '*Chaley*, why? Mind your own business.'

'Ah, but I want to also text her in case I get information,' Courage said in annoyance. 'Are you the only police officer in Ghana or what? Let me get the number.'

'OK, then ask Miss Djan for permission,' Dazz said with a wicked smile and a wink at Emma.

Courage looked at her. 'Can I get it?'

Emma shrugged her shoulders and looked at Dazz. 'Up to you.'

Dazz relented under Courage's glare and read out Emma's number to him.

'Where do you live?' Courage asked her.

'Madina,' Emma responded.

It was a sprawling town north of central Accra, just past the University of Ghana.

'Excuse me to say, but are you married?' Courage asked.

'No,' she said.

Dazz cocked an eyebrow at Courage. 'But why are you so nosy?'

'You too, are you her father or what?' Courage snapped back, sucking his teeth. He returned to Emma. 'You should be expecting my call. Very soon.'

'All right,' she said, her voice neutral. A woman doesn't show too much eagerness, after all.

'We won't keep you any longer, Emma,' Dazz said. 'Best of luck. Let's keep in touch.'

'Bye,' Courage said, smiling at her.

Emma turned back to the hotel entrance, where she was obliged to go through a metal detector like everyone else. She wondered if the Gabon president would have to do the same.

Passing through automatic doors, Emma entered Kempinski's gleaming lobby. Large works of art adorned the walls. In velvet and leather seats, dark-suited men and women sat meeting, or texting on their mobiles. A tall, curvy woman in a scarlet Kempinski outfit went sailing by on stiletto heels.

Twenty-first century Ghana, Emma thought, trying not to be overly impressed by the size and opulence. She took a seat in one of the high-backed blue velvet chairs and did what everyone else was doing: checked her phone and looked important. While working at the Apple store, she had bought a few decent outfits, one of which she was wearing. She hoped she looked reasonably chic in this environment.

She scanned the lobby, aware that she was a little nervous. She was embarking on a case that felt bigger than anything she had tackled up till now. A just-arrived Delta Airlines crew was checking in at the front desk as the bellman took care of the luggage. Someone was rolling out a red carpet from the front entrance into the driveway, presumably for the Gabon president's arrival. A group of officials who appeared to be the advance party were discussing logistics with the curvy woman in red and a Lebanese guy Emma thought was probably the manager on duty. Lebanese people in Ghana either managed places or owned them.

At a lectern on the other side of the lobby, a pretty

young maître d' in charcoal grey stood at the entrance to the outdoor Cedar Garden restaurant, where a few diners were having an early lunch. Emma rose and strolled over. 'Good morning, madam,' she said amicably.

'Good morning,' the maître d' replied, flashing even, white teeth. Her name badge said Zeneba.

'May I please have a look at the menu?'

'Certainly,' she said, handing Emma one.

'Thank you, Zeneba.' Emma looked through the items, relating to only one: vegetable soup for the price of thirty-six *cedis*, something that would cost one-sixth that much at a chop bar in Accra. 'I'm meeting a friend here,' she said casually, 'so I just wanted to get an idea of what you have.'

'Have you been here before?' Zeneba asked.

'No, my first time, actually.' She looked at the entrance where the presidential preparations had begun to appear more pressing. 'I'm a little worried because I thought my friend would have been here by now.'

'Maybe you can call him?' Zeneba suggested.

'I did try, but he's not picking up,' Emma said, getting out her phone. 'I was late myself, so I hope he hasn't left.' She gave a little laugh. 'You know these Americans; they can be a little impatient.'

Zeneba smiled, agreeing without agreeing.

'You've been here all this morning, right?' Emma asked.

'Yes please.'

'Maybe you might have seen him.' She brought up Gordon's photo – supplied by Derek – on her Samsung screen and showed it to Zeneba. 'Have you seen him, by any chance?'

'Oh!' Zeneba exclaimed. 'That's Mr Gordon!'

'You know him?'

'But of course. I remember him well. He was here with us a couple of months ago. He came to Cedar Garden often. He said our hummus is the best he's ever tasted.'

Emma hadn't the vaguest notion what hummus was. 'Oh, wonderful,' she said.

'You know,' Zeneba said, 'some guests I always remember because of how friendly and nice they are. Mr Gordon is one of those. He often used to get coffee in the mornings and sit over there reading the papers. Oh, a very nice gentleman. I thought he was going to stay longer, but it seems he had to check out earlier than expected.'

'Did he tell you why?'

Zeneba hesitated. 'No, he didn't, but it seemed sudden. Mr Gordon was having dinner here one night when he got a call. He said, "Who is this?" Then after some few seconds, he got up and left without even finishing his meal. That's the last I saw of him.'

'Ah, I see,' Emma said. 'Let me text him again.' Emma tapped out a faux message, waited a short while, and then allowed her shoulders to sag. 'What a shame. He can't make it tonight.'

'Oh, so sorry!' Zeneba said, appearing truly disappointed.

'But it wasn't all in vain,' Emma said, smiling sweetly. 'We had a nice chat. Thank you.'

* * *

Emma got out of the hotel just before the presidential motorcade came blasting through the gate. On the phone, she said to Yemo Sowah, 'Sir, it seems Mr Tilson might have received a significant phone call one evening, and he left the hotel very shortly after that.' Emma described what Zeneba had told her.

'Maybe some kind of threat, anonymous or otherwise?' Sowah said. 'If that's the case, who might have threatened Tilson, and why?'

CHAPTER THIRTY-THREE

18th May

At close of day, DI Doris Damptey still had the same backlog of cases as the beginning. The ragged files would remain stacked on her desk for the foreseeable future, and the pile would undoubtedly grow higher. It was like that at CID Headquarters. Cases lingered.

Damptey had been with the Vehicle Fraud Division for a couple of years, and now the CID bosses had transferred her to the newish Cybercrime Division, CCD, the brainchild of the IGP in concert with President Bannerman. Damptey was part of the Ground Enforcement Team, GET, whose role was to make the physical arrests resulting from online detective work. Honestly, there hadn't been that many. No one could pretend the CCD had been that active.

Damptey had completed a couple of assignments on the old, slow laptop the CCD had provided. The office, with a desk each for her boss and herself, didn't have much besides. An old photocopy machine, which was supposed to be a desktop model, sat squat on the floor in the corner of the room, not having worked in years. It had been a donation from the Dutch or Swiss or was it the Germans, but Damptey couldn't remember if the stupid device had functioned even once. Sometimes the *oburoni* countries dumped old, worthless machines onto the third world, which accepted them with fawning smiles only to discover they didn't work for more than a couple of months.

The CCD was supposed to be focusing on several areas – credit card fraud, gold, timber, oil concessions, romance cons, and so on. But actual prosecutions were few and far between because the division didn't have enough resources and training to stand up against the perpetrators' wide network, particularly since most victims were abroad.

The Bannerman government had also set up brand-new anti-cybercrime channels with the US and Europe. That was smart, because it was one way to get funding for cyber training courses, a couple of which Damptey had attended. The farthest she had been was Abidjan in Côte d'Ivoire, but she was hoping one day she'd get to attend a seminar in Germany or the UK.

She got to her feet and gathered up her handbag. Time to call it a day, even though she hadn't got much done. She turned off the light in the office and stepped out into the warm equatorial dusk.

She joined Nii Kwei at Nkrumah Circle chop bar, where he had already placed two orders – *fufu* and light soup for himself, boiled yam and *nkontomire* for Damptey.

While they waited, they talked, Nii checking his phone every time a notification buzzed in. 'You too, why?' Damptey snapped. 'Can't you leave that thing alone for even one minute?'

Nii smiled. 'OK, Mummy,' he said, putting the phone away. He called Damptey 'Mummy' in a teasing, half-affectionate way.

'The American man you were getting money from—' she said.

'You mean Mr Gordon?'

'Yes, him. His son is now here.'

They paused while their dishes arrived.

'What is he doing here?' Nii asked, washing and rinsing off his hands in the bowl of water provided.

Damptey did the same. 'He came to CID to report his father missing,' she said. 'I took his statement.'

Nii nodded and began eating with his fingers. 'And so, what are you going to do, Mummy?'

'You don't need to worry,' she said, staring at him. 'I will be delaying the investigation until he gets tired, and then he will go back to the States.'

Nii said, 'Why are you looking at me like that?'

'You always visit Kweku Ponsu, not so?'

'Yes,' Nii said warily. 'Why?'

'The American man also went to see Ponsu to ask about *sakawa* boys. And then something happened, and the white man went missing.' Damptey waited for a comment from Nii, but none was forthcoming. 'Do you know something about it?' she asked.

'About what?'

'That the white man went to see Ponsu. Did Ponsu tell you?'

Nii shook his head. 'No.'

'Are you sure?' Damptey pressed him.

'But why are you asking me all this?'

'If you want my protection, I have to know what you know.'

'Mummy, I don't know anything.'

Damptey started on her meal. 'Because people may come around asking questions. I must be prepared. Did you and Ponsu ever discuss what to do about Mr Gordon?'

'Never. I swear, Mummy.'

'What about your friend – Bruno?'

'No. Bruno is just a small boy. He doesn't know anything.'

Damptey licked her fingers, keeping her eye on Nii. 'It's getting more complicated now. More work for me.'

Nii's expression was something between weary and resigned. 'OK. I understand. Don't worry. You'll get more chop money.'

Damptey looked away, and then back. 'Double,' she said with finality.

CHAPTER THIRTY-FOUR

Bruno was sweating when he got to Kweku Ponsu's compound in Shukura past 5 p.m. In one hand he carried a sack containing two bound, squawking chickens. He was late because traffic everywhere in the city was worse than normal due to diversions and street closures for the international conference.

Bruno walked along a narrow alley, which branched to the left and ended in a courtyard with a single-room house along each of three sides. A muddy enclosure with two gigantic cows made up the fourth. The smell of cow dung hung in the air. A group of men sat in front of one house drinking mint tea, an Arab tradition. They were undoubtedly from Northern Ghana where the majority Muslim peoples were nomadic cattle raisers by custom – hence the cows.

One of the men asked Bruno what he wanted.

'Please, I'm looking for Kweku Ponsu.'

'He's not here.'

'Please, when will he come?'

'I don't know the time. You can wait for him.' The guy got up and dragged an extra chair over. 'Maybe you can call him too,' he suggested.

'Thank you,' Bruno said, putting down the sack. It shifted around each time the hens made a pointless attempt to break free.

Bruno sat and tried Kweku's number, but it went unanswered. He browsed through Instagram and Facebook for a while until his battery started to get low, at which point he switched off his phone.

The men played checkers in the gathering gloom until finally one of them switched on a bare bulb over the front door of the house. The time was almost 6.20 p.m. Bruno was wondering if he should wait any longer when one of the board game players received a text from Kweku saying he was almost there. In Ghanaian time, that could mean another hour, but fortunately he appeared after only thirty minutes.

In real life, Kweku was smaller than he had seemed to Bruno when he had seen him on YouTube. He walked quickly and his carriage was so erect as to appear angled slightly backward.

He glanced around the compound and spotted his guest. 'Are you Bruno?'

Bruno stood up. 'Yes please.'

'You brought the hens?'

Bruno pointed at the sack.

'OK,' Kweku said. 'You can leave them there. Come

with me.' Bruno followed as Kweku unlocked the door of the house.

'One moment,' Kweku said. 'Let me turn on the light.'

The naked bulb revealed a single room with a bed, an old chest of drawers, and in the corner, a battered chair to which Kweku pointed. 'Have a seat.'

With legs crossed, Kweku sat on the floor opposite Bruno and reached left to a pile of objects.

He held up one of them. 'Do you know what this is?'

It was dull tan in colour and shaped like a hammer with a short handle and rounded head.

'No please,' Bruno said.

'It's the thigh bone of a child,' Kweku told him. 'We do many things with it.'

Bruno hesitated. 'Please, how do you get it? The bone, I mean.'

'From the hospital morgue.' Kweku's diction was languid, quite unlike his rigid physical bearing. 'We know people there. If we ask them for something, they bring it to us.'

Bruno nodded. 'I see.'

Next, Kweku showed him another item, which was obviously the well-worn skull of some kind of bird.

'It's a hen's head from one of our sacrifices,' Kweku said. 'Like what you brought today.' He put that down. 'We also have special beads and cowry shells. Later, you will know what we use them for.'

'Yes please.'

'I know your friend Nii Kwei very well,' the priest

went on. 'It's good you are here, but what is your mission? What do you want?'

Bruno cleared his throat. 'I want to be powerful and get plenty Internet money.'

'Have you started doing the Internet thing?'

'Not yet. I have been training with Nii.'

'Good,' Kweku said, scrutinising Bruno. 'You want to be rich?'

'Yes please. I want Range Rover and Bentley and three houses.'

Kweku nodded. 'Then you will have to be very good at what you do. You must believe and be strong. You see, some of the things I do, if you don't take care, the power you get will be too much and it will take you down. Like the sea is a friend to a fisherman, but if the sea becomes rough, it can also overwhelm him. You get me? You must believe completely. If you have any fear – any fear at all – inside, you will *fail*.'

'Yes please.'

'And what again do you want?'

'Women. Plenty.'

'Everybody want that. That one be tough. For that one, you need this.' He leant over and reached under the bed, dragging out a huge skull that startled Bruno.

'This one,' Kweku said, 'is from a crocodile. If you wear this around your neck for one month, you will get women. In fact, you will be famous, and everyone will want to be with you.'

'Wow,' Bruno said, impressed. 'How did you get this big crocodile head?'

'We go to the Pra or Ankobra River,' Kweku said, sliding the skull back under the bed. 'We catch a baby one after it comes out of the egg and then we grow it here.'

'Grow it here?' Bruno echoed, glancing around as if a live crocodile might be in the room.

Kweku smiled. 'We have one outside. You want to see it?'

Bruno suppressed a flinch and nodded, already remembering the admonishment against fear. He followed Kweku outside around the cow enclosure to a sheltered cubbyhole full of rubbish, scrap metal, and a rusty bathtub. Kweku removed the rectangular plank and metal pan sitting on top of it, revealing a grate resting on the rim of the tub. With his phone, Kweku illuminated the reptile within. It was dark grey with a waxy hide and muscular legs pressed against its sides by the tub, which was altogether too small. A black, oozing fluid partially covered the beast's legs. For a moment, the crocodile didn't move, but all of a sudden it raised its snout, opened its jagged mouth and hissed. Bruno's hairs stood on end, but he didn't step back because he knew Ponsu was observing him for his reaction.

'It's big,' Bruno said.

'This is nothing,' Kweku boasted. 'It will grow even more. We call him Frankie.'

'Then you will have to find a bigger container for it. What do you give it to eat?'

'Chickens.'

'OK.'

'Can you face this crocodile?'

'What do you mean "face it"?' Bruno asked, looking at Kweku.

'For the best powers and the most success, you should wear the crocodile skull, but it has to be a crocodile you have killed. So, you will have to be the one to do it.'

Bruno licked his lips nervously. 'How?'

'I drag him by the tail on the ground, then when I tell you, you cut the neck with a cutlass. One strike only.'

Bruno nodded, his heart pounding. 'OK.'

A one-sided smile played at Kweku's lips. 'Are you sure? When I brought Nii Kwei to see the crocodile, he ran away.'

Bruno joined Kweku in laughter. He could just picture the scene. 'Please, I want to ask you something, Mr Ponsu.'

'Yes?' Kweku's phone beam was dying, so he switched it off. Now they were in almost complete darkness.

'Let's say,' Bruno began, 'me and you, we kill the crocodile.'

'Eh-heh? Go on.'

'If that be the case, then can I meet Godfather?'

Kweku released a small gasp, switched the phone light back on and trained it on Bruno's face. 'Heh! Who told you to ask me that?' Kweku grasped Bruno's bottom jaw. 'Who told you?'

Bruno shook his head. 'No one,' he tried to say. Kweku released him. 'You want to meet Godfather?'

'Yes please.'

Kweku snorted. 'You small boys, you think everything

205

is so easy, eh? Even after you kill the crocodile se'f, you won't be ready.'

'Then when, please?'

'You have to prove yourself,' Kweku said irritably. 'You have to be better than all the rest in order to see Godfather. Most of the *sakawa* boys are not good enough. Only those who make a lot of money or can do all the rituals.'

'OK, then I will do that.'

Kweku turned away with a grunt. 'You think it's so easy. But it's not.'

CHAPTER THIRTY-FIVE

19th May

Emma and Derek Ubered to the Flamingo Lodge in affluent Labone where Poem Van Landewyck had agreed to meet them. The house stood in a shady cul-de-sac of neem trees and frangipani. A wall topped with an electric fence encircled the property.

As the Uber driver dropped them off at the driveway, Poem was waiting for them just inside the entrance of the front gate. She was the tallest woman Emma had ever seen, elegant in a vanilla pants suit and swept-up blonde and grey hair.

'Welcome,' she said, smiling. 'You must be Derek.'

'Hello, Poem,' he said, shaking hands. 'Good to finally meet in person. This is Emma Djan, the private investigator I've hired to find my father.'

'Good morning, Emma,' Poem said with approval. 'Are you a solo investigator?' She had a Ghanaian-Euro accent.

'I'm with the Sowah Agency,' Emma said.

'I believe I've heard of it,' Poem said. 'Please come in. I

don't have a tenant for a couple of days, so we can sit inside.'

The house really was flamingo in colour and looked especially striking with its dark, energy-saving windows. As they followed Poem in, Emma couldn't help but admire the polished wood floors, soft leather chairs, and fluted window blinds. The kitchen had a large, stainless steel stove with a matching refrigerator. *I need a home like this*, Emma thought, and then checked herself for coveting 'thy neighbour's house'.

'This is beautiful, Poem,' Derek said. 'No wonder Dad chose you. How did he find you?'

'Google,' Poem said. 'Isn't that how everyone finds everything? Can I offer either of you some espresso?'

'Yes, *please*,' Derek said. 'I haven't had my coffee this morning.'

Emma, who wasn't sure what an espresso was, declined and took a glass of iced water instead. She didn't understand the whole coffee business and she stared with curiosity at Poem manipulating the gleaming, hissing machine on the kitchen counter. What on earth was she doing?

'Oh my God,' Derek said as he took his first sip and closed his eyes in bliss. 'This is amazing, Poem.'

She smiled, crossing her long legs. 'Thank you.'

'No, thank *you* for seeing us. We appreciate it.'

Poem rested her own cup. 'So, tell me how I can help because I want to. I enjoyed having your father here, and it's worrying that he's gone missing. It's why I called you and I'm so relieved that he put you down as his contact in case of emergency.'

'I am too,' Derek said. 'Did he tell you the story of what had happened to him?'

'After a couple of days here, yes – this so-called Helena he thought he was coming to meet. I was furious – not at him, but at whoever had pulled off the scam on him. It's happening more and more now, and it is really spoiling our name in Ghana. I asked your dad if he'd reported it to the American Embassy and he said he had, and that they had told him they would be forwarding the case to CID.'

Derek glanced at Emma. 'Speaking of which, did a CID detective called Doris Damptey ever get in touch with you, Poem?'

She wrinkled her nose. 'I believe that was her name. She called and we spoke on the phone once, but after that I heard nothing else.'

'Figures,' Derek said, shaking his head.

'And unfortunately,' Poem continued, 'in these situations of crimes against foreign nationals, standard procedure for the embassies is to refer the cases to CID. They can't do any investigating themselves – at least that's what their official policy is.'

'By any chance, did Dad give you the name of his contact person at the embassy?'

'No, I'm afraid not.'

'Sir,' Emma said to Derek, 'I think it will be good if we can track down the person your father spoke to over there.'

'I agree,' he said. 'I'll call the number on the embassy website. Poem, just so I know I have the dates right, would it be March 2nd that Dad arrived here?'

'Let me see,' Poem said, reaching for her phone and her glasses on the coffee table.

Looking through the lenses halfway down her nose, she scrolled through her iPhone calendar. 'Yes, that's the date I have. I spoke to him the evening before and he arrived in the morning.'

Derek looked at Emma. 'That would match up with what you found out at the Kempinski.'

Poem looked from one to the other. 'What's that?'

'Emma went to the hotel—' Derek cut himself off. 'Well, I'll let her tell you the story.'

Emma described to Poem what maître d' Zeneba had related about Gordon's apparently hurried departure after a phone call interrupted his dinner at the restaurant one evening.

'I see,' Poem said.

'You live offsite, right?' Derek asked her.

'Correct. Airport Residential.'

'So, you probably wouldn't have been aware if anyone significant came to see my dad here, am I right?'

'Well, yes and no,' Poem answered. 'It's true I don't live next door, but I come by the house almost every morning to check that everything's working correctly. I also touch base with the night watchman before he goes off duty. He would have told me if your father had any visits.'

'He went up to Akosombo on or about March 27th,' Derek said. 'Were you aware of that, Poem?'

'Yes, I was. Actually a few days before he left, he said

210

he was going there to talk to someone about these *sakawa* boys – someone who lives in Atimpoku, near Akosombo, and he wondered if I'd ever heard of the guy. I said no, but I strongly advised against going to see any shady characters.'

Emma asked, 'Madam, did Mr Tilson give you the name of the man he was going to see at Atimpoku?'

'I think he said Kweku or Kwame Pouncer – something of that sort.'

Emma snapped her fingers. 'No, not Pouncer. I think what he was saying was "*Ponsu*". Kweku Ponsu.'

CHAPTER THIRTY-SIX

'Kweku Ponsu does very well for himself,' Yemo Sowah said.

Emma and Derek had returned to the office after leaving Poem. That Gordon might have gone to Akosombo to make contact with Ponsu was significant.

'He's a charismatic but controversial guy,' Sowah continued, 'who often insults conventional clergy and other traditional priests, challenging them to what he calls "miracle contests" where he supposedly pits his powers against theirs. He's a lot of sound and fury. You either love or hate him, but he gets more than his share of love from his *sakawa* followers.'

'What does he actually do for them?' Derek asked.

'Supposedly he has an almost perfect record of turning *sakawa* boys into success stories. Accordingly, they flock to him and collectively they pay him a lot of money.'

Derek grunted. 'So, he's part of all these scams?'

'In that he enables the scammers, yes. But as far as I know, he doesn't practise the scams themselves.'

Derek looked perplexed. 'I still don't get how Ponsu helps the *sakawa* guys. He teaches them better techniques of ripping off people's money or what?'

'*Sakawa* boys will only say that Ponsu is one of their most effective intermediaries between the physical and spirit world,' Sowah said, 'and so he procures the best powers from the gods, so to speak.'

Derek snorted with derision. 'Sounds like hokum to me.'

'Well, it does to us,' Sowah said. 'We're not in that world, so it's difficult for us to understand.'

'It almost sounds like you're giving them some credibility.'

'Maybe, but not *legitimacy*,' Sowah responded. 'There's a difference.'

'You're right,' Derek said with a little more humility.

'Bottom line is,' Sowah continued, 'we have to find Ponsu and question him. He has two shrines – one smaller one here in Shukura in Accra, and a larger one in Atimpoku, his hometown and where he started out.'

'How soon can we do that?' Derek said.

'Emma and I will go to Shukura tomorrow morning, but if he's at Atimpoku at the moment, we'll proceed there immediately.'

'I'll come with you,' Derek said at once.

'I will not allow that, please,' Sowah said firmly. 'Part of my job is to protect our clients. If the path your father took put him in danger, we can't let that happen to you as well.'

'OK,' Derek said, but he was clearly disappointed.

He brooded for a while and then muttered to no one in particular, 'Why, Dad, *why*? Why didn't you *listen*?'

Sowah looked at Emma, and then back at Derek in sympathy. 'Very sorry about all this, Derek. We'll work on it until we have a resolution. I promise you that.'

'Thanks, Mr Sowah.'

'You're welcome. May I make a suggestion?'

Derek looked up. 'What's that?'

'That you go back to the hotel, relax – perhaps have a drink by the pool, and then a nice dinner. Something to take your mind off things. Let us do the worrying for you, OK?'

'That's not a bad idea.' Derek rose, smiling and looking marginally better.

The two men shook hands and Emma walked Derek to the front door. Outside, he faced her. 'Listen, I appreciate all your efforts, I really do.'

'You're most welcome, sir.'

'Now let me go get that drink,' Derek said, heading down the steps. He looked back at her with a playful smile. 'You should join me!'

Emma laughed. 'Have a good evening, sir.'

'No, no,' he said. 'Call me Derek.'

Emma watched him walk away before she went back in. As she returned to the detectives' room, she remembered she needed to call her mother, Akosua. Emma expected the usual harassment about why it had been such a long time since she had phoned, and she got it.

'*Ei!*' Akosua exclaimed. 'My one and only daughter!

What a miracle to hear from you. It's been so long.'

'Less than a week, Mama.'

'It seems like longer. But anyway, how are you?'

'I'm good, and you?'

'By God's grace, you know. We are managing. How is work?'

Sitting at her desk and speaking in Twi, Emma conversed with her mother for a while about the usual stuff: money problems (despite the stipend Emma sent her mother via mobile money every couple of weeks), the transgressions of this or that family member, and so on. When Emma wrapped up the conversation, fifteen minutes had passed, and it was about time to go home. As she packed up, a call came in from someone she had quite forgotten about: Courage, the SWAT guy.

CHAPTER THIRTY-SEVEN

20th May

Emma had requested Wednesday morning off to attend the Autism Centre's event honouring its most important patron, Mrs Josephine Akrofi. Emma arrived at 5 a.m. to help clean and decorate. There was sweeping, dusting, and scrubbing to be done. Auntie Rose, unsurprisingly, had arrived before everyone else. With some trial and error, Emma, Rose, and the other staff managed to suspend the welcome banner across the courtyard, but professionals took care of setting up the guest seating and the dais. Then it was time to dress the children up with the best combinations of donated clothing and whatever their parents could provide.

Kojo was restless this morning and rocking incessantly. He didn't want to wear a new outfit. He wanted only his regular Mickey Mouse T-shirt, which was badly soiled. Just as Emma was about to give up, Kojo agreed to don his red and white chequered button-down shirt and black pants.

'You look so smart, young man,' Emma said, kissing Kojo on his forehead, then laughing as the boy wiped her kiss away. Shows of affection were not his style, but he was difficult to resist. People only wished they could engage the gaze of his soft, big brown eyes, but Kojo avoided any visual contact whatsoever.

Families of the centre's children, their friends, and supporters were in attendance. Most were seated by the time Josephine Akrofi arrived just before eleven with an entourage of assistants and two officers – one male, the other female. A handful of media people materialised as well. Auntie Rose met them all at the front gate, shook hands all around and brought them in, where Emma and the other volunteers waited in a neat row beside one another. In person, Mrs Akrofi seemed larger than life. Tall and well-built, she carried herself with such flare in a scarlet outfit by Woodin.

Emma, who hadn't been present at the last visit, was meeting the Akrofis for the first time. Introducing her to the dignitaries, Auntie Rose described Emma as 'amazing with the kids'.

'God bless you, young woman,' Mrs Akrofi said with feeling, her eyes locking with Emma's. 'Dedicated and gifted youth like you are exactly what we need. People who are not afraid of these beautiful kids who badly need our care. Thank you very much, eh? Thank you.'

Emma felt gratified and somewhat overawed. She would never have anticipated that kind of praise.

Auntie Rose gave the guests a tour of the entire centre,

in and out, showing the Akrofis what had improved since the last visit and what still needed to be done. The police officers stayed unobtrusively in sight as Mrs Akrofi interacted with each of the children, giving each one her attention. But she made the most fuss of Kojo, who, after all, had been one of the very first at the Centre.

'He's growing up so fast, isn't he?' Mrs Akrofi asked.

'He is,' Rose agreed.

'How about school? Have you been able to mainstream him at all?'

'For about two hours a day,' Rose answered.

'That's really great,' Mrs Akrofi said, lightly bringing up his chin so he could look at her, but he didn't. 'Such a beautiful boy too.'

Emma glanced at the female police officer, vaguely recalling her from CID. She was short and squat – almost as wide as tall, it seemed. Once the speeches and ceremony were underway, Emma had a chance to hang back where the officer was. 'Good afternoon, madam.'

The officer smiled back, but only a little. 'Good afternoon. Haven't I seen you before at CID Headquarters?'

'Yes, madam. I used to work there. My name is Emma Djan.'

'Ah, OK. I'm DI Doris Damptey. Why did you leave?'

'It's a long story,' Emma said, smiling with discomfort. She pressed on hurriedly. 'So, you are doing special duty this weekend, madam?'

'This is outside work,' Damptey explained. 'Not directly connected with CID. You know, some of us moonlight here and there to make ends meet. It's not easy.'

Emma murmured her agreement, pausing to watch a poised Mrs Akrofi deliver her address from the dais. 'Because of fear and ignorance in our society,' she was saying, looking around at her audience, 'autism has been attributed to the devil, or curses, or punishment from God or the lesser gods. But *we* know that each and every one of these children belong to God just as any other child in this world. It is our duty to educate those who do not understand and those who fear.'

At the end of Josephine's speech, she presented the four new Samsung tablets to the centre to enthusiastic applause and the sound of camera shutters in concert. Auntie Rose then took to the microphone to express her gratitude.

'So where are you working now?' Damptey asked her a little above the volume of the speech.

'Sowah Private Investigators.'

Damptey nodded. 'Yes, I know it well. How is Mr Sowah?'

'Oh, he's healthier than I am, even,' Emma said, making them both laugh. She thought of something but hesitated to verbalise it. Was this the appropriate place? Maybe not, but she was going to try anyway. 'Please, do you remember a gentleman called—'

Her final two words got lost under the applause. Damptey signalled they should retreat outside the Centre's gates. Saturday morning traffic was going to and fro, taxi drivers leaning on their horns.

'You were saying?' Damptey asked.

'Do you remember a man by the name of Derek Tilson?'

Emma asked. 'I think you might have talked to him at headquarters.'

'What is your interest in him?' the DI asked, her face neutral.

'He came to us to report his father missing.'

'Why?' Damptey demanded testily.

'Why what?'

The DI was clearly annoyed. 'Why should he come to report that to you when we are already on the case?'

Emma knew she had to handle this carefully, like a piece of hot charcoal. 'Madam Doris, I think it's only because he understands the limitation of resources at CID. Just looking for some extra help.'

'Maybe,' Damptey said, relenting a little but not fully mollified.

'Madam, please, did you find out anything at all about the gentleman? I mean Gordon Tilson – the father. We understand he went to Akosombo on 27th March, so we were wondering if you were able to follow up there—'

'I have nothing to tell you,' Damptey interrupted, turning as cold as a Fan Milk popsicle. She glanced around, came closer to Emma, and lowered her voice. 'Listen, from one female investigator to another, don't get involved with this case. I respect Mr Sowah, but please tell him from me, this is best left for the police, and if he won't do that, then I advise you to request that he take you off the case.'

'Please, may I know why?'

220

'You don't need to know why,' Damptey said, shaking her head. 'You only need to know not to get involved. I must go back inside. I think the Akrofis will be leaving soon.' She walked away, but slowed down briefly to turn and say, 'Don't play with fire, eh? Or you will get burnt.'

CHAPTER THIRTY-EIGHT

That same morning in Shukura, far across town from the Autism Centre, Bruno waited at the edge of Ponsu's courtyard. His jaw tensed rhythmically and his right thumb dug into his left palm. Sweat streamed off him and soaked his muscle shirt.

'If I kill the crocodile,' he had told Sana Sana last week, 'I will get closer to meeting Godfather.'

Sana had reacted strongly. 'Kill a *crocodile*? No, I can't have you doing anything that dangerous. That thing will eat you alive.'

'Mr Ponsu will help me,' Bruno said. 'We'll do it together.'

'No.'

'Please, Sana,' Bruno said. 'You yourself told me this was never going to be easy. Now Mr Ponsu is providing a way to get to Godfather. I told him I can fight the crocodile. He's testing me. If I back out now, Ponsu will take me as a coward and then it will be all over. Please, I can do it. I have to.'

Concise and clear-eyed in his pitch to Sana, Bruno had convinced him that this was a chance they could not let go. But now the time had arrived and he was staring down the barrel of the actual task, Bruno was as terrified as an aquaphobe in the deep sea. He had made himself out to be a fearless young man who could combat a reptilian beast, and now it was going to take place.

Kweku Ponsu had erected a metal-slatted barrier along the open side of the courtyard, and quite a crowd – mostly boys and young men – had grown behind it to watch the spectacle. A rhythmic scraping sound was one of Kweku's men sharpening the machete for Bruno.

Ponsu beckoned Bruno to follow him to Frankie the croc's still-covered bathtub, where two assistants were getting ready to move it closer to the edge of the courtyard. Bruno and Ponsu joined in the effort and on the count of three they heaved the heavy bathtub over a few metres. Frankie didn't seem to object.

Kweku took up his position at the croc's tail end and directed Bruno to stand well to the right of the tub. The machete-sharpening guy, a wizened old man, came up to Bruno and handed him his weapon. 'Good luck,' he said, without much feeling. Bruno nodded dumbly. His legs were shaking uncontrollably and a chilly wave of fear swept through him.

Kweku told two of his men to slide the tub cover forward enough for him to reach in, grasp Frankie's hefty tail and straighten it out. The creature hissed but didn't resist. One of the guys, Issufu, stood at the front ready with a loop of rope tied with a slip knot.

'Bruno, get ready,' Kweku instructed. 'As soon as we move the top off, it will try to get out. Issufu will have to get the rope around the mouth. The crocodile will start to turn over and over. When the stomach is up, you have to cut the neck fast. That is the soft part. One time, sharp sharp! You get it?'

'Yes please.'

'Are you ready?'

Bruno nodded. His mouth was parched.

'Open the top,' Kweku ordered calmly.

Two of his men pulled the grate off the tub. Frankie raised his head to the sudden blast of sunlight and opened his mouth wide. Issufu dropped the loop down over the reptile's top jaw as Kweku pulled on the tail.

'Come back, come back!' Kweku said to Issufu. 'Pull, *pull*!'

The croc flipped out of the tub and landed on the ground with an earth-shaking thud. The crowd yelled in one voice. Bruno was horrified at how massive the creature was out of its cramped quarters – and it looked furious. It roared and jackknifed its muscular, armoured body around in a U towards Issufu and Kweku. Issufu yelled and jumped out of the way. Somehow the rope came off Frankie's snout, leaving him free. Kweku cursed and yelled, 'Get the rope on! Get it!' He held the tail fast and moved a quarter turn counterclockwise the same way as the croc. Two men from the courtyard rushed in to help hold the tail as Frankie whipped it to one side, throwing Kweku off balance.

'Get the mouth!' Kweku shouted at Issufu, but it wasn't safe and Issufu couldn't do it. Frankie's tail came out of the men's grasp and it made a dash for the metal barrier. The crowd disassembled in seconds. Frankie hit the metal hard, rolled over and darted for a tight corner beside the cows' enclosure where it stopped, its head under a rusty piece of corrugated tin roofing. Issufu started after it but Kweku stopped him.

'Wait, *wait*!' he snapped. 'You've messed the whole thing up. Give me the rope, you fool. You told me you knew how to do it, and now look!'

Issufu, squat and strong, suddenly looked small and crushed. Bruno, machete in hand, hadn't had even a second's chance to strike the crocodile. *Now what?* His heart was pounding and his entire body quivered.

'This is what we'll do,' Kweku said. 'I'll get on the wall from the other side to get the rope around the mouth. It can't move backward easily, but everybody watch out in case it does.'

Sitting astride the wall, Kweku inched the rectangular sheet of corrugated metal off Frankie's head. Its baleful eye seemed to be watching to see what would happen next. Little by little, at a painfully slow pace, Kweku had Frankie's snout in the clear. He lowered the noose slowly and, barely touching the croc's skin, he got the rope over the snout and both jaws. Kweku inched back along the wall for more leverage, then pulled.

Frankie abandoned any trace of docility and reared up against the wall as if to climb it. Kweku yelled and pulled his foot out of the way. The croc fell on its back with a bang, this time with its head towards the courtyard. It flipped over, hissed and charged. Kweku went flying off the wall behind the croc, but he held on to the rope.

'It's coming!' he shouted. 'Move away!'

As Frankie emerged into the courtyard again, it began the death spiral – flipping itself over and over to free itself. Instead it only tightened the rope around its jaws with each revolution. Kweku kept the tension on the rope. He couldn't see where Bruno had got to and he screamed out for him.

Out of nowhere, Bruno appeared brandishing the machete and moving almost in rhythm to Frankie's gyrations. As the reptile's sallow white underside appeared, Bruno struck, and the pale pink flesh of Frankie's gullet opened wide.

CHAPTER THIRTY-NINE

21st May, Akosombo, Ghana

Emma and Sowah arrived at Kweku Ponsu's compound to discover they had missed him by a few hours. He had left for Atimpoku early that morning. When would he return? None of the numerous, miscellaneous people hanging around knew.

'What next, sir?' Emma asked her boss as they stood at the roadside to hail a cab. Sowah often left his vehicle behind to avoid the headaches of finding a parking space in a city of chaotic traffic.

'Little choice but to go after him in Atimpoku,' he said, flagging down a rickety taxi. 'We don't know when he'll be back in Accra. We might as well go back to the office, pick up my car and drive directly there.'

They headed north to Atimpoku, eight miles south-east of the Akosombo Dam. At the last minute Sowah had also arranged to meet Mr Labram, the owner of the nearby Riverview Cottage where Mr Tilson had stayed before his disappearance.

En route, Emma said, 'Sir, I should tell you about what DI Damptey said to me yesterday at the Autism Centre ceremony.'

'Ah, yes?'

'She seemed upset that we are looking into Tilson's disappearance and she said I should please respectfully ask you to leave the case alone.'

Sowah tossed his head back and laughed. 'And if I don't, what will happen to me?'

'Please, she didn't tell me that part.'

Sowah sucked his teeth. 'Don't mind her. She's full of hot air.'

Well, Emma thought, *if the boss is not worried about her, neither am I.*

They arrived in Atimpoku a little after eleven Monday morning. The transport hub was alive with *tro-tros*, buses, taxis, and merchants swarming every incoming vehicle to offer bread, water, cold drinks, *abolo*, and the ubiquitous *one-man-thousand*, silvery anchovies from the Volta River deep-fried till crisp and crunchy.

Hungry, Emma and Sowah bought a packet of biscuits and some Alvaro soda to wash them down. They continued about a mile farther to the Riverview Cottage, which was down an incline in a picturesque and shady area not far from the Volta River's right bank. The lake itself, formed by the Akosombo Dam, was north of here. Emma noted how emerald green the environment was. Living in Accra in traffic and billboard purgatory made one forget what the natural world had to offer. She noticed the chirping of birds, a sound invariably drowned out in the urban environment.

Mr Labram had been expecting them. Fortyish, he was heavyset with a belly that spilt over his beltline.

'Very happy to meet you,' he said, shaking hands first with Sowah and then Emma. 'Please come this way into the house – you said you would like to look around. We have a tenant but they're out right now.'

They followed Labram along a shaded walkway with inlaid sandstone tiles. A breeze came off the river, glimpses of which they could see through a lush flank of trees.

'I'm glad someone is paying attention to this case,' Labram said, unlocking the front door. 'Mr Tilson was here for only a few days, but he was a kind, decent man. I also met Mr Derek when he came here looking to find out what had happened to his dad. Has Mr Derek returned to his country?'

Sowah replied, 'Not yet.'

Labram asked a little about the history of Sowah's detective agency and Emma noted how humble Sowah sounded in his response. His words conveyed a quiet wisdom born of years of experience. Emma hoped to be like that someday.

Labram must have been impressed as well. 'That is very good, Mr Sowah,' he said, nodding in approval. For his part, Labram was an Akosombo Dam engineer who had the option of free housing from the Volta River Authority. The Riverview would be his retirement home, but in the time being, he was reaping the benefits of Airbnb.

'I hope we can find out what happened to him,' Labram said, 'and that, God willing, it's nothing bad that has occurred.'

'Did anyone from CID get in touch with you?' Emma asked. Sowah wanted her to pose as many questions as possible, and she was gathering up the courage to do so in his avuncular presence.

'One lady detective,' Labram said. 'I think the name was Damptey – Dorothy or Doris – she called me and asked a few questions to confirm the dates Mr Tilson had arrived and was supposed to have left. She said she would send someone from Akosombo Police Station to interview me, but no one has ever shown up.'

'I see,' Sowah said, exchanging a glance with Emma.

The house wasn't as luxurious and modern as Poem's place in Accra, but it was comfortably furnished, and the air conditioner was running. The kitchen and dining area merged into the sitting room. Two bedrooms and a bath were beyond that, off a short hallway.

The trio crossed to the other side of the room where the patio afforded a view of the Volta River from a different, better angle. The calm, greyish-blue expanse of water looked powerful and deep, its ripples reflecting the sun in miniature explosions of light. Tranquillity belying strength was a quality Emma admired. A few fishing canoes, paddled by men solo or in pairs, bobbed up and down on the river's surface. Emma had a flash of childhood nostalgia. Her father often took her out in a canoe on Lake Bosomtwe in the Ashanti Region to teach her to swim and dive, not a skill the average Ghanaian father imparted to his daughter. But Daddy had never had a son, and Emma was tomboyish enough as a reasonable substitute. She certainly had not been a girly girl. Up till the present day, men especially were surprised to discover she was a powerful swimmer.

Looking southward, they could see the graceful arch of the Adome Bridge spanning the breadth of the river. Emma thought she could sit there for hours contemplating the view. But she snatched herself back to reality.

'Mr Labram,' Sowah said, 'could you recount for us what happened the day Mr Tilson disappeared and anything significant leading up to that day?'

'I will be happy to do so,' Labram said, shifting his weight and attempting to get comfortable in a chair that was on the skimpy side for his bulk. 'Mr Tilson planned to return to Accra on Tuesday 3rd April. He called me on Sunday – April Fool's Day – to let me know he would like to settle the bill on Monday, the eve of his departure. So, I came down around five on Monday afternoon and he paid the bill in full. We chatted for a little bit, and he told me he would leave around seven in the morning.'

Sowah looked at Emma, cueing her to ask a question.

Thank goodness she had one ready. 'Please, did Mr Tilson tell you anything about the problems he was facing – the reason he came to Ghana?'

Labram hesitated. 'He did. After he had been here a couple of days, he said he had come to Ghana looking for a woman he had fallen in love with online in America. When he arrived here, he found it was all a trick. He had given away thousands of dollars to a bunch of fraudsters.' Labram shook his head in disgust. 'These people are spoiling our country.'

Emma sensed his profound regret.

'Mr Tilson told me he was on a mission to find the culprit,' Labram continued. 'I felt a bit sorry for him because I didn't think he would be successful. Still, I prayed that he would be. If we can apprehend more of these people, perhaps others will be discouraged from doing these criminal things.'

'It's possible Mr Tilson came here looking for Kweku Ponsu, a traditional priest,' Emma said. 'Did he say something to you about that?'

'Yes,' Labram said. 'He asked me if I knew anything about Ponsu. I said very little except that he stayed in Atimpoku, his hometown, from time to time. However, I advised Mr Tilson not to get involved with such people unless someone in the know accompanies him. He said his driver knew his way around and would assist him.'

'You mean the driver Mr Tilson hired for the trip from Accra?' Sowah asked.

'Yes please.'

'By any chance, do you have the driver's contact information?'

'He gave his name as Yahya,' Labram said, taking out

his phone, 'but I didn't get his surname.' When he had located the number, he reached over to hand his mobile to Sowah, who wrote the number down in his small notebook, old school.

'While Mr Tilson was here,' Labram continued, 'Yahya stayed at a hotel in Atimpoku. On Tuesday morning, he arrived here before seven to meet Mr Tilson's absence. He then called me to ask if I knew where Mr Tilson had gone. I came down from my place and was very puzzled by his disappearance. Yahya and I went together to look for him at the Adome Bridge thinking he might have gone to take some photos. We even asked people in the Atimpoku area if they had seen an *oburoni* man early that morning or the night before, but no one had.'

'So, it means Mr Tilson disappeared sometime between five on Monday afternoon and seven Tuesday morning,' Sowah said.

'Yes, sir,' Labram said.

'And we understand that Mr Tilson's luggage was also not in his room,' Emma said. 'Is that correct?'

'Right,' Labram responded, his brow creasing. 'That made us worry about whether it was a robbery attempt and he had been harmed. Or even killed.'

'Those are the fundamental questions,' Sowah agreed. 'Could someone have heard something out of the ordinary overnight? Do you have servants' quarters?'

Labram shook his head. 'I have a house girl who comes to clean three times a week, but she lives in Atimpoku. If you want to question her, I can take you to see her.'

'We would like that, thank you,' Sowah said, smiling at how cooperative their host was. It wasn't always such smooth sailing for a private investigator. 'What about neighbours?'

Labram looked regretful. 'Unfortunately, the splendid solitude of this place, which is the reason why many visitors come to spend their holidays here and escape from hectic city life, is a disadvantage in this case. The next house from here is half a mile away. With the tree and vegetation cover, you can hear virtually nothing, even during the quiet of the night.'

Sowah nodded. 'May we see Mr Tilson's room?'

'But of course,' Labram said. 'Please come this way.'

They went to the hallway on the other side of the sitting room.

'The house girl has been here already to clean up,' Labram said, opening a door on the right. 'I'm sorry there's nothing much to see except the present tenant's belongings.'

The bed was neatly made. Some paper items and a Bradt *Travel Guide to Ghana* lay on the desk. A spinner suitcase stood in a corner.

'When did your present guest arrive?' Sowah asked, flipping over the luggage tag.

'Last week, sir,' Labram said. 'Him and his wife.'

'No reason to think they have any connection with Mr Tilson?'

'Connection?' Labram asked, looking surprised. 'Not that I know of.'

Sowah nodded. It was a long shot, not a serious thought.

Emma looked around, noticing a mosquito-netted porch outside the sliding glass doors. 'So, Mr Labram,' she said, 'you're certain there was no sign of forced entry onto the patio or through those doors that Tuesday morning?'

'No, madam,' Labram responded. They stood in silence a moment.

'This driver, Yahya,' Sowah said at length, 'how did he seem to you?'

'He was very agitated that we could not find Mr Tilson,' Labram said. 'He was almost in tears because with these car rental agencies, if anything at all happens to the customer, the driver is held responsible. I'm sure the company has sacked him by now.'

'We'll try to contact him once we return to Accra,' Sowah said. 'I think we're done here. Would you mind taking us to see your house girl, Mr Labram?'

'No problem, sir. We can go now. I'll drive us there so we can talk to her. Her name is Kafui.'

CHAPTER FORTY

While Emma and Sowah were in Atimpoku, Derek made some progress of his own, scoring a visit with Rachel Jones, one of the American Embassy's consuls. The building at 24 Fourth Circular Road was an impenetrable grey fortress with NO PHOTOGRAPHY ALLOWED warnings posted at every turn. The US Marines on duty on the grounds of the embassy were an additional reminder. Derek wondered what the consequences of snapping a pic would be.

Unsurprisingly in such an environment, Derek had to surrender his phone on entry, pass through a metal detector, get a pat down, and sign in at reception before proceeding. As Derek entered the heart of the building, which was deliciously chilled to US standards, he had a sudden twinge of home pride and felt a little embarrassed. He didn't want to be a rah-rah American.

A security guard showed Derek to a waiting room full of people of all shapes, shades, and sizes, many of whom, Derek guessed, were seeking the coveted American entry visa. After some twenty minutes, an attendant called his name and Derek followed him down the brightly lit hall to a door bearing Rachel Jones's name on a polished, brass plate. The attendant knocked, waved Derek in and then left. A diminutive, fiftyish, bespectacled white woman in a cream-coloured trouser suit stood up from her desk and thrust out her hand.

'Welcome, Mr Tilson. I'm Rachel Jones.' She indicated a couple of chairs off to the side and they sat opposite each other. She crossed her stubby legs. 'This is regarding your father, is that right, Mr Tilson?'

'Correct. Derek is fine.'

She smiled. 'Then you may call me Rachel in return. I'm assuming that since you've been in Ghana you've had no word on where he is?'

'None.'

'I'm sorry to hear that. When did you arrive in Accra?'

'May 2nd, about three weeks ago. I'm staying at the African Regent.'

Derek explained to Rachel his fruitless dealings with the police and his decision to go with a private detective agency. He saw concern flit over her expression.

'Be careful with that,' she cautioned. 'Some of these Ghanaian PI outfits are fraudulent. You might pay them a lot of money and end up with nothing at all in return.'

'I hear you,' Derek said. 'The agency I've hired is vetted by an international organisation. But I appreciate your warning me. I'm curious about exactly what my father said when he came to the embassy. I mean, what was the purpose of his visit?'

She nodded. 'Your father did visit the embassy in late February. I spoke to him in this very office and took a report about his experience with this scam. I sensed he was deeply hurt and angry. Unfortunately, these cruel online cons aren't uncommon, and I'm sorry we could not help your father to the extent of his expectations.'

'Oh? What was he expecting?'

'He wanted us to take action to address the prevalence of these scams, as in apply pressure on the police and the Ghana government to clamp down on this criminal activity. I'm sure you understand we can't do that. We're not in the business of law enforcement – especially not as guests in a sovereign nation such as Ghana. Furthermore, he wanted our FBI Legat to—'

'Sorry, what was that?' Derek interjected. 'The FBI what?'

'Apologies,' Jones said. 'I lapsed into State Department talk. The FBI maintains a presence in several countries as legal attaché offices, or "Legats". So, maybe Mr Tilson – your dad – had read something about Legats and he more or less – and I don't like to put it this way – *demanded* that our Legat start investigating his personal case. I explained to him this is simply not their role. As big a calamity as this thing was to him personally, it doesn't rise to the level of an international concern.'

'So, what exactly *is* the Legat's job?'

'They play a supportive role in cases that are of common interest to the United States and the host country. For instance, let's say CID has a need for sophisticated evidence collection and testing, that's an area we could assist; or, for instance – and I'm being entirely academic here – your father was in a hostage situation, we could *offer* the FBI hostage negotiation skills, if CID wanted them. Things like that. Beyond that, all I could recommend to your dad was to stick with the local police authorities.'

'Who, I'm sure you know,' Derek said, making a face, 'do absolutely nothing.'

'That's not *exactly* true,' Jones said. 'Prosecution of these fraudsters does occur. There have been a few high-profile cases like this one guy who used to ride around Accra in a candy-red Ferrari from all the money he swindled. But by and large, the steady drip, drip, drip of everyday scams is a colossal problem the Ghana police struggle to keep up with.'

'Is that the whole story? Isn't the truth more that the police are too corrupt to seriously investigate?'

'There's no doubt that corruption is rife in Ghana at many levels of society and government,' Jones said, and left it at that.

Derek blew out his breath. He felt deflated and helpless. Then he thought of something. 'By any chance, do you read the *Washington Observer*?'

'On occasion. Why do you ask?'

'I wonder if you might have seen an article there last month by Casper Guttenberg in which he talks about Ghanaian and Nigerian Internet con artists and uses my father as an example.'

Rachel shook her head. 'I must have missed that one. I'll confess we tend to read the *Post* around here.'

'No matter,' Derek said. 'I can find it and email it to you, if you're interested. Anyway, the end of the article mentioned that my father was remaining in the country to' – Derek air quoted – 'investigate who had swindled him. This was news to me. Did he say anything to you about his intention to get to the bottom of it?'

'He did not,' Rachel said firmly. 'If he had, I would have strongly cautioned him not to go down that garden path. It's not the kind of thing an American wants to get mixed up with, especially on foreign soil.'

'Right,' Derek said. 'I know Casper Guttenberg, the guy who penned the piece, and I asked him more than once if this was some scheme he and my father cooked up, but he denied it.'

'I wish I could help more,' Rachel said with a regretful smile. Clearly, delving into Cas's involvement was of no interest to her.

Derek stood up. 'Thank you, Rachel, for taking the time with me.'

When he was outside the building again, Derek felt empty. What had he found out from this meeting? That his father and Rachel Jones had met and talked, but very little else. And of Gordon's present whereabouts, Derek had learnt nothing at all.

CHAPTER FORTY-ONE

Emma and Sowah followed Labram into the heart of Atimpoku. It was a linear town hugging the road on either side in a north-south direction. Its eastern portion sloped down to the river, while the western part rose steeply uphill. Growth and expansion were apparent, with multiple new homes under construction on the hillside.

Labram's house girl lived on the east side of the town, sharing a compound with several neighbours. Conversing and laughing, three women were cooking in the open space while half a dozen kids of all ages ran – or crawled – around in play. A few goats chewed placidly on whatever goats chew on, chickens pecked at the dirt with exploratory noises, and skinny stray dogs cautiously approached the cooking area in the hope of a few scraps. A radio was playing religious highlife somewhere.

Labram greeted the group in Ewe.

They responded in unison and one of the women let out an exclamation of surprise when she saw him. She dropped what she was doing, wiped her hands on a rag, and hurried to where Labram and his two guests were standing. She shook his hand with a slight curtsy.

'*Ei, papa!*' she said, with a luminous smile. '*Woeizo!*'

Labram introduced her to Emma and Sowah. 'This is my house girl, Kafui.'

They exchanged greetings. Emma was staring at the baby on Kafui's back, an exquisite boy with a perfectly round head and big dark eyes with lashes that curled up as if by some kind of artificial device. *I want a baby like that*, she thought. 'What's your baby's name?' she asked Kafui in Twi.

'Please, his name is Yao.' Kafui glanced behind her to smile at her child snug and safe on her back, and then directed a couple of the older kids to place four chairs in a shaded spot.

'Please, have a seat,' Kafui invited her visitors, taking hers after them.

A girl about eight years old materialised with a tray of three sachets of water that she offered to the guests.

While it would have been rude for Labram to launch immediately into the purpose of the visit, neither was it Kafui's place to ask. The social hierarchy was sharply defined: Labram was her employer and a lot older than she was. So, the first five minutes were spent in pleasantries punctuated by some gaps of silence not considered awkward in any way.

It wasn't until Labram had drained his water sachet that he began telling Kafui why they were there to see her. 'Do you remember end of last March a certain American man came to stay at the house?' he asked.

Kafui cast her mind back. 'Please, do you mean Mr Gordon?'

'Yes, that's him,' Labram said.

'Oh, very nice man,' Kafui said with that easy smile. 'He was the only *oburoni* who would greet me and talk to me when I went to clean.'

It seemed to Emma that everyone – or almost everyone – had liked Mr Tilson.

'And you remember you went to the house the morning he left,' Labram said.

Kafui nodded. 'Yes please. Ten in the morning, I was there. By that time, he had already gone back to Accra.'

'Kafui,' Sowah joined in, 'did you notice anything different about the room compared to how you see it normally?'

She considered the question, apparently puzzled by it. 'No please.' Then, she sent Labram a worried look. 'Please, is something wrong with how I cleaned the room?'

'Not at all, Kafui,' he said. 'You are not in trouble. I will let Mr Sowah explain.'

Sowah took it up. 'Kafui, before you got to the cottage that morning to do your cleaning, the driver came to collect Mr Gordon around seven o'clock. But Mr Gordon had disappeared.'

Kafui raised her eyebrows. 'Disappeared? How, disappeared, please?'

'He has been missing since that time,' Sowah said. 'No one has located him or been able to reach him on the

243

phone. It seems something happened to him overnight.'

Kafui brought her hand up to her lips. '*Oh!*'

'Did you ever see Mr Gordon here in Atimpoku?' Sowah asked.

She shook her head. 'No please.'

'What about while he was staying at the cottage?' Emma came in. 'Did you notice anyone come to see him there?'

Again, Kafui's reply was in the negative.

'Do you know Kweku Ponsu, the fetish priest?' Sowah asked.

'Yes please,' Kafui said. 'Well, I know about him.'

'We understand Mr Gordon wanted to visit Mr Ponsu,' Sowah said. 'Did you see them together anywhere? Maybe between here and Akosombo, or by the river?'

Kafui shook her head, appearing regretful she hadn't provided any help so far. 'Please, maybe he has gone back to his country,' she suggested tentatively.

'No,' Emma said. 'Even his son has come to Ghana because Mr Tilson has not returned home.'

Kafui looked distressed. 'But what could have happened to him?'

Labram said, 'We are worried someone went to the house and took Mr Tilson away somewhere.'

It was at that instant that Kafui's expression changed abruptly. Apparently, something had struck her with the force of lightning.

'What's wrong?' Labram asked.

Eyes down, Kafui pressed her fingers to her lips as one

gripped by a sudden dreadful thought. 'I saw something.'

'You saw something?' Sowah asked. 'How do you mean?'

'Early that morning around two o'clock,' Kafui began explaining, 'Yao wouldn't sleep, so I took him for a walk to the roadside. While we were there, I saw an SUV turn onto the Adome Bridge. When it reached about halfway, it stopped, and I saw two men get out. They opened the boot and dragged out something in a long sack. The way they were carrying it, I could see it was heavy. It even looked like it could be somebody inside. They took it to the side of the bridge and threw it over into the river.'

Emma felt chills down her back.

'About how big was the sack?' Sowah asked.

'I'm not sure,' Kafui said. 'Maybe from there . . . to there.' She pointed out two spots on the wall about two metres apart – the length of a fairly tall person.

'You're sure it was the same morning that you went to clean the house?' Sowah asked. 'The same morning Mr Tilson disappeared?'

'Yes please,' Kafui said without hesitation. 'I remember it was a Friday and it was also Yao's birthday. I was planning to go to market the next day. On Thursday, Mr Labram called me to tell me I should come the next day to do a good cleaning for the next guest after Mr Gordon.'

Emma exchanged a glance with Sowah. Was this their first real break?

'Why did you think maybe there was someone in the sack?' Emma asked Kafui.

Kafui's eyes misted. 'I saw it move.'

For several moments, no one said a word. Kafui began to sniff and dab her eyes with a handkerchief. Clearly, she was feeling overwhelmed. Emma went to her side and dropped to her knees. 'Are you OK?'

'I pray it will not be the white man,' Kafui said, her voice shaking. She had just voiced what everyone in the small group was thinking.

CHAPTER FORTY-TWO

Nii Kwei had his audience of six *sakawa* boys, including Bruno, in the palm of his hand as he demonstrated brand-new software and hardware. The former had been downloaded and the latter was fresh off the plane, brought in by a friend from the US, and paid for online with a hacked credit card account used on Amazon Prime.

'This one,' he explained to his attentive colleagues, 'they call it Face2Face. It's a kind of real time facial re-enactment software.'

'*Ei!*' the youngest boy, Timi-Timi, exclaimed. 'Nii, you are killing us, oo!'

'Yeah, *chaley*,' another said, 'your words are too big. Come down small for us, please.'

Nii grinned at their joshing but got serious quickly. 'OK, shut up and listen. You already know how we use fake technology for Skyping. We download a video from YouTube and convert it to media file with ClipConverter or KeepVid.'

They bunched together behind him, watching his laptop screen. 'We go take as an example this one I already have of a beautiful Ghanaian woman I used for that American guy, Mr Gordon. Now, formerly I exported the file to ManyCam, and on Skype I use ManyCam as my fake camera instead of the real one. Do you get it?'

The students nodded.

'Then when I'm Skyping with the American guy,' Nii continued, 'he go see the video of this woman, but I can't make the woman really converse with him, and sometimes her expression no match what the man is saying. So, maybe she dey smile when he hasn't said anything funny. That's why we tell the guy that the laptop make old, the microphone is broken, and the network make slow, so because of that we can only text the conversation.'

'And some of them go suspect it's not real,' Bruno added. 'That's how we lose them.'

'Correct,' Nii said. 'Now, what if we can make the woman smile, laugh, and converse with the guy in real time?'

'Not possible,' Timi-Timi said, looking at Nii as if he were crazy.

'Just wait, OK? I'm coming. Now, instead of exporting our media file to ManyCam, we open Face2Face and import the file of the beautiful lady. Once we do that, we play the clip for about three minutes so that the software can learn all her facial expressions – her smile and all that stuff.'

While that was proceeding, Nii moved to the nearby table where the Face2Face camera sat. He turned it on, adjusted some settings, and returned to his laptop. 'Now we go to Skype. Instead of the real laptop camera, we click on Face2Face as our fake camera. OK, now you see the video of the woman.'

Nii returned to the Face2Face camera and sat in front of it, tilting it so that it captured his face within a frame on the screen. 'Bruno, you will be the American guy, OK? I'm going to call you and you get online.'

'OK,' Bruno said.

The call came through and once the connection was established, the image of the lovely Ghanaian woman appeared on the laptop's screen.

'Hello, my dear,' Bruno said in a brave attempt at an American accent.

Nii smiled broadly and batted his eyelashes, and so, correspondingly, did the beautiful lady on Bruno's phone. But through the magic of the software, it was *her* smile, not Nii's, and it looked natural.

'I'm fine, my dear,' Nii said, and with the tiniest delay, the lady on the laptop uttered the same words. Bruno jumped away; his jaw dropped. '*Ei!* Is it juju?'

'Don't be afraid, my darling,' the woman said, parroting Nii.

For a moment, the boys stared at this piece of wizardry in stunned silence and then pandemonium erupted. They screamed and jumped around as if Ghana had just won the World Cup.

'Wait, wait!' Bruno said to Nii in wild excitement. 'Let me try, can I try?'

Nii let him, and then each of the boys after him. Each time, the woman on the laptop responded. It was truly magical.

Later, Bruno accompanied Nii in his Range Rover to the spacious home he shared with two other *sakawa* boys and they ate *kenkey* and fish with *shito*.

'*Chaley*, Face2Face will change everything,' Bruno said. 'Money will flow.'

Nii nodded, eating with relish. 'It will be good, *paa*.'

'How did you find out about that Face2Face?'

'My friend in the States told me about it.'

'Ah, OK.'

They ate quietly for a moment, savouring the excellent quality of the *kenkey*.

'So, what about the American guy, Mr Gordon?' Bruno said. 'Tell me about that.'

'I made plenty money from him,' Nii said. 'He seems to be a very nice man. In fact, I even started to like him.'

'Is that so? But still you were taking his money.'

Nii shrugged. 'That's how it is. A nice *mugu* is the best *mugu*.'

'It's true,' Bruno agreed.

'Do you know he came to Ghana?' Nii said.

'Who? Gordon?'

'Yes. To look for the woman.' Nii found that funny and giggled. The first day he arrived in Ghana, he tried to call me and so I blocked him and changed my SIM card.'

'You should have answered the call and told him you were the lady's brother and that he should meet you at some place,' Bruno said. 'Then, from there, you rob him of all his money and mobile phone and everything.'

Nii frowned. 'No, because you never know he might bring police with him to trap you. Somebody you are dealing with online you should never meet in person, you get me. It's too dangerous.'

'OK.' Bruno broke off a chunk of *kenkey* with his fingers and scooped up a healthy amount of *shito*. 'So, this Mr Gordon, did he return to States?'

Nii shook his head. 'I heard he has gone missing and his son has come to town from *aburokyire* to look for him.'

'Really,' Bruno said. 'What has happened to the man?'

'I don't know, my brodda.'

'Maybe someone has butchered him with cutlass and buried him,' Bruno suggested.

'Maybe,' Nii said.

'Could you do that to someone?'

Nii looked up from the dish. 'Do what?'

'Kill someone,' Bruno said.

Nii frowned. 'It depends on the situation. What about you?'

'If I have to kill somebody – like I'm protecting my family or something like that, I will do it.'

'Yeah,' Nii agreed.

'Do you know I killed Kweku Ponsu's crocodile?' Bruno said.

'*Heh!*' Nii exclaimed in disbelief. 'Don't lie.'

'It's true. Kweku said because of that, I will be closer to meeting Godfather.'

Nii regarded him with new respect. 'Then you have tried, *paa*,' he said. 'You will be blessed. As for that crocodile, I will just urinate on myself if I face it.'

The two laughed till they were weak.

CHAPTER FORTY-THREE

Sowah, Emma, and Labram conferenced while Kafui went to change Yao's nappy.

'What Kafui related is ominous,' Sowah said. 'A large sack with something or someone heavy in it dumped into the river on the night Mr Tilson disappeared? I don't believe much in coincidences. I'll talk to DCOP Laryea to see if we can get some divers to search the riverbed around the Adome Bridge. But before that, I want Kafui to take us to the spot she thinks the SUV stopped along the bridge. Emma, please ask her if she can come with us.'

Kafui agreed. With Yao securely on her back again, she led the other three as she retraced her steps that night.

'I came to here,' she said, as they arrived alongside the green-painted Adome Hotel. A few metres away was the small roundabout with its three exit points south to Accra, north to Akosombo, and east across the bridge. Now the area was bustling with cars, *tro-tros*, trucks, and people, but of course the night Kafui had been there, the environment would have been quiet and still.

'I was standing here with Yao trying to make him sleep,' Kafui continued. 'Then, from the Akosombo side came the SUV driving fast.'

'Can you say the type of SUV?' Emma asked, while thinking how they all looked pretty much the same to her.

'Not at all,' Kafui said with regret. 'I didn't have time to see it well.'

'No problem,' Sowah said. 'Go on.'

'Then it went onto the bridge about halfway,' Kafui said, pointing.

'OK then,' Sowah said. 'Let's go there.'

They took the south-facing walkway – the righthand side of the bridge. The Adome – Ghana's only suspension bridge – dips slightly and then rebounds in response to traffic, particularly heavy-laden eighteen-wheeled vehicles.

About halfway to the other end of the bridge, Kafui stopped. 'It was around here.'

They looked down at the greyish-blue water. Rain clouds were gathering behind and above them, covering the sun and making the river look darker and more threatening. Still, fishermen were out plying the river.

'Makes sense to dump a body at this point I suppose,' Sowah said, looking from bank to bank. 'The water will be deepest at the centre of the bridge, not so, Mr Labram?'

'Yes, sir. At this point it's twenty to twenty-five feet.'

'Plenty of water to drown in,' Sowah commented.

'Yes, but what kills is the impact of the body with the water,' Labram said. 'It's ninety to a hundred feet from here to the river's surface. Only a miracle would save you.'

Emma shuddered.

'I'd like to see Kafui re-enact what she saw,' Sowah said. 'We might pick up something that wasn't apparent in her narrative.'

Kafui obliged. The most notable part of her performance was the awkwardness involved in lifting the sack over the top of the railing, which showed that the weight of the contents was substantial.

'How far do you think a body would float downstream from here since 3rd April?' Sowah asked.

'Not as far as you might think,' Labram replied. 'For a couple of reasons. One, the body or the sack containing it might snag on rocks on the riverbed. Two, you see those islands dotted all over the river? They aren't true islands at all. They are actually aquatic weeds.'

'Weeds!' Sowah exclaimed in surprise.

'Yes,' Labram said. 'They cluster together all over the river in thick, impenetrable clumps and present great challenges to the fishing livelihood. The point is, a resurfacing body could easily become trapped and concealed in one of those masses of vegetation. Third is the issue of nets.'

'Nets?' Emma asked.

'You might have noticed plastic bottles floating on the surface and thought they were rubbish,' Labram said. 'Actually, they mark the spot where fishermen have left their nets to trap fish over a period, like overnight. When they come back for the catch, they know which one is which.'

'Aha,' Sowah said. 'Simple but ingenious. So, at some point, the body could conceivably get trapped in a net.'

'Correct,' Labram said. 'That's why I recommend we talk to the fishermen and ask them to be on the lookout. Anything unusual, report to the police and get in touch with you. Which reminds me also, we should pay a visit to the Akosombo police as well. They took my statement when Mr Tilson disappeared and it's a good idea for you to make friends with them. You never know when you might need their help.'

Sowah agreed. Ghanaians made a big deal of 'greeting' the local authorities, whether that be the police or the traditional chief of a district. 'That is a great idea – thank you. But I think before we do that, we should pay Kweku Ponsu a visit.' He looked at Labram. 'Do you know where he lives?'

'Most people do,' Labram said. 'His house is at the top of one of the hillsides, so you can't miss it.'

Kafui asked to be excused as she needed to get back.

'Of course,' Sowah said. 'Thank you for everything, Kafui.'

He slipped her a few *cedis*, which brought a big smile to her face before she hurried away and left the other three to continue to Ponsu. They walked uphill between houses. Grazing goats and chickens in their path moved out of the way. The fragrant, reddish soil was soft from a recent rain shower and it appeared another was about to unleash itself.

Labram laboured somewhat from the upward climb, no doubt thankful when they reached a path oriented in a different direction and much less steep. From this vantage point, they had almost a bird's-eye view of Atimpoku all the way down to the river.

As they walked, Sowah looked at Emma. 'I'm glad you were there for Kafui,' he said. 'You established a good rapport with her, and I saw her look at you with admiration a couple of times.'

'Oh, thank you, sir,' Emma said.

'It's situations like this where a woman's finesse can be so helpful,' Sowah said. Emma had never felt so pleased.

Ponsu's home was indeed at the top of the hill. It wasn't shrouded behind a high wall and electric fence as Emma had imagined. With easy access to the sprawling area, Ponsu's three separate buildings were in plain view. Two of them were long, single-storey structures painted cream and brick red. The third was two stories and under construction. The land in front of the buildings was rough and unpaved. Ghanaians love big houses but don't care if it's a potholed road that takes you there.

A small crowd buzzed around five parked SUVs and a sedan as a two-person camera crew filmed and interviewed Ponsu showing off his vehicles. He was dressed in turquoise embroidered robes and layers of jewellery. Now he was demonstrating the beauty of the silver Escalade.

'Dis one,' he said, waving his horsetail whisk, 'I get it straight from America, you understand me. Very powerful! Look at the engine.' He directed one of his minions to pop the hood and open it up. 'You see? V-8; four hundred and twenty horsepower. *What!* No joke!'

'Massa, no joke!' one of his groupies echoed, laughing. 'Dis no be for small boys.'

'Where do you get all your money?' the interviewer asked.

'My money?' Ponsu said, hitting his chest. '*My* money? I earn it! People come to me for salvation, for healing, for blessings. You understand me. They pay me because it is worth it.'

'But is it true that sometimes you order ritual killings?'

The priest turned down the corners of his lips and shook his head. 'Never! Those who say that are just trying to destroy me because of their jealousy.'

'What about your enemies and rivals? Do you order them killed?'

Ponsu was offended. 'My friend, do you know the one who you are talking to right now? Right now, do you know who you are talking to, is what I'm saying. I am a healer and a man of God.'

'But you also believe in magical powers, don't you?'

'I believe in the powers given to me as divine gifts,' Ponsu declared, moving on to the black F-250.

Emma snorted with derision. 'What a buffoon,' she said under her breath.

Sowah looked at her with grim amusement. 'Indeed,' he said, checking his watch. 'I wonder how long this will go on.'

'Might as well be entertained,' Labram said.

In fact, whether by chance or design, Ponsu could be quite funny. Even so, thirty minutes of his antics were about all Emma and her companions could take, and just as they began to wonder whether to leave and return later, the TV journalists wrapped up the interview and began packing up to leave.

'Let's get to him before he launches into something else,' Sowah said.

They made themselves more conspicuous and a young man who looked like he could lift a building approached them to ask what they wanted.

'We need about ten minutes of Mr Ponsu's time,' Sowah told him.

'Wait here, please.' He went over to Ponsu and whispered in his ear. The priest glanced at the three waiting guests and nodded. The young man returned to them. 'Wait ten minutes,' he said. 'Then he can see you.'

'Thank you,' Sowah said. 'Your name, please.'

The man gave him a surly look. 'Clifford.'

There was a moment of confusion as a man, the exact double of Clifford, came out of the centre building. Emma's head whipped back and forth between the two men to be sure she wasn't seeing things. Clifford's twin, equally massive, walked up to them.

'That's Clement,' Clifford said. 'My brother.'

Evidently, Emma thought.

Clement said nothing, regarding the trio with little visible interest.

In the end, it was more like twenty minutes before Clifford and Clement led Emma, Sowah, and Labram to a kind of assembly room with some fifty chairs and a peculiar throne-like setup at the front. Ponsu had arranged himself and his robes apparently to appear as majestic as possible. Clifford and his twin stepped to the side and stood guard with identical stances.

'You are welcome,' Ponsu addressed them after shaking hands with them all. 'Please, have a seat.'

Clifford had pulled up three chairs. After sitting, Sowah introduced himself and his colleagues.

Ponsu nodded. 'Eh-heh, so what can I do for you?'

'Mr Ponsu,' Sowah began, 'Detective Djan and I are investigating the disappearance of an American man by the name of Tilson, Gordon Tilson. He has been missing since 3rd April and we have reason to believe that he might have visited you here in the four or five days prior to that date.'

'Before I even answer that,' Ponsu said, picking up his fly whisk, 'let me first ask you a question. Who gave you that information? That is what I want to know.'

'Well, the source is not that important, sir,' Sowah said. 'We—'

'Excuse me, please,' Ponsu interrupted, holding up a finger. 'Excuse me to say, but the source of the information is *very* important. Do you know why, please?' Sowah didn't answer, so Ponsu proceeded. 'The source is important because the information is not true. You understand what I'm trying to say. In other words, this person is telling you lies. Therefore, you must go back to that person, you understand me, and put him straight.'

Sowah waited a few seconds to be sure he wouldn't

260

be interrupted again. 'Perhaps I didn't make myself clear enough,' he said. 'What I said was that we have reason to believe Mr Tilson *might* have visited you, sir.'

Ponsu gave a long, slow blink that appeared to mean, *You think you're so smart, don't you?* 'And so, what if I say the *oburoni* was here?' he asked. 'Then what will you do?'

'We are trying every avenue to locate him, Mr Ponsu,' Sowah said. 'We talk to anyone he has been in contact with in order to gain some clues as to his movements and possible whereabouts.'

'I see,' Ponsu said, pressing his lips together. 'Well, let me tell you now that no such man of such description has ever been here.'

'Is it possible you might have met him or spoken to him, but you now cannot recall?'

The priest shook his head. 'I don't forget anything, and if he came here and I wasn't in, then Cliff and Clem would have told me.' Ponsu nodded at the twins.

'OK,' Sowah said. 'Mr Ponsu, sir, have you heard anything at all about this missing American – Mr Gordon Tilson?'

Ponsu regarded him deadpan. 'Nothing.'

'He was the victim of a romance scam,' Sowah went on. 'He came to Ghana looking for the woman he believed he had fallen in love with, only to find, of course, that it wasn't the case.'

'Ah, what a pity,' Ponsu said, with a creditable show of empathy. 'And why are you looking for him? What is your interest?'

'We have been contracted to locate him and find out what happened to him.'

'I see,' Ponsu said. 'Who is the one hiring you?'

'I'm not at liberty to comment on that,' Sowah said.

Ponsu lifted his palm and let it drop. 'Ah, well. So be it, then.'

'We are also looking into who was responsible for scamming Mr Tilson,' Sowah said, 'and so I would like to ask if you have connections with any *sakawa* boys, sir?'

Ponsu adjusted his robes. 'If I have a connection with *sakawa* boys,' he repeated with a laugh. 'Why are you asking me that?'

'All part of the investigation. You may decline to answer, if you wish. No one is forcing you.'

'You know, Mr Sowah,' Ponsu said, acquiescing, 'the boys come to me to ask for powers – powers to perform their work successfully.'

'And you help them even though they are involved in illegal activity?'

'Oh, *yes*!' Ponsu said, grinning. 'I don't pass judgement, you understand me. We all have our work to do, not so? If you are bringing the correct sacrificial animals and some money to me, then yes, I will help you.'

'And none of these boys has ever mentioned the name Gordon Tilson to you?' Sowah persisted from a different angle. 'Or maybe brought you a picture of the man?'

The priest shook his head. 'Never.'

An awkward silence followed. Sowah cleared his

throat. 'Thank you for your help, sir. May I keep in touch with you?'

'But of course,' Ponsu said, and recited his number.

'Thank you,' Sowah said. 'I also will flash you our contact info. In case you remember anything that could be relevant to the case, please call us.'

'And you too,' Ponsu said, 'if any of you have any spiritual or physical needs, feel free to get in touch. You can also go to my website, PonsuPower.com.'

Over my dead body will I use your services, Emma thought, but still, it was useful to have his phone number. With another round of handshaking, they thanked the priest again and left.

Emma waited until they were well out of earshot before saying anything. 'Do you believe him, sir?'

'No, I do not,' Sowah said without hesitation. 'All that braggadocio talk is just a front.'

'Ponsu is famous for that kind of language, though,' Labram pointed out. 'Watch his YouTube videos and you'll see that's his MO. I don't mean I necessarily believe him, just that his style of language might not point to his lying.'

Despite conceding Labram could be right, Sowah remained doubtful.

'So then, what next, sir?' Emma asked.

'We're not letting Ponsu off the hook, but what we need is another approach. We must find some kind of leverage to use against him. As it is, he'll just continue to deny, deny, deny. So that means we must dig up information on him. What is one possible link to him? The *sakawa* boys, of course. I know some of them, and I know people who know some as well. That's what we need to work on in the next few days.'

Now I'll have to tell him about Bruno, Emma thought. She didn't want to bring her family into the investigation, but here, she had no choice. Since her stepbrother was hanging around *sakawa* boys, Emma had a potential connection to them. She would tell Sowah, but she wanted to wait until she was alone with him.

She noticed he was limping. 'Sir, what's wrong? Did you hurt your foot?'

Sowah looked resigned. 'No, it's my old friend, the gout. He visits me every two months or so.'

Emma didn't know much about the disease – except that it hurt badly. 'Oh, so sorry, sir. Do you have any medicine to take for it?'

'Yes, back home. I need to hurry back to Accra once we're done here. After we talk to the Volta fishermen.'

'Sir,' Emma said, 'why not go home and take care of your foot, please? I will stay here overnight and go to the fishermen early tomorrow. In any case, most fishermen will be out on the river by this time. They return with their catch in the morning. And besides, rain is about to start.'

'You have a point,' Sowah said, looking torn. 'You'll be OK?'

'I'll be fine, sir.' Emma appreciated his concern but felt a little put off. She was a novice yes, but she wasn't *completely* helpless.

'I can take you to a couple of the fishing villages along the river,' Labram said to Emma.

'Thank you, sir,' Sowah said. 'We appreciate that. Where can she stay around here?'

'There are a couple of hotels we can check with and you take your pick.'

In the end, Emma decided on Benkum Hotel, the same place Mr Tilson's driver had stayed. It wasn't the cheapest available, but it was the best value for the money. The Adome Hotel was frankly awful.

Emma said goodbye to Sowah and wished him luck slaying the gout monster. Early the next morning, Mr Labram would come around to pick her up and they would set off. As much as Emma admired and adored Sowah, she felt it was time to do some detective work without his being present. In the privacy of her rudimentary motel room, she looked forward to the next day.

Before she went to bed, however, she had two calls to make: one to Derek, but before that, Bruno.

'Sis!' he exclaimed. 'Where are you?'

'Atimpoku.'

'Really? What are you doing there?'

'Just investigating something. I have a question for you. Has Nii Kwei or any other *sakawa* boy ever talked about an American man called Gordon Tilson?'

'No, why?' Bruno said, but Emma detected the slightest of hesitations.

'Are you sure?' she asked.

'Why do you want to know?'

265

Emma ignored the question. 'But you've heard the name, "Gordon Tilson", right?'

'Well, something like that,' Bruno said vaguely.

'Tell me more.'

'Agh, sis. You're killing me.'

'Bruno, come on. I've always had your back.'

Her stepbrother groaned.

'Who stood up for you against my father?' Emma pressed ruthlessly.

'You did,' Bruno said wearily.

'Exactly. So, help your sister out. What do you know about Tilson?'

'I can't say directly, but I can tell you who to ask. On one condition.'

'What's that?'

'That you didn't hear it from me.'

'OK. I accept. Who's the person we should talk to?'

CHAPTER FORTY-FOUR

21st May, Washington, DC

Cas was sipping black coffee in his flat with his feet up. The alcohol relaxed him, but he was still worried, riddled with anxiety like a corpse full of buckshot. Several weeks now, and still no word from Gordon. For some time, Cas had thought there could be a logical and simple explanation for his friend's silence, but the situation was now ominous.

On his laptop, Cas looked back at his 10th May article in the *Washington Observer*.

Out of Africa
An American delves into the lucrative African
underworld of Internet scammers

By Casper Guttenberg

PART TWO
Modern online romance scams, which often originate from countries like Ghana and Nigeria,

are premeditated crimes that steal millions – potentially billions – of dollars from vulnerable people all over the US, Canada, and Europe. Rarely caught or prosecuted, the scammers sit safely at computers while hunting for prey on social networks.

It is rare that American, Canadian, or European victims (some prefer the term 'survivors') of these scams travel to these countries to confront the conmen in person. GT, whom we met in Part One, decided to do just that. Travelling to Accra, Ghana's capital, GT embarked on a mission to find out who, using the fabricated name 'Helena', had duped him of some $4,000.

But GT found little help from the Ghanaian police authorities, themselves often mired in corruption, and he was compelled to seek other paths. Working with a local Ghanaian investigative reporter, Sana Sana, GT discovered that Internet scamming (commonly called sakawa *in local parlance) has infiltrated multiple strata in Ghanaian life, up to and including the high echelons. Along the way, GT has met a diverse, if not always pleasant, cast of characters including a voodoo priest and the wife of a top police official.*

He startled as his phone buzzed on the side table. It was Derek calling from Ghana, and Cas hoped and prayed he had good news.

'Hi, Derek. How are you doing?'

'Not that well.'

Cas's heart sank. 'What's going on?'

'The detectives are telling me that on the night Dad disappeared, an eyewitness reported what looked like a body being dumped over a bridge into the Volta River.'

Cas's immediate reaction was to push back. 'Yeah, but that could have been anything. We don't even know the reliability of this person. Eyewitness accounts are notoriously untrustworthy.'

'Seven weeks, Cas – seven weeks since my father was last seen.'

'I don't deny that it's troubling,' Cas agreed.

'I read the second part of your *Observer* piece, by the way,' Derek said. 'You know, now that I'm in Ghana, I'm seeing the articles differently than I did back home when I read the first part. I think I owe you an apology about the way I spoke to you about it back then.'

'No, that's all right, Derek. You were justifiably concerned. I just wish there was something more I could do.'

'Thanks. There's very little either of us can do but see what the investigators turn up.'

'Keep me posted. I'm keeping my fingers crossed.'

When the call ended, Cas sat still and stared into the fireplace without seeing, somewhere between numb and terrified.

CHAPTER FORTY-FIVE

22nd May, Atimpoku, Ghana

It had rained hard overnight, leaving the ground sodden. Fortunately, Emma had on her jeans and trainers. This was no time for a skirt. Besides the rain, something else came down heavily last night: her period, and she was cramping. She didn't ever want to be a man, but every month around this time she had transitory fantasies of a menstrual-free life. She'd have to wait a few decades for that.

Having washed up with the few toiletries she had bought from a convenience store, Emma was ready at a little past six when Mr Labram arrived in his four-wheel drive Toyota Prado, which he parked on the street.

'From here, we can walk down to the shore to speak with some of the fishermen,' he explained to Emma.

They crossed the road and descended towards the river, coming to a cluster of four thatched huts and a brick building a few metres from the water's edge. Three traditional canoes and a modern dinghy with an outboard motor were pulled up on shore.

A kilometre or so northward, the graceful arc of the Adome Bridge spanned the Volta. Looking across to the other side, Emma marvelled at the breadth of the river. It was at once magnificent and daunting. How in the world could they ever recover a body from these vast waters – if it was there at all? It could be anywhere along the river's course.

A shirtless young man of about eighteen was leaning against one of the canoes as he repaired a fishing net.

'Good morning,' Labram greeted him in Ewe.

'Morning,' he replied.

Labram continued in Ewe, introducing himself and Emma and explaining their mission. The man, whose name was Solomon, looked puzzled.

'Please, wait one moment. I will call my father.'

Emma recognised Solomon's speech was unusual – the pronunciation rather childlike, and she understood at once that Solomon might have a mild mental deficit. He went inside the brick house and returned a few minutes later with his father, Zacharia, a fortyish version of his son.

With the customary pleasantries, Labram told Zacharia what he did in the area, and after a complicated conversation involving names of people who had lived and worked where and when, it turned out that they were probably related. After much laughter and palm slapping between the two men, Labram got down to business.

'My brother, Madam Emma here, is a detective in Accra,' he said to Zacharia, switching to Twi for Emma's benefit.

'Oh, very fine, madam,' Zacharia said, looking at Emma. 'You are welcome.'

'We need help finding someone,' Labram said.

'What is it about?' Zacharia asked with interest.

'At the end of March this year,' Emma began, 'one gentleman from America came to stay at the Riverview Inn.'

'Ah, OK,' Zacharia said.

'He was supposed to leave on the 3rd April, but when his driver came to pick him up and take him back to Accra, he had disappeared.'

Zacharia frowned. 'And up till now he is still missing?'

'Yes,' Emma said. 'Now, around two in the morning of that day, 3rd April, one woman in Atimpoku saw an SUV on the Adome Bridge and two guys removing something from the back of the vehicle that looked like a sack with a human body inside. They took it and threw it over the side of the bridge into the river.'

'*Oh!*' Zacharia exclaimed, pulling back his head as if someone had jabbed him in the eyes with a garden fork. 'Ah! These people, eh? How can they do this? Is it the American man they threw in the river?'

'We don't know for sure,' Emma said, 'but we need to find out, and if he's been thrown in the river, we must find his body. His son has come all the way from the States to look for his father, and we are trying to help him.'

'God bless you, madam,' Zacharia said. 'If the American was thrown into the river, then by all means the body will come to float on top of the water.'

'Even if they put rocks in the sack?' Emma asked.

'Yes,' Zacharia said with certainty. 'It will float. Madam, you know one thing is that now the water is not as deep as in the old days, because of less rain every year. So, by all means, if the body is in the river, I think it will come to rest at a shallow area. But it can also get stuck on the riverbed or in some weeds, so that also might delay it small.'

'OK,' Emma said. 'Please, how long have you been a fisherman?'

Zacharia laughed. 'Since I could walk. My father was a fisherman, and his father too.'

'Oh, nice,' Emma said.

'But the fishing life is not so good any more, oo,' he said, turning regretful. 'The river doesn't flow as fast as before, so weeds get a chance to grow.' He pointed far out. 'You can see where bush is growing in the middle of the river. Those are all weeds, and the fish hide inside the weeds. So, we can't get them the way we used to.'

'I'm sorry,' Emma said. 'It makes life hard for you.'

Zacharia was grim. 'Even, my wife says we should go to live in Accra.'

Emma tilted her head side to side. 'Well, Accra too . . . that's another problem place altogether.'

The three of them laughed, but Emma noticed Solomon's expression changed little, if any.

'Mr Zacharia,' she said, 'we are asking if you can tell your fellow fishermen all about this. They should look out for something like what I described – a dead body, or a sack with something inside. Anything unusual.'

'By all means, madam,' Zacharia said, nodding vigorously. 'I will start to look for something like that all around the weeds and the riverbanks near Adome Bridge. Please, give me your number in case I see or hear something. I will call you at once.'

Emma obliged, and Labram gave out his number as well. 'Your boy is very quiet,' Emma said, smiling at Solomon.

'Yes,' Zacharia said soberly. 'You know, he has some small problems. He finds it hard to communicate.'

'I understand.'

'But he fishes very well,' Zacharia said, brightening.

'Very good,' Emma said. She dug in her pocket and pulled out a couple of bills, which she handed to Zacharia. At this rate, she was going to have nothing left. 'Thank you, eh? We appreciate it very much if you can help us.'

'Not at all, madam,' he said. 'I also thank you, and God bless you. If I find anything out, anything at all, I will call you or Mr Labram for sure.'

CHAPTER FORTY-SIX

22nd May, Accra, Ghana

On the afternoon of his day off, Dazz Nunoo stopped for a couple of hours at Busy Internet on Ring Road to use their printing service. Having decided to find a part-time job to boost his family income, he had updated his résumé. He was hoping he could find a position with an upscale security company. While waiting for his copies, he looked around the large, warehouse-like space occupied by row upon row of computer terminals and every seat occupied by people of all shapes and sizes. But young men predominated – students and otherwise. Dazz wondered how many of the 'otherwise' were *sakawa* boys, and with some grim amusement visualised himself walking down the aisle to ask each of them who was their overseas *mugu* of the day.

Résumé copies in hand, he stepped out of the air-conditioned environment into the humid warmth of the afternoon. Heavy, dark clouds gathering in the northern sky promised rain in short order and Dazz, like all bona fide Accra residents who pointedly reject the use of umbrellas, hoped he would reach home before he got wet. He hurried to the lorry park just before the Ring Road flyover, passing the Samsung electronics store he had once visited and promptly left on seeing the eye-popping prices. Now he slowed down as he spotted Courage, his SWAT buddy, exiting the store with two employees who were carrying a large rectangular box emblazoned on the side with the words, SAMSUNG SMART TV 52". They carted it to the bed of Courage's pickup lorry and secured it with cables. Wow, Dazz thought, a 52-inch Samsung? That ran a pretty penny.

Courage spotted Dazz and called out. '*Ei, chaley!* How be?' They gave each other a man hug.

'What!' Dazz said. 'You dey buy flat screen? Heh!'

Courage laughed with glee, showing every one of his teeth. 'Oh, *chaley*, yeah. Dis no be just flat, oo, i'be smart too!'

They guffawed and slapped palms.

'Wow, congrats!' Dazz said. 'When you go 'vite me your crib watch am small?'

'Oh, anytime, *chaley*, dis Saturday se'f. No, Sunday be better. Saturday, I get date with Emma.'

Dazz put his hand to his open mouth in mock astonishment. 'Already! *Ei*, you no dey waste time, *koraa*!'

More laughter, but Dazz added, 'But treat her well, OK? Emma, she's not a loose woman at all, so don't be trying to bed her, OK? You'll disgrace yourself.'

'Never you worry. I'm a gentleman.'

'For sure,' Dazz said, clapping his colleague on the shoulder.

'OK, boss, make I go now for house to install the TV.'

'No problem. You dey work tomorrow?'

'Yeah.'

'Cool. Tomorrow, then.'

Dazz was smiling as Courage departed, but he couldn't deny that he felt a twinge of envy over that 52-inch.

CHAPTER FORTY-SEVEN

Before Emma returned to Accra, her last call was the Akosombo Police Station, where Labram introduced Emma to the station commander, Inspector Bawa, a short man in his late forties.

'You are welcome, madam,' he said to Emma, smiling. 'Mr Labram and I have known each other for years.'

'Bawa, Emma is from Yemo Sowah's detective agency in Accra,' Labram said. 'They are investigating the disappearance of the American man.'

'Good, good,' Bawa said with enthusiasm. 'I wish you all the very best of luck. It's a big mystery. I'm sorry but I don't have any new information to give you. I wish I did.'

'Thank you, Inspector,' Emma said. 'We went to alert the fishermen in case they see anything.'

'Good idea. I hope your efforts are fruitful. Please, if you need any assistance, let me or Mr Labram know and we will try to help.'

Labram dropped Emma off at the junction and she

waded through the madness to find the right *tro-tro* back to the Accra station. From there she went directly back to work and to Sowah's office.

'Welcome back,' he said. 'Have a seat and tell me about the trip.'

Emma told him about the meeting with Zacharia. 'I think he's a solid man and he has promised to search around the riverbanks and other areas. I trust he will be alert to anything resembling a corpse and let us know. We also paid a visit to the Akosombo Police Station and talked to Inspector Bawa there.'

'Nice job, Emma.'

'Thank you, sir. And how is your foot now?'

'Much better, thanks. My doctor gave me some medicine for it.'

'OK, good,' Emma said. She hesitated. 'Sir, I need to let you know about something. I wanted to do it earlier, but I couldn't find the right moment. You see, I have a stepbrother called Bruno. My father never liked him and threw him out of the house many years ago. Since that time, he has been living on the streets, even getting in trouble sometimes.'

'I see,' Sowah said, even though it was clear he was waiting for the bottom line.

'But still,' Emma continued, 'we are close with each other. I like him very much, but what troubles me is that he can never seem to hold a steady job, and on top of that, Bruno has been hanging around some of these *sakawa* boys.'

'Ah,' Sowah said, light slowly dawning.

'OK,' Emma continued, 'so, I had an idea to find out if he had heard anything about Mr Tilson from some of the *sakawa* boys he has been associating with. I called him last night, and first he said he didn't know anything about it, but in the end he confessed he did, although he didn't want to personally tell me what he knows exactly. Instead he suggested we talk to the investigative journalist—'

'Sana Sana,' Sowah said, finishing her sentence.

'Yes, sir.'

'Interesting.' Sowah was staring at her, but it was a gaze lost in thought. 'So, does that mean Bruno is in contact with Sana?'

'Well, I think so, but Bruno neither confirmed nor denied, sir. All he kept saying was, "Ask Sana. He knows about everything." Do you want me to keep pushing him, sir?'

Sowah shook his head. 'I don't think we should alienate him – I don't know Bruno, and it looks like you have a good rapport with him, but we want to be able to go back to him if needed. No, I think we should act immediately on his tip without worrying him any further. I know Sana, and in fact, I'm remiss in not thinking of asking him about this. He's difficult to locate, but I will find him.'

'Yes, sir.'

'You've done some solid work in the past two days, Emma,' Sowah said soberly. 'Well done.'

She felt pride swell in her chest. 'Thank you, sir. Please, do you wish me to follow up something today?'

'Yes. The driver, Yahya. He was the first one we know of who arrived at the Riverview after Mr Tilson had disappeared. It's important we speak to him in person. See if you can meet him somewhere. We don't only want to know if he saw anything of interest there – a vehicle or a person coming away from the house, for example – but we also want to see his demeanour. Does he seem to be hiding anything? And so forth.'

'Yes, sir. I will do that.'

CHAPTER FORTY-EIGHT

At first, Yahya declined to meet up with Emma. 'Some lady detective has already come to ask me questions,' he said tersely on the phone.

So, the police *had* done some work, Emma noted to herself. 'Was it Detective Inspector Damptey who talked to you?' she asked.

'Yes, that one,' he said without enthusiasm. 'Are you working with her?'

'Not at all,' Emma said, explaining the difference between the agency and the GPS. 'Where do you live, sir?'

'Maamobi,' he responded. It was one of Accra's *Zongo* neighbourhoods – home to predominantly Muslim, Hausa-speaking inhabitants.

'Are you from Upper East Region?' Emma asked, taking a guess as she tried to warm him up.

'Bolga,' he said.

'I love Bolgatanga,' she said, even though she'd never been there. Much poorer than their southern sisters, cities of the north were often given short shrift.

'Is that so?' he said, with new interest in his voice. 'When did you go there?'

'Three years now,' Emma said without a second's thought. That she was lying with such facility was a little disturbing. 'Please, my battery is getting low, so can I meet you somewhere in Maamobi to talk? I'm not far away at all.'

He hesitated and gave a short sigh. 'OK. Do you know Maamobi General Hospital?'

'Of course.'

They agreed to meet outside the hospital in a couple of hours. *Now*, Emma thought, crossing her fingers, *if only he'll show up*.

Outside the hospital, a tree with buttress roots provided Emma and Yahya both shade and somewhere to sit. He was a little man, thirtyish, deeply black, and clearly dejected.

'They sacked me from my job,' he told Emma.

'Oh!' she exclaimed. 'Sorry. What happened?'

He shrugged. 'Ah, they said because the white man became missing – the one I took to Akosombo – it was my responsibility to keep him safe, so it's my fault.'

'Ah!' Emma exclaimed in indignation. 'How is it your fault?'

'Don't mind them,' Yahya said, angry now. 'It's because one of the other drivers didn't like me and he's the boss's boyfriend. Just looking for an excuse to sack me.'

'I see,' Emma said. 'What a shame. So, are you looking for a new position somewhere?'

He nodded. 'Trying to get another driver job. But the market these days? Hm, is not easy, madam.'

True, Emma reflected, the economy did seem stagnant. No money in the system, or more accurately, unequally distributed.

'What happened that morning when you went to pick up Mr Tilson to take him back to Accra?' she asked Yahya.

'Mr Tilson told me he want to leave at seven,' he said, 'so I arrive there by six-fifty. I text him say I'm waiting for him outside, but he don't reply. By five past seven, I went and knock on the door, but no answer. So, I call him on the phone. No answer again. So, I try the door and it's open. I went inside but no one is there. His bags – everything gone.'

'How many bags did he bring with him?'

'Two – a small one for his clothes and another for his laptop.'

'And his mobile phone and laptop were gone too?'

'Yes please.'

It could have been a robbery gone awry, Emma supposed, but she really didn't think so.

'I thought maybe he decide to get another car service,' Yahya continued, 'but why should he do that? I had Mr Labram number, so I call him and he came down. He was axing me, "Oh, did I see any other car here when I arrived?" and I say no. Even, I call my boss and ask her if any complaint or maybe Mr Tilson tell her he want a different driver, but she tell me nothing like that have happened.' Gaze downward, defeated, Yahya wiped his perspiring face and shaved head with a ragged washcloth.

Emma thought of Kafui's description of the SUV on the Adome Bridge. 'What kind of vehicle were you using to transport Mr Tilson?'

'Toyota 4×4.'

'What colour was it, please?'

'Black one.'

'OK,' she said. That would also fit Kafui's description.

Yahya looked up in some distress. 'Madam, I don't have anything to do with the *oburoni* make lost. For what reason? He was paying the company, paying my food and lodging every day and for that I will kill him and take his things? *No!* That lady detective Damptey over and over again she was axing me if I robbed the man and killed him and then buried him somewhere. *Ah!* How possible?' Yahya gestured at his body. 'Look! Do you see any muscles that I can kill this fat American man?'

'Did Madam Doris question you in person?'

Yahya shook his head. 'She call me on the phone. Mr Labram give her my number.'

'Did you know Mr Labram before now?'

'Yes, yes,' Yahya said. 'I know him well. We have been taking tourists to that Riverview house long time now.'

Was it remotely possible that the two men on the bridge had been Labram and Yahya, and the SUV could have belonged to either Labram or to Yahya's vehicle rental company? Both men had unimpeded opportunities to commit the crime, but what would be their *motive*? You don't amputate the hand that feeds you: Mr Tilson was a potential returning customer for both men. It simply didn't make sense.

'Do you know Kweku Ponsu?' Emma asked, trying another angle.

'The fetish priest?'

'Yes.'

Yahya came close to an eye-roll. 'Foolish man. I don't like him at all. He's a fake. If you want to see people with real power, come to Tamale or Bolga.'

Emma smiled. 'But do you know Ponsu personally?'

Yahya shook his head vigorously. 'I know where he live in Atimpoku, but that's all.'

'Did Mr Tilson ask you anything about Kweku Ponsu?'

Yahya nodded. 'Yes. First, Mr Tilson axe me questions about *sakawa*. I told him what I know – that they use juju to make money on computer and all that. Then he axe me if I know where Kweku Ponsu live and if I can take him there because he want to talk business with him.'

This is promising, Emma thought. 'Did you? Take him?'

'Yes, and I stay with him there because the customer is my responsibility.'

'I understand you,' Emma said. 'And so, Mr Tilson, did he meet with Ponsu?'

'Yes.'

'Do you remember the day?'

'Either 30th or 31st March.'

'What happened over there?'

'Ponsu's *macho men*, those twin guys, took us into his house to greet him. Mr Tilson axe him some questions.'

'What kind of questions?'

'About *sakawa* boys. And, if these big police people take part in *sakawa* too.'

Ah, interesting, Emma thought. 'And how did Ponsu answer the questions?'

Yahya grunted. 'First, he didn't say anything, then Mr Tilson gave him some money, but Ponsu still don't talk. Then Tilson get annoyed, and he say everyone lie to him and Ponsu challenge him to ask him if Tilson is calling him a liar too. Then, Tilson too, he tell Ponsu he doesn't fear him at all, and Ponsu say, "You should fear plenty other people before me." Tilson didn't understand him, but Ponsu just laugh and say, "White man, you will see." I tell Mr Tilson to relax small and we should go, otherwise plenty trouble start and those twins can beat us if we don't take care. So, we left from there, and the white man don't say anything after that.'

This was terrific information. 'Anything else you can tell me?' Emma asked.

'No please, madam,' he responded. Oddly, though, Emma caught the slightest shift in his gaze.

'Mr Yahya, thank you very much for all your help.'

They stood up simultaneously and shook hands. Emma gave him a few *cedis* – practically all she had left on her person – considering his plight and his cooperation. When they parted, Emma was certain Yahya had had nothing to do with Gordon Tilson's disappearance. Besides that, Yahya had supplied very important information: Tilson had indeed had a highly confrontational encounter with Ponsu, and Ponsu had said something that could well have been a threat to Tilson: 'White man, you will see.'

Emma saw Yahya as one of the 'good guys'. Just one thing bothered her a little. She wondered about that last subtle but visible change in Yahya's expression. Was he not telling Emma something?

CHAPTER FORTY-NINE

22nd May, Accra, Ghana

It was almost the end of Friday and DCOP Laryea was looking forward to spending some time with his grandchildren when the phone call came in. It was Commissioner Andoh and he wanted to speak to Laryea. Now.

Laryea went up the stairs as quickly as possible, which was decidedly slower than when he was a young man, oh so long ago. He knocked on the director-general's door and entered.

'Laryea,' Andoh said, signalling him to a chair at the side of his desk. 'I finished meeting with the IGP about an hour ago. He's concerned about this Tilson case – the American man.'

'Yes, I know of it, sir. It's DI Damptey handling it – under Chief Superintendent Quaino.'

'I want you to look into this. What are those two doing? It's almost two months since the American man has been missing, not so? What's going on? They need to give you a full update on the progress on Monday and I want your supervision thereafter.'

'No problem,' Laryea said. 'I will take care of it.'

'This is beginning to look bad,' Andoh grumbled. 'You know, Ghana's reputation is suffering with these increasing stories of Europeans and Americans defrauded of money by *sakawa* boys and the like. A lot of videos on YouTube now.'

'Yes, sir.'

'Now,' Andoh said, 'President Bannerman has given the IGP the task of cracking down on Internet fraud. Once he comes up with the blueprint, he will set up a summit to unveil the plan.'

'Yes, sir, I see,' Laryea said. 'Very good. I pray we succeed with this.'

Andoh nodded, but absently. After a pause, he said, 'But I hope we will see more than the customary lip service that we've experienced in the past.'

'We have to be serious about it, yes, sir.'

'And the question is whether we have the right people in place to implement these plans. You know, poor leadership leads to poor results.'

Laryea wasn't exactly sure to whom Andoh was referring specifically, and he was loath to ask.

'We have some hypocrites in high positions, Laryea,' he said with a surprising amount of bitterness. 'I won't name names, but they know themselves. They are just yes-men, puppets doing the president's bidding.'

'Yes, sir.' That's about as far as Laryea would commit himself.

'So that is it. I will let you know of any new developments. And of course, you know everything said in this room is to remain confidential.'

'But of course, sir.'

'How is the family?'

'Doing well, sir. Thank you, sir.'

Andoh smiled. 'That's good. Well, have a good weekend.'

As Laryea returned to his office to pack up for the weekend, he wondered what or whom the DG had been speaking of in his outburst, as cryptic as it was, when he talked about hypocrites, yes-men, and puppets in high places. The IGP? Did Andoh hold some grudge against Mr Akrofi?

Laryea dismissed the thought. It wasn't any of his business, and besides, he would never want to be caught up in that kind of contention. There was enough disarray at the CID as it was.

CHAPTER FIFTY

23rd May

Saturday night, Emma was undecided about what looked best with her skinny black jeans for her date with Courage. She was no fashion maven, and her closet was sparse – apart from the blunt truth that she was behind on her washing. The pile of dirty clothes in the corner was appalling.

She could go with a white sleeveless blouse or a filmy fuchsia long-sleeve shirt. She tried both on, watching her reflection in the full-length mirror as she made a 360-degree turn. Thin as she was, she could pull the outfit off OK, but she still thought she could afford to put a few curves and a couple of kilos on her frame.

Just as she settled on the sleeveless, her phone buzzed, and she had to dig under a pile of vetoed outfits on the bed before she located it. Courage was texting her to say he would be there in about ten minutes. Emma was just about ready, but should she go outside now, or wait for him to arrive first? She decided on the latter, stepping out the door only when he texted that he had arrived.

Courage, dressed in all black, was at the roadside standing next to a shiny, dark Rav4. 'You look so lovely, dear,' he said, as he opened the passenger door for her.

'Thanks,' she said. 'So do you.'

'You are so nice to say so. Thank you.'

He had on a strong but nice fragrance, which reminded Emma she had forgotten to put on any of her own.

As they headed south towards town, Emma thought Courage drove as crazily as a taxi driver.

'Where are we going?' she asked, holding on to the passenger armrest.

'Afrikiko,' he said, flashing a smile at her. 'Do you know there?'

'I've heard of it,' she said, 'but I've never been.'

'You'll enjoy it,' he said. 'Do you dance?'

'Not at all.'

'Don't worry. I'll teach you.'

Emma felt that mixture of excitement at the prospect of dancing and dread of 'looking funny' doing it.

'This is a nice car,' she said. 'It smells new.'

'Thanks. Yes, it's about six months old now.'

'I'm impressed,' Emma said, wondering where he found that kind of money.

She wasn't expecting Latin music at Afrikiko, but apparently Saturday was Latin night. Who knew there was such a thing in Ghana? Emma wasn't used to it – and certainly not at that ear-splitting volume. She could hear some similarities of the music to traditional Ghanaian highlife – the type her grandparents listened to, not the new stuff. Chairs and tables were arranged around a slightly elevated wood stage where couples danced away. It was obvious who the regulars were. They twirled and whirled in dazzling choreographic displays of agility that amazed Emma. Both she and Courage ordered non-alcoholic drinks. When they were through with the first round, Courage said, 'Let's dance.'

Emma opened her mouth to decline, but before she could say a word, Courage had her on her feet and they were nudging their way onto the crowded stage. They found a space, and Courage began to teach Emma to tango. She managed to make out his shouted instructions above the music.

At first, she was awful and got frustrated quickly by her clumsiness, but he was patient with her, and when she finally made her first turn, she found it exhilarating. After two numbers, she was dripping with sweat from her efforts while Courage was dry as a bone. They stopped for another drink and Courage ordered them a meal – goat kebabs for himself and Thai fried rice for Emma. She couldn't help noticing his wallet stuffed tight with fifty-*cedi* bills. Where was all this money coming from, or was he just trying to impress her?

After a couple of hours at Afrikiko, Courage took Emma to an ice cream parlour on Oxford Street in Osu. They sat outside on the open patio. The night was still humid, but it had cooled off a little. The club across the street was playing music, but not too loud that they couldn't talk at normal levels. Emma's ears were ringing slightly from

Afrikiko, and she was thankful for the relative quiet.

'So why don't you have a boyfriend?' Courage said, licking the rim of his strawberry cone.

She spluttered, taken by surprise. 'What?'

'You heard me,' he said. 'Attractive woman like you – why should you not have a man?'

'I'm not sure I'm that attractive,' she said.

'You are a whole lot lovelier than you realise. And anyway, you're supposed to say thank you, not try and reverse the compliment.'

'You're right,' she said. 'Bad habit. Thank you very much.'

'You are welcome.' He smiled. 'You still didn't answer my question.'

Emma shrugged. 'Basically, I don't know.'

'Really,' he said, apparently not satisfied with her response.

'Now it's your turn,' Emma said, adopting his tactics. 'Where's your girlfriend?'

He laughed, showing his nice set of teeth. 'She's now my ex – over a year now. I've just been dating, but I'd like to settle down sometime soon.'

She spooned up a mouthful of vanilla ice cream. 'That's good.' She realised she wasn't giving him much conversation fodder.

'Let's watch a movie tonight,' he suggested. 'I have a 52-inch TV at home.'

52 inch! 'Are you rich or something?' she asked.

He smiled and shook his head. 'I just know how to make use of my talents.'

'What does that mean?'

He continued the enigmatic smile. 'I'll tell you one day. Maybe. So, will you come to my place to watch a movie?'

Emma said, 'No, thank you. I have church tomorrow – the early service.'

'Really?' He looked at her askance.

'You don't have to believe me if you don't want to,' she said, amused.

'OK then. I believe you.'

Emma wanted to switch the general tenor of their exchange. 'There's something I'd like to ask you in turn.'

'OK.'

'What do you know about DI Doris Damptey?'

Courage looked disappointed. 'So, we have to talk about work?'

'Sorry. After this, I won't talk about it again.'

'Damptey?' He chortled with disdain. 'Every once in a while, that woman organises raids on *sakawa* boys just to look good to Director-General Andoh. Apart from that, she is one of the laziest women I know.'

'How does she get away with it?'

'A lot of people get away with laziness at CID,' Courage said with a smirk. 'In her case, she's sleeping with her boss, DCS Quaino, so she can do almost whatever she likes. Or nothing at all.'

Emma's spoon stopped halfway to her mouth. 'Sleeping with her DCS? How do you know that?'

'Open secret,' he said. 'Lots of people know, but no one says anything.'

'Does the director-general know, do you think?'

'He might,' Courage said, 'but you know the highest-ranking officers prefer to stay out of the gutter with this kind of thing, or else they just look the other way.'

Emma shook her head and shuddered, which made Courage chuckle. 'Why the shivers?'

'Your boss should never sleep with you. Ever. And I suppose DCS Quaino is married.'

'But of course! I've seen his wife at some of the events SWAT covers.'

'So, they're committing adultery as well.'

'It happens all the time,' he said. 'Maybe you've never been in that situation before, but believe me, when it comes around you may find yourself powerless.'

Emma immediately had a flashback to Director-General Andoh's assault on her and she felt ill. Her appetite for ice cream vanished.

'What's wrong?' Courage asked, noticing the change in her mood.

'Sorry,' Emma said despondently. 'I don't feel very well.'

Courage was concerned. 'Is it what we ate at the club?'

Emma shook her head. 'No, it's not that. Would you mind if we leave now?'

'No, problem.' Courage leapt from his chair and extended his date a helping hand.

CHAPTER FIFTY-ONE

DCS Quaino loved DI Damptey's big, overbearing body, her fat thighs and tremendous buttocks, and when she dressed in one of the dominatrix outfits her cousin had brought her from Amsterdam, he went crazy. Tonight, as she burst out of the bathroom in a red, see-through halter dress with strappy, elastic, webbed suspenders, black fishnet stockings, stiletto heels, and a tiny triangle of black patent leather over the entrance to her pleasure grotto, Quaino's eyeballs almost exploded from their sockets and he gurgled with excitement. For what had seemed an eternity, he had been lying on the bed waiting for her to emerge in all her glory. They had checked into Labadi Beach Hotel early that evening, he into 321, she into 418, and then he had joined her in her room. As far as their respective spouses were concerned, the two officers were on a highly confidential stakeout that was likely to go all night – don't wait up.

And Doris had a black whip. My God, that whip made Quaino's heart beat as if it was trying to break out of his chest. He lay spread-eagled on the bed in his boxers watching her every move as she sashayed around the bed. Her body was bursting out of its outfit – not in a curvy way, but as an undifferentiated mass of flesh, and he loved it.

She stood at the side of the bed and gave him a poke in the ribs with the end of her whip. 'You may speak.'

'Yes please, my Queen.'

'*Heh!*' she snapped. 'So, you don't know how to address me? How do you address me?'

'Em, is it my Queen?' he said, cringing.

'*Your Majesty!*' she bellowed.

'Yes, yes, Your Majesty. Please, I'm sorry. I beg you, don't punish me, Your Majesty.'

'You will *have* to be punished,' she sneered. 'You must be punished.'

'I beg you, oo, Your Majesty! I beg you.'

'I will whip you very well on your bottom.'

'Ohh, no please. Your Majesty. Have mercy on me.'

'Turn over on your stomach. Hurry up! I said, *turn over*.'

Whimpering, he obeyed.

'Pull down your shorts, you miserable subject!'

He shimmied out of them, exposing his round, bulbous buttocks.

'How do you call me?' she growled.

'Your Highness.'

'*No!*' She struck him across the buttocks, and he jumped and cried out. 'How do you call me?'

'Your Lordship.'

Whack!

'My Queen.'

Whack! Whack!

Quaino howled in exquisite ecstasy. 'My Lady.'

She hit him again and again. He was sobbing and laughing at the same time. 'No please, please, please.'

'Turn over,' she commanded.

'Yes please. Your Majesty.'

'*Ei!*' she exclaimed as he faced upward. 'Did I permit you to display such an egregious erection of your male organ?'

'No,' he stammered. 'No please, Your Majesty.'

'What is this thing, eh?' she said, softly stroking his tumescence. 'I think I have to punish it. How should I punish it?'

'Your Majesty,' he whispered, 'whatever pleases Your Majesty.'

She dropped the whip and clambered on the bed to straddle him. 'Like this?'

'Yes, Your Majesty,' he said, close to tears of joy.

'Don't touch me!' she said as he tried to reach for her body. She leant forward and pinned his hands at the side of his head while she bounced on him like a flabby rubber ball.

'You like to be punished, you bad man,' she said. 'Bad man.'

He began to tense. 'Yes, I like to be punished, Your Majesty.'

'Don't ejaculate in me,' she warned.

'No, no,' he muttered, just as he began to convulse. He struggled to pull out just in time.

He let out one last moan and fell asleep almost instantly.

Doris rolled off him and propped herself on her elbow to observe him snoring. 'Men,' she said, shaking her head. 'Hopeless.'

Early in the morning while it was still dark, Quaino rolled over, opened his eyes, and stared at the ceiling.

'DI Damptey,' he said.

She popped her head up. 'Yes, boss?'

'Sit up. I need to talk to you.'

'Yes please,' she said, scrambling upright in bed.

'We are in a little bit of hot water,' Quaino said.

'Please, meaning?'

'Yesterday at close of business, DCOP Laryea called me about your case – the missing American. He's getting pressure from Director-General Andoh, and he in turn is feeling the heat from the IGP. Laryea wants to see both of us on Monday.'

'Oh,' she said. That was serious.

'Yes,' Quaino said. 'And you know Laryea doesn't joke around. I fear him more than the director-general.'

'Yes please.'

'I haven't checked with you about the case lately,' Quaino said, worried. 'Are you about to make any arrest?'

'Arrest?' She went hot in the face. 'Not as yet.'

'Why not?' he said.

'I'm still working on it.'

'We have to get something – somebody,' Quaino said, 'by Monday morning.'

'We don't have any evidence tying anyone to the crime,'

she stammered. 'I don't even know where the American is.'

He grunted and they stayed silent awhile. Now he sat up. 'But we *do* have evidence!' he said. 'It has been staring us in the face. Come on, get dressed. We have an arrest to make.'

CHAPTER FIFTY-TWO

24th May

Sunday morning, Emma was dragging because of her late night, but she still got up early for the 8 a.m. church service, which was the short one – an hour. The 11 a.m. service ran into three hours and then there was additional Bible study after that.

In the *tro-tro*, Emma reflected on last night. Yes, she had to admit she had enjoyed herself more than she had in a long while. As for Courage, well, she wasn't too sure about him yet. Much too early to say. She would wait and see, but she wasn't in a hurry for anything serious, and as for sex – well, he could forget about that altogether.

Anyway, today was a new day, and Emma didn't want to dwell much on the events of the evening. Right now, she was eager to get to the Autism Centre to try out the new Samsung tablets Mrs Akrofi had donated. When Emma arrived, Grace, another volunteer, was outside supervising four children.

'Morning, Emma,' she said. 'Kojo is inside with Auntie Rose.'

Emma found Rose feeding the boy breakfast, a slow and laborious process, since Kojo didn't like eating and had limited food preferences.

Rose was glad to see Emma. 'How are you, dear?'

'I'm good, thank you, Auntie,' she said. 'Would you like me to take over?'

'Yes please,' she said with relief. 'I'm going to church, now.'

'No problem,' Emma said, sitting down next to Kojo, who had begun rocking. 'Kojo. Less back and forth, OK?'

Twenty arduous minutes later, Kojo had cleaned his cereal and fruit plates. 'Good job,' Emma said. 'Let's wipe our mouths. You remember?'

Kojo flapped his hands multiple times.

'Here you are,' Emma said, handing him a napkin. The boy wiped his mouth, but barely.

'OK,' Emma said, laughing. 'Good enough.'

She unlocked the cabinet with the tablets while Kojo stood in the middle of the floor repetitively rubbing the thumb of his right hand against his fingers.

All the tablets were enclosed in solid, thick protective jackets and a screen protector. The kids were instant wreckers of anything delicate – especially expensive electronic devices.

'Come, big man,' Emma said. 'Here, sit next to me.'

She placed all the tablets on the table in front of her and Kojo let out a few short, piercing shrieks.

'Stay cool,' Emma said. 'OK, let's explore.'

Three of the tablets were the same, but the fourth was different in that it had a stylus pen for drawing on the screen. She doubted Kojo would take much to that, since he'd hardly ever been drawn to paper and pencil, but it might be worth the try.

A free autism aid app designed by a group of Ghanaians a couple of years ago was available, but no one had downloaded it onto any of the devices. Two tablets were almost out of battery power, so Emma plugged them in and began the download. The other two had enough juice for now, including the one with the pen. She set the latter where Kojo could reach it and at the same time tried out the stylus. At first, it was an odd experience drawing on the slick screen – nothing like sketching on paper. On the side of the tablet were several icons to change the thickness and texture of the lines. Emma valued these donations from the IGP's wife, but she felt the drawing tablet was a little too advanced for any of the children here and she could see the stylus pen being destroyed in a matter of days.

Kojo made a noise and reached for the stylus.

'OK, but be careful,' Emma said.

Left-handed, Kojo began scribbling a few lines, his head bent studiously over the screen.

Emma checked the other devices, where the pace of the downloads was agonising. She was pretty sure the Wi-Fi at the centre was still only 3G. She noted how still Kojo was sitting and how focused he was on his task. It was unusual for him. As the minutes passed, Emma followed the strokes of his hands in growing incredulity.

He had even figured out how to use the digital eraser. A head was taking shape, and then the body of a woman.

'Who is that you're drawing?' she whispered.

He had found colour on the app, which Emma hadn't even yet discovered. She held her breath and slipped her mobile phone out of her pocket. She began to video Kojo as he was sketching a head of hair, large eyes, and a big smile. For thirty minutes, Kojo did his work and Emma recorded.

'Grace?' she called out, her voice cracking. '*Grace!*'

She ran in from outside. 'What's wrong?'

Emma pointed at the tablet. Kojo had put down the stylus and was rocking.

Grace came around to their side. 'It looks like . . . It looks a little like Auntie Rose,' she said, looking at Emma and then at Kojo. 'Who drew it? You?'

'No, *he* did,' Emma said.

His drawing was not an exact likeness of Auntie, but it was recognisably her. For a while, Emma and Grace stared at it in silence.

'But he's never done anything like this before, has he?' Grace said.

'Not that I know of,' Emma said. 'Auntie Rose would have talked about it if she had seen it before.'

'What about Abena?' Grace suggested. 'Let's check with her. Maybe she's seen Kojo draw at home but hasn't attached much significance to it.'

'I doubt that very much,' Emma said, picking up her phone from the table. 'But I'll call her now. I'm sure this is going to be as much a surprise to her.'

CHAPTER FIFTY-THREE

DCOP Cleophus Laryea was very fond of his nephew Inspector Dazz Nunoo, who was much more like a son to him. Dazz had benefitted from his uncle's high position in the GPS, not for lack of intelligence or talent, but just because it never hurt to have a senior officer help steer you up the river of promotion. The current was *always* against you.

Most Sundays after church, Dazz would come over to Uncle Cleo's spacious house in Cantonments for lunch. Today, the two men's wives had left on an outing with Dazz's two young daughters. Uncle and nephew sat on the cool back porch to relax and drink beer.

Laryea had some news for his nephew. 'IGP Akrofi has asked me to join President Bannerman's task force on elimination of corruption.'

'Congrats!' Dazz said. 'You must be happy about that, Uncle Cleo. You've wanted something like that for a long time.'

'These commissions and task forces on corruption have come and gone,' Cleo said, wiping a line of beer foam from his upper lip, 'but this may be the first of our presidents who is deadly serious about it. Others have merely paid lip service.'

'Let's hope it works this time,' Dazz said. 'But what if Bannerman doesn't get back in power?'

'He's almost certain to. Evans-Aidoo, the standard bearer of the opposing party, is dead. His running mate doesn't have anywhere near Aidoo's magnetism.'

'That's certain.'

'How is the Panther Unit treating you?' Laryea asked.

'Everything is fine, Uncle.'

Laryea rose as his phone began to ring from somewhere in the sitting room. It took some searching to locate it under a pile of newspapers. It was Yemo Sowah calling.

'*Ei*, Yemo!' Laryea said. 'Good morning! I'm doing well, and you?'

Both men slipped into Ga, their mutual mother tongue. Laryea wandered back to the patio as he was talking and sat down again. They chatted as old friends about this and that.

'I've been meaning to ask you how Emma Djan has been working out at the agency,' Laryea asked, as the conversation drifted inevitably towards work – something they tried, and always failed, not to do.

'She's very good,' Sowah said. 'Thank you for referring her to me. I'm grateful.'

'Did she ever reveal the real reason she left CID?' Laryea asked.

'No,' Sowah answered, 'and because of what you told me about her meeting with the commissioner, I didn't ask her. You and I both know the rumours concerning Andoh and young female recruits. I pray nothing untoward happened to Emma in that regard. If she wants to talk about it, I'm happy to listen. Apart from that, I think it would be too awkward to ask about it.'

'Agreed,' Laryea said. 'What cases are keeping you busy these days?'

'You've heard about this American man – Tilson – who has disappeared?'

'Yes, I have. He came to Ghana supposedly to meet a woman he met online – or someone he thought was a woman. I'm curious how you came to be on that case, because our DI Damptey is also working on it.'

'Tilson's son, Derek, came to us,' Sowah explained. 'He was dissatisfied with the way Damptey was responding – or not, I should say.'

'I see,' Laryea said. 'DI Damptey can be sluggish. I'll find out what's going on. Meanwhile, if you learn anything that you can share with CID, I would appreciate hearing about it.'

'Of course, my friend. Well, as you mention it, there *was* something. We have reason to believe Mr Tilson paid a visit to Kweku Ponsu, the fetish priest, a few days before his disappearance, but we don't know what the purpose of the visit was.'

Laryea frowned. 'Ponsu? What would Tilson have to do with him?'

'That's the question, my brother. When I find out, I will let you know.' They wished each other a nice Sunday and a productive upcoming week.

'That was Yemo Sowah,' Laryea told Dazz.

'I gathered,' Dazz said. 'So, you know something about Emma Djan leaving CID and joining Sowah's agency?'

'Long story,' Laryea said cryptically.

Dazz smiled, aware he wouldn't get anything more than that out of his uncle. 'I saw her a few days ago while we were on SWAT duty at Kempinski Hotel,' he said. 'She was working on that case, the American guy – Tilson? I'm not altogether familiar with the story. What happened, exactly?'

'Well, that's the question,' Laryea said. 'The gentleman lives in the US and was duped by one of these online romance scams. He came to Ghana supposedly to meet the woman he had fallen in love with, only to discover she doesn't exist. Instead of returning home, Tilson decided to stay in Ghana for some time. But as of 3rd April, he has disappeared.'

Dazz raised his eyebrows. '3rd April? That's a long time to be missing.'

His uncle nodded. 'I fear he may have got into trouble. Yemo was telling me on the phone that he has reason to believe Tilson intended to pay a visit to Kweku Ponsu.'

Dazz frowned. 'Ponsu? For what?'

'That's what we don't know, but if we put two and

two together, we know Ponsu deals with these so-called *sakawa* scammer guys, so could it be that Mr Tilson went to talk to him about that and then got into trouble?'

'Ponsu should be questioned,' Dazz said. 'Who has the case?'

'DI Damptey.'

Dazz palmed his forehead. 'Oh, God.'

'Yes, her. DCS Quaino is her direct superior.'

'I'm not sure that helps,' Dazz said with a snort. 'What is going on with those two?'

Laryea glowered. 'I prefer not to think about it. We have a lot of dead wood floating around CID – people I would love to get rid of but can't. More than ever, we need smarter and smarter police officers. To an extent, I think that's happening slowly at CID. We have more university graduates than before and along with improved technology, I believe crime will suffer.'

'Is Ghana becoming more violent?' Dazz asked.

Laryea said, 'It's only recently that the police service has begun digitising crime statistics, so at first glance, armed robbery, rape, and murder might appear to be increasing, but it may be a function of improved records. We'll need a few years to study the trends. What worries me is a possible increase in crime sophistication. For example, the assassination of Bernard Evans-Aidoo. That was a deadly, pre-planned attack by an expert marksman.'

'Who is investigating?'

'Technically, CID in conjunction with the Bureau of

National Intelligence. But the BNI, as usual, is trying to dominate.'

'Who do they suspect, do you know?' Dazz asked.

'No, I don't, but the implications of a sniper eliminating the one threat to President Bannerman are dire. This is no small boy acting on his own. It's more like a killing contracted by someone high up.'

'But a sniper, Uncle?' Dazz said. 'Where would someone like that come from?'

'The BNI says they have reason to believe there could be secret assassins-for-hire in the ranks of military and SWAT units,' Laryea replied.

Dazz frowned. 'Seriously?'

'Yes,' Laryea said, his jaw hardening. 'So, bear that in mind. I'm not asking you to spy on your SWAT colleagues, but, you know, just be alert.'

'Well, if I hear anything,' Dazz said cautiously, 'I'll let you know.' He hoped he *never* heard anything.

'I don't want to put you in any awkward position, though,' Laryea said quickly, as if reading his nephew's mind.

'I understand, Uncle Cleo,' Dazz said. He hurried to fill the slightly awkward silence. 'How much would an assassination job pay?'

'Upward of three thousand *cedis*.'

'Wow,' Dazz said. 'Impressive.'

'So, if I notice you buying a whole lot of expensive toys,' Laryea said, winking at him, 'I'll have questions.'

Dazz laughed. 'Don't worry, I would never take such a job.'

Laryea beamed. 'Of course. I know that, and I trust you.'

Dazz smiled, but then his blood froze to ice as something struck him. Courage buying that 52-inch TV fitted the profile Uncle Cleo had just depicted: a sniper with money to spend on expensive toys.

CHAPTER FIFTY-FOUR

25th May

Mid-morning Monday, Sowah burst out of his office and came to Emma's desk. 'Let's go,' he said. 'I've located Sana Sana and he's willing to meet.'

Emma jumped up and followed the boss out of the building. His gout had cleared up and he was walking faster than Emma had ever seen.

'How did you find him?' she asked.

'Not by phone,' Sowah said. 'I used a network of street contacts who worked through the weekend.'

'Outstanding, sir.' She got into the passenger seat of his nice but modest Kia. Sowah simply wasn't a flashy kind of man. 'Where do we meet him?'

'Somewhere around Circle,' Sowah said, 'but I don't know the exact location. Once we get there, we'll park, I'll call his guy, and he'll take us to another location. Sana doesn't meet or live in one place all the time. He's constantly on the move.'

'What a life,' Emma said, shaking her head. 'I don't know how he does it.'

'Nor I,' Sowah said. 'How was your weekend?'

'Fine, sir,' she said, not planning on talking about her date. 'In fact, it was special.'

She related the story about Kojo's newly discovered talent. 'He's never liked paper and pencil, or even crayons. But because he's so drawn to anything with a screen, I suppose the tablet liberated his gift, in a way.'

'Perhaps so,' Sowah said. 'You seem to love working with the children.'

Emma smiled. 'It's sometimes a lot of frustration, but the small rewards make it worth it. Like Kojo.'

'I imagine he teaches you a lot about being patient.'

Emma nodded. 'He does. And gives me practice in peering inside someone's mind.'

'That's why you'll make a good detective.'

'Thank you, sir.'

They parked near Ernest's Chemists on the north-east side of Nkrumah Circle and Sowah made the call, telling the guy on the other end where they were. He showed up after five minutes, a lanky man of about nineteen wearing ratty slide slippers. He didn't say much except 'Morning,' and they followed him off the beaten track into a deeply set huddle of residential shacks built on treacherous terrain. Walking down ever-narrowing passages, they came to a small, vomit-green house. Outside the door was a security man with a mass of knotted muscles. He patted Emma and Sowah down before holding the door open to let them in. They entered a musty, semi-dark room where it took a few seconds for their vision to accommodate.

'Good morning, Mr Sowah.'

At first, they didn't see where the voice came from, but then they realised that Sana Sana was sitting in a corner dressed in black.

'Morning, Sana,' Sowah said, stepping forward to shake hands. 'It's a while since we've spoken. This is my assistant, Emma Djan.'

'You are welcome.'

Sana was not wearing his iconic cap with a concealing curtain of beads attached to the visor. Instead, he had donned a lifelike human mask. He gestured towards two guest chairs in front of him. Sowah and Emma sat.

'I'm sorry it's been difficult to get hold of me,' Sana said. 'I've been away for a few days.'

'No problem,' Sowah said. 'You are a very busy man.'

'How can I help you, sir?'

'We are trying to find out what has happened to an American gone missing in Ghana, one Gordon Tilson. He came to Ghana on the 15th February and was in touch with people back home in the States up until 3rd April, at which point he disappeared and has not been heard from since. His son, Derek, arrived in Ghana at the beginning of May and is now our client. As you can imagine, he is desperate to find his father.'

Sana nodded. 'Naturally.'

'We're consulting you because you have your ear to the ground and know a lot about what's going on in the country at any one time. We're curious if you have any information – no matter how small – about Mr Tilson, and his disappearance.'

317

Sana paused before his response. 'It's very interesting that you come here today because I have also been very interested in what has been the fate of Mr Tilson. I had heard that he had disappeared and that the police were investigating, and the reason why it has been of interest to me is that Mr Tilson came to see me.'

Neither Sowah nor Emma could hide their surprise. 'He did?' Sowah exclaimed.

'Yes, sir. He contacted me via Facebook Messenger and told me he had read a lot about me and my reporting on Internet fraud and *sakawa* boys. Now, I don't respond to everyone who messages me, but his situation interested me because I've been working to collect enough cases in which defrauded individuals come from abroad to confront the people who have ripped them off. There aren't many of them. OK, so, that's one aspect of what I'm doing. The second is what I call the Big One. That is to name, shame, and jail high officials in the police force and elsewhere in the government who are secretly aiding and abetting *sakawa* boys to continue in this illegal, money-making enterprise.

'So, clearly, we had a common interest, Tilson and I, and we agreed to meet somewhere around 5th March, I think it was. But before that, I spoke to Tilson on the phone and advised him to move out of the Kempinski Hotel.'

'Ah,' Emma said. 'We wondered who it was. Why did you advise him as such?'

'Kempinski is a high-visibility place with extraordinary security in place. I call it a political hotel. Unless you're a harmless tourist, I wouldn't recommend a journalist, detective, or any kind of investigator stay there. I suspect in some cases the rooms are bugged. But that's just me.'

'Interesting,' Sowah said.

'Yes. So, at the time we met,' Sana continued, 'I had expected Gordon to be concerned mostly with catching the person or persons who had tricked him, and he had already gone to the police about it. What surprised me was he asked if he could help me in my goal to name, shame, and jail the *sakawa* big wigs, as I call them.'

'What role did he want to play?' Sowah said. 'I mean, what could he do?'

'That's exactly the point. He was overeager – like a sprinter off the starting block too soon. I have a method of working and I use my own people. I didn't want a co-investigator, I only wanted to know what had happened to Mr Tilson and take it from there. He said he had a possible contact who could give him access to top-ranking officials in the police service. I told him, if you start at the top, you have nowhere to go from there. Start at the bottom and work your way up. For example, I told him about Kweku Ponsu, the fetish priest, who has contact with both *sakawa* boys and powerful people. No one will admit it, but MPs, commanders, commissioners, and CEOs alike go to Ponsu for spiritual guidance to make money, get promotions, destroy political opponents, and so on. Ponsu has a foot in one world and the other foot in another. He is the kind of player we want to engage and court, but it's a slow process.'

Sowah exchanged a glance with Emma. 'Now we know how Mr Tilson found out about Ponsu. What was his response to your recommendations about Kweku Ponsu?'

'Something to the effect that he wanted to work as fast as possible,' Sana said. 'That he didn't want to stay in Ghana "for ever". Americans are very impatient, you know. They always want to do things fast. So, when they come to Ghana, they don't understand why things take so long.'

'Were you aware Mr Tilson went to see Ponsu at Atimpoku?' Sowah asked.

'Not at the time, but I learnt about it later. I don't like to engage in "I told you so", but I had advised Mr Tilson to stay away from Ponsu. After that, I never spoke to him or heard from him again.'

'We now know from the driver, who took Mr Tilson up to Atimpoku, that Tilson had an ugly verbal altercation with Ponsu,' Sowah said.

Sana said, 'I don't doubt it.'

'What do you think has happened to Mr Tilson?'

Sana shook his head slowly. 'I doubt he's still alive.'

'Murdered?'

'Look, if he was in a car crash or something of that nature, we would know by now. So, the question at hand now is who murdered him and where is he? Buried somewhere? Thrown over a cliff? I don't know.'

'How about thrown over a bridge?' Sowah said. 'We have an eyewitness who saw something that looked like a body being dumped over the Adome Bridge into the Volta on the night of Gordon's disappearance.'

'Really.' Sana leant back in his chair, discomposure showing even with his mask hiding his expression. 'Oh. That's not good at all. Have you informed the police?'

'This morning I spoke to DCOP Laryea about possibly getting some divers to search the river, but things move at a snail's pace at CID and I don't expect anything to happen soon in that regard. Meanwhile, Emma has asked some local fishermen to keep a lookout while they're on the river.'

'Good,' Sana said.

'I'm curious, Mr Sana,' Sowah said, 'have the police ever spoken to you about Tilson?'

'No, they haven't,' Sana said. 'Like you, they probably didn't know of any connection between the two of us. Besides, on this issue they might want to avoid me like the plague if they're the ones responsible for Tilson's death.'

Sowah looked startled. 'What do you mean?'

'Consider it. If indeed there are top police personnel involved in these scams, and I'm positive there are, and Mr Tilson went to Ponsu asking probing questions about some of these same high-level cops that Ponsu is regularly in touch with, that sets up a potentially dangerous situation for Tilson. I don't need to tell you that one messes with high authority at one's peril, and one should leave it to the professionals.'

'Do you have a specific person or persons in mind?' Sowah asked.

'No one definite yet,' Sana said. 'But I'm working on it.'

Sowah looked at Emma. 'Did you have any questions? Anything I missed?'

She leant towards him and said in a low voice, 'His whereabouts.'

Sowah nodded, stood up, and stretched out his hand to Sana. 'We will take our leave, now. Thank you very much for your time. This has been very informative. Just one more thing—'

'On 3rd April,' Sana interrupted, 'I was in the States doing some TED talks. There are some recent YouTube videos of me with a verifiable date. Is that what you wanted?'

'It is,' Sowah said. 'Thank you, sir.'

CHAPTER FIFTY-FIVE

DCOP Cleo Laryea generally did not like Mondays and he was already grumpy when, as he had promised the director-general, he summoned DCS Quaino and DI Damptey to his office.

They entered his frigid, air-conditioned office like a pair of guilty children due for a spanking, giving the customary civilian salute by stiffening briefly with closed palms facing backward.

'Sit,' Laryea said curtly from behind his desk. They kept their eyes down until he began to speak. 'We have this American man missing since April. That is your case, correct, DI Damptey?'

'Yes, sir.'

'Update me on your progress so far.'

'Yes please,' Damptey said. 'After the man's son – I mean Mr Tilson's son, Derek – came to CID to report his father missing in middle of May – around there – we started to work diligently on it while following several leads—'

'What leads? Be specific.'

'Please, we were in touch with the locations where the gentleman – Mr Gordon – was residing here in Accra and also at Akosombo.'

'What did you learn?'

'At first he was staying at a certain hotel, em—'

'Kempinski,' Quaino prompted.

'Yes, Kempinski, and then he moved to another place one European woman owns. When I talked to her at March ending, she told me Mr Gordon Tilson had left for Akosombo to stay at someone's home, but he never returned after that. So, then we called the homeowner and spoke to him. We found out that on the morning Mr Gordon was supposed to leave, he was absent from his room and all his possessions were gone.'

'Did you find any signs of struggle in the room?'

Damptey, shifting her weight and appearing uncomfortable, seemed to have lost her tongue.

DCS Quaino came to her rescue. 'Please, due to transportation issues, we have not as yet been able to visit the Akosombo site—'

'*What?*' Laryea's eyes blinked rapidly. 'A possible scene of the crime and you haven't seen it in person?'

'Please, we couldn't secure a vehicle—'

Laryea cut him off. 'Don't try that old, worn-out excuse because it doesn't work on me. What about Derek Tilson? Did you ask him to assist you with transportation costs?'

'Sir,' Quaino said, firming up, 'we asked him, but he was annoyed because we were asking him to cover our transportation costs. He doesn't understand how our system works.'

'What system?' Laryea asked icily. 'What *system*? Derek Tilson is right to be annoyed! Why should he pay our transport costs? That is not a system. That's your laziness, pure and simple. Oh, you think because now I'm a DCOP I've forgotten how officers make up these inflated transportation costs and pocket the change?'

The two flagellated officers sat as still and silent as they could. If only they could magically disappear.

Laryea sighed wearily and ran his hand back and forth over his hair, of which there was less and less these days. 'So, where are we with the case at this moment?'

'Sir,' Quaino said, taking over, 'from the beginning, Mr Gordon's driver has been a person of interest.'

'What driver?' Laryea said, frowning.

'Oh, sorry, sir. I didn't explain it well. Let me start from the beginning.'

'Please do.'

'Mr Gordon went to Akosombo on 27th March with the intention of staying five days at a private lodge by the Volta River. He rented a vehicle from a business called Executive Fleets here in Accra. They provided him with a driver called Yahya Azure. While Mr Gordon was at the lodge, Yahya stayed nearby in Atimpoku. On the morning of 3rd April when Mr Gordon was to return to Accra, Yahya told us that when he arrived to pick up Mr Gordon, the gentleman did not respond to his texts or calls. Yahya claims the front door of the lodge was open, so he went inside to discover that Mr Gordon was nowhere to be found and his luggage was also not there.'

Laryea nodded. This was how a narrative was supposed to be done. 'OK, go on.'

'So, Mr Yahya called the owner, one Mr Labram, who came down to also have a look and confirmed that Mr Gordon had disappeared along with his luggage and laptop and phone and everything.'

'You spoke to Mr Labram yourself?' Laryea asked.

'Yes please. On the phone.'

'What happened after that?'

'Mr Yahya returned to Accra and his employer sacked him, saying he was ultimately responsible for the safety of the clients.

'DI Damptey and I then conducted a search of the vehicle that Mr Gordon had used, but we found nothing – no traces of blood or anything like that. Mr Yahya also gave us permission to search his house in Shukura and at first everything was normal until DI Damptey, to her credit, found a dark brown jacket of fine quality that Yahya had been keeping in his room in a plastic bag. When we asked him about it, Yahya said Mr Gordon had accidentally left it in the rental vehicle on the eve of their departure from Akosombo, and so Yahya kept it with him in the bag with the intention of giving the jacket back to Mr Gordon in the morning. But, of course, in the morning, the white man was gone and Yahya held on to the jacket for safekeeping, so no one at the car rental would steal it.'

'What did Yahya plan to do with it eventually?' Laryea asked.

'He said he wasn't sure,' Quaino said. 'But anyway, we confiscated the jacket as evidence and asked the forensics lab to check for bloodstains. They didn't find any. We were still not satisfied, so a few days later, we questioned Mr Yahya again and, on this occasion, his story changed in that now he claimed Mr Gordon had given him the jacket as a gift.

'It was on Friday after you called me, sir, that I went over the case carefully with DI Damptey and we realised that Yahya was not really in the clear. On Saturday morning, we went to see him to ask again how Mr Gordon's jacket had come into his possession and how he discovered Mr Gordon had disappeared. He became confused when I asked him why Mr Gordon should give Yahya a jacket that is oversized for his small stature. I then arrested him for property theft and brought him to CID to question him more closely.

'We questioned him on Saturday afternoon. Eventually he broke down and made a signed confession that very early on the morning of 3rd April he went to the lodge with the intention of robbing Mr Gordon of all his possessions. During his attempt, Mr Gordon accosted him, and a struggle ensued. Yahya knocked him out and took all his belongings including the luggage, his laptop and mobile phone.'

Laryea leant back in his ergonomic chair. 'And where are those items, then?'

'We believe Yahya sold them but either forgot to get rid of the jacket or simply decided to keep it.'

'Yes, but then where is Mr Gordon?' Laryea asked, mystified.

'OK, this is another strange part,' Quaino said. 'Yahya admits to overpowering Mr Gordon, knocking him out and taking all his things, but says he left Gordon in the lodge lying on the floor. Yahya says he doesn't know what happened to Gordon between the time he left him unconscious in the lodge around three in the morning and when he returned about four hours later to supposedly collect Mr Gordon back to Accra. We don't believe him. We believe in fact that Yahya murdered the American and has disposed of the body somewhere. He's just afraid to confess to the full crime, but we believe he will do so in due course.'

Laryea blew his breath out through his cheeks. 'You have a perfectly decent job as a driver and then you rob and murder a client? It makes no sense.'

'He's uneducated and also a little bit stupid, sir.'

Laryea grunted and contemplatively rested his temple against a closed fist. 'Just one thing, though. If Yahya had a struggle with Mr Gordon, there must have been signs of it, surely? Furniture scattered, table lamps overturned – things like that. Did Mr Labram say anything about that?'

'No, he didn't, sir.'

Laryea was doubtful. 'Well, we'll see if Yahya confesses to anything further, but I'm afraid your case is not that strong, Quaino. It's very blurry around the edges. You understand what I mean by that? It's not solid at all.'

'Yes, sir.'

'The motive is not well-defined, and if this jacket is the only physical evidence tying Yahya to the crime of murder, it won't stand up well in court.'

'But he will confess,' Quaino said with confidence. 'I am certain of that.'

CHAPTER FIFTY-SIX

3rd April, Akosombo, Ghana

Gordon Tilson hadn't smoked in decades and he didn't know how or why the urge had suddenly materialised. Standing at the side of the Riverview Cottage, he puffed away at his second cigarette for the night. The bubbling sound of the river was soothing, and he needed that. One o'clock in the morning and he couldn't sleep.

His visit to Akosombo had been eventful but he couldn't say successful, exactly. He had met with Kweku Ponsu four days ago, but it hadn't gone as well as Gordon had hoped. At first, under the watchful eye of the twins Clifford or Clement, the conversation had been easy-going enough – where Gordon was from in the States, how long he had been in Ghana and where he was staying in Akosombo, and so on.

When Ponsu asked Gordon about the purpose of the visit, Yahya quickly answered for Gordon in some local language and the response appeared to have satisfied Ponsu – something to the effect that Gordon was writing a book about traditions in Ghana.

Gordon wanted to learn about Ponsu's involvement with *sakawa* boys and how the system worked. What, specifically, did they come to Ponsu for? What did they pay him? How did Ponsu communicate with the gods, and so on?

Ponsu's responses were evasive and unhelpful. He sat there, passive as a block of wood. Gordon tried to entice him to say more by initially handing him a hundred dollars in crisp bills.

'Mr Ponsu, do you know the director-general of CID, Commissioner Alex Andoh?' Gordon asked.

'No, sir. I do not.'

'Do you know of him being involved in *sakawa*?' Gordon asked.

'Not at all.'

'What about Inspector General Akrofi?'

'What's your question?'

'You know him? Does he do all this *sakawa* stuff too?'

'Why don't you ask him?'

And on it went. Gordon asking more questions and Ponsu remaining as impenetrable as Fort Knox. And then Gordon lost it. He was frustrated and angry. Ponsu was a liar. Of *course*, he knew all these top guys – MPs, police commissioners, and the like.

'The truth will come out,' was Gordon's parting shot to Ponsu. 'And then we'll see how the whole corrupt system works.'

Another minute and the muscle twins might have thrown Gordon out, but Yahya had ushered him away in time to prevent such an occurrence. Initially after the meeting with Ponsu, Gordon had been despondent, bitter, and at his wit's end. What was he doing here in Ghana? What was the point of it all? He wanted to go back home to DC. He had been here six weeks and that was long enough.

But yesterday, his resolve began to creep back with a little help from Cas, who reminded Gordon that he had never been a quitter. That was true, and in fact, now Gordon was feeling more in command and he had a lot more fight in him. He felt he had a mission to complete.

The cigarette had kept the mosquitoes at bay, but now that Gordon was done with it, he could feel and hear them mounting an attack. He went back inside the chalet and got into bed, turning over several times as he tried to get comfortable. He drifted off and wasn't sure how long he had been asleep before he woke to a light tapping on the front door. What, or who, was that?

He got out of bed and tiptoed to the door. It was definitely someone knocking. A male voice said, 'Mr Tilson?'

'Yes?' he answered warily. 'Who is it?'

'It's Mr Labram, please.'

'Uh, is something wrong?'

'Small problem, please.'

332

'Oh? Well, yes. Sure.'

Gordon unlocked the door, looked out cautiously and saw the silhouettes of two men.

One of them had a club, which he swung hard against Gordon's skull.

CHAPTER FIFTY-SEVEN

28th May, Akosombo, Ghana

Zacharia and his son Solomon had paddled upriver in their sixteen-foot canoe. The Adome Bridge was straight ahead. Eleven in the morning, the sun was powerful but not yet at full strength. Solomon was at the stern steering while Zacharia at the bow was casting the net.

They were halfway between banks near a thicket of river weeds so dense it appeared solid. A few other canoes – single- and two-man – were out on the river at various distances.

The bright reflection off the water reduced visibility, but Solomon made out a greyish mound nestled in the weeds.

'Papa,' he said.

'Yes?' Zacharia answered, looking back.

Solomon pointed and his father followed his finger to the mound.

'*Bola*,' he concluded.

'No,' Solomon said, turning the canoe and paddling for the island.

'Agh,' Zacharia said with annoyance. 'Where are you going?'

Solomon said nothing and sidled the canoe up to the bundle. When he poked it with a stick, it barely moved. They detected a stench now. A bag of dead fish? But that made no sense.

Solomon leant over to tug at the object, which was heavier and larger than it seemed. Most of it was beneath the surface and appeared to be attached to the weed clump.

'We have to pull it to the shore,' Zacharia said, getting into the water.

He disappeared under the surface for a few seconds and struggled to free the object from the vegetation, which proved difficult. Solomon joined him in his efforts until the two men could finally secure their cast net around the mass, and then Zacharia got back in the canoe to help paddle it to the nearest available space onshore. Solomon jumped out and pushed the canoe securely onto land. Wincing from the odour, they rolled the thing up onto dry land. It was a coarse, sodden greyish-brown sack about three metres in length and swollen with its contents. They could make out the shape of rocks at one end, but the rest was a firm, unyielding, rubbery mass.

'It's the man,' Zacharia said, breathing hard from their efforts. 'The American they said was thrown in the river.'

Solomon looked back and forth between his father and the grisly find. Zacharia stared at it awhile, then took out his fish knife. He cut a long slit in the sack at its bulkier end and took a brief peek inside. The odour assaulted him so strongly that he recoiled as though jabbed with a spear. He'd seen enough, in any case.

'My phone,' he said to Solomon, who always safeguarded his father's device. Solomon gave it to him and Zacharia squinted a little at the phone's screen as he looked for Emma's number. Finally, he found it. He took a deep breath and called.

CHAPTER FIFTY-EIGHT

3rd March, Accra, Ghana

On multiple occasions, Gordon had considered calling Josephine and then put it off. Cas was pressing him to do so, but Gordon had wrestled with how he would 'look' to Josephine: stupid, a sucker, some kind of crazy white guy with a lust for African women so strong that he'd allowed himself to be hoodwinked by a bunch of kids?

He had to swallow his pride, though. As Cas said, Gordon knew the wife of Ghana's top cop, so how could Gordon *not* get in touch with her.

His heart was in his mouth as he dialled her number. Josephine didn't pick up the call, but she returned it minutes later.

'Hello?' she said. 'May I know who is this, please?'

Gordon was using a local line, so she would not have recognised it or had him in her contacts.

'Hi, Josephine,' he said brightly. 'How are you? This is Gordon.'

There was the slightest of pauses, and then she said, 'My goodness, Gordon! You're in Ghana?'

'I am. In Accra.'

'*Akwaaba!* How long have you been in town?'

'Just a couple of weeks.'

'Are you at a hotel?'

'I was at the Kempinski, but I moved to a bed and breakfast yesterday. More privacy here and it's a lovely home.'

'I'm glad. Oh, what a lovely surprise.'

'It would be nice to see you,' Gordon said hopefully.

'Same here,' she said. 'We must definitely set something up. Listen, I'm in a hurry to an appointment, but can we meet later?'

Josephine expected to be in Achimota, another mushrooming suburb of Accra, until about five, and then she would be free.

'Meet me at the Achimota Mall around then,' she suggested. 'There's a coffee shop called "Second Cup" that I like.'

'Great,' he said. 'I can't wait to see you.'

Second Cup really was a nice coffee place – popular and packed to capacity with Ghanaians and expatriates. The background buzz and the music gave it the right atmosphere. Gordon had arrived before Josephine did and had bagged a table. He waited only about ten minutes more before she came in looking around to see if he had arrived. He waved and she smiled and hurried to the table.

In a formfitting turquoise-and-black dress, Josephine's hourglass shape was a study in perfection. Gordon still had plenty reserves in his lust storage tank.

'It's so good to see you,' she said as they embraced lightly. 'Welcome to Ghana.'

'Nice to see you too,' Gordon said. 'You look amazing.'

'Thank you so much.' She was glowing as they sat down, and Gordon noticed her brand-new short haircut with the hair tucked behind each ear to show off a single pearl.

'We have some catching up to do,' he said. 'But first, can I get you anything?'

She wanted a mochaccino. Gordon stuck with a more ordinary cafe au lait. Once they had their drinks in front of them on the table, they began to talk.

'So, I'm dying to know what brings you across the pond our way,' Josephine said eagerly. 'What a surprise I got when you called this morning.'

'I figured you would be,' Gordon said. 'At the moment, I'm just enjoying a few weeks of vacation.'

'All by yourself?' She was surprised.

'I'm afraid so, yes.' Gordon's mood was moving towards the negative column. He felt gloomy.

'Did you suddenly get nostalgic about Ghana?' She smiled and winked at him. 'Did I cause that?'

They had a small laugh, but Gordon said, 'In some ways, yes. I suppose I remembered how wonderful the company of a Ghanaian woman can be.'

She inclined her head. 'Aw, that's so very sweet. Are

you enjoying yourself? Where have you been so far?'

'Just Accra, really.'

'I see.' Concern came to her expression. 'Is everything OK, though? You don't seem as happy as I remember you.'

'Josephine, I wanted badly to see you,' he said, 'but at the same time, I've been dreading this meeting because of what I'm going to tell you.'

'Oh,' she said, looking both curious and worried.

'When I met you in DC, I had been talking online to a Ghanaian woman called Helena, located in Accra. She contacted me through a Facebook page for widows and widowers, and over the months between November last year and February this year, we talked a lot via Skype and so on. Helena, or the person I *thought* was her, looked absolutely beautiful and I fell in love.

'There's no other way to say it, and by February I really wanted to see her. She was going through a rather difficult patch, including her favourite sister having been very seriously injured in a highway crash. So, I was helping Helena and her family out with the finances associated with this catastrophe.'

Josephine sipped her drink as she kept her eyes intently on him. Her expression was entirely non-judgemental now, but Gordon wondered how much longer that would last.

'I finally took the plunge and travelled to Ghana. I got into Kotoka International on Saturday, February 15th. Helena was to meet me there. I probably don't need to tell you that not only did she not show up at the airport, she never materialised at all.'

Josephine was staring at him and slowly shaking her head. Gordon braced for the 'You mean to tell me you haven't heard of these Internet scams?' but instead, she said, 'It makes me furious that someone would take advantage of your kindness in this way. These damn *sakawa* boys! How much did they steal from you?'

'Almost four thousand dollars.'

She put her hand over his and squeezed. 'I'm so very sorry, Gordon. I even feel like apologising on behalf of the whole country for this.'

He cracked a smile. 'You shouldn't feel that way. This is entirely my stupidity.'

Josephine disagreed. 'Don't come down so hard on yourself. How were you to know the level of sophistication these Internet criminals have achieved? You've reported this to the police?'

'Yes, but they don't seem to be doing much. Or anything, for that matter.'

'How long do you plan to be in Ghana?'

Gordon sipped his coffee before continuing. 'Until the middle of April, tentatively. It partly depends on how much headway I make.'

'With the police?'

'Well, yes and no. I'm not expecting great things from them.'

Josephine shook her head. 'We won't accept that. I'll talk to James about it. He can apply pressure to Commissioner

Andoh at CID. I feel sorry that you didn't get in touch earlier, but it's OK. We'll make up for the time.'

'Thank you, Josephine.'

'Call me Jo. All my friends do.'

'I'm happy you consider me a friend,' he said. 'After . . . you-know-what.'

She tossed her head. 'Whatever happens in DC . . .'

He laughed. 'I got it. Don't worry, I'm on my best behaviour.'

'Good.'

'I had a question for you,' Gordon said, 'and you don't have to answer if you can't or don't want to.'

'I'm all ears.'

'Have you heard anything, or do you know anything about whether there's any truth to the claim that some senior officials, including in the police force, may be in cahoots with these *sakawa* boys?'

'Cahoots in what way?'

'Well, they support the system and receive money from those lower down on the chain.'

'Oh dear. I must confess I don't know much about that kind of thing.' Josephine was still smiling. 'I make it a point not to talk to James about work. He's in such a sensitive position, being that close to President Bannerman. I don't ever want to create a conflict of interest for my husband, so, as they say, don't ask, don't tell.'

'Gotcha,' Gordon said.

'I'm curious why you asked.'

342

'I just wondered. I read some stuff online—'

'Can't believe everything you read,' she cut him off with surprising swiftness. 'Especially online. And *certainly* not from that Sana Sana – if that's who you've been reading.'

'Full disclosure,' he said. 'I have.'

'He's a sensationalist and a dishonest journalist,' Jo said, her tone sharpening. 'What he calls investigation is pure entrapment of innocent people.'

In Gordon's mind, that wasn't exactly accurate, but he had no desire to argue with her over this. 'OK,' he agreed. 'Then I'll take whatever I read from him with a grain of salt.'

'I just want you to be careful, that's all.'

They smiled at each other but Gordon detected a change in Jo's mood. He shifted the topic to talk about his granddaughter and show Jo pictures of Simone on his phone. But now, Gordon felt awkward. Jo wasn't the same woman he had met in DC. Or maybe that wasn't it. The woman was the same, the circumstances were radically different. Now Gordon was on *Jo's* turf, where she belonged to a certain elevated class and was in complete control. Here, the world was hers and she was James's wife. Her body language was clear. There was no romance. She would not be having any sort of sexual liaison with Gordon in Ghana. He knew that was appropriate, but a morsel of him felt somewhat hurt.

He could tell that as far as Jo was concerned, Sana Sana was a piece of shit. Hence Gordon deliberately did not mention that next Thursday, he would be meeting up with the man.

Battle lines were being drawn. Looking at it from Cas's point of view – and to an increasing extent, Gordon's as well – this was going to make an excellent story.

CHAPTER FIFTY-NINE

28th May, Accra, Ghana

Before Kojo's mother, Abena, left for the Autism Centre to pick up her son at the end of the day, Auntie Rose called her. 'An important visitor will be here when you arrive. We have some great plans to discuss with you.'

'Is that so?' Abena couldn't imagine what she could mean, but it sounded exciting.

'We'll see you when you come. Hurry!'

When Abena arrived, Grace and two other staff members were outside in the yard holding an arts-and-craft session with the children.

'Hi, Abena,' Grace said. 'They are waiting for you in the playroom with Kojo.'

'Ah, there you are,' Auntie Rose said, as Abena entered. 'Come in.'

Sitting with Kojo at her side was Josephine Akrofi in the most beautiful pale pink dress Abena had ever seen. She had met the IGP's wife now again during her visits to the centre.

'Good afternoon, madam,' Abena said.

'Hello, Abena,' Mrs Akrofi said with a welcoming smile. 'It's nice to see you again. How are you?'

'I'm fine, please,' Abena said. 'Thank you, madam.'

Kojo was rubbing thumbs and fingers together, but was otherwise calm.

'Have a seat, Abena,' Rose said, indicating one of the two empty chairs at the table.

Abena noticed a Samsung tablet on the table. She wondered if Mrs Akrofi had brought it just for Kojo.

'Abena,' Rose began, 'I invited Mrs Akrofi here today and she has been very kind to join us to talk about your Kojo.'

'Oh, OK,' Abena said. 'Thank you, madam.'

'He is a special boy,' Mrs Akrofi said, her voice warm. 'I know how amazed and happy you were when he drew the picture of Rose on the tablet. This kind of ability in an autistic child – well, any child, really – is not a small thing.'

Abena glowed.

'What we want to do from now on,' Mrs Akrofi continued, 'is collect as many of Kojo's drawings and make videos of him while he's doing it. I know so far he's drawn only one, but I'm sure more will be forthcoming. We want to bring world attention to his talent. In turn, that will raise awareness about the Autism Centre and attract funding. This is the most important thing right now – the survival of the Centre.'

Abena nodded. 'Yes please. I think that will be a very good plan.'

Rose was elated. 'Yes, yes, it's wonderful. So, Abena, we want to get your permission to make a documentary about Kojo. One day next week, some people will come to film the Centre and what we do here, but they will be concentrating mostly on Kojo.'

'OK, madam. No problem.'

'Also,' Mrs Akrofi added, 'we will have a section showing you and Kojo together and include a short interview with you and me. The interview with me might be done at my home, but I will let you know.'

Abena became a little teary. Out of the blue, her son had become special. He had a talent that had been hidden away all this time, and to Abena, that was a thing of joy.

CHAPTER SIXTY

Even in a relatively mellow, cannabinoid state, Bruno was becoming agitated. 'Please, why?' he demanded of Ponsu. 'I killed the crocodile, which is very tough, and now what again?'

Nii Kwei, sitting quietly at his side in Kweku Ponsu's Accra courtyard, sent Bruno a warning look. *Don't argue.*

Ponsu, opposite them, curled his lip. 'So, you think you're a big man just because you killed the crocodile?' he said. 'You don't decide what you must do to meet Godfather, *I* do. I know him, he knows me. People just can't meet him like that. They must prove themselves. Nii Kwei is a loyal *sakawa* servant. He makes plenty, plenty money, much more than most of the boys. But you, you are far away from that. So, you must do something else as proof of your loyalty. Otherwise, you can forget.'

Bruno's jaws clenched and released repeatedly. He looked at Ponsu with resentment and doubt. 'Is this the last task?'

'Yes,' Ponsu said. 'This last one, and then you meet Godfather and become one of the special boys – like Nii.'

Bruno took a deep breath and let it out. 'OK,' he said, resigned but still irritated. 'What is it you want me to do?'

'You are to bring me the shirt of a devil child,' Ponsu said.

Bruno frowned. 'Please, what is that? A devil child?'

'They can't talk and you can't tell what they are thinking, but inside they have power to control you.'

'Like deaf and dumb?' Nii Kwei suggested.

'No, it's not deaf and dumb,' Ponsu said. 'They can hear, but they don't understand. And they won't look at you too. Just turning the eyes round and making strange noises.'

'Do you know what he means?' Nii asked Bruno.

'I think so,' he said. 'My sister takes care of those children at some place. They call it otistic or something like that.'

'Then you can ask her to bring one of those children,' Nii suggested.

Bruno shot him a withering look and then turned back to Ponsu. 'Please, what will you do with the shirt of the devil child?'

'You bring it first and you will see.'

'Please, do you have something else I can do instead?' Bruno begged. 'This one, I don't know.'

'*Kwasea!*' Ponsu shouted. 'Don't come here and waste my time if you can't do anything. If you like, refuse this one and see what happens to you. You go die.' He dusted his hands in a gesture of finality. 'Just you try and see.'

He got up and walked into his house without another word.

Nii Kwei was angry with Bruno. '*Chaley*, you can't just refuse him like that! What's wrong with you? Don't play with this man. He has powers he can turn against you. You better go tell him you'll do whatever he says.'

Bruno rose and went to Ponsu's door. He knocked. 'Please, I'm sorry, OK? What you want me to do is no problem. I will do it.'

CHAPTER SIXTY-ONE

Derek opened the door of his hotel room to Emma and Sowah.

'Hello, Derek,' Sowah said. 'May we come in?'

He must have read their expressions because his face fell. 'Yes, of course.'

They sat in a triangle.

'As I told you,' Emma began, 'I asked some fishermen on the Volta River to look out for anything strange. Today, I heard from one of them, who told me that they have found a sack with a body floating in the river.'

Derek nodded. His face was neutral. 'OK.'

A short silence fell over them, then Emma cleared her throat. 'I'm not saying it's your dad. But to investigate this fully, we must ask you to view the body to either confirm or deny the identity. We'll be going to the mortuary up there in a couple of hours. Can you come with us?'

Derek said, 'Yes, of course.'

* * *

The Volta River Authority Hospital was relatively well-funded with proceeds from the hydroelectric dam, but it still lacked resources. The morgue was overcrowded with more than one body per refrigerator drawer. Only two autopsy tables were available. Dr Anum Biney, who had been the chief medical officer there for decades, met Emma, Sowah, and Derek at the front entrance.

He had a startling white moustache curled at its tips and shocking white hair to match. Accompanied by a police officer from the Akosombo Police Station, they followed Dr Biney along a veranda flanking long, low-profile wards. The sky had opened and let loose a torrent that nearly soaked them as they crossed the uncovered space between the wards and the morgue.

Emma loathed the typical morgue smell – human decay mixed with bleach and formaldehyde. She felt nauseous with it as they entered the building. Before they went into the autopsy room, Biney stopped to address them. He had a calm, baritone voice, which gave the impression that no situation, no matter how dire, could ever fluster him.

'We have now washed the body of dirt and other river debris,' he said. 'Nevertheless, I must caution you it is still a severe sight – among the worst I have ever seen. The odour also, some of which you might already be detecting, is very powerful and penetrating. That is why I suggest you all put some Mentholatum underneath your nose. We have some for you.'

A morgue attendant brought them a small jar of the thick, pungent ointment that Emma's mother often used during her relentless asthma attacks. The odour brought back a flood of bad memories.

'OK,' Biney said when they had all applied the stuff, 'let's proceed now.'

He held open the door and they filed in. The body on the autopsy table was covered with a stained grey sheet. The Mentholatum did not cut the odour much, in Emma's opinion. She felt unwell and steeled herself for a sight she knew would be hard to bear.

The attendant rolled back the sheet and Emma saw it was even worse than she had imagined. Had not a head and outstretched arms been present, Emma would not have thought it human. Eyes popped out from a blue-green face that had become slimy, bloated, and pushed off to the side like a badly fitted mask. The mouth was open with the lips forming an oval as in a silent scream for help. Some of the skin on the arms and chest had turned deep purple and had sloughed off – or was about to.

Emma shuddered and averted her eyes. Derek retched, turned, and ran out of the room. Sowah looked at Emma and they both went after Derek. He was outside the building leaning against the wall in the rain. 'Sorry,' he said. 'I couldn't take it in there. That's the most revolting thing I've ever seen.'

'Yes,' Sowah said quietly, his own face contorted with revulsion. 'Come this way out of the rain.'

'It's not Dad, though,' Derek said as they took shelter along the corridor. 'Thank God.'

'It's not,' Emma said, half question, half statement.

'No way,' he said, shaking his head.

'OK,' she said, but she doubted the question was settled. 'You're sure?'

He frowned. 'Of course, I'm sure. If that's the guy you say got dumped over the bridge that night, it's not my father.'

They watched him for a while. He was hyperventilating and not making eye contact with them.

'Derek,' Sowah said, 'did your father have a wedding band?'

'Yes. He never took it off, even after Mama died. Why do you ask?'

'Would you be able to identify his ring?'

'Of course. It's white gold with three inlaid diamonds. But why, though?'

'The person in the morgue has a wedding ring.'

Emma was startled. How had Mr Sowah noticed that in such a short space of time?

'If I take a photo of it and show it to you,' Sowah continued, 'would you be able to say whether it belongs to your father or not?'

Derek shrugged. 'You can if you want, but it won't be Dad's, I can tell you that right now.'

'OK, sure,' Sowah said. 'Just to double check and make it official.'

He went back in. Emma put her hand on Derek's shoulder and rubbed it lightly. 'I'm sorry.' Tears pricked her eyes. She felt sick with a heavy sense of doom.

He smiled weakly. 'Thanks.'

Sowah returned, phone in hand. Emma was dreading this moment, even more so as she saw how grim and sorrowful Sowah appeared. He exchanged a glance with her that told her that the worst possible nightmare was unfolding.

Sowah went to Derek's side. 'Can you please take a look at the photo?'

Derek looked at the image of the wedding band almost nonchalantly, as if there was no point but he would oblige. The ring was shiny, despite its presumably long period of immersion in water, and it had three inlaid diamonds.

Derek snorted. 'Someone with the same ring as my Dad's? That's ridiculous.'

He looked up at the sky. 'Ah, this is so stupid, the whole damn, fucked-up situation.'

'Yes.' Emma took his hand in both of hers.

His legs began to quiver. Sowah grasped his arm and guided him to sit against the wall.

Emma sat beside him, watching him closely.

'What I don't understand,' Derek said, his voice shaking, 'is why he had to do *any* of this. The whole coming to Ghana thing, trying to track down who did this to him, and it was all so unnecessary, right?'

Emma nodded.

'And I *told* him, I said, "Dad, just come home. We might have had differences, but I still love you, Dad. I still do." And I don't know if he believed that. I don't know. But I do. I love you, Dad.'

'Yes,' Emma said. 'I know you loved him very much.'

'It's him in there, isn't it?' he said, looking up at her. She nodded.

Derek crumpled and shrank, as if trying to disappear inside himself. Emma put her arms around him and brought him closer as his sobs came one after another like wave upon stormy wave.

CHAPTER SIXTY-TWO

The day had been long, troubling, and draining for Emma. Yes, Gordon Tilson had been found now, but this was the most dreaded end. Crawling into her narrow bed with every muscle tense and aching, Emma felt a dark, awful heaviness. Who could have done this to Mr Tilson? One name repeatedly came to her mind: Kweku Ponsu.

She thought of Derek, his heart ripped from his chest, his spirit destroyed. He would never unsee his father on the autopsy table, monstrous from the putrefaction and prolonged aquatic immersion. Dr Biney had offered to do an autopsy but Derek had declined. He wanted the body flown back to DC as soon as possible and have the post-mortem done there instead. It was understandable. If Emma had been in his position, she would have wished the same. The American Embassy would assist in airlifting Gordon home.

Her phone rang – Courage calling. She debated whether to answer, and against her better judgement perhaps, she did.

'I'm checking on you,' he said, his voice much softer

than she'd ever heard it. 'I heard the American guy's body was found. And in terrible condition.'

'I've never seen anything so horrible,' Emma said.

'Are you OK?'

'Yes, I am. Well, I will be. Thank you.'

'I know this is hard.'

She appreciated his sympathy.

'Do you want any company?' Courage asked. 'I'm available.'

'Perhaps another time,' she said without much interest reflected in her voice.

'I would love to see you again,' he said.

She hesitated.

'Can I?' he pressed.

'Courage, I don't think we're a good match.'

'Oh,' he said, sounding so crushed she felt sorry for him. 'But we had fun together.'

'That's true, but—'

'But what?'

She sighed. 'Let's talk another time, OK? I'm very tired.'

'All right, then. I'm sorry I bothered you.'

'No, it's OK, really.'

'Goodnight, Emma.'

Just as Emma was hoping she could get a little rest, the phone rang yet again. This time it was Sowah.

'I just received some more bad news,' he said. 'They arrested Yahya Azure on Saturday and now they've charged him with the murder of Gordon Tilson.'

* * *

By 9 a.m. the following day, Sowah and Emma were at the charge office on the ground floor of the CID building to look for Yahya. Sowah explained to the charge officer why they were there. He looked a little uncertain, but Sowah's senior, authoritative demeanour had a lot of pull. The officer yelled back for the prisoner to come up to the front. A motley crowd of arrestees were packed into the jails behind the charge desk.

Yahya came forward. He looked scared and even smaller than when Emma had met him. When he saw her, his expression lit up. Emma feared he might be thinking she was here to secure his release.

'Good morning, Yahya,' she said.

'Good morning, madam.'

Emma introduced him to Sowah.

'How do you feel?' Emma asked, although it was already clear. He was despondent, frightened, and bewildered.

He shook his head. 'I don't understand what is happening.'

Given the racket in the place, there wasn't much chance of their conversation being overheard, but Sowah nevertheless beckoned Yahya farther down the counter to put some distance between them and the charge officer's station.

'Who arrested you on Saturday?' Sowah asked Yahya.

'The policeman, Quaino, and the woman, Damptey.'

'About what time was it?'

'Around ten in the morning, please.'

'When they arrested you, what did they say?'

'First, they axe me regarding the jacket. They stand one on my right side and the other on my left side, shouting on me with the questions and then Quaino was slapping me too.'

'Slapping you?' Sowah repeated.

'Yes, every time he axe me a question, he slap me here,' Yahya said, touching the left side of his head.

Emma and Sowah exchanged glances, reading each other's minds. If Yahya was telling the truth about the abuse, and they believed he was, then any kind of confession on his part was suspect.

'Then they arrest me and bring me here to the cell,' Yahya continued. 'In the afternoon they take me to some room in the big building and they started the questions all over again, shouting on me.'

A wretched, crushed Yahya stared at the counter in silence. Emma felt terribly sorry for him.

'Did Mr Quaino and Madam Damptey have you sign a statement?' Sowah asked.

'On Saturday night, they said if I sign a statement, the judge will be lenient with me and not send me to Nsawam Prison.'

'What did the statement say?' Sowah asked.

'They didn't give me chance to read it,' Yahya said morosely. 'Or maybe I read it and I forgot what it said. I was tired. I felt like I was having fever too.'

'OK, Yahya,' Sowah said. 'Let me see what we can do. We will try to talk to the officers who arrested you and get back to you.'

Yahya's eyes sprang to life with hope. 'Thank you, sir. God bless you, sir.'

Emma and Sowah left the charge office and headed upstairs to DCS Quaino's office.

Climbing flights of narrow, worn steps to the fourth level, Emma cringed. She was physically separated from Commissioner Andoh's office, but mentally and emotionally, she might as well have been right there. The image of him, his smell, the sounds he made – they were all still vivid in Emma's mind. She had to consciously block them out.

Neither Quaino nor Damptey was in. Sowah and Emma decided to give them an hour or so. At the seventy-five-minute mark, they were about to call it quits when the pair appeared on the floor.

Damptey saw Emma and a flicker of recognition betrayed her deadpan expression. She clearly did not want to see Emma, and she would have continued walking by had Emma not stood up and sidled into her path. 'Good morning, Madam Damptey. Good morning, sir.'

'Good morning.' Damptey said, without interest. 'Yes? Can I help you?'

Sowah was close behind Emma and she introduced him to the two officers.

'*Ei!*' Quaino exclaimed. 'Are you the Yemo Sowah who used to work for CID?'

'Yes, I am.'

'Wonderful! My father is Christopher Quaino. He was also in CID but is now retired. He used to talk a lot about you. He admired you very much.'

'Yes, yes!' Sowah said, laughing. 'Thank you. Chris Quaino – of course. We worked some cases together.'

'Oh, very nice to meet you, sir,' Quaino said. 'What an honour. You are welcome to your old stomping ground.'

Laughter all around, and even Damptey managed a titter, but she didn't look happy. 'I think you have a private investigation agency, isn't it?' Quaino asked.

'Yes,' Sowah said, 'for many years now.'

'Oh, very wonderful,' Quaino said.

'Thank you very much. Do you have time to discuss a case with Miss Djan and me?'

'Of course, of course. Come this way.'

They followed him to his office, which was air-conditioned – a perk an officer got once past the rank of chief inspector.

Emma let Sowah do all the talking. The link between each other that he and Quaino had discovered was handy because the rapport was instant, but from the corner of Emma's eye, DI Damptey appeared tense.

'That's the way we came to be following this case,' Sowah said, after explaining how Derek had come to them and the events that had followed.

'Yes, I see,' Quaino said. 'Well, thank you for that, sir. I believe DI Damptey tried to explain to Mr Derek that these investigations take time. Sorry he had to trouble you, Mr Sowah, sir.'

'Not at all,' Sowah said, waving it away.

'Yes, I was working closely with Derek Tilson,'

Damptey chimed in, 'but he was too impatient.'

Emma doubted that very much. In her judgement, Damptey was an inadequate police officer who wouldn't hesitate to cover her poor performance with a lie, whether big or small.

'And I understand you've arrested the gentleman, Mr Yahya?' Sowah said.

'Yes, that's correct,' Quaino said with an air of importance. 'We found him in possession of the jacket he stole from the American man, and he's now confessed to it.'

'And you also suspect him of murdering Mr Tilson?'

'Yes please.'

'But do you have physical evidence tying Yahya to Tilson's death?'

'Well, the jacket, sir—'

'That ties Yahya to Mr Tilson, not his death,' Sowah pointed out.

'He will confess, sir,' Quaino said with conviction.

'Just be sure it's not under duress.'

'Duress?'

'Be sure it's non-coercive because the law doesn't take kindly to that. You see what I mean?'

'Yes please. You are right. Thank you, sir.'

'Well, good,' Sowah said, placing his hands on his thighs and looking at Emma. 'Did you have anything you wanted to ask?'

'No, thank you, sir,' Emma said. 'I think you've covered it very well.' They got up and so did Quaino and Damptey.

'By the way,' Sowah said, as if by afterthought, 'is DCOP Laryea around?'

'I'm not sure, sir,' Quaino said. 'I haven't seen him today.'

'He's a good man,' Sowah said. 'He was also my mate in the good old days, along with your dad. I'll stop by and say hello.'

'He's on the fifth floor. Will you like me to take you there, sir?'

'Don't trouble yourself at all, Mr Quaino. We'll find our way. Thank you so much.'

Outside, Sowah waited until they were clear down the hall before commenting. 'This is preposterous,' he said grimly. 'They've made Yahya an easy scapegoat and bullied him into a confession. We're not going to allow this to go any further.'

CHAPTER SIXTY-THREE

25th March, Accra, Ghana

James Akrofi summoned the director-general. In Akrofi's office at the top of the Police Headquarters, which was a separate entity from the CID building, he showed Andoh a letter of great concern.

> *James Akrofi*
> *Inspector General of Police*
> *Ring Road East, Accra*
>
> *March 21st*
>
> *Dear James Akrofi:*
> *On February 14th this year, I arrived in Ghana under the impression that I was to meet a woman I had been communicating with. I then discovered that such a woman did not exist and that during the months of January and February, I was being defrauded of thousands of dollars by an Internet*

romance scam, which I'm sure you are familiar with.

I filed a full and detailed statement with CID. My hope was that the person or persons responsible for scamming me and stealing my money would be apprehended. The case was assigned to a Detective Inspector Damptey. To say that I have been disappointed by her performance would be an understatement. After more than a month now, there appear to be no results whatsoever from what I even hesitate to call 'an investigation', or if there have been, I have not been made aware. Every call I have ever made to DI Damptey has been met with evasion and prevarication. I get the impression that she has taken no interest whatsoever in my case.

What I am learning from people like investigative reporter Sana Sana is that the lack of any meaningful investigation into Internet scams, of which mine is only one, is most likely due to the collusion of police officials themselves, including those in high position. More revelations in this regard are likely to be forthcoming, but the phrase 'name, shame, and jail' does come to mind. I read in the media that President Bannerman has engaged you in his initiative to eradicate corruption. I sincerely hope the house you clean first will be yours.

I was in Ghana decades ago while in the Peace Corps and I had a most engaging and fulfilling time, including meeting the Ghanaian woman who *became my wife. It has been a tragic experience for me to observe the negative changes that have overcome this nation and turned it into one of greed and monetary gain at any cost. Along with a writer from the* Washington Observer, *I intend to write an extended piece about my experiences and incorporate, if possible, some of the names Mr Sana will come up with in the next few months.*

Yours truly,

Gordon Tilson

Andoh was appalled. In the first place, there was something treacherous about people who went straight to the top with their complaints. Why hadn't this man come to Andoh first? Second, the letter was full of outright hostile language.

'Sir, this . . . this is ridiculous,' Andoh said. He looked at the letter again. 'How dare this man? "I sincerely hope the house you clean first will be yours"? It's insulting. And what is he trying to do, threaten us by telling us he's working with Sana Sana? And that he'll be writing something in the what? *Washington Observer?*'

Akrofi chose to disregard that for the moment. 'Where is DI Damptey with the investigation?' he asked.

'I have to get an update from her supervisor, DCS Quaino, but they have been questioning different *sakawa* boys, both in custody and on the street, to see if there's a connection with the American man. It's not true what he's saying about Damptey not taking any interest.'

'Was there any kind of personality clash between Tilson and Damptey, to your knowledge?'

'No, sir. Not that I know of.'

'All right, listen,' Akrofi said calmly. 'This man, Tilson, needs to be checked. I don't care who he thinks he is. The best way, in my opinion, is to invite him down to your office, have a courteous meeting with him and tell him you will make his case a priority, but for that to take place, he needs to cease and desist from all this nonsense. What he is doing here is not proper at all. If he wants to behave this way, he can go back to the US and find trouble there.'

'Yes, sir, of course,' Andoh said. 'On top of it all, this mess he finds himself in is all his own doing. What galls me is his collaboration with Sana Sana, who is probably encouraging him to behave in this arrogant manner.'

Akrofi looked at his watch. 'I have a meeting with President Bannerman.' He stood up. 'As always, keep this discussion completely confidential, please.'

'Yes, sir.'

'Bottom line, you need to stop this Tilson in his tracks. Quickly.'

Back in his office, Andoh brooded. Regarding Gordon Tilson, he agreed with Akrofi on what needed to be done, but Andoh had not always seen eye to eye with the IGP. In such situations, however, the director-general had to hide his feelings and kowtow to his superior. That was just how police hierarchy worked, not to mention Ghanaian society. Andoh didn't think Akrofi was much good, really. Take the issue of the

Cybercrime Division as an example. It was more than nine months ago that Andoh had alerted the IGP to the dire need for more funding. What had Akrofi done? Nothing. In fact, he hadn't even followed up with Andoh about it. Not a word.

Besides the lack of faith in Akrofi's professional effectiveness, Andoh harboured a well-hidden, years-long personal grudge against the IGP. It sat stubbornly in his psyche like an immovable mass of unrefined cement. But Akrofi was completely unaware of this resentment and even more oblivious to its origin.

CHAPTER SIXTY-FOUR

25th March, Accra

Josephine was getting off the phone after a long, trying conversation as James came in from work to find her in the bedroom lost in thought.

'What's wrong?' he said, stopping in the doorway.

She looked up. 'I was talking to one of the administrators at Kwame's care home, and she's saying he'll have to go to a higher level of care.'

'Oh?' James came in, peeling off his jacket and loosening his tie. 'What's going on?'

'His behaviour has become more aggressive,' Josephine said glumly. 'They don't know exactly why, but they can't handle him any more.'

'Where are they saying he should go?' James asked, sitting beside her.

'There's a couple of locations – she'll send me the links so we can take a look.'

'More expensive, I assume?'

'Of course. When does anything get cheaper?'

He put his arms around her, and they lay back on the bed. 'It will be OK,' he said.

'The finances?' she asked timorously.

'Of course. You have nothing to worry about. We can manage it just fine.'

She nodded, looking up at the ceiling. A tear ran from the corner of her eye down the side of her face. 'I love that boy so much. I want only the best for him.'

'And he will always get it,' James said, wiping the tear away. 'Why are you so anxious?'

'Because if President Bannerman loses power, I know you'll be asked to leave your IGP post. And then all the perks we have right now will vanish.'

'First of all,' James said, 'Bannerman is not going to lose the election. He and the party are way ahead at the polls now that Evans-Aidoo is gone. Second, you act as if we'll suddenly turn broke. I'm a lawyer, I'll go back to practising law in the private sector and we'll have our other source of funds as well, so we'll be OK, my love.'

He kissed her on the cheek.

'Have they made any headway with that?' she asked. 'I mean, in finding out who was responsible for Evans-Aidoo's death?'

'No,' James said, sitting up. 'They have not. The BNI is heading up the investigation and as far as I'm concerned, they are a bunch of incompetents – except for a few of them.' He shook his head and got off the bed to undress. 'I'm going to take a shower.'

'OK. Dinner will be ready by the time you get out.'

* * *

Around 11 p.m., after they'd watched the late TV news together in bed, Josephine and James switched out their respective bedside lights and slipped under the covers. The air conditioner was set at a comfortable level for the night.

James always slept better than she did. Nine times out of ten, his breathing would settle into a light snore within a few minutes and he was away in dreamland long before she was. She slept on her side while he was always face up. She watched the silhouette of his profile against the faint light coming into the window from the garden lamps. She could tell he was wide awake instead of dozing off.

'What's wrong?' she said.

'Hm?'

'It's my turn to ask what's worrying you, because I know something is.'

He heaved a sigh. 'I received the strangest letter today from an American man in Ghana.'

Josephine lifted her head slightly off the pillow. 'A letter? About what?'

'The gentleman is a victim of a Ghanaian Internet scam. He came here to meet the woman he thought he was talking to, and now that he's discovered what a fool he's been made of, he's irate and trying to throw his weight around.'

Josephine's muscles tightened involuntarily. 'What's his name?'

'Gordon Tilson.'

Her stomach flipped and plunged. She was silent for a moment. 'Well . . . but what did he say in the letter exactly?'

James quoted it as faithfully as he could from memory. 'I'll show it to you tomorrow,' he added.

Josephine lay very still. Then she said, 'That is outrageous.'

It disturbed her to no end that Gordon had written this letter. It felt like a personal assault, a cannon strike to the walls of her castle, where she was normally snug and secure. But at the same time, she realised she might have staved off this attack. At Second Cup, she had promised Gordon she would bring his situation to James and thereby, she hoped, get CID moving on the American's case. This letter might not have ensued if she had done as promised. But she hadn't, because during her meeting with Gordon at Second Cup, something had happened. The moment he launched into that line of questioning over whether top police officials were in cahoots with *sakawa* boys, her sympathetic attitude towards Gordon had evaporated. His giving credence to Sana Sana had added insult to injury. Had she overreacted? Perhaps. At any rate, now she certainly could not reveal to James that she knew Gordon, especially with the memory of the Washington tryst hanging over her head like a shroud of guilt.

'I spoke to Alex Andoh about it,' James said, bringing her out of her thoughts. 'He'll take care of Mr Tilson.'

She looked at his silhouette again. 'What does that mean?'

'Well, with these things, it's always good to start diplomatically,' he said.

And then what? she wondered.

CHAPTER SIXTY-FIVE

8th June, Accra, Ghana

Emma had an expanding lump of panic in her throat. It was almost 9 a.m. and, running late to the airport, she was afraid she would miss Derek. He would already be inside Terminal 3 beyond the PASSENGERS ONLY sign. With an air of confidence, Emma flashed her Sowah PI Agency badge at the guard at the entrance. 'CID detective,' she said. 'Here to arrest a suspect.'

He was confused for a second. 'What? Heh! Wait!'

'There's no time,' Emma said over her shoulder. 'I have to catch him before he boards.' She scanned the check-in areas ahead for Derek and spotted him at the Delta counter.

Moving closer to the gate entry point to be sure she didn't miss him, she waited for him to be done. As he walked up with one hand holding his travel documents and the other wheeling a spinner carry-on, he saw her, and his face lit up. 'Emma!'

'Hi, Derek. I was scared you had already gone in.'

They embraced.

'Thank you for everything,' he said in her ear. 'You've been wonderful.'

They were both teary as they separated and looked at each other.

'You know you have my deepest condolences,' she said.

He nodded. 'Yes, I do. I can't thank you enough.'

She squeezed his hand. 'I will keep working on this. It's not over at all. Sowah and I will find who killed your father.'

'I know you will,' he said.

'Did they airlift him home?'

'Yes, he arrived in DC yesterday and they'll do the autopsy in the next few days. I'll forward the report to your email.'

'Please do.' She smiled sadly at him. 'Will you ever come back to Ghana?'

Derek sighed. 'I'm not sure. It will take me some time to heal.'

'I understand,' Emma said. 'I would feel the same way. But please stay in touch, and if you ever return, be sure to look me up.'

'I will.' He hesitated. 'Emma, it's possible the FBI will look into Dad's death once he arrives in the States. If anything comes up, I'll let you know.'

'Good,' Emma said. 'Thank you. Bye, Derek.'

They hugged again briefly. Emma watched him going up the escalator to the gates, and then he disappeared. She wiped away the tears that had welled in her eyes.

In another world, Derek would be her husband. Oh, well. She turned away to the terminal exit where the same guard she had encountered on the way in said sarcastically, 'I see you made your arrest.'

She blew him a kiss.

CHAPTER SIXTY-SIX

10th June, Washington, DC

The second day after Derek's return home, he was horrified at what he saw when he went to pay a visit to Cas. His bony frame was now beyond skeletal. Gordon's death had deeply affected him, obviously, but Derek wondered if anything else was wrong. Cas was coughing continuously – a ghastly, phlegm-filled cough.

'Should I take you to the ER?' Derek suggested.

Cas shook his head, trying to get through another fit of hacking. 'It's just a cold,' he managed to get out. 'What's the doctor going to say? Rest, drink plenty of fluids.'

'The results of Dad's autopsy should be ready this week,' Derek said when Cas managed to quiet the paroxysms for a while.

Derek was sitting opposite him in the sitting room. Outside, even before the official start of summer, DC's heat and humidity were already brutal.

Cas grabbed a handful of tissues and dabbed at his eyes. 'It's tough to lose a friend.' His voice quivered. He looked at Derek and smiled wanly. 'And a father, of course.'

'Yes. Thank you, Cas. This isn't easy for either of us.'

'I'm sorry, Derek. I've done an awful thing.'

'How do you mean?'

But Cas had doubled over in another fit, so violent that it sent him to the floor.

'Cas?' Derek got to his feet. 'Cas?'

Cas tried to sit upright. 'I shouldn't have—'

But there was no point his trying to talk any further. As the paroxysm worsened, he slumped forward with a kind of whimper, his face now ashen and lips slightly blue.

'Oh, fuck,' Derek said.

It had been a long wait outside in the ER waiting room at MedStar Georgetown University Hospital. Derek had called 911 and after getting to the hospital had to explain his relationship to Cas. They asked, did Cas have any next of kin?

'You're looking at him,' Derek said. 'His wife's in a nursing home with dementia, his only child hasn't spoken to him in thirty years, and neither he nor I know where the hell she is. So whatever policies and procedures you have regarding next of kin, you better make this work.'

For two hours, Derek had no idea what was going on in there. Staff came and went, people got called, patients went in and came out. Derek's butt got so sore from sitting he had to get up and walk. He was numb with misery. His father dead, his father's friend sick with only God knew what.

Finally, a young – very young – female doctor came out to Derek. Was he getting old or was this a child prodigy?

'We had to intubate Mr Guttenberg,' she explained. 'He was hypoxic breathing on his own. Looks like he has pneumonia, or it could be lung cancer, or both. He'll be going up to the ICU as soon as we get a bed.'

'Is he going to be OK?' Derek asked. 'In other words, should I stick around for a while?'

She wiggled her lips around. 'We're not sure of his prognosis just yet, but I would say he's stable for now. I mean, you could go home and get some rest, come back in the morning. If anything comes up, we can always call you, but at this point there's not much you can do.'

Derek nodded. 'Thanks. I'll come back tomorrow, then.'

As he drove home, Derek wondered how and why life had become so sad and grim. Had he been a religious man, he would have asked if God was punishing him. Now Derek recalled something that had been buried in the excitement. Cas had been trying to say something before becoming completely overwhelmed by his coughing fits. 'I've done an awful thing,' he had said. And after that, he started to say he shouldn't have . . . what?

CHAPTER SIXTY-SEVEN

18th June, Accra, Ghana

Sowah called Emma into his office after the morning brief. 'Have a seat, Emma. I want to talk to you about the Tilson case.'

'Yes, sir.'

'We've found Mr Gordon Tilson as his son requested. This was a classic missing person case with a terrible outcome. We wish it could have been a happy ending. Unfortunately, it was not.'

'Yes,' Emma said. 'Very sad.'

'Despite that,' Sowah continued, 'we have fulfilled the task Derek assigned to us. The rest, namely finding who actually killed Gordon Tilson, is now in the hands of the police.'

Emma felt her dismay rising as she realised what Sowah was driving at. 'You mean we're not going to keep on investigating?'

'As I said, it's now in CID's court. Let them handle it. We are under no obligation to investigate, especially now that DCOP Laryea is overseeing Quaino and Damptey. Laryea is a straight shooter. He will see to it.'

'Oh,' Emma said, defeated.

'Why so downhearted?'

'I promised . . .'

'Promised what?'

'I promised Derek we would find the culprit.'

'And we will. Maybe not you and I specifically, but the culprit will be found.'

'Yes, sir.'

'I can see you're disappointed,' Sowah said, smiling a little. 'I know you would have liked to be the one to bring Mr Tilson's murderer in, but I would rather we don't tangle with murderers if we don't have to.'

'Of course, sir. You're right.'

'In the meantime, I have a brand-new case for you.'

At her desk, Emma wrestled with her feelings of profound let-down. She agreed that the flavour of the case had changed: a missing person was now a murdered one, and her boss didn't want her exposed to some potentially dangerous men, but she felt empty and unfulfilled leaving it at that. The logical next step after finding Gordon so hideously murdered was to find out who did it.

Emma's phone rang and, to her surprise, it was Bruno. He almost never called her.

'Bruno, what a miracle,' she said dryly.

'Oh, *chaley*.' He laughed. 'How be, sis?'

'By God's grace. And you?'

'I'm good, oo. Are you at work?'

'Yes, I am. What's up?'

'I have a question for you.'

'OK,' Emma said. 'Go ahead.'

'You go to some place every Sunday – what is it called?'

'Autism Centre.'

'Ah, autism. I see. Those children, they can't talk, or what?'

'Some do, some don't. For example, Kojo, my favourite, is thirteen years old and up till now, he doesn't speak, but he can draw very well. Why do you ask about it?'

'Some guy told me they be devil children. Is it true?'

'No, it's not,' Emma said. 'As for we Ghanaians, as soon as we fear something or don't understand it, then we call it juju, or the devil, or curses. But it's not like that.'

'Ah, OK. What about his mother and father?'

'His father, I have no idea where he is,' Emma said. 'But Abena, his mother, is a very nice woman. Normally, they visit me on Sunday evenings. Why don't you come to my house this Sunday to meet them?'

'OK,' Bruno said, with a slight hesitation. 'I will do that.'

When Emma ended the call, she toyed with a happy fantasy that Bruno would be quite taken by Kojo and might show an interest in helping at the Autism Centre. Somehow, though, she didn't believe that would happen.

CHAPTER SIXTY-EIGHT

19th June

After much back and forth, a court order to the Apple Corporation granted the American Embassy Legat office in Accra access to Gordon Tilson's iCloud emails. Had those emails never been stored in the cloud, the FBI would never have seen any of these messages no matter how hard they tried to persuade Apple to enable them to break into Tilson's phone.

Gordon Tilson
24th February at 8.05 a.m.
Re: Ghana
To: CGuttenberg

Hey Cas – thought about what we discussed, but seriously, I feel like I should cut my losses and just get the hell out.

Casper Guttenberg
24th February at 12.32 p.m.
Re: Ghana
To: GTilson

OK, got it. I guess I understand, though I'm disappointed – not in you personally, that's not what I'm saying, but occasionally, a chance to make an impact comes along, and I was hoping you would take that chance.

There are signs that lots of Internet scam survivors are taking back the power by going to Ghana and confronting them. Watch this YouTube clip https://bit.ly/2CFEDi8 in which a European woman went to Ghana to hunt down her scammer. She got him, he was arrested and his house and car, both ill-got, were sold off by the authorities and the funds returned to the her. Very satisfying.

Gordon Tilson
24th February at 8.57 a.m.
Re: Ghana
To: CGuttenberg

Outrageous how luxurious the scammer's house was on that video. And an Escalade parked outside no less. I wonder what kind of car my scammer drives.

Casper Guttenberg
24th February at 2.16 p.m.
Re: Ghana
To: GTilson

Makes one's blood boil to think of these guys living in the lap of luxury all financed by stolen money. Well, maybe you can find out what kind of vehicle your scammer drives! It's rumoured some of them have Lamborghinis. How is that even possible? Still think you should at least try get in touch with the Sana Sana guy. And maybe Josephine, as well.

Gordon Tilson
27th February at 7.22 a.m.
Re: Ghana
To: CGuttenberg

You get my text yesterday? I reached Sana Sana via his FB page, kind of surprised he responded, but he's interested and, whatever it's worth, wants to meet with me next week on Thursday, March 5th.

Casper Guttenberg
27th February at 12.07 p.m.

Re: Ghana
To: GTilson

Outstanding you'll be meeting with Sana! I think it's worth at least a discussion with him. I'm betting he has a lot more resources at his disposal than we know. How about Josephine? Still undecided whether to reach out to her?

Gordon Tilson
1st March at 1.46 p.m.
Re: Ghana
To: CGuttenberg

Sana called today recommending I move out of the Kempinski Hotel to somewhere more 'sequestered', as he put it. He said Kempinski is one of those places to be 'noticed', whether intentionally or not, and if Sana (or anyone else) wanted to come to visit me in private, Kempinski is exactly the wrong place. Not to mention their rigid security here – guards everywhere for these big shots who breeze in and out of the hotel. They notice everyone who enters and leaves. I'm moving to another location tomorrow morning.

Gordon Tilson
2nd March at 8.42 a.m.

Re: Ghana
To: CGuttenberg

At my new accommodations, now, a B&B called Flamingo Lodge owned by a Dutch woman who's lived in Ghana practically all her life. Lovely woman, and her place is great with all the amenities including meals cooked on the spot by a chef, and a great espresso machine.

And you'll be proud of me: I'll be meeting with Josephine tomorrow.

Gordon Tilson
3rd March at 6.31 p.m.
Re: Ghana
To: CGuttenberg

Very interesting meeting with Josephine Akrofi today. We met late afternoon and had coffee. Of course, she looked incredible, but in the different setting of Ghana as against Washington, she seemed very different. It's all context, I guess. She's the master of her domain, confident, competent, and quite rich. She didn't pour scorn over me at all, in fact, she bemoaned the present state and extent of Internet scams and the pain people like me are being put through. Indirectly I asked her about possible collusion of highly placed officials – government

*or otherwise – in the scams, and she became
kinda defensive about it. In the same breath, she
castigated Sana Sana – ripped him to shreds really
– even without my having brought him up. I didn't
have the heart to tell her that I'll be meeting Sana in
a few days. I don't want to antagonise her, but it's
clear whose side she's on – her husband's, the IGP,
and the 'establishment', and why should she not be?
She lives a really cushy life with all the trimmings
and perks. Talk about the one per cent!*

Casper Guttenberg
4th March at 2.09 a.m.
Re: Ghana
To: GTilson

*Fascinating. Would be intriguing if her
'defensiveness' has something to do with her own
knowledge of highly placed people who are in on
these online cons. She's not going to squeal on
them if they belong to her inner circle. You're in
the driver's seat obviously and I don't want to
be a backseat driver, but I would mention your
meeting with Josephine to Sana when you see
him. Tell him you have a possible 'in' on this via
Josephine. I feel you shouldn't avoid her, even
if she seems a little distant to you compared to
when you met her in Washington.*

Gordon Tilson
5th March at 11.11 a.m.
Re: Ghana
To: CGuttenberg

I met the famous/infamous Sana today at a secluded, wooded area outside of town. He had his signature 'cap and beads', and at first it was a weird experience talking to him, but after a little while I got accustomed to it and it even felt kind of normal. He took down all the details of my story and asked me to forward my WhatsApp conversations with 'Helena'. He seemed a little surprised by my interest in the wider scope of my being conned, i.e. how far up this thing all goes. He said most white people just want to catch the con artists, get their money back, and get the hell out. I suppose it has to do with my connection with Ghana. I spent a great two years of my life here as a Peace Corps guy, I met my wife here, I came back to Ghana with her multiple times to visit, and on top of all that, when you think of it, Derek is half Ghanaian. So, when I see all this crap ruining this country, I guess I basically care more than the average 'oburoni'.

Sana told me some chilling stories of how groups of 'sakawa boys' now organise into factions based on their location where they can then exercise control over the local police or even chiefs in that specific area. Someone high up in the government or police force can then oversee a cluster of these factions and make money off them in return for protection. Reputedly, at the top of the whole pile is one guy whose name is, appropriately, 'Godfather', but I'm not sure if that's just urban legend.

Casper Guttenberg
7th March at 7.11 p.m.
Re: Ghana
To: GTilson

This is some amazing work you're doing, Gordon. I think we have enough for me to begin drafting the first write-up. Great job, my friend.

Gordon Tilson
22nd March at 11.36 a.m.
Re: Ghana
To: CGuttenberg

Started with diarrhoea last night, something I ate, I guess. Feeling pretty lousy. I'll go get something from the pharmacy down the street. The pharmacies are very well stocked here. Beginning to feel I should call it quits in Ghana and come home. I don't know how much more I can get out of this quest I'm on, and it's not as important as it felt back in February.

Casper Guttenberg
22nd March at 12.45 p.m.
Re: Ghana
To: GTilson

Sorry to hear about the stomach upset. Hopefully you'll feel better soon. Regarding the 'quest', you should do whatever feels right for you, Gordon, but I think if you could see the witch doctor guy Sana told you about, that could really round up the story and tie up some loose ends. If a lot of the sakawa boys go to consult this man, maybe he might know about who duped you in particular. Maybe he'll let on if you offer him some serious money. Just think if you could nab the guy who did this to you! I get you're tired and I agree you should come home soon. Just don't give it up too prematurely. I've written up Part One, and it looks great. I'll send it to you once Marc has taken a look and you can make changes or additions if you see fit. Feel better, my friend!

CHAPTER SIXTY-NINE

21st June

On Sunday evening Abena and Kojo visited Emma as they did most Sundays. Reproducible routine was important to Kojo, and this was one that he liked.

Emma welcomed them at the door. 'Come in, come in. Kojo, how are you?' He didn't respond or look up at Emma, but she sensed his acknowledgement instinctively. 'I've started the *nkontomire*,' she said to Abena as they went to the kitchen.

Emma left the main door open while closing just the screen door to allow some air to circulate through the tiny house and release food fumes from the matchbox kitchen. Abena sat Kojo down on a mat in the corner. 'I brought his tablet to keep him calm,' she said.

'Is that one from the Centre?' Emma asked.

'No – Mrs Akrofi gave him a new one.'

'That's nice of her. When will you go to her house with Kojo to do the video?'

'I don't know yet,' Abena said. 'They want to film

him at the Centre first. I know they're hoping Kojo will draw something again, but since the first time, he hasn't done anything.'

'He will do it when the spirit moves him,' Emma said, beginning to grind fresh chillis on a large, flat stone. The fresh, piercing odour tantalised her. 'My brother Bruno was asking about autism today. I told him he should visit this evening and meet Kojo. I wish I could get him interested in doing something good in his life – maybe volunteer to work with autistic kids.'

'That will be really great,' Abena said. She looked over at her son, who was sitting cross-legged on his mat.

'Have you ever had a full night's sleep since Kojo was born?' Emma asked.

Abena pulled a face. 'No, I don't think so.'

'He can sleep on my bed when he's ready,' Emma offered.

Late that afternoon, Bruno had asked Nii to take him to Emma's house in Madina.

'She said Abena and her son will visit her this evening,' Bruno explained. 'So, I will see if I can get one of the boy's shirts.'

'How are you going to do that?' Nii asked.

Bruno chewed on the inside of his cheek. 'I don't know.'

He was quiet almost the entire journey as he thought it over. Traffic from town to Madina was impossible. As they waited in the gridlock that plagued the stretch from the 37 Roundabout up to the Accra Mall interchange, the customary itinerant traders plied the lanes between vehicles waving food and cheap goods in the windows for a quick, on-the-run sale. Bruno was idly watching a vendor ahead of them with a skyscraper load of children's clothes balanced on her head when a brainwave struck. He lowered the window and emitted a sharp whistle to catch her attention. Her merchandise was still rock steady on its human perch as she ran up eagerly to Bruno. He asked for a T-shirt to fit a thirteen-year-old. He had no idea how big or small Kojo was, but he would take his chances.

He chose a canary yellow one as cars began to move forward. 'Do you have another one, same size?' he asked her.

Rummaging through her collection while half-trotting alongside the vehicle, the trader found a duplicate and Bruno paid her just as traffic finally began moving.

It was almost seven when they reached Madina. Nii parked, but looked unsure whether he was getting out or not.

'What are you waiting for?' Bruno asked, shooting Nii a look.

'I'm shy of your sister,' he confessed.

Bruno laughed and sucked his teeth. 'You are not serious. She won't do anything. Come on, let's go.'

They walked along the uneven pathway between houses until they came to Emma's. Bruno knocked and called out, '*Kokoo ko!*'

Emma came to the door. '*Ei*, Bruno! So, you came after all. I thought maybe you weren't.'

'Sorry, sis. Traffic. Nii brought me.'

'Come in, come in,' Emma said. 'Hi, Nii. Thank you for coming.'

'Good evening,' Nii muttered.

'He's shy,' Bruno said, laughing.

Nii glared at him and gave him a mock slap to the back of his head. 'Shut up. I'm not.'

Emma laughed at them. 'Silly boys. Come and meet Abena and Kojo.'

In the thick of cooking, Abena offered her wrist to the two men instead of a full handshake on introduction.

'This is Kojo,' Emma said, kneeling next to him.

Bruno followed her cue and addressed Kojo. 'How are you? Give me five.'

Kojo, glued to his tablet, ignored him.

Emma smiled. 'He has to get used to you first.'

'I brought something for him,' Bruno said to Abena, producing the new T-shirt, still in its shrink wrapping.

'Oh!' Abena cried. '*Medaase!*'

'That's so nice of you,' Emma said to Bruno. She was genuinely surprised at his gesture. She would not have predicted it of him.

Abena washed her hands hurriedly, opened the package and unfolded the shirt for Kojo to see. 'Look,' she said. 'See what your Uncle Bruno brought you.'

Kojo grabbed it, apparently attracted to the bright colour.

'Yellow is even his favourite colour,' Abena said, delighted.

'Let's see how it looks on him,' Emma said.

'I hope the size is correct,' Bruno said, getting his phone ready.

'Oh, I think so,' Abena said, pulling off Kojo's present shirt. She put it aside and Bruno discreetly took a picture of shirtless Kojo.

Abena persuaded her son to let go of the garment and then put it on him with a mother's practised deftness. 'It's perfect,' she said, laughing. 'Bruno, thank you so much.'

'Take a pic of us together,' he said, handing Emma his phone. He crouched beside Kojo and made a cool finger sign.

'Such handsome young men,' Emma said, snapping several images.

'Yes, that's very true,' Bruno agreed. He looked at Kojo and gave his head a friendly rub. The boy did not appear to mind.

CHAPTER SEVENTY

Next morning, Bruno and Nii were ready to take Kojo's yellow T-shirt to Ponsu, but Nii was uneasy.

'Be careful,' he cautioned. 'Maybe Ponsu has the power to know that the boy didn't really wear it.'

Bruno said, 'Is that so?' Then he shook his head and dismissed the notion. 'He won't know. And if he challenges me, I will challenge him back. Let's go.'

Still, they were in some suspense as they watched Ponsu examining the garment. Bruno then showed Ponsu the before and after phone pics. He grunted and nodded. 'OK,' he said, apparently satisfied. He turned and yelled, '*Ama!*'

A young woman came running. 'Yes, Papa?'

Ponsu handed her the T-shirt. 'Take this, burn it, and make into a powder and bring it back.'

'Yes, Papa.' She went away.

'One of my daughters,' Ponsu said with pride to the other two men. 'She's here from our hometown.'

Bruno and Nii murmured appropriate approval. Ponsu excused himself and disappeared around the corner somewhere. He seemed to have been gone for a long time, but when he returned, he had a black powder in an old chipped bowl in one hand and a sachet of water in the other. He sat down and silently mixed the water in slowly with the black powder.

'Please, that's the boy's shirt?' Bruno asked. 'You burnt it?'

Ponsu nodded, mixing diligently. Bruno shot Nii a knowing look of disgust. He knew what was coming next.

The priest held out the dark concoction. 'If you don't fear to become a madman like the boy, drink it.'

Bruno hesitated. Ponsu was pushing him past his limit. He felt like punching the priest in the head. But where would that get Bruno? Nowhere. He took the potion from the priest, took a breath, and drank it. It was grainy, bland, and bitter all at the same time. Bruno pulled a face and gave the bowl back.

'You are good,' Ponsu said, showing a level of approval that had been absent until this point. 'Now you have power. The *mugus* can't control you, but you can make them do whatever you want. From this day on, when you are asking money from the *mugus*, you will see they will become confused and send you money no matter how much you ask for. The *mugu*'s family will even be telling him to stop, but he won't be able to help himself.'

'That's great,' Bruno said. 'Please, what about Godfather?'

'You can go with Nii the next time he will visit.'

That put a big smile on Bruno's face. 'Yes please. Thank you.'

When Bruno met with Sana Sana the next time, he wasn't alone. Along with his two bodyguards, four of his other investigators were present, each of them to discuss their latest progress and to receive further instructions.

In Bruno's case, Sana wanted to know when the tentative meeting with Godfather would take place.

'I don't know yet,' Bruno said. 'I think it will be soon, but I will hear from Nii before.'

He thought the golden beads cascading from Sana's boonie hat in front of his face was one of his most attractive getups. Sana rose from his seat and beckoned to Bruno.

'Come and sit here.'

Bruno, afraid something was wrong, sat down warily.

'Up till this time,' Sana said to him, 'I have not shown you my face because I have been waiting to be sure you can be trusted. That time has come. You are a good man, a hard worker, courageous, and above all, trustworthy. So, from this day forth, you will now know what I look like.'

Bruno was riveted as Sana pulled the beads to one side and slowly removed his hat. The others in the room began to laugh as it became clear that Sana was wearing a lifelike mask under that.

'OK,' he said, chuckling. 'This time, I'm really going to reveal myself.'

He snatched the latex mask off and Bruno saw a man in his early forties with a lean, angular face, a small tribal mark on his left cheek, short hair, moustache and goatee. While Bruno had imagined an intense, fierce gaze, Sana's eyes were very much softer – kind, in fact.

'Wow,' Bruno said.

'Yes, so now you know,' Sana said. 'You may now give me my chair back.'

Bruno jumped up stammering, 'So sorry, please,' much to the amusement of the others in the room.

'This is the secret camera you'll be using to film Godfather,' Sana said, holding out a watch to Bruno, who took it gingerly.

He feasted his eyes on the device. It was thick and beefy with four buttons on the chrome bezel – three on the right and one on the left. The face was matte black with two chronographs.

'This has a camera?' he asked in wonder. 'Where is it?'

'At the six,' Sana said.

Bruno peered closer. 'I can't even see it.'

'Let me show you how to operate it.'

Bruno gave it back and Sana showed him which buttons to push for photo and video as well as the charging port. 'Wear it and use it so you can accustom yourself to it and learn how to get the best photos and videos. For example, if you're sitting down opposite the person, you rest your forearm on your thighs with the wrist turned outward.'

Bruno nodded. 'Yes please.'

'But be very careful with it. It's expensive.'

Bruno carefully fastened the watch to his wrist. 'Thank you, my boss.' He felt full of pride.

'Let me know as soon as you hear from Nii Kwei,' Sana said, 'and we will meet again to plan some more. I will be giving you dollars to take to Godfather. You'll tell him it's money you made from the *mugus*. You will pay him that money, and it's very important that you get that on video. We must show him accepting money in return for your protection from law enforcement all so that the *sakawa* system can continue to flourish.'

He looked around. 'All of you men are my faithful warriors. I'm your leader, and I care about what happens to you. That's why I never stop reminding you that these are dangerous times. In the past few months, the death threats against me and my film crew have been on the rise. Yesterday alone, I've received four on Messenger, and one of them mentioned *sakawa* and warned me to stop investigating it.' Sana looked at the two bodyguards. 'Next week, I will attend the UNESCO Conference on Press Freedom and we will need to be careful. After that event, I'll be lying low until we're ready to present the *sakawa* story to the world.'

CHAPTER SEVENTY-ONE

27th June

The new Centre Against Corruption (CAC) was President Bannerman's brainchild. A month after completing its construction on the premises behind the CID building, the grand opening, evening gala, and fundraiser were in full swing. Cream in colour, the floodlit, colonnaded edifice appeared luminescent and classic against the night sky. The courtyard within accommodated hundreds of well-heeled partygoers coiffed and dressed to the nines. Everyone who was anyone in Accra was in attendance, most of them undoubtedly keen for a chance to chat with the president. Getting to him was easier said than done, however. Apart from his entourage of closest associates, he had a flank of personal, armed bodyguards.

In general, with military and SWAT present, security was heavy. Both Dazz and Edwin were on duty, Dazz on the rooftop and Edwin patrolling the grounds. At midnight, Edwin would switch places with another team member at the front entrance.

James and Josephine Akrofi were among those lucky enough to be in President Bannerman's inner circle. The Akrofis were big donors to the new centre and their names were already up on the brass-plated list of patrons. The conversation was lively and the champagne bubbly. A DJ was spinning tunes and there was a small dance floor. Shortly after midnight, Josephine whispered to James that she needed to get something from the car. He nodded.

When Josephine reached the front, Edwin was keeping an eye on the car park and surroundings.

'Madam, can I help you with anything?'

'Please escort me to my car, officer.'

'Yes, of course, madam.'

He walked alongside her. Their shoes created an irregular rhythm on the asphalt. 'How are you, Edwin?' she said quietly.

'I'm fine, Mummy. And you?'

'I'm good. It's been quite some time since we spoke. Why don't you call more often?'

'Sorry. I should do that. You look very nice tonight, by the way.'

'Thank you.' She smiled at him as they passed a row of shiny SUVs, still the vehicle of choice for the well-off. A few chauffeurs were hanging around talking to pass the time.

'Where are we going?' she asked him.

He pointed ahead. 'Over there.'

At the end of the car park was a not-yet-open garden of shrubs and shade trees, a seating area with tables and chairs, and what was to be a bar with soft drinks and snacks for the centre's employees. The only illumination of this corner came from the lamps in the parking area. Now, Edwin and Josephine were in the shadows.

They sat down together.

'Do you ever speak to your father?' Josephine asked.

Edwin grunted. 'He doesn't even mind me. Even at CID, it's like I'm not even there.'

She squeezed his hand. 'Don't worry, eh?'

'I'm not at all worried,' Edwin said.

'That's good.'

'And Kwame, how is he?'

'He seems to be much better in his new spot,' she said. 'He had become tough for the old place to manage, so we had to move him out. He's adjusting well.'

'Great to hear that,' Edwin said, smiling. 'I'll never forget that day when he was a baby, long before you took him to UK, how you brought him to see me and I was holding him in my arms. It was so nice.'

Josephine nodded slowly as she thought back on it. 'Yes, it was. Whenever I think of that time, I wonder what it would have been like if he had been normal.'

'I know what you mean,' Edwin agreed, 'but praise God, Mummy, he is getting very good care in *aburokyire*.'

'Yes, we thank God,' she said. 'How is work – and your friends, Courage and Dazz?'

'They are doing great.' Edwin paused. 'Mummy, I want to move to a new place.'

'Oh? Where?'

'On Spintex Road. Two bedrooms. They want two years' rent in advance.'

That was against the law, but all the landlords did that.

'How much, my dear?' Josephine asked.

'It comes to seventy thousand.'

'Is it a nice place?'

'Very,' Edwin said. 'Just a little repair work here and there, which will be easy for me. I can pay some of it – maybe about five thousand.'

'All right, dear,' she said. 'I'll transfer the rest to your account on Monday.'

On the roof, Dazz had noticed Edwin escorting the IGP's wife. The area inside the perimeter of the CAC was secure, so accompanying the ladies was a courtesy and formality, really, as well as an opportunity for tips, sometimes good ones. The tips made these after-hours events worth their while. Dazz didn't keep exact track of the time since he had seen Edwin with Mrs Akrofi and when he put his night-vision goggles to his eyes, it was not for the purpose of 'checking up' on them. But as he slowly scanned the perimeter of the property, he passed two figures in the garden area at the far end of the car park and came back to focus on them. Dazz's head jerked back with surprise at first. He returned his eyes to the goggles to double check that he had really seen what he thought he had seen. Yes, it was indeed Edwin and Mrs Akrofi locked in an embrace.

CHAPTER SEVENTY-TWO

23rd March, Accra, Ghana

Meandering around the Internet, Gordon came across a Facebook page titled 'Sakawa Boys'. Among the video shorts was one of a reputedly filthy-rich Internet fraudster standing on the second-floor balcony of the West Hills Mall outside Accra while showering elated shoppers below with hundreds of *cedi* bills. Eventually, the clamour turned into a dangerous stampede in which people got hurt. The comments below the clip ranged from 'This is shameful' to 'This is either totally fake or a publicity stunt'.

Gordon noticed an answer to the latter comment from someone called Susan Hadley. She wrote, 'It could be real! I've encountered one of these *sakawa* guys and they really do make that kind of cash. It's not as easy a life as one might think, though.'

Gordon clicked on Susan Hadley's name and sent her a private message. 'I don't know your location, but would you be willing to talk to me about *sakawa*? I'm in Accra but originally from the States. One of these guys duped me. I'm here to find him and I want to know everything about their world.'

Susan replied several hours later. 'I'm in Accra as well. I have some experience with *sakawa* boys. Call me.'

She had left a phone number, and so he did. She told him she was in Ghana for a short vacation. 'So, you were scammed by an Internet fraudster?' she asked him, cutting to the chase.

'I was,' Gordon said, 'and now I'm learning to own it and face it head on.'

'I'd like to hear about it,' Susan said. 'Want to meet for coffee?'

'Sure, absolutely.'

She suggested a time and place: that evening at a coffee and sandwiches place called Ci Gusta! in the Airport Residential area.

Gordon and Susan found an isolated table in Ci Gusta!'s farthest corner. The decor was bright and modern, the atmosphere cheerful. Outside on the patio sat a mixed crowd with a heavy presence of chain-smoking Lebanese.

Gordon ordered a pistachio ice cream while Susan had a raspberry froyo. He sized her up quickly as a burning-out blonde at the point where ageing was about to usurp her attractiveness.

Once they were settled, she said, 'So, I'm eager to hear your story.'

He told her, and she listened without a word till the very end.

'Quite a tale,' she said. 'Unfortunately, not that uncommon.'

'So, what's the "experience with *sakawa* boys" you said you've had?' Gordon asked.

'Four years ago,' Susan began, 'I came to Ghana for a two-year visiting professorship in physics at the University of Ghana. I met a political science student, and we got romantically involved with each other. Nii – that's his name – was poor as a church mouse then. Fast forward a couple of years, I come back to Ghana in February this year and Nii has transformed himself. He has expensive clothes and he's driving a fancy car and living in a near mansion. Unbelievable. I knew there was no way this could be legit money. When I first asked him about it, he was evasive, but after I badgered him almost to distraction, he admitted he was a fraud boy, or *sakawa* boy – whatever term you prefer.'

'What was his con game of preference?'

'He's done a little of everything – the rom-cons, like yours, and so on, but the most lucrative for him are the gold scams. They make thousands of dollars, and with a strong dollar they reap a boatload in local currency.'

'You think I could meet this guy – Nii? You're still in touch with him?'

'In a way,' she said cryptically. 'Not like before. I felt uncomfortable about his lifestyle and livelihood.'

'Why didn't you turn him in to the authorities?'

409

Susan fixed him with a look. 'You're kidding, right?'

Gordon turned sheepish. 'Sorry, bad question. Anyway, can I meet this guy?'

'Depends what you're looking for.'

'I'm hoping he might know who ripped me off.'

Susan was doubtful. 'Given how many fraudsters there are in Ghana and their unwillingness to snitch on each other, I'd say the likelihood of your finding that out is small, but we could try.'

'What about how police and other government officials are in on the game?' Gordon asked. 'Could he help me there?'

She pursed her lips. 'Maybe, but we'd need to sweeten this up a lot.'

Gordon nodded. 'I fully expected that. How much do you think he would want?'

'It's hard to make Ghanaians name a price upfront, but I would say three hundred and fifty would be reasonable.'

'Three-fifty *cedis*?'

Susan looked amused. 'Dollars.'

'Of course. What was I thinking?'

'You have dollars with you?'

'I have some back at the hotel, yes.'

'If you're short, you can give the rest in *cedi* equivalent. You want me to text Nii now?'

'That would be great.'

Susan did, and about ten minutes later, her phone rang.

'Hi, Nii,' she said, and Gordon was impressed by

how instantly her voice switched to tones of honey. 'How are you? I'm fine, thank you. I have a very dear friend from the States I'd like you to meet. He needs help, and I told him I know exactly the person.'

CHAPTER SEVENTY-THREE

Independence Day, Washington, DC

Cas's body was being ravaged by metastatic lung cancer. He had almost died of respiratory failure in the hospital ER and had spent ten days in the ICU. That could enervate even the most robust of patients, never mind one riddled with malignancy. By the time Cas was back on the recovery ward, he looked like a bag of bones.

Derek was his durable power of attorney and next of kin by default. Once Cas was strong enough, he would go to an assisted living centre to spend the short time he had left on earth. At the bedside of the dying man, Derek felt pity for him and a kind of sad anger.

'I'm sorry I couldn't attend Gordon's – your father's – funeral,' Cas said, his eyes closed, his voice feeble and his words muffled by the oxygen non-rebreather mask over his nose and mouth.

'You were in no state,' Derek said.

Cas nodded. 'Did you ever get the autopsy report?'

'Yes.' Derek knew it by heart. 'The cause of death

was drowning subsequent to blunt force trauma to the left parietal region of the skull. The mechanism of death was asphyxia. In other words, whoever killed Dad, bashed in his skull first, and then threw him into the river, where he drowned.'

A flash of pain registered on Cas's face. 'God,' he whispered.

'I know the part you played in his death,' Derek said after a moment.

Cas's eyes fluttered open. 'What?'

'Urging my father to stay in Ghana. I'm not sure if I should call it encouragement or egging him on to dig deeper and deeper into the case. I don't know this for sure, but I feel that if not for you, Dad would most likely have safely returned to the States.'

Cas kept his gaze fixed on the ceiling, where there was nothing more interesting to see than hospital white, and after a while, tears broke the dam and rushed down his hollow, weathered cheeks like water into a craggy canyon. 'How did you know?' he whispered.

'Your emails between you and Dad were all in the cloud,' Derek said. 'That's the only morsel Apple grudgingly tossed to the FBI. So, they dug it up and notified me.'

'Derek, I didn't think anything like that would happen to Gordon.'

'But you were willing to risk it just so you could get a feature in the *Observer*?' Derek asked, his voice sharpening.

'I knew I had cancer,' Cas said. 'I knew I was going to

die. One last round before I go. One final article to leave the world with. That's what I was thinking.'

'But what I want to know,' Derek said, voice shaking, 'is did you give a thought to what kind of trouble Dad could have got into, and did? I mean, did you use him without a second's thought?'

Cas turned his head slightly in Derek's direction. 'I took it as a collaboration between us. I didn't feel I was coercing him. He was free to say no. He wanted to help me the way I helped him get started in Washington.'

Derek's lip curled. 'So, he owed you, is what you're saying.'

'No.' An odd, wheezing noise emanated from Cas, the sound of him weeping and trying to say something at the same time.

Derek leant forward. 'What?'

'Kill me. Please. Take my oxygen off and I'll die in ten minutes.'

Derek looked at the oxygen meter on the wall. It was set high at fifteen litres per minute.

Cas followed Derek's gaze and nodded, *Yes, that*. 'Turn it off.'

Derek drew in his breath and shook his head. 'I can't do it. I won't.'

Cas's eyes beseeched him. 'Forgive me.'

Derek didn't answer. Perhaps in time, he thought, straightening up. 'I have to get going now. I have power of attorney whether I like it or not. All your affairs will be taken care of.'

When he reached the door, Derek half turned as he heard Cas try for the last word. He had moved his oxygen mask to one side and now he said, in a strikingly stronger tone, 'I left everything to your dad. And in his absence, it all goes to you.'

CHAPTER SEVENTY-FOUR

25th March, Accra, Ghana

Nii Kwei didn't know much about Susan's American friend: the man was doing research for a book and wanted to know something about how *sakawa* works. Nii was fine with it as long as Susan had reassured him the guy was OK. Best thing was there'd be some cash in it for Nii as well.

At seven-thirty in the evening, he pulled up in his white gold Audi Q7 to Champs Sports Bar on Ring Road Central. The parking attendant waved him into a secure spot and Nii gave him a tip to keep an extra watch on his gorgeous vehicle.

Inside, the bar was alive with music, rowdy conversation, and laughter while an English Premier League football match was playing on the wide screens. Nii looked around and saw Susan waving. He walked over to her table where she and her friend were sitting. Susan stood up to embrace Nii before the introductions.

'This is my friend, Gordon. Gordon, meet Nii.'

The two men shook hands. Nii thought Gordon seemed familiar, but frankly a lot of white guys looked the same, so initially he didn't think too much of it. The white man seemed to be scrutinising him from top to bottom.

Susan ordered a carafe of white wine while the two men had a Stella Artois each. She did a good job breaking the ice, but Nii felt awkward and imagined the white man did too.

'So, yes, Nii,' Susan said. 'Gordon here is writing a paper on the *sakawa* phenomenon and I told him you have experience in that world.'

Nii only smiled.

'I hope it's OK to ask you a little about it,' Gordon said politely.

'No problem at all,' Nii responded, but he felt a chill pass through him like the hot ice of a malarial attack. It was all coming together – hard to believe, but impossible to deny. The voice, the face he recalled from Skype, and the name. *Gordon*. This was one of his *mugus*, right here in Ghana talking to Nii live. What did he want? What was he looking for?

'How long have you been dealing with the *sakawa* phenomenon?' the white man asked.

'Just a few years.'

'Lucrative, huh?'

Nii shrugged, 'Anyway, somehow.'

Susan interjected. 'Nii, I was telling Gordon the *sakawa* life is not as easy as it's sometimes portrayed on the Internet.'

'That's true,' Nii said. 'Sometimes the priest or *mallam* can make severe demands – like tell you to commit incest or dig up a coffin from the grave and sleep in it every night for two weeks.'

Gordon looked both incredulous and revolted. 'Oh, my God.'

'And even,' Nii continued, 'those are the easy ones. Every month, the *sakawa* gets a new ritual he must do. To be rich, you have to do some of the ultimate rituals.'

'How do you mean?' Gordon asked. He had finished his beer and signalled one of the waiters over. 'Get me a Smirnoff on the rocks, please.' He turned back to Nii. 'What is an ultimate ritual?'

'It involves removing highly treasured parts of the body and giving them to the priest,' Nii said cryptically.

'You're talking about things like genitalia and so on, right?' Gordon said.

'Yes please.'

'And those are the ones that make you the richest? How much are we talking?' His Smirnoff had arrived, and he started on it.

'Depends on the person,' Nii said, 'and what he's willing to do.'

'And if you don't fulfil the assigned task?'

'Terrible things can happen.'

'Like what?'

Nii sipped his drink. 'I know one guy, the priest told him to sleep with his sister and he refused. After a few days, he had boils all over his body.'

Gordon snorted and shot a dubious look at Susan, but her eyes were down, fixed on the table.

'Please, you say you are writing an article?' Nii asked Gordon.

'Right,' he said, sipping.

'An article for what, please?'

Gordon sidestepped. 'What I don't get is how doing all this ritual stuff can make you more successful at swindling people online.'

'My Audi is outside,' Nii said simply. 'You can go and look at it, if you like.'

'I'll pass,' Gordon said. 'I may not understand *sakawa* completely, but what I do know is it's out of control. It's a menace to society.'

The Smirnoff was unleashing Gordon's tongue and his feelings. Susan's eyes came up and flicked Gordon a warning.

Nii was wondering what was going on. Was Gordon on to him? 'Has something happened to you, please?' he asked Gordon. 'I can see you are very upset.'

'Upset? Me? No, not all. I'll tell you why I'm not upset. Because' – he grabbed his phone from off the table and began to fumble and scroll – 'because I came to Ghana to meet this lovely lady. Here she is. See?' He thrust his phone out to Nii. 'Yeah, this so-called Helena doesn't even exist. So why should I be upset?'

'Sarcasm isn't used much here,' Susan said in a matter-of-fact tone.

Gordon flapped his hand backward. 'OK, so I *am*

upset, OK? No money is free, Nii. *Ever*. You might steal some, or even a lot, but one day it's all going to backfire on you. And all you guys – the *sakawa* boys, the police, and government big wigs you're in league with? I can't *wait* for you to be exposed, and I'm going to play whatever part I can to make sure that happens.'

Susan rested her forehead in her palm. 'Jesus, Gordon.'

Nii stared at Gordon. 'Please, the way you are talking is not correct at all. We Ghanaians are hospitable to a point, but after that, the hospitality dries up like a stream in the Harmattan.' He stood up.

'Nii,' Susan said, half standing, 'please don't go. I'm sorry.'

But Nii did walk out, and in disgust. This is what he came for – to be insulted by this white guy? He got into the Audi, slammed the door, backed out, and gunned the engine. The tyres screeched and painted a layer of rubber on the driveway.

Gordon's affront gave Nii's defensiveness a boost, a branch to swing from. Someone like that *deserved* to be conned, and Nii wasn't one bit sorry about it. He voice-dialled a number on the Audi phone, and when the person at the other end picked up, Nii said, 'That man Tilson is in Ghana, and he's becoming a problem.'

420

CHAPTER SEVENTY-FIVE

5th July, Accra, Ghana

The International Trade Fair site, not far from Labadi Beach, is 120 acres of open space, part history as an Nkrumahera relic of 1960s Ghana, and part modern with its event spaces for anything from weddings to international conferences. As such, it's an odd mix of updated design with deteriorating infrastructure.

The Africa Pavilion, with a capacity of up to three thousand people, was the setting for the UNESCO Conference at which Sana was to speak. Dignitaries were arriving at the grand entrance where the Information Minister and other officials welcomed them to the first day of the meeting. Sana Sana was the keynote speaker for the morning plenary session.

Security at the event was medium, with uniformed armed police and military at the entrance and minimally armed guards in the car park. The gaggle of photographers was normal, but on this occasion, the tension and sense of excitement were high because Sana Sana was expected.

About five hundred metres away ran an enclosing wall and behind that a robust mango tree dense with leaves and ripening fruit. It wasn't the best place for the assassin to securely position himself and his long-range rifle, but it was the only available fixture in this otherwise rather barren stretch of land. It was an underdeveloped area begging for developers to get their hands on, and indeed, several investors had made a bid for it.

The assassin had climbed the tree before dawn. He wore a cap that he would pull down low over his face as soon as the mission was completed. The intelligence was that, by arrangement with the organisers of the conference, Sana would use the rear, secret entrance of the pavilion, bypassing all the reporters who fully anticipated his arrival at the front, where everyone else was.

The wait was long, and the assassin's quadriceps were aching from locking himself firmly into the tree's anatomy. He had a secure Y-shaped junction of two branches on which to rest the rifle, but when he fired, there must not be a millimetre's accidental shift in his stance. This was a far less certain target than Evans-Aidoo had been.

The assassin came to attention as the black Escalade Sana often used appeared on the access road to the Africa Pavilion and sped towards the rear entrance. The vehicle's windows were blacked out with the deepest tint possible. It came to a sharp halt in the no-parking zone in front of the entrance. The assassin readied himself. Sana would spend very little time moving between the SUV and the pavilion. One of his bodyguards hopped out, looked around, and then opened the rear door of the vehicle. For a moment, nothing happened, but then Sana, wearing a black Fedora with a curtain of dark beads hanging from the brim, stepped out and walked towards the building with a bodyguard following him. The assassin was a little surprised there weren't two. He had Sana's left temple isolated in the scope's field.

It was Sana's decoy who had alighted first from the SUV. The real Sana stayed inside the vehicle with the second of his two bodyguards. The driver kept the engine running.

A couple of seconds later, there was a sharp crack and the decoy collapsed instantly.

'*Drive! Go!*' the bodyguard shouted, pulling Sana down to the seat to shield him. The driver gunned the Escalade, which took off with a roar, tyres squealing. The bodyguard waited until they'd completely cleared the fair site before letting Sana up. 'Are you OK, my boss?'

'I'm fine, fine,' Sana said shakily.

He had survived yet another attempt on his life. It wouldn't be the first time. Nor the last.

CHAPTER SEVENTY-SIX

6th July

News of Sana's escape from death was all over the media within half an hour. The UNESCO Conference was immediately adjourned until the following day. In Sowah's office, no one was getting any work done. Emma and her colleagues were glued to their phones and the lounge TV. Radio discussions were exploding with theories about who might have been responsible for the assassination attempt. Sana's decoy had been struck not in the head as had probably been intended, but in the back. Fortunately, he had been wearing a bulletproof vest and would survive just fine.

Emma's phone rang and her heart jumped when she saw it was Derek calling from the US.

'How are you?' she said. 'It's great to hear from you and you sound much better.'

'I am doing better, thanks. And you, Emma? How's life?'

'No complaints really.'

'I wanted to share something with you,' Derek said. 'Do you have a moment?'

'Yes, of course. Let me move to somewhere quieter.' Emma went to the waiting area where there were no clients at the moment. 'OK, what have you got?'

'The FBI agent working on my father's case shared some emails with me. They're between my dad and his friend and I'd like you to look at them because there could be information you or the police or someone could use. Can I forward the emails to you?'

'Thank you, Derek. I'll call you back after I've had a look.'

The emails came in after some fifteen minutes. Emma sat at her desk riveted to her computer screen as she read the back and forth between Mr Tilson and his friend Cas. Derek was right. Cas had gently but firmly encouraged Mr Tilson to soldier on, but what jolted Emma was that Gordon knew Josephine, having met her in Washington – Emma had no idea in what capacity – and he met her again in Ghana on 3rd March. *Very interesting meeting with Josephine Akrofi today. We met late afternoon and had coffee.*

It seemed to Emma that the meeting might have been a little tense, what with Mr Tilson asking about 'highly placed officials – government or otherwise' who might be benefitting from Internet cons.

Then came another surprise.

Gordon Tilson
27th March 9.36 a.m.
Re: Ghana
To: CGuttenberg

Susan, the American I told you I discovered on FB, set up a rendezvous with a sakawa *boy called Nii Kwei – 'boy' isn't accurate, this is a full-grown man with money – at a sports bar. The plan was to say I was writing a magazine or online article on Internet scams, which is kind of true anyway, and that I would only ask general questions. But I kind of lost it after one too many drinks and I blurted out my story to this Nii, and then let loose with some sanctimonious crap about how I was going to expose a whole bunch of Ghanaians. In other words, things didn't go too well. I messed it up.*

So, Mr Tilson had met Nii Kwei! Emma would like to know more about that. And who was this Susan who facilitated the meeting? The net Mr Tilson had cast was much wider than Emma had thought. It included Kweku Ponsu, Josephine Akrofi (and therefore, possibly *James* Akrofi), Nii Kwei, and Sana, not to mention everyone he was in touch with at CID – Detective Inspector Damptey and the rest. How much of a nuisance, or threat, was Mr Tilson posing to people on that list?

Emma needed to get this information about the emails to the right place, of course, and she should start with the man she trusted the most – her boss. He was out of the office now, however, so Emma would have to meet him the following day. For the time being, she wanted to talk to Bruno, who was becoming a kind of bridge to everyone and everything.

When she reached him on the phone a few minutes later, she asked when next he would see Nii Kwei and whether she could go with him. Bruno immediately made an insinuating noise.

'No,' Emma said flatly. 'I'm not interested in him like that.'

'Are you sure? I think he likes you too. He always asks of you.'

'Just answer my question. When will you be going to see him?'

'Maybe even tonight. I will call him and let you know.'

'Don't mention I'm coming, OK? I want it to be a surprise.'

'Oh, is that so? Hmm.'

'Shut up,' Emma snapped. 'It's not that.'

CHAPTER SEVENTY-SEVEN

Nii was happy to entertain Bruno and Emma that evening – it was a chance to show off his new Audi and the sprawling house he shared with two other guys in upper-middle-class Dzorwulu.

The sitting room, three times the size of Emma's entire living space, had bright red leather chairs and a gigantic widescreen TV – the kind she had only seen at the mall. Despite all the space, boys would be boys, she recognised. There was no tasteful decoration of any kind anywhere, and as large as the kitchen was, it was a mess with dirty dishes in the sink and an overflowing rubbish can, which by the smell of it, needed disposal.

Nevertheless, Emma laid on the praise thick, showering Nii with expressions of awe and admiration. He was clearly flattered and very pleased. Emma imagined he was not unaccustomed to admiration of young women, many a lot more glamorous than her.

Nii's housemates had moved to the den to play video

games, leaving Emma, Bruno, and Nii in the sitting room. The two men had a bottle of beer each while Emma had fruit punch. The evening news was on TV in the background.

'Emma,' Nii said, smiling at her. 'How are you? Do you still work at the mall?'

Apparently, Bruno had not told Nii that Emma was now with a detective agency. She wasn't about to tell Nii either.

'No, I moved from there,' she said. 'Now I'm at an agency.'

'Ah, OK. Travel agency?'

'Something like that.'

The sports segment of the news showed a football clip, which inevitably brought up the traditional football rivalry between Accra's Hearts of Oak and Kumasi's Asante Kotoko and who would win the next big match.

Emma listened to the banter between Bruno and Nii for a while until she interjected bluntly, 'But Sana Sana has already shown us that these referees are corrupt and have been fixing the games, so what's the point of all this argument?'

Nii Kwei sucked his teeth. 'Stupid Sana. That man will die. They are trying to kill him and one day they will succeed.'

'Who is trying to kill him?' Emma asked.

Nii Kwei shrugged. 'Take any of his enemies. They're too many to count. Sana goes out and deliberately offers money to people and when they take it, he says they're corrupt.'

'They wouldn't take it if they weren't corrupt, would they?' Emma said.

'But maybe they never accepted anything like that before and in a weak moment they succumbed to the temptation,' Nii argued. 'It doesn't mean they have been corrupt up until now, and to this day, Sana has not made any definite connection between the referees taking money and the outcomes of the match. So, it's a failure of his investigation. The problem is he is too arrogant to admit it.' Nii looked at Bruno. 'What do you think?'

Bruno shrugged, said nothing, and Nii winked at Emma. 'He doesn't want to disagree with you, so he won't say anything, but I know he hates Sana.'

'And so, when Sana comes out with his new report about *sakawa*,' Emma said, 'aren't you afraid of how it will affect you?'

'What report?' Nii said, his expression and tone changing.

'Don't pretend you don't know,' Emma said kindly. 'It's all over GhanaWeb.com that he's working on finding out all the police and government officials who are benefitting from *sakawa*.'

Nii shook his head. 'He can't prove anything.'

Emma studied him. 'Really? So, it won't affect you?'

'Not at all. Maybe he'll expose one or two people, but it won't make much difference.'

'OK,' Emma said, feigning relief. 'I was worried about you and this *sakawa* thing.'

'Is that so?' Nii said, his eyes softening with appreciation.

'Thanks.'

'And so, are there *sakawa* girls too?' Emma asked.

'Of course,' Nii said. 'Just not that many. But they are becoming more and more now. We guys want more of them because we often depend on women to help us attract the *mugus*.'

'What is a *mugu*?' Emma asked, aware that Bruno was eyeing her. What was her sudden curiosity surrounding *sakawa* all about?

'The person we target for the money in Europe or the States or wherever,' Nii said, in answer to Emma's question.

'So, then, if for example I was a *sakawa* girl,' Emma said, 'how would you use me with a *mugu*?'

'Why?' Nii said. 'Are you interested?'

Emma nodded. '*Chaley*, I need to make some extra money just like everyone else.'

Nii sat back and looked authoritative. 'For example, if I'm doing a romance scam, I can use your picture for it, or use you to answer the phone or Skype with the *mugu*.'

'Oh, I see.' Emma became as wide-eyed as possible. 'Have you had one like that before?'

'But of course,' Nii said smoothly. 'Many of them.'

'And you made a lot of money?'

'Anyway, somehow,' he said cagily.

'So, when can I do one?'

Nii winked at Bruno. 'Will your sister make a good *sakawa* girl?'

Bruno nodded. 'Yes, of course. You can trust her and *mugus* will like her *paa*. Like, we should make a company, the three of us.'

'Yeah,' Nii said as the idea immediately began to grow on him. 'It's true.' He looked at Emma. 'What do you think?'

'I'm in. What should we call it?'

'Our initials, NBE,' Nii suggested.

'No, why not NEB?' Emma said. 'Or BEN. The BEN Company.'

Nii nodded his approval. 'Nice. Then let's shake hands.'

After that little ceremony, the *sakawa* entity of BEN was born.

CHAPTER SEVENTY-EIGHT

After Emma and Bruno had left Nii, they walked in silence for a while towards the closest *tro-tro* stop. Their footfall crunched rhythmically along the unpaved pavement. Somewhere, a nightclub was blaring music.

Then Bruno said, 'Are you investigating something for Mr Sowah? Because I know you really have no desire to be a *sakawa* girl. You're trying to find something out. What is it?'

Emma looked at him and then at the ground before answering. 'Yes, you're right. I'm trying to find out what, if anything, Nii knows about the death of that American man, Gordon Tilson, last April. Nii met Tilson at a sports bar sometime in March.'

'Oh, really. That I didn't know. I see you've been working diligently on this case.'

'To be honest with you,' Emma confessed, 'Mr Sowah told me to drop it, now that Tilson's body has been found.'

'Then why are you disobeying him?'

Emma blew out her breath through her cheeks. 'I don't know. I can't let it go.'

'My stubborn sister,' Bruno said knowingly. 'You get something inside your mind, and you won't let go of it. You've always been like that.'

'I used to annoy you when we were kids, right?' Emma said with a laugh.

'Yes!' Bruno exclaimed, affecting abject despair. 'Very much. But it's OK. You're still my girl. Let's sit here for a while.'

Outside a Stanbic Bank, they sat on a low wall after acknowledging the night security guard patrolling the grounds. Security guards don't like to be ignored. Traffic sped by. The aroma of *kelewele* wafted over from somewhere, reminding Emma she hadn't had much to eat all day.

'Look, I know my looking into Nii and the *sakawa* thing might be a problem for you,' Emma said.

Bruno's gaze was fixed ahead of him. 'Well, not really.'

'How do you mean?'

'You can keep a secret, right?'

'Of course.'

'I'm working for Sana Sana.'

Emma jumped to her feet. 'What?'

'Yes. That's why I didn't say anything about Sana when Nii was talking about him.'

'No, Bruno. Are you serious?'

'Yes.'

'How long have you been working for him?'

434

'Almost two years.'

'Oh, my God.' Emma said. She walked away a few paces shaking her head and then returned. 'I wish I'd known.'

'Sometimes I've felt like I should tell you,' Bruno said, 'but the fewer people who know, the better. Not just for me, but for others as well.'

'So, is your friendship with Nii part of Sana's probe into *sakawa*?'

'It is. That's the way I found out that Nii is the one who scammed Mr Tilson.'

'Wait a minute. Nii did that?' Another shock for Emma. 'Then the meeting between them at the sports bar – was that for Tilson to confront Nii? Maybe he discovered Nii was responsible for duping him.'

'Maybe,' Bruno agreed, 'but how would Tilson have found out?'

'I don't know,' Emma said, reflecting. 'There is a woman, Susan, an American, who apparently set up the meeting. Do you know anything about her?'

'I think that's the lady Nii was having a love affair with,' Bruno said. 'He mentioned her a couple of times when he was training me.'

'Can you find out more about her from Nii?' Emma asked. 'And also, the meeting at the sports bar?'

'Yes, I can do that for you the next time I see him, which will be soon. We are setting up for Nii and myself to meet Godfather, the man on top of this whole *sakawa* empire. I will expose his identity by secretly recording him accepting money from us.'

'Oh,' Emma said, alarmed. 'That could be dangerous. Are you sure you want to do that?'

'It's not whether I want to or not. It has to be done.'

That gave Emma very little comfort. 'Then be careful. That's all I'm saying.'

'I appreciate that.'

A thought struck Emma. 'By the way, did you ever meet the American man?'

Bruno shook his head. 'No, but Sana told me that Mr Tilson came to consult him. He and Sana had a quarrel and went their separate ways.'

A thought entered Emma's head from a side door. Could the acrimony between Tilson and the journalist have been so bad that Sana might have wanted to get rid of him? She put the notion in her back pocket for now.

'What about Kweku Ponsu?' she asked Bruno. 'What have you found out about him?'

'Besides how much I hate him? Well, he controls the destinies of a lot of *sakawa* boys and on the other side, MPs and top policemen and so on. Some people say even President Bannerman consulted him and participated in a ritual that made him win the election.'

'Really,' Emma said, not sure whether or not to believe that. 'Well, whatever the case, now that someone has shot Evans-Aidoo, looks like Bannerman will take the presidency again.'

Emma and Bruno looked at each other, reading each other's minds. An assassination organised by the president and/or his henchmen was not an impossible scenario to imagine.

Something struck Emma at that moment. 'Bruno, have you been tempted to do *sakawa* on the real? Tell the truth.'

'No,' he said without hesitation, 'and do you know why? These boys and girls who go into it find themselves trapped. If you happen not to be successful, and you want to get out, it's very tough. If you make a mistake or woe betide you, you have conflict with the fetish priest, you can suffer badly. When you live by spiritual powers, you can also die by them. So, no – I will not go inside, even if I wasn't working for Sana Sana.'

Emma nodded. 'Because I don't want you to do it.'

He put his hand on her shoulder. 'I know you don't.'

Bruno's phone rang. 'Nii, watsup?' He listened for a moment. 'Thursday, right? OK, no problem.' He ended the call and looked at Emma. 'Nii and I will meet Godfather tomorrow night.'

CHAPTER SEVENTY-NINE

On Thursday morning, Nii reflected he might have rushed into this so-called BEN partnership a little too quickly. Maybe Emma had charmed him so much that he had lost his head? Technically, Nii should have told Ponsu about Emma so he could vouch for her by spiritual means. Ponsu would need to see a picture of her and fortunately Nii had snapped a selfie with her and Bruno. But with the all-important Godfather meeting looming that evening, the Emma question could wait a couple of days.

Like any major hotel in Accra, the Mövenpick Ambassador Hotel where Bruno and Nii were to meet Godfather was already revving up for a weekend of parties, weddings, and conferences.

Beautiful people dressed to kill swarmed the lobby with its high ceilings and glistening marble floor. A live band accompanied the laughter and clink of champagne glasses. Bruno took it all in with envy, keen as a knife. *Look at all these people enjoying life.*

'Come on,' Nii said. 'This way to the lifts.'

They took one to the top floor where Godfather's suite was guarded by an armed police officer.

'Good evening, boss,' Nii greeted him.

'Your identification,' he said, deadpan.

He looked at their IDs, and then up again at them before handing the cards back. 'Remove your backpacks. Stand there, arms up and legs apart.'

He patted them both down, searched their packs, and when he was satisfied, he picked up his phone.

'Good evening, sir. Mr Bruno and Mr Nii Kwei here. Yes, sir.'

Bruno, nervous as the officer opened the door, quickly and surreptitiously checked his watch that the tiny LED video recorder indicator was on. The door shut behind Bruno and Nii and they took in the view. It was a vast room with a bar, dining area, and sitting room. The floor and the furniture gleamed. Bruno had never seen anything quite like it. The surroundings were impressive and overwhelming.

A baby-faced man in a dark suit appeared. 'Good evening.' He gestured to the sofa in the sitting room. 'Please have a seat. My boss will be with you shortly to speak to you.'

Bruno and Nii sat down meekly, almost not daring to move. A movement from the corner of the room caught their attention. A man, tall, well-built and bulky around his midsection, appeared. He wore glasses and a royal blue silk caftan with cream-coloured pants. This was Godfather? Bruno didn't recognise him. He and Nii stood up.

He sat opposite them without a word, and then raised his hand at the man in the suit, signalling he could leave. When the front door closed softly, Godfather looked at the two young men.

'Good evening, gentlemen.'

'Good evening, sir,' they chorused. Bruno, sweating a little bit and still edgy, unobtrusively rested his left forearm on his lap with the watch aimed in Godfather's direction.

'How are you, Nii?' Godfather said. 'I see you have brought your protégé with you.'

'Yes please. This is Bruno.'

'High praise about you from Mr Ponsu,' Godfather said to the protégé. 'You are very dedicated and have shown a lot of courage in your rituals.'

'Thank you, sir,' Bruno said.

'But you know this is not the end, this is the beginning. Now that you are wrapped in spiritual power, you must use it to gain riches with the aid of Priest Ponsu and your mentor, Nii. Do you understand?'

'Yes please.'

'You must follow the example of Nii Kwei, who makes a lot of money every day, every month, every year. Through Kweku Ponsu, I will monitor how well you are doing. Listen to Mr Ponsu, do all his rituals as he tells you, and you will be showered with blessings and live well.

'I'm expecting great things from you. The consequences of failure are great. You can ask Nii about that.'

'Yes please.'

'One final thing,' Godfather said, 'I think you already

know that you don't talk about anything that happens here to anyone outside. You do not speak about me; you do not mention me or describe me. If you do that, you will be sorry. My people are everywhere. You get it?'

Bruno's heart was pounding. He felt a little sick. 'Yes please.'

'Very good,' Godfather said. 'I think you have something for me, not so?'

The two young men went into their backpacks and took out a bundle of cash each. There was a moment of uncertainty as to who should offer the money to Godfather first. Thinking on his feet, Bruno gave his share to Nii, who handed over the combined portions. That way, Bruno would have a clear video of the transaction taking place. They could produce multiple stills from the clip.

Godfather nodded and put the cash down on the table beside him. 'Come, both of you. Kneel here.' They knelt before him and he touched their heads. 'You are now both my sons. God bless you. You may go now.'

Bruno and Nii left in silence and closed the door behind them. The military officer and the man in the suit eyed them.

'We too, we need water to drink,' the suit said pointedly.

'By all means,' Nii said. He got out his wallet and gave them each a fifty-*cedi* bill.

CHAPTER EIGHTY

On Friday morning, bathing in the afterglow of the successful meeting with Godfather, Nii texted Ponsu that things had gone very well. Hours later, the priest, not the fastest texter in the world, replied to say Nii should come to his compound that afternoon before Ponsu headed to Atimpoku for the weekend.

'OK, Daddy,' Nii said.

As was typical for Ponsu, he kept Nii waiting at the compound for an eternity before showing up. He had been to a funeral and was resplendent in crimson and black cloth. He seemed unusually preoccupied as Nii followed him into the house.

'Have a seat,' Ponsu said, casting around for the remote for his new air-conditioning unit. To his annoyance, he couldn't locate it, so he sat down on the bed. 'So, talk about Godfather. How is he?'

'He's fine. He was happy to see us.'

Ponsu rolled down his cloth to his waist to help cool

off. 'What about Bruno? Did Godfather say something about him?'

'He was praising Bruno. Very happy. And Godfather blessed the two of us.'

'Good, good. Now, Bruno will see the money flowing.'

'Yes please,' Nii said. 'Daddy, I want to ask you about a certain woman who was at my house yesterday—'

'One of your girlfriends?'

Nii laughed a little. 'No, this one is just a friend. Bruno's sister.'

'Eh-heh? And what?'

'Please, she wants to do *sakawa* too.'

'Is that so? Bruno trusts her?'

'Yes please.'

'Her name?'

'Emma.'

'You have a photo?'

'Yes please.' Nii went to his recent pics. 'Here.'

Ponsu took the phone and studied the photo. 'It seems I know her,' he said.

'Please, spiritually?'

'No,' Ponsu said. 'I've seen her before somewhere.'

'Oh, OK.'

Ponsu rubbed his forehead. 'Wait, wait. It's coming.' His head snapped up. 'This girl is a detective.'

Nii stiffened. 'Please, you say what? A detective? What kind of detective?'

'She's something like an apprentice with that guy's

private investigator agency – Yemo Sowah. Both came to see me in May asking me about the white man, the one who was your *mugu*. This is the woman you say wants to be *sakawa*?'

Nii was in state of confusion. 'Please, are you sure this is the same woman?'

Ponsu looked one more time and returned Nii's phone. 'Yes, it's her. What did you tell her?'

'Bruno trusts her,' Nii said, 'so I told them it's OK for her to come inside with us and I can start to show her things.'

Ponsu's eyes narrowed. 'And what else?'

Nii said, 'She asked me if I ever used a woman before to get money from a *mugu* and I told her yes.'

Ponsu leant forward and slapped him hard. '*Kwasea!*'

Nii jumped not only at the impact of the priest's hand but the very idea that Ponsu had struck him. It had never happened before, and he felt tears prick his eyes.

'You should know better,' Ponsu said. 'This woman is investigating you, don't you see? Because she's fine, she has blinded you. You know you have to consult me first about these things.'

Emotionally wounded, Nii was almost crying. 'Please, I think she's real. Even if she was a detective, she wants to do the *sakawa*.'

Ponsu seemed to halfway consider that as a possibility but then he returned to his preceding stance. 'Don't talk to that girl any more. Do you still trust Bruno? Why didn't he tell you the girl is a detective?'

'Please, I don't think he even knows the kind of job she does. They don't see each other often.'

Ponsu was sceptical. 'Find out about her, you understand?'

'Yes please. I will do that.'

'OK, look,' Ponsu said, softening. 'I'm sorry for slapping you, eh?'

'No problem.' Nii managed a smile.

'Just be careful in the future.'

'Yes please.'

'And I think you have some cash for me today.'

Nii Kwei met DI Doris Damptey at their usual spot, and as always, he treated her to a massive meal, this time of *fufu* and groundnut soup. The woman's appetite was boundless, and she ate with relish.

'I want to ask you something, Auntie,' Nii said.

'What?'

He showed her his selfie with Emma and Bruno. 'Do you know this woman?'

She sucked her fingers. 'Emma Djan. She used to be with CID.'

'What does she do for a living?'

'Private investigator now. With Yemo Sowah. She's too inquisitive. I don't like her at all.'

'You're sure she's still a private detective?'

'Yes, isn't that what I said? Are you doubting me?'

Nii grinned. 'I would never doubt such a wondrous woman as yourself, Auntie.'

'Please.' Damptey rolled her eyes. 'So, what about Emma?'

'She was at my house yesterday asking questions about how she can become a *sakawa* girl. Kweku Ponsu thinks she's investigating something about me.'

'And he's right!' Damptey said heatedly. 'This girl a *sakawa*? Don't mind her! She and Sowah were looking into what happened to that white man who drowned in the Volta River. Once they found the body, Sowah told my boss that they won't be trying to investigate this any longer. So why is this girl still doing it? And Bruno, too – what is he doing with her?'

'I don't know,' Nii said. 'I thought I trusted him, but I'm not so sure now. What should we do?'

'I'm going to report that girl to our DCOP Laryea. He'll take it from there.' Damptey sucked her fingers and smacked her lips.

'As for Bruno, well, find out if he's working with that girl and warn him to stop.'

In the morning, Damptey found out DCOP Laryea was out of town and otherwise unavailable. She wasn't sure what to do, so she consulted DCS Quaino. But he didn't want to get involved.

'Mr Sowah was my father's mate,' he said. 'How do you think I'm going to call him with a complaint about his employee? That's disrespectful.'

'Yes, sir,' Damptey said. After lunch, she decided to take it to the top and put in a request to Sergeant

Thelma for a meeting with Director-General Andoh. He saw Damptey a couple of hours later in his office and listened without comment while she described the problem of meddlesome Emma Djan.

'Why didn't you report this to DCOP Laryea?' Andoh asked.

'Please, he's not in. I think he has left for the weekend.'

The director-general eyed her with disfavour. 'And this couldn't wait until Monday when he returns?'

'Please, I thought one of my superiors should be alerted.'

Andoh scowled at her and heaved a sigh. 'You let the DCOP know when he returns on Monday. Don't trouble me with this kind of trivial issue. You are dismissed.'

Damptey left feeling useless and embarrassed. In retrospect, it did seem a petty issue to take to the director-general, but to *her*, it was still very important. Damptey strongly resented Emma Djan. She needed to be silenced.

Back in his office, Andoh got on his phone and called the IGP. 'Good morning, sir. Yes, sir, thank you, sir. I wanted to keep you updated regarding the *sakawa* investigation. No, sir, not exactly a new development, but it seems the lady investigator from the Sowah Detective Agency is continuing the enquiries. Yes, Emma Djan. As far as I was aware, sir, her boss informed DCOP Laryea that they would relinquish the investigation to us. Yes, sir. So, I'm not sure if Sowah was telling us a lie, or has changed his mind, or whether the girl is doing this on her own accord . . . OK, sir. Yes, sir. Thank you, sir. I'll take care of it.'

CHAPTER EIGHTY-ONE

On the way to work on Friday, Emma called Bruno to find out what had transpired during the Godfather meeting. She could barely wait to hear. He didn't answer initially but returned the call soon after Emma had got down at her *tro-tro* stop.

'Yes, we met with him,' Bruno told her, 'and I think I got a good video, but his face wasn't familiar to me, so I can't tell you who he is.'

'And Nii doesn't know either?' Emma asked.

'Nii always calls him "Godfather", nothing else. But Sana will recognise who the man is as soon as I show him the video this morning.'

'OK, then call me later.'

No sooner had Emma arrived at her workstation, Beverly called out to her from her desk.

'Someone on line two for you, Emma. I asked who's calling but he doesn't want to say.'

'Thanks.' She pressed the line two blinking button. 'Emma Djan speaking.'

The voice from the other end sounded as if it were emerging from a tin can. Emma couldn't say whether it was male or female. It said, 'Stop looking into Mr Tilson, stop looking into *sakawa* unless you want to die.'

'Hello?'

The line cut. Emma felt a wave of icy heat pass through her. She put the receiver down. So, it's come to this, she thought. *Threats to her life.*

Bruno delivered the watch to Sana, who was preparing to move to a new location with his team. Everyone was jumpy after the assassination attempt. For a while, Sana would be moving around more frequently.

Bruno gave an account of the visit with Godfather chapter and verse.

'Thank you, my brother,' Sana said. 'You've done well. Beautiful job. We are packing up now to go to our new location near Achimota Forest. When we're there and have set everything up, probably by tomorrow morning, I'll call you and give you directions. By that time, I will have downloaded your video along with some of the clips from the other investigators. The project is coming together nicely.'

'Yes please. Thank you, Sana.'

He had some cash in a crisp envelope for Bruno, who smiled and thought he would have some fun this weekend. Perhaps he might even go to Mövenpick.

When he returned to his room at Cocobod, he felt strained and tired and lay down to take a nap. He had no idea how long he had been asleep when his phone next rang.

'*Ei*, Nii Kwei,' he mumbled. 'How be?'

For a moment Nii didn't answer and Bruno thought the call had dropped. But then Nii spoke.

'*Chaley*, what's going on?'

'Oh, everything cool. I dey take some small nap.'

'Your sister, Emma. I found out today she works for that Yemo Sowah detective agency.'

Bruno's stomach plunged. 'To be honest my brodda,' he said, 'she didn't tell me where she works.'

'Has she talked to you today?'

'No, not at all,' Bruno lied. '*Chaley*, what's wrong?'

'Your sister is a detective and she was here asking me all kind of questions and now you ask me "What's wrong?"'

'Nii, don't worry. She's not after anything bad. I don't know where she works, but I know she wants to be a *sakawa* girl for sure.'

Nii was silent again for a few beats. 'Watch out, Bruno. Be very careful.'

The call ended. Bruno looked at his phone screen for a moment as if that would reveal what in the name that had all been about. Then he called Emma and told her what had just occurred.

'And someone called the office a couple of hours ago and when I answered, he hung up,' Emma said. 'It must have been Nii.'

Bruno was alarmed. 'Sis, don't do anything more with the American man's case unless you let me know, OK? Sana

451

will see my Godfather video tomorrow and from there, we can see what to do.'

Emma hesitated. 'OK. We'll talk soon, then.'

When Bruno hung up, he was surprised to see it was already six-thirty in the evening. He was famished. He slipped on his *chale-wote* and went outside where the town was loud and alive. Food sellers were out in force to feed the hungry thousands. Delicious food smells mixed with car exhausts. Music from chop bars competed for people's ears above the hubbub of humanity. Bruno felt like *kenkey* and crisp-fried fish with lots of fiery *shito* and he walked to his favourite seller over the rough, unpaved pavement. She had sold from the same spot for years, but nowadays one got a smaller amount of chop for almost twice the price it was when Bruno was a little boy. But the aroma from the steaming ball of *kenkey* still held the power to make his salivary glands contract, and he was in a hurry to get back to his room for the feast.

Bruno was unlocking the door when he had a sense that something was wrong. He began to turn around but never completed the motion. Something struck the back of his head and he thought his skull had been split open. He fell forward, hit the doorframe and bounced backward onto the ground. He rolled over and tried to sit up, briefly glimpsing the silhouettes of two powerful men. They half dragged, half lifted Bruno to the rear of his shack.

'We know what you are doing,' they said together in Twi, punching him repeatedly in the face. His nose cracked and he tasted his salty blood. He fell back and they kicked him in the head and in his guts. 'You better stop or we kill you next time.'

Bruno waited for the next strike, but it didn't come. He was suddenly alone. His mind told him to get up, but his body refused, and he sank into unconsciousness.

CHAPTER EIGHTY-TWO

On Saturday morning, Emma went to Madina Market to shop for the week. The frenetic hustle and bustle were typical of any Saturday and everything was selling from pots and pans to freshly butchered goat meat to widescreen TVs and microwave ovens. At a fabrics shop, Emma was irresistibly drawn to a gorgeous purse made of red leather and a contrasting black-and-white strip of *kente* along one edge. She bargained obstinately with the vendor until she got the price she wanted. Returning home laden with heavy shopping bags, Emma wondered when Bruno might call her. Perhaps in the afternoon after he had viewed his secretly recorded video with Sana Sana.

Having put her provisions away, Emma texted Bruno and waited about twenty minutes before trying both a voice and video call. Still no response. She began cooking, but not hearing from her stepbrother was bothering her. After trying one more time, she made up her mind. She needed to go to Cocobod to find him.

* * *

Emma knocked on Bruno's door, but no one responded. She looked around and then walked over to the marijuana-smokers' corner. Bruno was nowhere. She went back to his door and banged harder this time.

'Are you looking for Bruno?'

Emma turned to find a man in his mid-forties. She remembered him as one of Bruno's neighbours. 'Yes,' she said. 'Good afternoon. Do you know where he is?'

He looked pained. 'Oh, sorry to tell you. They found him this morning at the back of the house and took him to the hospital. Somebody beat him very badly last night.'

Emma drew her breath in sharply. '*Awurade.*'

'I think they took him to the Military Hospital.'

'But, but was he OK?'

'Anyway, I can't say exactly. He could talk a little bit, but his face was very bad.'

Emma felt sick. 'Thank you for letting me know. I'll go there now.'

When Emma got to the Military Hospital, someone told her that Bruno was most likely in the Trauma and Surgical Emergency ward. Emma wandered into the middle of a chaotic place with patients in varying degrees of distress and pain lying on beds in the open ward. Young long- and short-coated doctors worked on patients alongside senior physicians. A nurse told her she was supposed to be back in the waiting room.

'I'm looking for—'

'*Go!* You can't be in here, don't you understand?'

Emma went back and found the receptionist's desk, where she asked for Bruno.

'He's not here,' the receptionist said flatly.

'Please, do you know where he is?'

'They took him to the general medical ward. You can go there.'

After some confusion over where that was, Emma located it and again asked for Bruno at the front desk. 'He's on the other side,' the receptionist said, pointing behind her and then adding, 'but it's not visiting hours, so you can't see him.'

Emma ignored her and went looking. They would have to drag her out if they wanted to make her leave. She put her head into each of three open wards and thought she saw Bruno at the far end in the third. But she wasn't positive. She gingerly approached and looked at the name on the foot panel. It *was* Bruno. He lay on his back, his shirt off. His face was swollen and almost unrecognisable with one eye completely shut and multiple sutured lacerations. There were black and blue bruises all over his torso. Emma caught her breath in shock.

Bruno opened the good eye and when he saw her, he attempted a smile. 'Emma,' he whispered.

Tears streaming, she took one of his hands as gently as if it might break. 'How are you?' she said, choking on her voice.

'Don't cry,' he said. 'It's not as bad as it looks.'

That attempt to reassure her only intensified her

shock, grief, and the pain she felt for him. She sat at the side of the bed and leant closer. 'Who did it?' she whispered. 'Did you see?'

'Not well,' he said through inflamed lips, 'but it was two of them, I think. Very strong. I went to buy *kenkey* and when I returned, they were waiting for me. They dragged me to the back of my place and beat me there.'

'Did they say anything to you?'

'I should stop what I'm doing, or next time they'll kill me.'

'Stop what you're doing? Meaning your secret investigations?'

'It must be,' he said, grimacing as he gingerly touched his face. 'Now that Nii knows you work for the detective agency, he must have got the idea that I'm collaborating with you.'

Emma agreed. 'And so, then he must have reported it to Ponsu, who sent his macho men after you to frighten you away. You said it was two tough guys, right? Have you ever met Ponsu's bodyguard twins, Clifford and Clement?'

'No, I haven't.'

'They match the description you gave me. If it's them, Ponsu is definitely behind this.'

Bruno nodded, but barely, because even the smallest movement was painful. 'And remember Nii took a selfie with us. I'm sure he showed it to Ponsu.'

Emma winced. 'You're right. I didn't even think of that.'

'When I went to buy the food,' Bruno said, 'I left my phone in the house. Can you get it for me? My house key is in my pocket here.'

She extracted the key. 'OK, I'll go for it. Are you OK for now?'

'Yes, but I want to turn to the side a little bit.'

As Emma helped Bruno shift position, a nurse walked in and asked Emma what she was doing there. Didn't she know visiting hours were not until this evening?

'I'm leaving now,' Emma said. 'Bruno, I'll be back.'

'Be careful,' he said.

As she left the ward, she felt the full weight of her outrage at what had been done to her stepbrother and her determination cemented. She would get to the bottom of this and whoever had perpetrated this violence upon Bruno would pay. Two people were on her mind right now. The first, Mr Ponsu, she would avoid for now. The second, Nii Kwei, was the person she wanted speak to as soon as possible.

CHAPTER EIGHTY-THREE

By the time Emma returned to the hospital, visiting hours were back on. She sat at Bruno's bedside while he scrolled through his phone texts using his one good eye. Sana, who had been expecting to see him earlier today, had texted him twice asking where he was. Bruno tried Sana's number, but received no reply, so he sent a short text message to call him as soon as possible.

Bruno and Emma chatted on and off. She was glad to see small glimpses of his impish humour returning, even here where it wasn't easy to be cheerful. The ward, as in most Ghanaian hospitals, was an open one with little to no privacy, meaning everyone's pain and suffering was on full display. Directly opposite Bruno's bed was a woman with a chest tube who moaned with every agonising breath she took. At another bed, a group of Jehovah's Witnesses had gathered around a post-op patient to pray for his speedy healing. At intervals, they broke into religious song.

Emma turned her attention back to Bruno, noticing that some of his facial swelling was already receding. He had finally had a CT scan, which, apart from a broken nose, had shown a mild degree of brain contusion, but doctors expected him to do OK ultimately.

'I hope Sana calls you while I'm still here,' she said. 'I want to talk to him.'

But by the time the bell rang for visiting hours to be over, there had been no word from Sana. Emma prepared to leave.

'Will I see you tomorrow?' Bruno asked her, sounding hopeful.

'Yes, of course. I'll come after church. Should I bring you some fresh clothes?'

'Yes please. Thank you, Emma.'

Nii reached Emma on his second attempt.

'I was just about to call you,' she said.

'About Bruno?'

'Yes. So, you heard?'

'One of his neighbours at Cocobod called me just a few minutes ago to tell me he's in the hospital,' Nii said. 'Said he was beaten up very badly. I tried to call him, but he wasn't picking up, so I thought of getting in touch with you.'

'I just came from seeing him,' she told him. 'He's at the Military Hospital.'

'Will he be OK?' Nii asked.

'Probably, yes.'

'Thank God,' Nii said.

'I need to talk to you,' she said.

'Me too,' Nii said, his voice a little shaky. He steadied himself. 'What's happened to Bruno is serious. Can you come to my house now to discuss everything?'

'Yes, I'm not that far away. I'll take a cab.'

'Then I'll see you soon.' Nii put the phone down and turned to look at his three guests, Ponsu, Clifford, and Clement. 'She's coming,' he told them.

Ponsu smiled. 'Good job. Why are you shaking? Relax.'

The twins laughed, but Nii didn't find it funny. Nothing had been funny within the past half hour. Clifford and Clement had pushed him around and roughed him up while Ponsu had watched with a sick grin. It could have been worse, of course. The twins could have snapped Nii's neck like a chicken.

As Emma got to Nii's house, she texted to say she'd arrived.

'Wait, I'm coming,' he said. After undoing multiple locks on the other side of the door, Nii opened it, she entered, and he locked up again behind her.

'How are you?' he said, as they went to the sitting room. His roommates weren't in sight but the place smelt of weed so Emma imagined they were somewhere around smoking.

She sat next to Nii on the red sofa.

'How was Bruno when you left him?' he asked her.

'He seems to be getting better,' she answered. 'So,

461

what's going on? What do you need to talk to me about?'

'First, you tell me what you are investigating,' Nii said. 'I know you work with Mr Sowah now.'

'Was it you who called the agency yesterday to see if I was there?'

'Yes,' he admitted.

'I'm investigating a lot of things,' Emma said. 'Who killed Mr Tilson is the first. Who attacked Bruno is the second, and I'm curious to know why yesterday you called him and warned him to be careful.'

'I was afraid for him,' Nii began, 'because someone saw the selfie I took with you and Bruno and recognised you, saying you work with Yemo Sowah's detective agency.'

'Who is that someone? Kweku Ponsu?'

Nii didn't answer. He seemed awfully jumpy and tense. For a moment Emma wondered if he was on something else besides the marijuana.

'Look,' she said, 'I know you're always in contact with Ponsu. There's no point in you pretending. Did he tell you to warn Bruno off?'

Nii shook his head. 'No. I did that on my own. I was angry that it seemed Bruno was secretly working with you, but at the same time I didn't want anything to happen to him.'

'So, you're saying Ponsu didn't tell you he was planning an assault on Bruno?'

'Yes, that's what I'm saying.'

She noticed his eyes darted briefly to a point behind

462

her and she instinctively turned. No one was there. She came back to Nii. 'But it could be he commanded the twins to do it.'

'Well, of course. They do whatever he tells them to. If Ponsu doesn't like you and he sets the twins upon you, it's bad.'

'Then it must have been bad for Gordon Tilson.'

'Who is that?'

'Gordon Tilson. You know him. Don't bother lying. He was the guy you scammed on the Internet, the same one you met at a sports bar – Champs, I'm guessing. Everyone knows Champs. And a lady called Susan was also there.'

Nii appeared shaken. 'Who told you all this?'

'It's true, isn't it? And then, somehow, Mr Tilson ended up dead in the Volta.'

Nii clamped his jaw. 'I heard he drowned, but I don't know anything else about it, OK?'

'So, how did you come to meet Mr Tilson at the bar?'

'He was just a friend of Susan's, and I knew Susan from university.'

'Did he know you were the one who had been scamming him?'

'No, and at first I didn't know either. He said he wanted to learn something about *sakawa*, so we discussed it. It was as we were talking at Champs that I realised who he was.'

'But the discussion turned sour.'

'No, *he* made it so,' Nii said indignantly. 'Started to say he was going to expose *sakawa* boys and the big men who take part in it. He was talking shit and I didn't like it.' Nii kissed his teeth.

'And so, you called Ponsu and told him all about it?'

'I mentioned it to him.'

In this context, Emma found the word 'mentioned' amusing. 'What did Ponsu say he was going to do about Tilson?' she asked.

'He didn't say anything.'

'Sure?'

'Positive.'

'I'm begging for your help, Nii,' she said, softening her voice, 'but you don't want to. Why?'

'You don't understand,' he said. He seemed miserable.

'I do. You don't want to put yourself in danger. But at the same time, if Kweku Ponsu has committed a crime – whether to do with Mr Tilson or Bruno – he has to be held accountable.'

Nii was cracking his knuckles in rapid succession. Emma thought she might be getting to him, but she was wrong.

'Leave it alone,' he said sombrely. 'Leave everything alone. I respect you, but please, both you and Bruno – stop. It's the best thing to do.'

They were silent for a moment as Emma tried to divine what was going on in Nii Kwei's head. At length, she said, 'Have you heard from Ponsu today? Where is he right now?'

'I don't know.' He avoided her eyes.

'I know what's bothering you is your allegiance to

Mr Ponsu,' Emma said, 'but at the same time, you and Bruno and I are friends. Just join us and let's get to the bottom of this thing.'

He was staring at the floor, his jaw working.

Emma stood up. 'Think about it. Sleep on it. Call me tomorrow.'

Nii went to the door with her. His shiny Audi was parked outside.

Something occurred to Emma. 'Do you have another SUV? Black or a dark colour?'

'No. Why?'

'No special reason,' Emma said, but she was thinking of Kafui's description of the vehicle she had seen the night of 3rd April.

Then, Nii looked quickly behind him, put his finger to his lips and came close to her. 'They're here,' he whispered. '*Run!*'

That's when Emma saw the hulking shadow of one of the twins coming up behind Nii. She turned to bolt, but the other twin was waiting for her and she smacked into him. With an open palm, he struck the side of her head with the force of a wrecking ball. She collapsed in a heap.

CHAPTER EIGHTY-FOUR

Nii was horrified at the sight of Emma lying motionless on the ground. Was she breathing? He tried to go to her, but Clement shoved him away.

'But why did you hit her so hard?' Nii cried.

The other men ignored him. 'Get the car,' Ponsu told Clement. 'Clifford, start tying her up.'

Ponsu's SUV was parked in the back of the house. Clement drove it around to the front and opened the boot.

'Where are you taking her?' Nii demanded.

'None of your business,' Ponsu said. 'It's better you don't know, anyway.'

By the outside veranda light, Clifford had finished binding Emma at her wrists and ankles. Ponsu found a rag in the boot and handed it to Clement, who opened Emma's mouth and stuffed the rag in as far as it would go.

Nii shrank away, watching with dismay as the twins picked Emma up and swung her into the boot as if she were a dead goat.

Ponsu turned to Nii scowling. 'If you say anything about this to anyone, I swear, we will come back and get you and you'll regret you ever opened your mouth.'

Clifford opened the rear door of the vehicle for Ponsu to get in, and then he took the driver's seat. Clement joined him on the front passenger side and they pulled away, tyres kicking up dust.

Nii stared after them until the rear lights had disappeared. Then he turned away and went back in the house feeling sick. One of his housemates, who was quite high on weed, asked Nii what was going on.

'Nothing,' he muttered. 'Go back to your room.'

The housemate shrugged. He had been planning on doing that anyway.

Nii paced the living room, then sat down rubbing his head in despair. He didn't know what to do. Yes, it's true that he didn't like the idea of Emma investigating Mr Ponsu, but this was no way to treat her. On the other hand, Nii couldn't go to the police for help, and that included Auntie Doris. She didn't like Emma and wouldn't lift a finger to help her.

Nii took out his phone. The battery was in the red zone so he cast around for a charger. He had so many of them, why could he not find one when he needed it most? When he had located a charger stuck between the sofa cushions, he plugged it in and called Bruno, praying that he would pick up. He did.

'Nii, what's up?' Bruno said. 'You know I dey hospital, right?'

'Sorry, oo. Look, I didn't know they were going to do this to you, I swear.'

'You mean Ponsu's guys?'

'Yeah. *Chaley*, they've taken Emma too.'

'What? When?'

'Just now. They forced me to call her to come here so I can talk to her and they hid themselves and listened to what she was saying. When they heard how much she knows, they knocked her out and tied her up.'

'And where are they going with her?'

'I don't know,' Nii said, his voice shaking with emotion, 'but I think they're taking her to the Adome Bridge.'

'Shit,' Bruno said. 'Let me call you back.'

Emma came to in pitch darkness. She was in motion but wasn't sure if she was moving forward or spinning. Her head ached. Her wrists were tied behind her back, the bindings cutting into her flesh. Her ankles were fastened together as well and her mouth was stuffed with a rag that tasted of fuel.

She drifted in and out of consciousness with no concept of time or place. Her skull seemed to be humming and then she realised it was the noise of the vehicle in which she was confined. She was lying on her right side and found she could barely shift position. Faint voices came from some direction as well as percussive white noise she recognised as heavy rainfall. The ride felt like that of a large car or SUV. Every slightest bump jarred Emma's pounding head. She felt nauseous and dizzy.

Emma struggled to remember what had happened, but her recollection was only faint. She had been at Nii Kwei's house, but what after that? She began to feel like she was suffocating, and panic grew. *Stay calm. Stay calm.*

The vehicle slowed to a halt and two men began to talk. From where Emma was, their tones were muffled and obscured by the downpour and she could hear only snatches of what they were saying. The vehicle doors slammed. The boot clicked ajar. The moment the men put their hands on her, Emma began to fight. They grunted and cursed as they pulled her out. She twisted and writhed, and they had trouble holding onto her. She realised that she had a bag of rocks tied to her ankles to weigh her down, which made sense because now she knew where she was – on the Adome Bridge, and the twins were about to throw her over.

The pavement lamps illuminated the rain so that it looked like a thousand silver daggers coming down at a slant. Emma also saw who the men were – the twins. They carried her to the side of the bridge and Emma collided with the railing. She heard the bubble of river below and the noise of rain upon it. This was where Gordon Tilson had met his end, and now it was Emma's turn to die. In seconds, she would strike the water with force enough to tear her insides apart and shatter her spine. Suddenly, her resistance was spent and she resigned herself. Clifford and Clement hitched her onto the top of the railing.

CHAPTER EIGHTY-FIVE

The squawk of a police vehicle rang out and Clifford and Clement found themselves silhouetted in headlights. They let go of Emma and ran, leaving her bent at the waist across the railing, her head on the deck side and her feet pointed down at the water. She tried to kick to propel herself towards the safe side, but the rocks fastened to her ankles made the effort futile. Slowly, she began to slide backward towards the water, and then to accelerate.

She closed her eyes as she began the long plunge. And then she seemed to stop in mid-air. She was being dragged upward. *What was happening?* Was she spinning? She thudded against a flat surface, but it couldn't have been water.

'Miss Djan? Are you OK?'

She opened her eyes. She was on the ground on top of a brawny policeman. His arms were still wrapped tightly around her and he was breathing just as hard as she was. Looking up, she saw two other rain-soaked officers standing over her.

'Are you OK?' they repeated.

She wasn't certain.

One of them said, 'Untie her.'

Once Emma was unshackled, the policeman sat up, but she wouldn't let go of him. She began to cry like a baby.

'You're OK, eh?' he said. 'Don't cry. You're safe now. Can you stand up?'

He helped her. She was unsteady on her feet, still dizzy and plagued with a relentless headache.

'Put your arms around my neck,' the policeman said. He lifted her as if she were as light as a feather and carried her to the police vehicle.

Inside, it was warmer, but Emma was shivering. The officer who had pulled her from the brink sat quietly in the back beside her. The other two sat in front. The officer on the passenger side turned towards Emma and she recognised him.

'Inspector Bawa!'

'Madam Djan,' he said. 'That was a very close call.'

'But how?' she said, mystified. 'I don't understand how you came to my rescue.'

'We received a call from Sana Sana,' he told her. 'He said he knew from reliable sources that an attempt on your life was imminent and the MO was likely to be the same as in the Tilson case. By the time we got the call, we were even afraid we were too late.'

His two-way radio buzzed and he listened to it for

a few seconds before turning back to Emma.

'My officers have nabbed the twins at the other end of the bridge.' He chuckled. 'They didn't have many escape options.'

'Oh, thank God,' Emma said fervently. 'What about Mr Ponsu?'

'We believe he's still in Accra. Someone will be dispatched to his compound. Do you wish to go to the hospital before we go to the station to take your statement?'

'I'm fine,' she said, which wasn't completely true, but she didn't think a hospital would help. 'I can't thank you enough, Inspector. And you, Constable.' She turned to her new hero and took his hand. He wasn't much older than Emma, and now, no longer in rescue mode, he was quite bashful.

'OK, then,' Bawa said to the driver. 'Let's go to the station.'

As Emma wrote out her statement at the police station, another familiar face appeared: Mr Labram.

'How did you know I was here?' she asked in surprise.

'News travels fast around here,' he said. 'Inspector Bawa called to inform me what had happened. Thank God you are OK. When you're done here, my wife says you must come to stay the night at our house and get some rest.'

CHAPTER EIGHTY-SIX

A light tap on the door of the Labrams' guest room woke Emma in the morning. She sat up, forgetting for a moment where she was.

'Good morning, Emma.' The voice on the other side of the door was Mrs Labram's.

'Good morning, please.'

'Sorry to wake you, but someone is here to see you.'

'OK, thank you. I'm coming.'

Emma looked at her phone. Goodness, it was almost ten. She considered sleeping this long in someone else's home to be poor form. She got up and realised someone had washed, pressed, and folded her wet clothes from the night before and set them neatly on the chair beside her bed. So nice of them, she thought. She went to the bathroom and washed up quickly. The left side of her face and head were still puffy from the impact of Clifford's (or Clement's) blow, and her wrists and ankles still raw and tender.

As she came into the sitting room, Emma couldn't imagine who might be waiting for her and she least expected Bruno, but there he was chatting with the Labrams. His face, too, was still swollen, but much better than before. He smiled and stood up when he saw her.

'*Ei*, Emma! So good to see you, sis.'

They embraced. Bruno took a step back and peered at the side of her head. 'Ouch. Now we look more alike,' he quipped.

She giggled. 'Silly boy.'

They sat next to each other and munched on the cookies with fruit punch that Mrs Labram had laid out. Emma was still fuzzy about the sequence of events the night before.

'Nii Kwei called me to tell me that Ponsu and the twins had kidnapped you,' Bruno explained. 'There's only one person in the world I know who can act fast enough, and that's Sana. So, I called him. The only problem was that at first he wasn't answering his phone, so I was very worried. Finally, he called me and I told him what was going on. He called the Akosombo police. A lot of people may not like Sana, but when he says something is up, everyone knows it's real. So yes, they moved quickly.'

'Thank you, Bruno,' Emma said. 'You really did save my life.'

'Thanks, but in the end it's Nii, actually, right? If he had not called me, you would now be at the bottom of the Volta River.'

'You're right.' Emma contemplated that scenario for

a second and shuddered. 'How did you get here this morning, Bruno?'

'I needed to be sure you were OK,' Bruno said, 'so I sneaked out of the hospital very early and took a *tro-tro* to Atimpoku. I went straight to the Akosombo police station to find out what had happened. I met Inspector Bawa there and he said you had survived and were staying with the Labrams.'

'God bless you, Bruno,' Mrs Labram said. 'What you have done is noble – considering you yourself were still in the hospital.'

He smiled coyly. 'Thank you, madam.'

'That's my brother,' Emma said with pride, taking his hand and squeezing it. But the excitement of last night and the elation over being alive had begun to plunge and Emma began to experience an odd despondency in the aftermath. She concealed it from the Labrams, however, all smiles as she and Bruno thanked them and departed.

Bruno and Emma took a cab to Nii's house from the *tro-tro* station. This being Sunday, traffic was thankfully light. Nii's housemates were home, he was not.

'He didn't tell you where he was going?' Bruno asked.

'No. When we woke up this morning, he was gone. We tried to call him but it seems his phone is off.'

Emma tried Nii's number, and so did Bruno, but neither received a response. According to the network, Nii's phone was off.

'Probably he might have gone to his family home in

Bukom,' George, one of the housemates suggested. Bukom was one of the oldest parts of Accra and home to the Ga people, of which Nii Kwei was very much one.

'Ah,' Emma said, lighting up. 'Do you know where the family house is?'

'Anyway, somehow.'

'What do you mean, "anyway, somehow"?' Emma asked, frowning at George. 'Do you know his place in Bukom, or not?'

'He took me there one time,' George said vaguely. 'We can go if you like and I can try to find it.'

Emma looked at Bruno, who nodded. 'Yes, let's go.'

CHAPTER EIGHTY-SEVEN

That Sunday afternoon, Abena was with Kojo at Josephine Akrofi's home where the documentary on Kojo was struggling to come together. The film crew had completed the sequences at the Centre, but the segments with Josephine interacting with Kojo at home were proving to be a headache. For two days running, Kojo had been restless and difficult to manage with his hand flapping, finger rubbing, and high-pitched screaming disrupting the repeated takes. Abena and Auntie Rose had a lot of patience, but Mrs Akrofi's was wearing thin. Her idea had been to show Kojo interacting quietly with his tablet in her home. She would enter the scene, sit next to the boy, and explain how she often welcomed him and other children from the Centre to her home (which wasn't entirely true). The idea was to put an 'international face' to the appeal and boost the Centre's new website and crowdfunding campaign. Josephine's theory was that well-off people are more likely to donate if they could 'see themselves' in the video – if they could 'relate' to a well-heeled, fashionable woman contributing to such a noble cause.

'It's the very opposite of showing malnourished African kids in refugee camps with bloated bellies and flies buzzing around their faces,' she reasoned. 'People in the West are tired of seeing all those images. They have compassion and donor fatigue. So now let's put a splash of glamour into charitable giving.'

However, nothing was working. The whole of Saturday, the day before, the director and camera crew had been at the Akrofis' home, trying but failing to get some usable footage. They had returned this morning with hopes of knocking out a good video segment, but it looked like it was to drag into Monday. Despair and frustration had begun to take hold of everyone, including the object of their attention: Kojo. Abena and Rose agreed with each other that he could not take any more overstimulation.

'I'll take you home, Abena,' Rose said.

'I have a better idea,' Josephine said. 'Abena, you can stay in the servants' quarters overnight. We have an extra room that's not in use. That way we can begin the filming early tomorrow morning – no later than seven. My husband is away until tomorrow evening and I would like to have everything finished by then. He's not particularly fond of disruptions in our home.'

All parties agreed to that. Abena retired with Kojo to the servants' quarters at the side of the home. Mrs Akrofi provided dinner in containers that Abena took with her to the quarters. She bathed Kojo, fed him, and lay him down to rest. He was quiet with none of the repetitive behaviour of before. Abena finally had a chance to eat in peace. Araba, Mrs Akrofi's house girl, had prepared sumptuous *banku* and okro stew.

After dinner, Abena took a quick shower. Kojo wouldn't wake up for another two hours. She tried reaching Emma, but the call didn't go through. Abena lay her head down to sleep and she prayed this project of Mrs Akrofi would end soon. She could understand the purpose and she approved of it, but the stress being put upon her and Kojo was beginning to wear them down.

Voices from behind the servants' quarters woke Abena. What time was it? Her phone said ten minutes before midnight. From one of the two windows in the room Abena looked out several metres to the hibiscus garden, which – as was the case with most well-appointed homes – was illuminated brightly with security lights installed along the enclosure wall. She saw Mrs Akrofi in her dressing gown speaking to a man. She seemed upset. Her chin was thrust forward, her voice rose and fell in both pitch and volume, and she gesticulated with her hands. They were both speaking in Twi, but from where Abena stood, she could make out only a few words here and there.

The man had an odd-looking facial scar. His hand gestures indicated defensiveness and frustration as Mrs Akrofi argued with him. Towards the end of the almost ten-minute discussion, the man's head dropped, and he appeared crestfallen. Mrs Akrofi did an about-face and marched away back to the house, leaving the gentleman to see himself out.

Who was the man, Abena wondered, and what had the heated discussion been about? The question didn't occupy her mind for very long, however. It wasn't really any of her business. She went back to bed and fell asleep again.

CHAPTER EIGHTY-EIGHT

On Monday, CID headquarters in Accra brought in Clifford and Clement from Akosombo Police Station, which didn't have enough space to keep the twins much longer. Aware of the strong bond between the twins, Commissioner Andoh kept them apart to throw them off balance and render them more vulnerable to questioning.

A constable brought Clifford to the commissioner's office and stood to one side to keep watch over the handcuffed muscleman. Clifford appeared sullen but nervous. The commissioner told him in Twi that anything he said might be taken down and used later as evidence in court. 'Do you understand?'

'Yes please,' Clifford said, but he looked uncertain. He was out of his depth. A person of means might have refused to answer questions without a lawyer present, but Clifford didn't know anything about that.

'How old are you, Clifford?' Andoh asked.

'Twenty-four, please.'

'Where did you attend school?'

Clifford muttered a name and then admitted he and Clement had never completed high school.

'You are always together, you and Clement, eh?' Andoh asked.

'Yes please.'

'You feel like you are one person – or part of each other.'

'Yes please.'

'Well, I will do my best to bring you together again,' Andoh said, 'but only if you are honest with me and you don't waste my time. You understand me? In other words, if you and Clement tell the truth, all will be well, and you will be with each other again. Otherwise, we will have to keep you apart and keep questioning you.'

'Yes please.'

'Clifford, I want to ask you about last Saturday night. Where were you and Clement?'

'Please, we were at Kweku Ponsu's house.'

'Where? In Accra or Atimpoku?'

'Accra.'

'But we know you also went to the house of one Nii Kwei on Saturday night.'

Clifford stared at the ground and didn't reply.

'We don't want Clement to get hurt,' Andoh said. 'Some of my men are not as kind as I am, so I don't know – they might beat him or something like that. But if you tell me everything, I will order them not to beat him or harm him.'

Clifford flinched with visible pain at the possibility of causing the infliction of pain on his brother. 'Yes, we went to Nii Kwei's house,' he confessed.

'You and Clement and who again?'

'Mr Ponsu.'

'And what were the three of you going to do there?'

Clifford searched Andoh's face, appearing unsure what to say.

'I'm here to help you,' the commissioner pressed gently. 'I know that you and Clement are good people. You always do what your boss tells you, so no one is going to blame you and Clement for doing what your boss said. Probably he was even shouting at you and telling you he won't pay you any more if you don't do what he says. Do you think he won't try to blame you for everything? He will! So you better tell the truth before we catch him and he gets a chance to tell lies.'

Confused, Clifford rubbed the back of his head.

'Would you like some water to drink?' Andoh asked. 'Constable, bring Clifford some water.'

'Yes, sir.' The constable left.

'Relax, OK?' the commissioner said, smiling at Clifford. 'Let's wait for the water first before we continue.'

Clifford drank down most of it. 'Thank you, sir.'

'You're welcome, my friend,' Andoh said. 'So, you were saying you and your twin brother and Mr Ponsu went to Nii Kwei's house, and then what happened?'

Clifford cleared his throat. 'Mr Ponsu told Nii to call that girl, Emma Djan, to talk to her. At first, Nii didn't want to do it.'

'So, how did you persuade him?'

'Well, Mr Ponsu said by force, Nii had to do it.'

'Did you beat Nii to convince him?'

Clifford squirmed. 'We just made some rough-rough on him.'

'Like you pushed him around? To scare him?'

'Yes please.'

'And then?'

'Then Nii called the girl, and she came to talk with him.'

'Where were you and Clement and Mr Ponsu at that time?'

'Clement stayed with Mr Ponsu, hiding in the kitchen to listen to what all she was saying. I waited outside. When Emma was leaving, I think Nii secretly told her we were there, so she tried to run away, but I was there.'

'And what happened?'

Clifford cleared his throat again. 'I gave a blow here.' He touched his temple. 'We tied her hands and her feet. First we went to Kweku Ponsu's house—'

'In Accra?'

'Yes please. Mr Ponsu said he was going to stay there, and then we tied a bag with some rocks around the girl's feet.'

'What was that for?'

'Mr Ponsu told us to drown her in the Volta River.'

'By throwing her off the Adome Bridge.'

Clifford kept his head bowed. 'Yes please.'

Two floors down in the DCOP's office, Laryea was questioning the other twin.

'Clement, on 3rd April, a certain white man called Mr Tilson was thrown into the river from the Adome Bridge. Was that what Mr Ponsu told you to do? The same thing as the lady last night?'

Clement leant on his forearms and cracked his knuckles repeatedly, trying to imagine what Clifford would say. In his mind he could hear Clifford saying there was no point in trying to lie, especially if that would cause them to be separated for ever. Clement could not bear to be apart from his brother.

'Ponsu told us to go to the white man's house in the night,' he began.

'Around what time?'

Clifford cast back. 'Around two or three. In the morning, I mean. He said we should go there and pretend we are Mr Labram, the one who owns the house, so that the white man will open the door, then we should beat him and take him to the bridge.'

'And throw him inside the river?'

'Yes please.'

'And so that's what you did.'

'Yes please.'

'Where was Mr Ponsu at that time?'

'In the house. At Atimpoku.'

'So, after you threw the white man in the river, what did you do?'

'We returned to the house and report to Mr Ponsu that we have done everything.'

'And then?'

'We went to sleep.'

CHAPTER EIGHTY-NINE

At Monday morning briefing, Emma was subdued and her heart was in her mouth. She was about to face Mr Sowah to tell him the entire story of how she had disobeyed him and continued to investigate the death of Mr Tilson. But she imagined Sowah knew something about it already because Dazz had heard her story from Laryea, and she was sure the DCOP had informed Sowah as well.

At the end of the meeting, Sowah beckoned her to come with him to his office and she felt like she was walking to an execution.

They sat down together on the sofa.

'First of all,' Sowah said, 'how are you feeling? Are you OK?'

'Yes, sir. I feel fine. So, you know what happened?'

'DCOP Laryea called me and gave me the gist, but you will need to tell me everything from the beginning. And don't leave anything out.'

Emma had a sense of relief to be unburdening herself. The day she stepped into the quicksand and found herself being sucked under was when she had seen Gordon Tilson's emails that Derek had shared with her. Her discovery that Nii Kwei had met Gordon had intrigued her and she had asked Bruno if she could meet Nii. At the time, she had still entertained the possibility of mentioning the emails to Mr Sowah. Then she had found out what her stepbrother was *really* doing – working undercover for Sana Sana. She hesitated sharing that with anyone, including, she confessed, Mr Sowah, because she didn't want to blow her stepbrother's cover. Then, exactly what she didn't want to happen did: Bruno was beaten up by, most likely at the time, the twins. One thing led to another – Emma's night visit to Nii, the attack, the Adome Bridge, Emma's brush with death. And now, here she was. Battered but alive.

'Bruno and I went to Bukom with one of Nii's housemates yesterday,' she added, 'but we didn't find Nii anywhere. I'm worried about him. How do we know Ponsu didn't get to him?'

Sowah nodded. 'It's a possibility. Ponsu can't be located either; Interpol notified the Togo and Benin police because it appears he's crossed into Togo. They'll get him eventually. So, now to the crux of the matter, that you independently decided to start collaborating with Bruno after I had expressly asked you to relinquish any investigation related to Gordon Tilson's death.'

She nodded. 'Yes, sir. I was wrong and I'm sorry I disobeyed you. I have no excuse.'

Sowah eyed her, but did she catch the hint of a smile? 'When I give those kinds of instructions,' he said, 'there's method to my madness. The very reason I didn't want you to go any further with the Tilson affair is the same one for which you were almost thrown into the river.'

'Yes, sir.'

'On the other hand,' Sowah said, leaning back with a sigh, 'your actions have led to the arrest of two out of three people responsible for the murder of Mr Tilson. So, I'm both shaking your hand and shaking my finger at you.'

'Yes, sir. The bottom line is that I put myself in danger and it's only by the grace of God that I'm here.'

'Amen.'

'Please, if you wish me to resign at once, I will do so.'

Sowah smiled. 'Well, I don't need to throw the baby out with the bathwater.'

'Come again?'

'It's just an expression. In other words, if I sack you just because I'm annoyed by your disobedience this one time, I may – no, *will* – be depriving myself and the agency of a talented, courageous, moral, and all-round good detective. And what would be the point of that?'

Emma broke out into a broad smile. 'Thank you, Mr Sowah. Thank you very much. God bless you.'

CHAPTER NINETY

Monday evening, Dazz and Courage helped Edwin pack up his belongings and furniture to move from his house in the suburb of Dansoman to the new place on Spintex Road – definitely a step up. Spintex was an area of high economic activity with houses and strip malls materialising apparently every day. Unfortunately, road paving never happened as quickly as buildings were erected, so the ride to Edwin's place in his pickup was a jarring test of the vehicle's suspension.

Neither Courage nor Dazz had seen the house yet, and they were suitably impressed. Unfurnished, it would take a few more chairs and sofas to fill up the sitting room. Two bedrooms, each with a modern bathroom, a kitchen with much more than Edwin's meagre cooking abilities would ever require, and a backyard with enough space to have a good party.

'What!' Dazz exclaimed, each time they followed Edwin into another impressive space.

'This is nice,' Courage agreed. 'Congrats.'

After they had moved and carried things around, the guys walked to the corner to buy *kelewele*, then returned to the house to devour the delicious meal and wash it down with some beer. Edwin had already set up his TV, so they watched music videos for a while and then switched it off.

'I really like the place,' Courage said.

'Yours is even better, Mr Bill Gates,' Edwin teased.

'No, it's not. This place is bigger.'

Dazz said, 'What am I doing wrong? You guys have nice places and I'm stuck with two tiny rooms for a house.'

'Look, Dazz,' Courage said, 'I know your uncle is the DCOP and he's honest to the last *pesewa*, but you need to do things for yourself and not worry about what he thinks. I know the guys at the top say we're not supposed to do certain private jobs for ministers and embassies and so on, but many of us do, and so should you. You can't make money in the GPS until you get very high up – like the commissioners and so on. And even *they* have money-making schemes on the side.'

'Yeah,' Edwin said dryly. 'Like *sakawa*. But I agree with what Courage is saying.'

Dazz sat forward. 'Edwin, what's your story?'

He frowned. 'What do you mean?'

'I saw you and Madam Akrofi together at the CAC party. I told Courage about it.'

'What are you talking about?' Edwin said defensively. 'I only walked her to her vehicle.'

'No, no,' Dazz said. 'I saw the two of you embracing. In the garden there by the car park.'

'Sugar mummy, Edwin?' Courage said, winking at him. 'How long, and how did you meet?'

Edwin eyed his two friends without a word.

'We're not judging you,' Dazz said, 'but we do want to know.'

'Why shouldn't you get something out of fucking her?' Courage said with a shrug.

'Shut up,' Edwin said, his features clouding. 'You don't know what you're saying.'

'Then what?' Dazz said.

'Mrs Akrofi isn't a "sugar mummy", as you call it,' Edwin said. 'She's my *real* mother. My biological mother.'

'What?' Dazz and Courage said together.

'Yes,' Edwin replied.

'Are you serious?' Dazz said.

'Of course I am.'

'But you've never talked about it,' Courage said, incredulous. 'I mean, this is not your ordinary mum who lives in some tiny village somewhere in the hinterland, this is an important lady around town. The IGP's wife!'

'I don't talk about it,' Edwin said, 'because *she* doesn't talk about it. And she doesn't talk about it because her husband doesn't know she had a child before she met him, and she's always kept it from him.'

'But is it something to be so ashamed of?' Courage asked.

'Maybe not to you, but to my mother's mother, yes. She said I was the product of sinful lust, so she sent me

492

to Techiman in the Brong-Ahafo Region to grow up with my aunt – my mother's sister. That way, I was out of sight, out of mind. It was only when I reached manhood that I returned to Accra. My grandmother was dead and gone by that time, anyway. But Mummy supported me even while her sister was bringing me up. She paid my school fees and used to send money to my PO box at the post office. Sometimes, even, those wretched people at the post office would steal my cash. Once we got mobile money, Mummy used that method. So yes, she paid most of the rent due for this house. She loves me, but I think the real thing is she's trying to make up for the guilt of sending me away.'

'Listen, *chaley*,' Courage said, 'I'm sorry for what I said about . . . you know.'

Edwin dismissed it. 'Don't worry about it.' He seemed troubled about something else. 'You know, my mother is complicated. In fact, her whole life is complicated. My half-brother, Kwame, has autism and he's in an institution in the UK. Before Mummy sent him away, she took him to some fetish priest somewhere to see if he could cure Kwame. This was after she and Mr Akrofi had taken the boy to several doctors who didn't know what was going on.'

Dazz and Courage were silent as they tried to absorb all of this. It was a lot.

'Who is your dad, then?' Dazz asked.

Edwin gave a dry laugh. 'I knew that was coming next. I'm not even sure if I should say. You've already had quite a few surprises for one night. Are you ready?'

The other two nodded.

'You know my father quite well,' Edwin said. 'He's Commissioner Andoh.'

They were struck dumb for a moment. Then Courage said, 'Wow, you are right. You have a lot of surprises.'

'I'm truly short of words,' Dazz muttered.

'Mummy met Daddy before she met Mr Akrofi,' Edwin continued. 'I was an accident, to put it in a frank way. The commissioner wanted to marry Mummy, but she was already in love with Mr Akrofi. So, now you can imagine the way my father treats me.'

'I guess not well,' Dazz said. 'You represent the woman he lost.'

'You could say that,' Edwin said, with a hint of bitterness. 'He hates Mr Akrofi, but I don't think the IGP knows that. And me? I've spent a long time waiting for the day my father will approve of me. That's why I became a policeman. But I'm done with trying. I don't care about him any more.'

Dazz and Courage looked at Edwin with some – not complete – understanding. They could see why Edwin was sometimes moody and introspective.

'We aren't worried about any of this, Edwin,' Dazz said. 'You are still our good friend and colleague, OK? In fact, I feel our friendship is even stronger.'

'Agreed,' Courage said. 'Let's have some more beer and drink to that.'

CHAPTER NINETY-ONE

The Saturday after Edwin moved, he held a housewarming party, which gave Courage an excuse to invite Emma out. She accepted. Although not authorised to do it, Courage had told Emma beforehand about Edwin's secret: the parents very few people knew he had and his formative years growing up as a kind of adoptee.

'That's quite a story,' Emma had commented. But honestly, it wasn't that remarkable, she reflected later. The Ghanaian's concept of 'family' was quite fluid. Kids often went away to stay with aunts, uncles, grandparents, and even distant relatives for financial, catastrophic, or other reasons. It was normal. Words like *brother*, *sister*, *mother*, *father* were used quite loosely.

Around thirty people were at Edwin's party, most of which he held in the backyard. But the guests spilt over into the sitting room and the kitchen. Emma recognised a few faces from CID, but apart from the host, Courage, and Dazz, she knew very few people. Edwin introduced Emma to Ginger, a glamorous woman somewhat above his age who appeared to be his girlfriend – well, for the evening, at least.

Plenty of lavishly catered food and drink were on hand, accompanied by a loud hiplife music playlist. Emma chatted within reach of Courage. He was being neither possessive nor indifferent to her – somewhere in the middle – and Emma was fine with that.

Here and there, she heard a snatch of a comment about how nice the house was and 'Does Edwin earn that kind of money?' Inevitably, the phrase 'sugar mummy', which Emma despised even more than the 'daddy' version, came up. At any rate, if Edwin was aware of murmurings, he didn't seem to care. He was having a good time. Emma noticed what a 'babe magnet' he was, and that it didn't seem to bother Ginger. Emma decided that she couldn't be a 'serious' girlfriend.

Apart from gossip, bad jokes, and general partying behaviour, one common topic of discussion was going around, and that was what jaw-dropping scandals Sana Sana's new exposé, scheduled for Sunday night as all his features were, might bring to light. People were taking wild guesses and making even wilder predictions about who the infamous 'Godfather' would turn out to be, but others played down the potential impact of the show, especially Sana's detractors, and he had many.

A smarmy man had been eyeing Emma from the bar and she was not comfortable with it. She turned and positioned herself out of his line of sight, soon forgetting about him.

'I'm going to the washroom,' she told Courage. He nodded.

The one downstairs was occupied, so she went to the upstairs guest bathroom. Coming out, she was about to return to the party when she heard voices from the room at the other end of the landing. Curiosity got the better of Emma and she tread lightly up to the door, which was open just a crack. Still, it was enough for Emma to see Edwin and the smarmy man talking quietly and looking at something on the bed. Emma adjusted her eye's view and saw part of what they were studying: a large case containing a rifle, a handgun, and multiple firearm accessories neatly tucked into fitted cut-outs.

'You say you'll only take dollars?' the smarmy man said.

'Yes,' Edwin said. 'I don't deal in *cedis*.'

'And is the rifle and everything working well?'

'Perfectly.'

'Then why are you getting rid of it?'

Edwin shrugged. 'Don't need it any more.'

'What about the paperwork?'

'What paperwork? *Chaley*, no any paperwork! If you want the thing, then bring the dollars and it will be yours. Simple as that.'

'OK,' the man said sullenly. 'I call you.'

This is where I leave, Emma thought, departing for the stairs and still thinking about the formidable weaponry Edwin had been showing the man.

Downstairs again, Courage found her. 'I was looking for you.'

'I had to go to the upstairs washroom.'

'Are you having a good time?'

'Sure,' she said.

'What's on your mind? You look distracted.'

She shook her head. 'Nothing. I'm fine.'

'You're strange sometimes, you know that?'

'Yes,' she said.

He put his arm around her. 'Come on, let's dance.'

CHAPTER NINETY-TWO

Traditionally, Sana's exposés always aired Sunday nights at 8 p.m. Emma had invited Bruno to watch at her house along with Abena, who would be over for the usual Sunday dinner. At 8 p.m., with Kojo safely in bed, they gathered in front of the TV in anticipation of Sana Sana's new blockbuster, *The Sakawa Story: Power, Corruption, and Deceit.* Bruno knew in advance about the big IGP reveal at the end, but he hadn't let on to Emma or Abena.

There was far more to the feature than just video clips of people accepting money. It reintroduced the viewers to Sana's work, which had an increasingly global perspective. His signature slogan, 'Name, Shame, and Jail', was repeated often. The show went on to examine *sakawa* from its early beginnings in Nigeria, where it was called '419' after a section in Nigeria's criminal code. The origins dated to much earlier than most people realised – as far back as 1920. Now, the notorious old 419 scams with Nigerian 'princes' were all but gone, replaced by more effective Internet scams. Over the decades, online fraud transformed itself from a clunky, unreliable *tro-tro* to a powerful Bentley.

Sana showed how many millions of dollars *sakawa* was now worth, and why it was too much of a good offer for politicians and corrupt law enforcement to refuse. The essential infrastructure for corruption in Ghanaian society was already well in place and primed to take *sakawa* on, like a highway with an available extra lane.

How and why does Internet fraud involve *mallams*, traditional priests, and the like? Because they are the people who can invest the Internet fraudster with the magical powers that will bring the money pouring in. The documentary showed a clip of Kweku Ponsu performing some of his *sakawa* rituals, including one in which he whirled around hundreds of times while dressed in ceremonial cloth and covered in white powder from head to toe.

Then to the heart of the feature where prominent members of society were exposed one after the other. The *coup de grâce* was Bruno's segment from the Mövenpick penthouse, where 'Godfather' made his appearance. Although Bruno had not recognised him at the time, he now knew. Godfather was none other than James Akrofi, the IGP. Abena jumped out of her chair in shock. Emma, for her part, was speechless. Bruno, his face almost back to normal, smiled with secret pride. It was, after all, *he* who was responsible for the stunning footage to the world. But by agreement, neither Bruno nor Emma would reveal that to Abena. The less people knew, the better.

At the end of the movie, there was so much for the trio to discuss. They argued furiously with each other until they were exhausted.

'But you know one funny thing?' Abena added. 'In the video, that guy – the fetish priest, what's his name, Kweku Bonsu?'

'Ponsu,' Bruno said. 'What about him?'

'I thought I had seen him before and now I remember where. He came to see Madam Josephine last week when I was at the house in the servants' quarters.'

'Is that so?' Emma said. 'He came to see her for what?'

'I don't know,' Abena said. 'She was angry and shouting at Ponsu about something, but I couldn't hear what she was saying.'

Emma said, 'Oh,' and looked at Bruno. 'But I had no idea that she knew Kweku Ponsu.'

'Neither had I,' he said.

'The question never even came up,' Emma murmured. 'How did we miss that?'

CHAPTER NINETY-THREE

Before Sana's blockbuster aired that Sunday evening, the Office of the President had an advance viewing. When the revelation came that James Akrofi, the IGP, was the Godfather who made money off fraud boys and the network of *sakawa* operatives, President Bannerman went rigid and found himself unable to speak for several minutes. His chief administrative assistant sat and waited until Bannerman looked up and said quietly, 'Please summon Commissioner Andoh to the palace.'

James was enjoying a pre-dinner beer while his wife was busy in the kitchen. She had already let him know that she had no intention of watching Sana Sana's film scheduled to air in a couple of hours. She detested the man and wouldn't dignify him by watching his nonsense.

Someone knocked on the door and James got up to answer. He was surprised to see Commissioner Andoh on his doorstep holding his police cap respectfully to his chest.

'Alex!' James exclaimed. 'What a surprise. Is everything all right?'

'Good evening, sir. Yes, fine, sir.'

'Come in, come in and take a seat. Would you like something to drink?'

'No, sir. I'm not staying long. Please, I have been directed by President Bannerman to summon and escort you to Jubilee House.'

The IGP was puzzled. 'Is this an emergency meeting? Why wasn't I informed?'

'A situation of high emergency has arisen, sir. Please, if you can come now? I will wait here for you, sir.'

'Well, yes, of course,' James said, mystified. 'Give me a moment. I'll get dressed.'

President Bannerman's soul was shattered in a thousand pieces, like crystal on a stone floor. In the sanctuary of his office with James Akrofi and Commissioner Andoh, Bannerman played Sana's video again. There it was: Akrofi accepting money from Nii Kwei, a *sakawa* boy of note.

'That is you in the video,' Bannerman said, turning to James. 'Is that not so?'

The IGP was frozen in place. He stared at the president, his mouth opening as if to speak, but nothing came out.

Bannerman was in visible pain. 'But, why, James? *Why?* I trusted you. This is a devastating betrayal. We've been friends, colleagues, partners . . .' He trailed off, words failing him.

'I feel shame,' James whispered. 'I've felt it for a long time.'

'But what use was that shame if it still allowed you to go on doing what you were doing?'

James bowed his head. 'I'm sorry, Mr President. I can assure you right here and now – even take an oath – that I will stop using my position to enable the *sakawa* systems that infiltrate our society and our neighbourhoods. I pray you will pardon me, sir.'

Bannerman was trembling. 'No!' he cried. 'No. I can't do that, James. Can't you even see how immoral that would be? What will the people of this nation say? That certain individuals are above the law? That my relatives and cronies can get away with the same corruption I've been preaching against like an evangelist? No, James, that I cannot do. To maintain my integrity and that of my government, I must do the right thing. Commissioner Andoh, please take over.'

James looked at Andoh. 'Am I under arrest?'

Andoh put his hand lightly on the IGP's shoulder. 'Yes, sir.'

CHAPTER NINETY-FOUR

The morning after Sana's sensational film, the newspaper headlines screamed out who the infamous 'Godfather' was. The IGP himself. Some papers branded him '*Sakawa*-in-Chief'; 'Head Con Man'; 'Inspector Greedy of Police'; and a host of other names.

When Emma got to work, the workroom was alive with discussion about Sana's TV event, which had broken all previous viewership records. The number of corrupt officials identified had been staggering, but nothing topped the revelation that the IGP, who, word had it, was being confined at a secret location, had been profiting from online fraud. Mr Sowah came to the workroom to join the discussion, but he also had an announcement.

'DCOP Laryea called me to say they've arrested Mr Ponsu at the Togo border. He was trying to sneak back into Ghana unnoticed.'

Emma and everyone else clapped.

'So, have we wrapped up the Tilson's case?' one of the detectives asked.

'In a funny way, yes,' Sowah said, giving Emma an amused, bemused look. She smiled sheepishly. 'The point is,' he continued, 'they have two solid, independent confessions from the twins which corroborate well with each other. Ponsu doesn't stand a chance. And so, it turns out Ponsu was so bothered by Gordon Tilson and our very own Emma coming close to the truth, he had to get rid of them. Luckily, Emma came out of it alive.'

Before Emma could object, they gave her a standing 'hip hip hooray' cheer.

Getting back to work was difficult for everyone in the office. It felt more like a day to sit around and gossip about everything that was going on.

Her phone rang. It wasn't a number she recognised.

'Hello?'

'Emma, it's me, Nii Kwei.'

'My God,' she said. 'Where are you?'

'In Accra,' he said cryptically. 'I just wanted to call you to find out how you are.'

'I'm fine, thanks to you. I know you called Bruno and then he called Sana. I want to say thank you for that. How are you too?'

'I'm good. I heard Ponsu and the twins are in custody.'

Emma suspected he knew that from DI Damptey. 'Yes. They murdered Mr Tilson.'

'I feel sorry for what I've done,' Nii Kwei said. 'I'm

going to sell my Audi so I can return Mr Tilson's money to his son.'

'It's the honest thing to do,' Emma said. 'Thank you.'

'We'll talk soon.'

He ended the call abruptly. Emma reflected what an odd situation this was. Nii Kwei was a criminal, but he had also played a large role in saving her life. She was glad he hadn't told her where he was, thus avoiding a possible conflict of interest for Emma. If anyone asked her if she knew where Nii Kwei was, she could truthfully answer that she didn't.

She sat thinking about the case. Something was bothering her, but she couldn't put her finger on it.

At the end of the day, Emma got hold of Yahya, the driver, on the phone. He sounded happy to hear from her.

'Madam, long time!' he said, laughing. 'How are you, please?'

'I'm well, Yahya, and you?'

'Oh, by God's grace, madam.'

'Did you manage to find a new job?' she asked.

'Yes please. Now I'm a driver for the director of the State Housing Company.'

'Wow, that's so great. Congrats.'

'Thank you, madam. I'm very happy. Please, how is the case of the white man going?'

'We are getting somewhere with it, but I wanted to ask you something that might help us some more.'

'By all means, please.'

'You remember when we met and you were talking

about how you took Mr Gordon to see Mr Ponsu?'

'Yes, madam.'

'You said Mr Ponsu told the American man he should be afraid of someone. I don't quite recall the exact words.'

'Eh-heh, yes. I remember it very well. The white man tell Mr Ponsu, "Do you think I'm afraid of you?" and then Ponsu too said to the white man, "There are people before me you should be afraid of."'

'OK. And then?'

'The white man say, "What do you mean?" and Mr Ponsu just laugh and tell the white man, "You will see." And then we left and that was all.'

'I've got it,' Emma said. 'Thank you very much.'

'You are welcome, madam. God bless you.'

When Emma was off the line with Yahya, she went down the hall to Mr Sowah's office, but only Beverly was there restocking the printer with new paper. 'He's already gone for the day,' she said.

Emma stopped to think for a moment, and then she called Dazz.

CHAPTER NINETY-FIVE

At almost ten-thirty at night, light streamed from Edwin's windows, indicating he was home. Once Emma had reached Dazz, it had taken a while to find his uncle, who had absent-mindedly switched off his phone.

Edwin was surprised when he opened his door to find Laryea, Dazz, and Emma.

'How are you, Edwin?' the DCOP said. 'May we enter, please?'

'Of course,' he said, stepping aside to let them in. 'Is something wrong?'

'Let's sit and talk for a moment,' Laryea said.

They went to the sitting room. Edwin looked tense and suspicious as he and the others took seats in a square formation.

'What's going on, sir?' Edwin asked Laryea.

'Sorry to disturb you so late,' the DCOP said. 'It's about the firearm you have in your possession.'

Edwin appeared puzzled. 'Firearm, sir? Which firearm is that?'

He's probably sold it already, Emma thought with a doomed feeling. We'll never find it now.

'Someone witnessed you on Saturday night offering to sell a long-range rifle to one of your party guests,' Laryea said. 'You and the man were seen in the upstairs bedroom with the weapon out in the open on the bed.'

'Who told you that, sir?'

'That's not important right now.'

'No, I'm very sorry, sir. There must have been some mistake.'

Laryea nodded. 'Then you don't mind if we search your bedroom?'

Edwin's eyes twitched. 'On what grounds? Excuse me to say, sir, but don't you need a search warrant?'

The DCOP smiled. 'No, Edwin. Section 2.1.1 and 2.1.2 of the Ghana Police Procedure manual states that a police officer above the rank of Assistant Superintendent of Police may conduct a search without a warrant if he or she believes that a person has concealed an article that has been stolen or unlawfully obtained, or an article in respect of which a criminal offence has been, is being, or about to be committed.'

Emma sensed Edwin's panic, but he was still shielding it well.

'OK,' he said, quickly shifting tactic. 'Yes, I do have a rifle, but it's completely legal and I have a permit to use it from the Ministry of Interior.'

'Why didn't you just say so before?' Laryea asked, frowning at Edwin. 'I mean, if it's been legally obtained, what were you worried about?'

'Sorry, sir,' Edwin stammered. 'Sorry, I just got a bit confused.'

The DCOP stood up. 'Show us the way to the item, please.'

In silence, they trooped up the stairs to the same bedroom Emma had seen Edwin and the other man haggling over the weapon. Emma doubted very much that it was legal. One had to apply to police authorities for ownership of a gun *before* the purchase could be made. Of the two million or so firearms floating around Ghana, only about half were registered correctly.

Edwin unlocked one of the closets in the bedroom, removed the case, and placed it on the bed.

'Open it, please,' Laryea said.

Edwin undid the clasps along the side of the case and flipped up the lid. Close up, the weapon looked formidable to Emma. Laryea studied it for a while. 'There's an empty space where the handgun should be,' he observed. 'Where is it?'

'The handgun didn't come with the set,' Edwin said at once.

Laryea grunted, shut the case again and snapped the clasps closed. 'Edwin, we will have to check the veracity of your statement and conduct a further search for that handgun,' he said. 'We'll start here.'

Edwin stood and watched as Dazz and his uncle looked through drawers and closets. That wasn't difficult, because Edwin had still not finished unpacking all the boxed materials from the move. That was where the work really was, and it took over an hour to carefully search through the crates and boxes in the bedrooms, sitting room, and garage. In the end, Laryea and Dazz were satisfied that there was no handgun in the house.

'What now, sir?' Edwin asked the DCOP.

'We will need to confiscate the weapon while we run a check on it. We will let you know tomorrow and if everything is correct, we'll return your property to you intact.'

'Very good, sir. Thank you.'

CHAPTER NINETY-SIX

At eleven the following morning, Dazz, Courage, and Emma hung around the CID general detectives' room waiting for news on the status of Edwin's weapon. Their mood was sombre and Emma understood how the two men must be feeling. Edwin was their colleague. It was demoralising that he was under investigation for illegal possession of a weapon. Emma wondered how they felt about *her*. She was the one who had alerted Dazz about Edwin's rifle and his apparent move to sell it, and then he had called his uncle. They must have been experiencing mixed feelings, she suspected. But they had nothing to chastise her about. The law was the law, criminality was criminality, and they knew that.

Dazz's phone rang. He listened for a moment then turned to Courage and Emma. 'The DCOP is ready to talk to us.'

They all filed into his office feeling anxious. In the room with Laryea were Damptey and Quaino.

'Have you been in touch with Edwin this morning?' Laryea asked Dazz.

'No, sir,' Dazz replied. 'What's happening, sir?'

Laryea was grim. 'His weapon is illegal. DI Damptey has been at the Ministry of Interior all morning long. No such long-range rifle is registered.'

Emma glanced at Damptey and thought, *Goodness, so you really are good for something.*

'It likely came in concealed at a port of entry,' Laryea said, crossing to a cabinet in the corner of the room. He removed a bulletproof vest. 'Dazz and Courage, get your gear on. We need to go for Edwin. I'm worried he has the missing handgun on his person.' Laryea held out a spare vest to Emma. 'That's for you.'

But when Laryea, Dazz, Courage, and Emma arrived at Edwin's home, he did not appear to be in. His car was gone from the garage and no one answered their repeated knocking. A constable with a battering ram had accompanied them, but the DCOP didn't want to take that measure yet.

'Try his phone again,' Laryea suggested to Dazz.

Dazz did, but shook his head. 'It's off.' He looked at Emma.

'His mother's place,' she said. 'Mrs Akrofi.'

The fact that Josephine was Edwin's mother was no longer a news item for the DCOP. He had not known beforehand, but Dazz had now informed him.

Laryea nodded. 'You're right. Let's go there now.'

* * *

Edwin's vehicle was parked in the Akrofis' driveway.

'He's here,' Courage said.

They piled out of the car and knocked at the front door. It opened and a young woman looked out. She appeared terrified already and her alarm visibly grew as she saw the armed policemen.

'Who are you?' Laryea asked her.

'Araba,' she whispered. 'The house girl.'

'We would like to come in, Araba.'

She opened the door wide and stepped aside to let the visitors in.

'What's wrong?' Laryea asked her. 'You're shaking. We're not going to harm you. Are you afraid of us?'

'No please,' she said in her tiny voice. 'It's just that a certain man called Edwin came and he's holding a gun. He took Madam Josephine with him into the bedroom.'

'The missing handgun,' Dazz muttered, looking at Emma. Her heart plunged.

'Show us the bedroom where they are,' Laryea said curtly.

They followed Araba upstairs and she pointed to the end room. 'They are in there.'

Laryea lowered his voice. 'Thank you, Araba. Please return downstairs to a safe area. Do you have servants' quarters?'

'Yes please.'

'Then go there and remain until we tell you otherwise. Emma, for now, please stay at the bottom of the stairs for safety.'

Emma complied, but not completely. She stopped halfway down the stairs so she could still see and hear what was going on. Laryea and Dazz went to the bedroom door first while Courage and the constable hung back.

'Edwin!' Dazz called out into the door. '*Chaley*, what's up? How be?'

Silence.

'We just want to check on you to make sure you're fine.'

Edwin replied, but from where Emma stood, she couldn't hear what he said.

'Are you in there with Mrs Akrofi?' Dazz asked.

This time, Edwin shouted his answer. 'I'm with her. Don't come in. I'm armed.'

'We just want to talk to you about everything that's going on,' Dazz said.

Silence.

Laryea beckoned to Dazz and they pulled back to where Courage and the constable stood.

'Ask Araba if she knows if there's a long ladder you can use to take a quick look through the window from the outside to see what the situation is.'

As Courage hurried downstairs and Dazz and Laryea returned to the bedroom door, Emma took a calculated risk and sneaked back to the top of the stairs. She wanted to be closer to the action. But she stayed low and flat.

'Edwin,' Dazz called out again. 'Is the door locked? May we open it and enter? We don't want any problems. We just want to chat with you, OK? Please.' Dazz waited for an answer, but none came. That could mean Edwin was undecided and considering options. '*Chaley*, we're friends, right?' Dazz continued. 'I know you've had some tough things happen in your life, but you're a good man. You've come a long way and you're one of our best policemen. I've seen that with my own eyes. Please, Edwin.'

Dazz looked at Laryea, who signalled him to keep going. Keep the pressure on.

'Edwin,' Dazz continued, '*chaley*, we can make it fair so that everything will come out right for all of us and no one has to get hurt. Talk to me. Tell me what's wrong. What's troubling you?'

'The door is open,' Edwin said.

Laryea whispered something to Dazz and he relinquished his automatic weapon to the DCOP, who stood out of sight in a small alcove in the hallway a few metres from the bedroom door. Courage had returned from outside shaking his head to indicate *no ladder*. He took a position next to Emma but insisted she back down a couple of steps.

'I'm not armed, Edwin,' Dazz called out into the bedroom. 'I'm going to open the door now, OK?'

Emma saw Dazz shut his eyes for a second, as if sending up a quick prayer. He pushed down the door handle and slowly opened the door.

CHAPTER NINETY-SEVEN

Edwin had Josephine close beside him on the sofa, his left arm loosely around her waist. His right hand held a semiautomatic pistol. Josephine, in a house dress and headscarf, sat rigid and terrified.

'Hello, Dazz,' Edwin said.

Dazz stood with his hands clearly visible. 'Hi, Edwin. How are you?'

Edwin snorted. 'Funny question. I've been expecting you.'

'Is that so?'

'The rifle is unlicensed, I know. And this handgun too.'

'Put it down and let's talk,' Dazz said.

Edwin laughed. 'Are you forgetting I'm a SWAT guy? I know about negotiation tricks. You'll get me to drop the gun and then you'll arrest me. You're not taking me anywhere. And Mummy is not going anywhere either.'

'Edwin,' Josephine whispered. 'Listen to him. Please. We can work something out. I can help.'

'How?' he said, his voice laced with contempt. 'Your husband, the big chief, is out of the picture. Commissioner Andoh hates both you and me. And you are inside this thing too. How are you supposed to help? Or are you just trying to betray me now? I release you and then you turn on me and blame me for everything?'

'What is he talking about?' Courage whispered to Emma.

She thought she knew, but she wasn't sure and she didn't answer the question.

'What is it she will blame you for?' Dazz asked Edwin.

He looked at his mother. 'Tell them, Mummy. Tell them what you made me do.' He pressed the muzzle against Josephine's neck and she began to shiver with fright.

'Edwin,' Dazz said. 'Edwin, look at me. Put down the gun. Think about this. It's not really worth it, right?'

'And all that just because you wanted your husband to remain IGP so you could continue your life of luxury,' Edwin said to Josephine, the muzzle still pressed into her neck. 'Tell them what the ballistics will show, Mummy.'

'But I've been supporting you all these years, dear,' she said, beginning to cry.

'The money isn't your love,' Edwin said, his voice cracking. 'It's your *guilt*. Guilt that you let your mother send me away to Techiman to stay with your sister, guilt that you never let me come back into your life. Even autistic Kwame is OK to be in your family, but me? Nothing but *shame* over me.' He had begun to cry with her and Emma had a feeling that the situation was spinning out of control. Edwin was getting more overwrought instead of more reasonable.

'Edwin,' Dazz tried again, 'you know as well as I do that we can do things to cool down the situation. You have a lot of people on your side – me, Courage, all your colleagues.'

'No, no,' Edwin said. 'You think I don't know? You'll turn against me the moment I'm in jail.'

'Why would you think that?' Dazz asked, and Emma caught a slight tremor in his voice. It was important that he stay rock steady, but she wasn't sure how much more he could take.

'Why should you think that of your friends?' Dazz repeated.

Edwin brought the gun down away from his mother's neck. Emma prayed. *Please God. Make him drop it and surrender.*

'I just don't know what to do,' Edwin said, sounding like a small, lost child. 'Nowhere to turn. Nobody to trust.'

'That's why I say we can help you,' Dazz said urgently. 'I beg you, Edwin. Please. Let us help you through this.'

'I don't know what to do,' Edwin said again, bringing the gun back up to Josephine's neck again.

'*No*—' Dazz said.

What happened next was almost too quick to see. A shot rang out and a starburst of blood erupted. Josephine screamed and fell to the floor from the couch while Edwin launched backward. Dazz let out a guttural cry of horror and Courage and the DCOP sprang into the hallway and started towards the bedroom. Emma followed Courage, who had his weapon raised and ready. Dazz stood frozen in the doorway.

Josephine was crying out, patting her body all over and looking for the gunshot wound. But she didn't have one. And then she saw her son splayed on the back of the sofa with mouth open, eyes staring up, and brain matter on the wall behind him. She shrieked, '*No!*' and scrambled up to go to Edwin.

'No,' Dazz said, diving for her. 'Come away, madam. Come away.'

Weeping, she resisted as he removed her from the scene. She began to collapse, but Emma was there to catch her.

'I've got her,' she said to Dazz. 'You go do what needs to be done. I'll take care of her.'

Emma held onto Josephine and coaxed her downstairs. She had never seen the IGP's wife without make-up or in anything except a beautiful outfit. Now she was plain and vulnerable and distraught beyond anything imaginable.

'Come, Madam Josephine,' Emma said. 'Let's sit down.'

She sat with her arms around Mrs Akrofi, who wept until she had no energy left. Then she was quiet, appearing dazed, detached even. Soon Araba, her own face tearstained, came to sit with her employer in an attempt to comfort her. Within the hour, the crime scene team appeared in their otherworldly outfits, going up and down the stairs to process the carnage.

Emma thought about the unbearable sadness of it all, and about the bitter truth that was yet to come. She had understood it now, and it was all very clear.

CHAPTER NINETY-EIGHT

Exhausted, Josephine had slept for a short time on the couch in James's study. She sat up, unsteady and bleary-eyed and saw Emma in the doorway.

'Looks like you really needed that rest,' Emma said, smiling at her.

'Yes,' Josephine said. She gasped and dropped her head into her palm. The memory of what had happened must have just hit her like a pile of rocks.

'I can only say how sorry I am about Edwin's death,' Emma said.

'Thank you,' Josephine said stiffly.

'Would you like to come outside?' Emma asked. 'I can have Araba bring you something?'

'Just water, please.'

Josephine was surprised as she emerged to find DCOP Laryea in the sitting room. 'Oh. Hello, Mr Laryea.'

'Good afternoon, madam,' he said, standing from his chair. 'I hope you're feeling better?'

'Yes, thank you,' she said, taking a seat slowly, as if she had suddenly aged decades. 'Well, I mostly feel numb, really.'

Araba came in to give Josephine a glass of water and then left. Emma took a seat in a chair to Laryea's right.

'Sincere condolences for your loss, madam,' he said. 'He was a fine SWAT officer.'

'Yes,' Josephine said, staring at the floor, her water untouched. 'Why would he kill himself? I just don't understand.' She looked at Emma in anguish. 'You knew Edwin. Did he tell you anything? I mean, was something troubling him? If you know, please tell me.'

'Mrs Akrofi,' Emma started, 'this is very difficult. Edwin was living with a lot of pain.'

She looked surprised. 'Pain? What pain? How?'

'It started when, as a child, he was sent away to live with his aunt in Techiman.'

Josephine reacted quickly. 'But it wasn't my decision.'

'Oh, Madam Josephine,' Emma said, smiling kindly at her, 'I'm not levelling any accusations or criticisms against you. We're talking about Edwin now. Up till the time he died, he felt banished and abandoned, whether justifiably or not, by both you and his father.'

'But I supported him,' Josephine objected, her voice rising. 'I sent him money regularly.'

'What he needed from you more than that,' Emma said, 'was love. Remember what he said today before he took his life: he had never felt that the money you supported him with represented your love for him; he felt it was your *guilt*. Guilt over your sending him away to Techiman to stay with your sister, guilt over your not letting him back into your life. In his mind, you were keeping him *away* with the financial support. You never lost the shame your mother laid on you for having a child out of wedlock.'

'I felt no shame at all,' Josephine denied. 'None. Edwin was always welcome.'

She refuses to admit the truth, Emma thought.

'Madam Akrofi,' Laryea took up, 'during our attempts to make Edwin put down his weapon, he made reference to your having made him do something. Do you know what he meant by that?'

'I made him do something?' Josephine was evidently nonplussed. 'I'm sorry, I don't remember him saying that. It's all a blur now. A terrible blur.' Tears trailed down her face.

Emma snatched a couple of tissues from the box on the centre table, handed them to the IGP's wife, and sat next to her.

'What am I supposed to do now?' Josephine whimpered, almost to herself. 'My husband is gone; my son is dead. My world has collapsed.'

'And I know how much you wanted to keep it together,' Emma said. 'To keep Mr Akrofi in his elevated position and protect all his secrets. To keep having the ability to travel to the UK several times a year to see your little boy, Kwame. And when that stability was threatened, you had to act.'

Josephine stopped dabbing her eyes. 'I'm not sure I understand what you mean.'

'Bernard Evans-Aidoo posed a serious threat to President Bannerman's re-election,' Emma said, 'and if Evans-Aidoo defeated him, your husband would be out and both of you would lose the many perks and privileges that come with the IGP position – the travel allowances in particular, which was how you jetted so frequently to Europe, the US, and to the UK to see your autistic son.'

'Why are you saying all this?' Josephine asked with a frown.

'When Edwin said, "Tell them what the ballistics will show, Mummy,"' Emma continued, 'he was referring to the rifle we found at his home. The same one he used to kill Evans-Aidoo.'

Josephine pulled back. 'What? Edwin didn't kill anyone.'

'To protect Bannerman's re-election and your husband's continued post as the IGP, you needed Evans-Aidoo dead,' Emma said. 'You pressured Edwin to carry out the assassination. You made him feel the obligation to do it for you, his mother. And what son doesn't feel a duty to his mother?'

Josephine looked bewildered. She looked at Laryea. 'I don't know what she's talking about. Do you know?'

'And the assassination attempt on Sana Sana was by Edwin as well, wasn't it?' Laryea said. 'Sana Sana was getting too close to the truth, so again, you asked Edwin to eliminate him. Fortunately, he was unsuccessful.'

The IGP's wife sat up ramrod straight and moved away slightly from Emma. 'Why are the two of you attacking me like this?'

'Because you are guilty of a very serious crime,' Laryea said.

'No, no,' Emma said, reclaiming Josephine's attention. '*He* may be attacking you, but I am not. I'm on your side in the sense that you have a God-given right to protect your husband and your way of life.'

Laryea said, 'Miss Djan, please leave the room. *Now.* You should not be here in any case.'

'Madam Akrofi is a good woman, sir,' Emma said, turning to him. 'She's responsible for all of the success of the Autism Centre. She cares about every single child there as much as she cares for her own Kwame in England. Isn't that right, madam?' Emma lightly touched the other woman's shoulder. 'I know how much Kwame means to you.'

Josephine nodded, tried to say something, but choked up.

Laryea rose from his seat and started to move menacingly towards the sofa on which the two women sat. 'Miss Djan,' he said quietly, 'if you don't leave now and allow me to handle this myself, I will arrest you on the spot.'

Emma jumped up and stood in front of the DCOP as if to bar him from taking another step in Josephine's direction. 'Wait, sir. *Please.* You're telling me a mother shouldn't be able to see her autistic child when she wants? Do you know the kind of pain Mrs Akrofi went through when she had to abandon Kwame in the UK?'

A stifled noise came from Josephine and she began

527

to weep, her chest and back heaving with every pained breath. 'I didn't abandon him,' she struggled to say. 'It's not fair of you to accuse me of that.'

Emma hurried back to her. 'Madam, no, no. I didn't mean it like that. I'm sorry to have upset you. The way you feel about Kwame is something I understand because I have that kind of deep love for Kojo at the Autism Centre, and he's not even my son. If I was in your position, I would move heaven and earth for him. No one can take away your right to use your husband's position to Kwame's benefit.' Emma gave Josephine another wad of tissues. 'And no one should ever try to bring your husband down. Not Sana, not Mr Tilson.'

'Mr Tilson,' she said blankly. 'What do you mean?'

'He was nosy, not so?' Emma said. 'Going around asking all kinds of questions about whether high police officials, including your husband, were involved with and supportive of Internet fraud in cahoots with *sakawa* boys. And Mr Laryea has also told me about the obnoxious, threatening letter Mr Tilson wrote to Mr Akrofi – and I know you don't take well to threats, either to you personally or your family.'

Josephine smiled very slightly. 'No, I don't.'

'And Mr Tilson even went to Kweku Ponsu to ask questions that were none of his business,' Emma continued. 'Madam, you've known Kweku Ponsu a long time, have you not? Abena saw you and him having an argument the night after I was supposed to have drowned in the Volta River. You were angry with

Ponsu, of course, for having failed to get rid of me.'

Josephine stared at Emma. 'Have you taken leave of your senses?'

'I had no idea you and Ponsu were acquainted,' Emma continued, 'but Edwin told Dazz, Courage, and me that you took Kwame as a child to a traditional priest to try to banish the autism, and I guessed it was Mr Ponsu you consulted. Am I right?'

'I was desperate,' Josephine said, almost indignantly. 'I had to do something. Ponsu said he could cure Kwame but failed.'

'You must have been devastated,' Emma observed. 'Were you angry with Ponsu?'

'I wouldn't say angry,' Josephine said, twisting the used tissues around in her fingers. 'He did his best.'

'And over the years, you kept in touch with Mr Ponsu?'

'Off and on.'

'When Mr Tilson went to Ponsu's shrine in Atimpoku,' Emma said, 'they had a verbal tussle in which Ponsu warned him, "You should fear plenty other people before me." By that he meant people with power and privilege like yourself. Once Mr Tilson had left, Ponsu must have called you to tell you all the American man had said. Tell me if that's correct, Mrs Akrofi.'

Her jaw set, Josephine looked away and said nothing.

Emma shifted position, kneeling on the floor where she was back in Josephine's line of sight. 'I'm not judging you, madam. This is only a matter of the truth. You have more wisdom than I do, so I don't need to tell you that the truth will set you free. The burdens you're carrying right now – your husband's arrest, your son's suicide – those *alone* are too much to bear. Don't add another load on your shoulders.'

Josephine's face betrayed no emotion, but she was fidgeting uncomfortably.

'Mrs Akrofi?' Emma prodded. 'Please, let's get through this together, eh? What do you say?'

The room was silent for what seemed a long time before Josephine shrugged and spoke in a low, husky voice. 'He became the enemy.'

'Mr Tilson, you mean,' Emma said, her eyes fixed on the other woman's face.

Josephine nodded. 'Yes, him – Gordon. He changed, became a different person. I had enjoyed his company while I was in Washington, but when he came to Ghana, I hated what I saw in him. He was like a garden spoilt by weeds. Because of his experience with the scam, which I felt was entirely his fault, he was bitter and vindictive. Worst of all, he joined forces with Sana Sana.'

'That could not stand,' Emma agreed.

'And no one threatens my husband,' Josephine added. '*No one.*'

'I hear you,' Emma said, 'so when Ponsu revealed Gordon's threats and his attempts at intimidation, you were outraged?'

Resigned and drained, Josephine said, 'Yes.'

'So, you took action, of course.'

'Well, at that point, there was only one thing to do,

530

wasn't there? I told Kweku to get rid of Gordon. I didn't care how he did it. I just wanted that American gone.'

Josephine sat slumped, her bottom lip trembling and her eyes welling.

Laryea came close to her and gently rested his hand on her shoulder. 'Josephine Akrofi, I am arresting you as a co-conspirator to murder and attempted murder, and an accessory to murder. You do not need to say anything further, but anything you do say may be taken down and used in evidence against you in a court of law.'

Josephine put her face in her hands and wept quietly.

Laryea nodded at Emma, who went to the door and opened it. Dazz was waiting.

'She's ready,' Emma said.

Dazz came in and helped Josephine from the sofa. 'Come along, madam,' he said gently.

He led her away.

Laryea looked at Emma. 'Well played,' he said, but there was no gloating in his tone. 'Thank you.'

'And you too, sir,' she replied. 'Very well played.'

CHAPTER NINETY-NINE

After Mrs Akrofi's arrest, Emma took a cab to CID, where Thelma Bright had scheduled a meeting with Commissioner Andoh. Traffic en route was predictably slow and it gave Emma enough time to call someone she was dying to talk to. Derek picked up after three rings. 'Emma! So good to hear from you. How are you?'

'I'm very well, thanks. Is this a good time?'

'For you, any time is good.'

She smiled. 'That's sweet of you. I'm calling with news.'

'Is it good?'

'I would say so, yes. Do you remember a woman called Josephine whom your father mentioned in his emails to Casper?'

'Yes, the woman Dad had met here in DC.'

'Yes, they were friends there, but in Ghana your dad became a danger to Josephine. He was getting closer and closer to knowing the truth about how high the *sakawa* scams went up the chain and Josephine was afraid of her husband being exposed. That would threaten their whole life as they knew it, and she couldn't abide by that.'

'So, you're saying . . . she had my father killed?'

'Yes.'

'My God.'

'She conspired with Kweku Ponsu and his bodyguards to have your dad attacked and dumped into the river.'

For a moment, Derek was silent. Then he said, 'That's so sad, so pitiful. I don't understand it.'

'Mrs Akrofi even targeted two other people she considered a menace,' Emma said. 'One was assassinated – presidential candidate Evans-Aidoo, while the other, Sana Sana, escaped the attempt. Again, Derek, I can't tell you just how deeply sorry I am that this has befallen you and your father.'

'What about you?' he asked. 'You told me how you were almost dumped in the river yourself. Was that Mrs Akrofi's doing as well?'

'No. That was just Mr Ponsu getting tired of me all on his own.'

'All on his own?' Derek snorted. 'Funny way of putting it.'

He fell quiet again and Emma gave him a moment before asking, 'How do you feel?'

'I suppose I'll go through different stages,' he said. 'Right now, I feel a kind of satisfaction that these people have been caught, but a sense of sadness and futility as well. But above all, I'm grateful to you for keeping your promise and even risking your own life to get to the bottom of this. I'm for ever in your debt. Thank you, Emma.'

'You're so welcome. Thank you for bringing the case to us.'

Thelma opened the door of the director-general's office to let Emma in.

Andoh was at his desk talking on the phone. At length, he hung up and looked at the two women in front of him. 'Yes?'

'Do you remember me, sir?' Emma asked.

He frowned. 'I don't think so. Who are you?'

'Emma Djan is the name. May I sit, sir?'

Andoh gestured at a chair on the other side of the desk, but instead of sitting there, Emma picked up the chair and brought it next to him. *Then* she sat down.

Andoh moved away. 'What are you doing?'

'Remember in January how close we sat at this desk, and how you put your hand on my thigh?'

Andoh looked at Thelma. 'What is going on? This is outrageous.'

'And then,' Emma said, standing up, 'you asked me to follow you here.' She rose and walked to the door of his secret chamber. 'We went inside, you told me to sit in the chair in the middle of the room, and then you attempted to rape me.'

'Nonsense,' Andoh snapped. He looked at Thelma. 'Get her out of here.'

'But what she says is true, sir,' Thelma said. 'I've worked for you for many years and learnt a lot from you. But what prevents me from wholeheartedly respecting you is what I suspected about how you treat young female recruits – what you do to them. It was that night in January when you attempted to rape Miss Djan that I finally had the evidence. I was returning to the office to get something I had left behind when I heard voices and Emma's screams. I crouched behind your desk as she came running out, and then I followed her to the washroom and talked to her from the other side of the stall door. I know this happened, sir.'

Speechless, Andoh stared at them.

'Thelma and I will be spreading this on social media and TV and radio,' Emma said.

Andoh looked both incredulous and disdainful. 'Who will believe you?'

'A lot of people,' Emma said. 'Especially women. And the way President Bannerman is feeling right now, I suspect he will too.'

'What do you want?' Andoh demanded. 'Money? I can give you money.'

'No, sir,' Emma said. 'We want nothing more than a public confession and apology to the women you've assaulted.'

Andoh snorted. 'Stupid. Do you think I will submit to this extortion?'

Emma pulled out her phone and went to her Facebook page. 'You see this, sir?' she said, flipping the phone around so he could see the screen. 'I'm prepared to send the information out right now.' She took Andoh's picture. 'Thelma will also post. After that, it will only be a matter of time before many other women you've assaulted come forward. You have until tomorrow to make your mind up. If Thelma doesn't hear from you, we'll post the alert everywhere.'

Andoh got up abruptly, knocking his executive chair backward. 'Get out.'

'Thank you, sir,' Emma said. 'We'll be listening for your public revelation and apology tomorrow. Thelma can book your TV appearances, I'm quite sure. Goodnight, sir.'

GLOSSARY

Abolo (*ah-BO-low*): slightly fermented, slightly sweet, dumpling-like preparation made from rice and corn flour

Aburokyire (*ah-bu-ro-CHEE-RAY*): overseas countries, particularly North America, Europe, etc.

Akwaaba! (*ah-KWAH-bah*): welcome! (Twi)

Asantehene (*ah-san-tay-HAY-NAY*): king of the Asante people of Ghana

Awurade (*Ay-woo-rah-DAY*): God

Bola (*BOW-lah*): rubbish, trash

Cedi: Ghanaian monetary unit

Chaley (*cha-LAY*): bro, dude, pal, buddy. Also, *chale*

Chale-wote (*cha-LAY-wo-tay*): flip-flops (literally, 'Let's go, buddy', for the ease with which one slips on this footwear)

Chop money: euphemism for bribe

Ete sen? (*eh-tih-SENG*): how are you? (Twi)

Ewe (*EH-way*): language and peoples of coastal south-eastern Ghana (Volta Region) and southern Togo

Fufu (*foo-FOO*): staple made by pounding cassava, plantain or yam into a soft glutinous mass. Also available pre-made, simply add water

Ga: people of the Accra Metropolitan Area and several coastal regions

Grasscutter: bush rat, the meat of which is used in soups and stews

Juju: of and relating to magical powers and the occult

Kelewele (*kay-lay-way-lay*): ripe plantain cut into cubes and deep-fried with ginger and other spices

Kenkey (KEN-kay): staple dish of fermented cornmeal dough

Kente (ken-TAY): silk and cotton fabric of interwoven colourful cloth strips, native to the Akan peoples of Ghana

KIA: Kotoka International Airport (Accra)

Koraa (krah): at all (Twi)

Kpakpo (pah-POH): small (Ga)

Kwasea (quass-ye-AH): fool, idiot

Macho man: thug

Mallam (MAL-lam): honorific title for an Islamic scholar

Medaase (mih-daah-sih): thank you (Twi)

Mugu (moo-goo): scam victim (lit. fool)

Nkontomire (in-cohn-TOE-me-ray): spinach stew

Nyame adom (nya-may-A-dome): [By] God's grace, [I am well.]

Oburoni (*obu-ro-NEE*): white person or foreigner

One-man-thousand: tiny anchovies caught and cooked in large amounts

Paa (*pah*): a lot, very much

Papa (*pa-PAH*): father (respectful)

Pesewa (*peh-say-wah*): monetary unit, 1/100th of a *cedi*

Sakawa (*sah-kah-wah*): Internet fraud backed up by supernatural powers

Shito (*she-TAW*): chilli pepper sauce

Tatale (*tah-tah-lay*): deep-fried ripe plantain batter, appearing similar to pancakes

Twi (*chwee*): predominant Akan language spoken widely in Ghana

Waakye (*wah-chay*): rice and black-eyed peas

ACKNOWLEDGEMENTS

I am greatly indebted to friend and private investigator Yahya Azure in Accra, Ghana, for helping me research the *sakawa* phenomenon, a core aspect of this novel. He worked diligently to set up meetings with traditional priests and *sakawa* boys. In that regard, many thanks to Mallam Salisu Raji and Musah Yahya for their assistance.

Randy Torgerson, PI, in Los Angeles, generously shared his experiences with cases he investigated while in Ghana.

To my terrific editors at Soho Press – Juliet Grames and Rachel Kowal – and to Ben LeRoy, who stood in for Juliet while she was away: thanks for your guidance and collaboration in bringing to life a brand-new African female detective.

Finally, my heartfelt thanks to Allison & Busby and editor Kelly Smith for bringing this novel to UK readers with the opportunity to meet West Africa's newest female private investigator in fiction.

KWEI QUARTEY was born in Ghana, but moved to the USA to complete his medical training. He practised as a physician for more than twenty-five years while simultaneously writing, before deciding to become a full-time novelist in 2018. His previous work has been published to great critical acclaim and has appeared on the *Los Angeles Times* bestseller list. *The Missing American* is the first novel in a brand-new series featuring Private Investigator Emma Djan.

kweiquartey.com   *@kweiquartey*